PERSEPHONE & HADES II

by Tabatha Grove

Cover design by: Tabatha Grove
Photography by: Christopher Grove
ISBN: 9798860685710
ASIN: B0CJVLN6VL
Imprint: Independently published
Printed in the United States of America

Dedication

*This book is dedicated to my brother, Christopher Grove,
who has hung in there with me through so many drafts and
concepts they all began to blend. Without his reason and
steady ear to listen to my madness, my work would not have
a direction. I must credit him for Persephone & Hades II book
cover photography as well as my author bio pic. Indeed,
his skills are unmatched, and he fulfilled my vision with his
abilities, for which I am eternally grateful.*

Thank you, brother.

Acknowledgment

To my mom, Joyce Grove, who has always been my biggest supporter and fan. To my brother Tyrell Grove, who continues to encourage me to write and always offers great wisdom and critique. And to all of my family who continue to support my dreams of sharing my stories with the world.

Thank you.

CONTENTS

CHAPTER 1 MAIDEN

Persephone cursed the saddle horn digging into her hip as she fought against his hand that cupped her ass holding her in place. Soon, they slowed into an unbearable trot, making her curse even harder until they finally arrived at a blessed halt. Lifting her by the back of her dress as if she weighed nothing, even as she thrashed her arms and legs in resistance, someone set Persephone's feet firmly on the warm stone ground. They wobbled as she found her footing. She flipped her matted tangles off her face and looked around with her heart pounding as she turned around, trying to assess where she was. The walls were dark, barely lit by a few torches. The rough surface glistened in the light. Persephone could see no sky, no sun, nor feel any cool breeze on her cheeks. Like a warm embrace, she felt a whisper welcome her as it echoed in the distance, barely audible but in her mind. It was unmistakable. This power exuded a warm energy that wrapped around her body like a mother would her arms to a child. She shook her head to clear it. Feeling the powerful male's energy behind her, she turned to face him. Looking up into familiar eyes, Persephone gasped.

"Hades?" Frantically searching the foreign surroundings

for anything recognizable. Persephone found nothing. "Where are we?"

"We're home," Hades replied with a wicked grin.

"What... What have you done?" She asked with a tremble in her voice.

His boots made a thud like a heavy weight on the stone floor. Hades led Aethone down to her stables as Persephone followed, stomping her bare feet behind him. He handed the reins to a stable worker, closed the stall door, and then turned, stopping abruptly with the angry goddess blocking his way.

"Hades, you have to take me back," Persephone demanded. "My mom will lose her mind not knowing what's happened to me."

"Nothing has happened to you. Yet." Hades' eyes were so intense her breath quickened.

From anger? Fear? Lust? She couldn't differentiate any of her emotions.

A quick pet of Aethone's mane and Hades left her standing mouth agape and walked back toward the room where the booming sounds of laughter, music, and revelry, perhaps even some fighting, rang through the cavern.

"Hades, take me back!" Persephone protested from behind him. "Or I swear I'll...."

"You'll what?" He whipped around and stared down at her, daring her to continue. "Cry out for mommy? Go ahead. See if she hears you from down here."

Blinking in astonishment, Persephone stood frozen. "You're just fucking with me, aren't you?" She said incredulously. "This must be some sort of joke. An illusion or spell. Hecate!?" Her anger built like a rumble before the lightning strike she wished she possessed. "This is a dream. It can't be real."

When her eyes closed and reopened, she thought maybe things would change, and she would wake up. Persephone turned away from him, placing a palm against her sweat-slickened forehead, and groaned at her circumstances. This place was real, and she was trapped.

"Hecate isn't here. At least, not right now," Hades chuckled in a deep, menacing tone that made her step backward as her heart began to race. "I assure you, this is very real, and you're not going anywhere except maybe my bed later tonight," he said, leaning down with almost a whisper in her ear, seducing her with his deep tone, her stomach fluttering as the feeling the hairs on her neck respond to his lips mere inches away. "And I promise you. You'll be begging me for more in the end."

Before she could exhale, Hades walked away toward the light at the end of the corridor, leaving her struggling for air.

"You can't do this," Persephone said through gritted teeth, stomping in her bare feet after him. "Demeter won't allow it!"

His sudden stop forced her to halt her pursuit, almost knocking into him.

"Allow?" Hades growled dangerously, narrowing his gaze on Persephone over his shoulder. "I don't have to ask anyone permission to do whatever I want. I never have. I've only ever done so in the past out of courtesy for you and your father. And after all the humiliation and foulness from Demeter that I've endured, my patience has ended. To say nothing of being reduced to a mere guardian for weaker gods. It was beneath me, and Zeus knew it. I only agreed because we seem linked by some prophecy that if I could change, I would. But I've made a decision. The prophecy may play out, and if it does, then the world can end for all I care." He stepped closer to her, his eyes wavering to the gentleness she remembered, and reached out but stopped, closing his hand into a fist as he flexed his jaw with clenched teeth. "No one will ever take you away from me again. Ever."

"You can't go against Zeus' command if my mother gets to him," she replied, folding her arms.

Hades walked one step deliberately at a time toward her, stopping inches of them touching, and leaned closer with a look she had never seen. It was chilling her to the bone, making her shiver slightly. Her arms absently dropped to her sides, where she clenched them tight.

"If Zeus tries to take you from me," he said with a chilling darkness in his tone that caressed her spine. "I'll kill him myself."

They stared one another down, both refusing to break eye contact. His dominating presence was making her waver in her convictions. She was trapped, and she knew it. That didn't mean she was going to let him see it. And she wouldn't back away no matter how terrifying he would have been to anyone else. Hades would never hurt her, and she would use that against him.

A ghostly gray billow of smoke formed beside them as she opened her mouth to object but instead paused. A powerfully built, dark-brown-toned god emerged bare-chested but for a cloak that wrapped over one shoulder held by a silver clasp. He bowed to Hades, revealing his firm muscles beneath the tight leather pants from the back. The shortened scythe was folded and strapped to his back, where his long black locks brushed the silver hilt.

"My lord. I see we finally have our guest of honor," he said with perfect white teeth.

His charm was intoxicating. At least it would have been had Persephone not been so furious.

"I present the Goddess of Spring, Persephone," Hades said, softening his eyes for the first time since her arrival when he looked at her. "Persephone, meet the God of Death and my top general, Thanatos."

"We've been expecting you for some time," Thanatos said, eyeing Hades and clearing his throat.

"So you've planned this obduction?" Persephone said quietly to herself, then shook her head. "I should have known it was a lie that you'd let me choose. You're no better than Zeus."

Hades glared at her, all traces of softening now gone.

"Prepare her quarters next to mine and get her something more appropriate to wear."

"Of course," Thanatos replied with a curt nod. "Goddess, if you would follow me..."

"Appropriate, huh?" Persephone glared up at Hades, crossing her arms. "Appropriate enough for a goddess stolen away from her mother and brought to this... This dread of a place? What could I possibly wear that would make any of this appropriate?"

"That's up to you."

"You're going to pay for this, Hades." Persephone flared her nostrils, glaring up at him. "When my mom finds us, she will destroy this place until she gets me back, and you know it...."

"After you've changed, you will join me at the feast in the Great Hall," Hades said in a bored tone, ignoring her ire.

Persephone scoffed. "I'm not feasting on anything with you so long as I am a prisoner here."

"If that's how you wish to see it, so be it." Hades turned to Thanatos. "Get her ready, then meet me in the war room."

"Hades, don't you dare disappear on me," Persephone warned.

Hades narrowed his eyes, grabbed her by the back of her head, and pulled her into an aggressive kiss. Persephone was too stunned at first to fight. Missing the way his lips felt was weakening her. No. Don't give in, Persephone! Her mind screamed at her as her body betrayed her. She shoved at his chest, trying to push him away, but he held her firmly against his hard body. The moment she felt her will give in to his, he released her and disappeared in a cloud of black smoke, leaving the last thing to vanish. That wicked grin she hated so very much.

"Hades!? Get back here! I'm still not finished with you, damn it!" She bellowed as loud as she could.

"My queen?" Thanatos coughed into his hand and gestured for Persephone toward the hall with the light. "If you would follow me, please, I will show you to your new chambers."

"Thanatos, I don't want new chambers. I want to go home." Persephone ran her hands through her loose curls of red and pink with some gold strands still hanging in front of her face. "You have to talk to Hades and get him to let me go."

"I'm afraid that's impossible," he said, shaking his head. "When the Dark Lord makes a decision, nothing will sway him. Down here, Hades is law and king, and everyone, even you must submit to him."

Persephone narrowed her eyes. "I will do no such thing."

Thanatos shrugged. "You are here until my lord says otherwise. I suggest you get used to it and find a way to accept your fate, my queen."

Persephone squared her shoulders, pointing her nose up. "I will never do that."

"Are you so strong in your convictions?"

"I am."

"I see. I wish you the best of luck with that," Thanatos smirked down at her. "Still, until you change his mind, will you follow me? Please."

His words hung in the air, stagnant, making her feel like the walls were closing in. Thanatos turned and walked into the large cavern. She could hear music and drums echoing. She had never heard anything like it. It was so primal and raw. Compared to her mother's music or that of Olympus, which was often light and played with mostly string instruments, the base resonated throughout the ground, vibrating her bare feet as they entered another hallway that led away from the festivities.

They passed the entrance to a new cavern where Thanatos led Persephone down to the lower levels. The passage wove in and around the stalagmites that formed, rising upward toward the ceiling with matching stalactites as though reaching to touch one another. They neared a fog-rolled passage. It stopped Persephone in her tracks, mesmerizing her, beckoning her to go down there where the whispers said her name softly.

"Persephoneeee...," something whispered to her from behind, making her turn to see nothing.

Thanatos gestured her past the sound to follow him.

"What's down there?" She asked, looking back.

"That is not a place for you to go...ever," he warned.

"Why not?"

"There are far more frightening things down there than even your dreams can conjure."

"I don't know. I have a pretty vivid imagination. I have been to Olympus, after all." She wanted to ask more, but he pulled her away, relieving her trance and bringing her back to reality.

"Olympus is a vile place, to be sure, but what's down there can only be experienced, not described." Thanatos turned to begin walking again. "So you must ask my Lord to take you himself."

"Why couldn't you take me?" She asked, pulling her arm from his grasp.

Thanatos gave a heavy sigh. "Because Hades is the only one who can permit anyone to enter or leave that domain."

"There we go again with his permission," Persephone grumbled.

Thanatos only smiled and continued to walk and guide them through the veined chambered hallways glimmering in the firelight. They soon arrived in a cavern opening that vented the heat through holes above them. She realized that she was standing in a volcano and found it fascinating.

In the center was a bright pit with fire licking at its sides as the hot magma whirled and moved in tumbling churns. A walkway led straight across with organic shapes creating the rails of stone. Thanatos led them to two great stone doors with detailed carvings of the Titan wars. The Largest doors showed the scene where Hades, in particular, battled the Titans. With his helm of invisibility, he charged the beings with his sword drawn and a vicious battle cry etched on his face filled with rage. It was much the same as she had seen on Olympus on his door, only this scene was different. His claws and fangs were sharp, and his body was much larger than the others.

She realized this must be his complete form. Dark clouds billowed out from him and around, drowning the lower creatures in darkness and something resembling fire, but she didn't know what kind. She stopped and reached out to touch the image.

Thanatos cleared his throat, pulling her attention away, and signaled for her to follow to the opposite brightly lit hallway. As they walked, smooth carved rock walls seemed to breathe in the firelight. Thanatos opened the door at the end with a flower garden carved into it with the flower she had picked in the meadow adorning the center. He knew I'd find that flower, she thought to herself. Her anger began to boil up again.

The heavy doors creaked as they entered a room that made her uncomfortable with its opulence. Having lived a humble life in a cottage, and even with Zeus' abundant accommodations, it was a shock to see everything draped in jewels, gold, and rich fabrics. Chandeliers adorned in hanging pearls and prisms of diamonds and crystals made the light dance on the obsidian walls. The bedding was a dark tyrian color, somewhere between wine and purple, with golden lining and jewels elaborately woven into the cover over a large round bed surrounded by Corinthian columns made of gold. The light lavender sheer drapes blew softly from a breeze from another attached room.

Persephone investigated the massive space that led to a large spring steamed with hot water she desperately craved after all she'd been through. She'd give anything to settle her nerves and aching bones, but she was too upset to think of relaxing. Persephone looked down at her slightly torn lavender dress that now came up to her knees from being so rough with the light fabric. She held the delicate material and looked at the harsh and bold colors. She wrenched her hands together, turning to the god still behind her.

"Thanatos," Persephone said with a deep sigh. "This room is way too grand for someone like me. And how did you get a bold color like this?" Everything was so dark. It felt like the cave was closing in on her.

"My lord had this fabric made for you as a gift. He says the dye comes from the secretion of the ocean's sea snails."

"It's beautiful," she said with sadness while marveling at how the color complimented the gold.

The craftsmanship in these rooms was enchanting, to say the least, she thought to herself. How the stone and wood worked together to mimic the nature above was a true marvel for her. Someone with incredible talent carved delicate flowers in the golden furniture. But it was all an illusion and nothing like her home. It was beautiful, but it was still a prison.

"I'm sure he will be pleased to hear it."

Persephone pulled her hand back from touching the soft fabric. "Don't say anything. Please."

Thanatos looked down and smiled. "I'll let you tell him when you're ready."

"Thank you." Persephone clasped her hands together. "I hope you won't take my anger personally. You're not catching me in my best light."

"I wouldn't dream of it, my queen." Thanatos' genuine smile charmed her out of her anger for the moment. "Perhaps you're what we need to bring light into such a, what did you call it? A dread place?"

"I probably shouldn't have said that about your home. Truly, I have no quarrel with you. Only Hades." Persephone frowned, standing near the dresser with a mirror, looking at her ragged appearance. "Please don't take my anger as a reflection of how I feel about you or anyone else."

"I will keep that in mind." Thanatos bowed and moved to leave. "Now, please excuse me. I have much to do before the party."

"What do you mean?" Persephone felt nervous being alone and wasn't sure how she would prepare for a party she didn't want to attend. "You're leaving me here alone?"

"I have prepared your wardrobe for your arrival. I hope it's to your satisfaction," he said, gesturing toward the smaller room behind the bed. "My lord, Hades, ordered these clothes prepared for your arrival. You are to choose whatever you like."

Persephone scoffed. "What choices do I have here?"

Thanatos raised a brow at her question. "That is also up to you to decide."

"And what if I don't want to attend? Will I be forced to anyway?" she asked, walking over to the wardrobe.

Thanatos smiled gently. "I have no idea what my lord has intended for you, but I do know that he hasn't slept, eaten, or even indulged in what he typically enjoys since he returned with the sky queen."

"He hasn't?" She asked, feeling her stomach ache at the mention of Hera.

"No." Thanatos looked away. "My lord has been different these past six months. His rage is seldom quelled even with reason." Thanatos looked back at her and smiled. "I'm hoping you can help with that."

It was a slight comfort knowing he was miserable while she was away. Her smugness faded with a hollowness in her gut that longed to take away his pain. No, Persephone! She scolded herself. He is a monster, just like what your mom said.

"I'll make no promises." Persephone sighed. "My only desire is to return home. Can you help me find a way?"

"I wouldn't dream of assisting your escape if I want to keep my head, my queen."

"He would actively kill Death?" She scoffed. "For me?"

"My queen," Thanatos gave her a look so intense she knew he was telling her the truth. "For you, Hades would destroy the world."

"I don't want any of his favor," Persephone said with eyes narrowed. "Nor do I plan to obey his rules."

"Fair enough." Thanatos furrowed his brows at her coldness. "Now that you know the way, I'll leave you to prepare for tonight's event. We dine at sunset."

Thanatos bowed, then disappeared in a dark gray cloud that dissipated as the fog left her alone to her thoughts.

Looking down at her torn lavender chiton garment, Persephone felt regret. The last thing she had said to her mother were words of anger and insisting that Hades was nothing like Zeus. Persephone cursed herself for believing those lies.

"You must be sick with worry about me," Persephone said, laying her head in her hands and focussing on breathing. "And what of the nymphs? They must have been so scared."

It infuriated her that she couldn't find a way to tell her mom that she was alive or ensure her friends were okay. After what happened with Hera, Demeter would never stop looking for her. Somehow, Persephone knew she had to find a way out. But she'd need a plan and an ally. Damn it! Where was Artemis when she needed her so much right now? Her best friend would know everything about this place and a way out. The one rule Persephone remembered from their conversations was to never eat from the underworld, or she would be trapped forever.

"Is this why you've planned a feast for me, Hades?" She sneered at his name on her lips. "To ensure I would have no choice but to remain here forever? Well, that's not going to happen. So long as I remain a prisoner here, I will consume nothing."

Persephone turned away from the new wardrobe and resigned herself to wearing what she had on, down to her bare feet and wild hair. If he wanted her to look like a queen, she would sour his plans and remain as she had arrived. Disheveled and unyielding. If Hades didn't like it, she didn't give a damn. He would regret mistaking her kindness for weakness. No matter what, he would pay for this, and she didn't know if that was a good or a bad thing as her feelings were conflicted. A part of her felt he deserved it, while the other side wanted to destroy anyone who dared.

CHAPTER 2 KING

Hades sat staring at the floor, his right hand pressed against his lips in thought. He knew she would be angry. Maybe even for a century or two. Who knows how long? It didn't matter. He would wait for her head to cool over time. It had been agony the past few months waiting for her to wake up. Barred from her home, he was unable to even inquire about her. He suffered each hour that passed with no word whatsoever. Day by agonizing day, Hades waited. His temper had grown, and his usual comforts were impossible even to consider when she was injured, and he couldn't protect her.

The image of Persephone as she lay limp in her mother's arms played over in his mind. Arms that should have been his, he thought to himself. Hades cursed under his breath for letting things get as far as they had. The blame was all his. Persephone could never have calculated Hera's treachery. He should have, knowing what he did about Hera. At the time, he wanted to believe there was hope. Hades clenched his fist, digging his nails into his palms. He would never forgive himself for what happened. That Persephone survived was a testament to her strength. At that moment, when she vanished, he found his weakness. His chest ripped apart, and he'd wanted to tear out his heart to stop the pain.

A gut-wrenching pain struck him like a specter hand had ripped out his heart the days prior. Hades fell to his knees, shaking. His eyes darted back and forth, trying to find the source of his pain. But he knew. She was gone. He screamed in agony, collapsing from exhaustion only to wake alone, shivering on the warm stone floor with only the light in the fireplace to see. He paced endlessly, rubbing his chest to make the ache go away. The feeling of Persephone being gone had subsided, yet the anger and madness began to take over him. He began to rage at anyone in his presence, never knowing what was happening to her nor finding solace or peace in his mind.

Hades destroyed his personal chambers. He ripped apart the war table from its stone base after he broke it in half while bellowing at his generals over something he didn't even care about. Repairs to the obsidian statues carved out of the rock adorning the cracked stairs leading up to his throne were underway, illuminated by the large fire pits at the base of the stairs for all to see his unchecked fury.

His throat was always dry with a lump no amount of wine would swallow; it remained a desert. He refused sexual company. The last time Mynthe had come to him, he had her by the throat before she could speak and almost killed his once favorite nymph. He wanted no comfort because there was none without the one he couldn't have.

The moment he'd sensed Persephone's energy vibrate in his core, he froze in place, stone cold, the rage leaving his body instantly. Hades stared at the sky he couldn't see. Hope. The seed, now bloomed, was sending a signal, causing his whole body to resonate with a powerful drive of energy screaming at him to go to her.

Hades dropped his accusing hand, pointed at the daemons before him, and stood from his throne when he felt her. The court froze and turned to whisper in confusion why he stopped screaming at them when Hades immediately transported to Aethone's stall directly next to her.

"It's time," Hades said, holding out his hand, creating his black saddle with silver stitching and silver reins—a simple nod from Aethone with her bit forming in her mouth assured him she was ready.

Hades pulled himself up and squeezed his thighs to hold on. Aethone spurred into action with a forcefulness that almost left him behind. Her hooves raced faster than they had ever traveled before. Hades couldn't breathe as he led Aethone to the opening he felt in his core. It grew stronger as they closed in.

At last, the light appeared ahead in the total darkness. Hades could tell that the crack wasn't wide enough, so he pulled his bident and extended it, feeling the dark power flow through him and explode through the weapon. Hades sent a beam of blue fire to rip it open as wide as he could. As he released the beam, the hole began to close slowly. Hades realized it might close behind him if he didn't move quickly, so he used his power again to make it wider to give him enough time.

His heart pounded as hard and fast as the hooves that barreled through the fissure and landed in a bright, sunlit, flowery meadow. Hades blinked and raised a hand to shield his eyes when he saw her red hair whipping in the wind as she ran from him. He kicked Aethone into action. Knowing he only had moments before Demeter would come, Hades rode Persephone down. Instead of talking, asking, or questioning his actions, he grabbed Persephone by her belt as she dropped her shawl, threw her over his lap, and turned Aethone around to run as hard as the mare could.

With one last look back, he realized he'd been spotted by one of the nymphs running toward them with her arms out, crying for Persephone. Too far from her spring, the nymph collapsed and transformed into a river that flowed from her gasping form, still reaching out until she was all but water sinking into the soil. Persephone was going to be devastated when she found out. There was no time to save the nymph anyway. Even so, there were thousands of nymphs Persephone could replace one with. His only focus was to reach the fissure just before Persephone could cry out.

They landed harder than he intended when they reached his realm. Persephone was furious with him. At least she was alive and now in his care. Her words were adorable, cursing and insulting him. Persephone was angry now, but he knew she would have no choice but to give in and become queen, as he had seen in the vision what seemed ages ago.

His relief was short-lived when he realized Helios, riding across the sky in his golden chariot as the blazing sun, indeed the god would have witnessed what Hades had done. Hades shook the dark thoughts of what to do from his mind, deciding to worry about that at another time.

Thanatos appeared next to Hades, distracting him from his thoughts.

"My lord, Persephone is safely in her chambers and is dressing for tonight."

"She is?" Hades asked with a slight squeak in his voice, then shook his head and cleared his throat. "I mean, good."

"My lord, our queen doesn't seem too happy about her arrival."

Hades said nothing.

"Are you sure this is a good idea, my lord?"

"Are you questioning my orders?" Hades straightened his shoulders.

"Of course not," Thanatos cleared his throat nervously. "It's just that it doesn't seem she was pleased with anything in the room."

"She will be," Hades replied, narrowing his eyes at Thanatos. "Give her time."

"As you say," Thanatos said with a short bow. "How long before Demeter finds out she's here?"

"Only two beings saw us," said Hades, clenching his

jaw. "Helios, who would have undoubtedly seen me from his elevated perspective."

"And the other?" His general asked with an arched brow.

"She's of no concern," Hades said, waving a hand dismissively. "Just a nymph who turned to water when running too far from her spring. She's become a river and won't be telling anyone anything."

Thanatos nodded. "I see. Do you think he will tell Demeter if she asks him?"

Hades shook his head. "It's unlikely. Helios never comes close enough to speak to us. She would have to go to him."

Hades was trying to remain calm. He tapped his finger repeatedly on the arm of his throne. Hating the idea of Demeter finding her too soon, Hades was determined to keep Persephone hidden until he could find a solution to their problem. He would always find her. The question that hung over his head like a cloud was, would she stay? And if she did, would she be able to obey his rule? In his realm, he was king and bowed to no one. They came to him. Eventually, so would she, he growled to himself.

He could hear the whispers and talk from the Chthonic court murmuring questions of where she was and what their queen would look like. He expected she'd be dressed by now in full regalia befitting her station as his bride. His muscles tensed, wondering where she was and what was taking so long.

"Where is she?" Hades asked in a threatening tone to Thanatos.

"When I left, she was choosing an outfit. I'm sure she will be here soon," Thanatos assured.

"You prepared appropriate garments for her?" Hades asked, narrowing his eyes at the empty hallway of her presence.

"Of course." Thanatos nodded. "The goddess has everything she could desire. I left nothing to chance based on your specifications."

"Good." Hades tapped a finger on his armrest while outwardly seeming relaxed, leaning back into his throne.

As they waited, a few fights broke out, and some sensual activities began taking form, but Hades stopped it with little more than a glare. His disapproval was palpable as the court did their best to wait for their new mistress.

"I'm going to the war room," Hades growled. "Alert me when she arrives."

Not long after entering the room behind his throne, he heard an insistent knock.

"Enter." Hades called out.

Persephone walked beside Thanatos in her wild appearance, far removed from what he expected. Her hair was messy, and her lavender dress was in tatters up to her knees. Keeping her gaze locked on his, Hades watched secretly, wanting to smile at Persephone's defiance as she glared up at him.

Thanatos came in, closing the door discreetly behind him. Saying nothing, Persephone walked over to Hades' chair by the fireplace and next to a table with wine, and instead of filling her glass, she crossed her legs, flexing her toes and staring him down. As uncomfortable as she was trying to make him, he was grateful her eyes had life enough to appear angry or not."

"You haven't changed," Hades said in a measured tone.

Persephone rolled her eyes. "And I'm not going to."

"You will if I command it," he replied, thinking two could play this little game.

"You may have control over everyone here, but you will never control me. So If I say I'm not going to change my dress, there's nothing you can do about it." Persephone's curt reply was amusing, but he remained level despite her jabs.

Hades opened his mouth to speak, then stopped. He realized she didn't feel she had much control. Perhaps this was her way of exerting what she could.

"Fine. Wear whatever you want."

"I will." Her lips quivered with pursed tension.

He wanted her even when she was angry. Gaia, help him. She was even more beautiful when she was enraged.

Thanatos cleared his throat for attention, interrupting their stare.

"Hermes is here with a message. You've been summoned to Olympus to speak to Zeus," Thanatos said.

Hades clenched his fists. "Let me guess, Demeter has already found out Persephone is here."

"Not to my knowledge. From my sources, Demeter still seeks her daughter far from here. I think it's regarding Hera."

Hades noticed Persephone visibly shuddered, and she seemed to crawl into herself at the name, crossing her arms with a hand placed tenderly on her chest. Hades barely held back his rage, thinking of Hera's name. He didn't even know if what he feared was true.

"Tell him that I'm not going anywhere. I'm staying here, and so is Hera. Leave no mention of Persephone being here. Is that clear?"

"I cannot lie to Zeus; you know he won't like the refusal of his command," Thanatos warned.

"That's not my concern," Hades barked, baring his teeth. "You remember who your master is and obey at once, or your role as death will end in Tartarus."

"Hades!"

Hades turned to see Persephone standing with eyes wide from his outburst. Clenching his jaw, Hades took a deep breath and then calmed himself. "Send a message that I declined his gracious invitation due to important pressing matters here but will attend later." Hades inclined his head. "Is that better?"

"Your will is mine, my Lord," Thanatos said, looking at the floor with his head bowed. In a cloud of gray, he disappeared, leaving them alone.

Persephone placed her hands on her hips, inclining her head. "Is that how you speak to all of your court members?"

"Only those who disobey my orders," he said, narrowing

his eyes at her.

"Is obedience what you want? Or do you simply enjoy exerting power over others?"

"You have no idea the level of power I possess here," Hades said, tilting his head with eyes narrowed. "You've never seen what my full power even looks like."

"Yes, I have," she replied. "The Chimera attack was unforgettable, to say the least."

"That is a fraction of my power that you witnessed with your team," Hades said, leaning against the table. "You may have seen my darkness but have yet to witness my fire."

"Is fire and darkness what you plan to use against my mother and Zeus?"

"If it comes to that, yes."

"What are we going to do?" Persephone asked so quietly he almost thought it a whisper.

Seeing her sit back in the chair and curl up her knees to her chest, holding them, looking at the stagnant wine lost in memory, made him quell his aggressive energy. Hades walked over to her and knelt in front of Persephone. He reached up, brushed the hair on her cheek back behind her ear, and softened his eyes at her.

"You don't ever have to worry about what will happen to you. I will protect you now. No one will ever hurt you again." His hand rested on her cheek as she leaned into it for comfort.

"Not even you?" Her wide, large eyes looked up at him, filled with sorrow.

He was helpless to that look. A combined innocence with accusation all at once. Her eyes began to glow, tears filling them and falling in long streams down her cheeks. She was stunning in her sadness.

His thumb reached up instinctively to wipe them away. "From now on, you're mine, and I will always protect you."

Persephone shook her head away from his hand. "She's going to burn it all down until you give me up."

"I don't care," Hades said, wishing he could alleviate her

fears. But he couldn't. "I'm not letting you go."

He would if he could find a way to make it all work and everyone be happy. But that wasn't the world they lived in. Someone would lose, and he would make damn sure it wasn't him. Even if Persephone hated him for a thousand years, he would take her punishments willingly as penance.

Persephone pulled away from him. "That's the problem. I want you to care, and I want you to respect my decisions for my life, not fight against me."

"You want me to agree to let you go?" Hades swallowed hard, trying to remain composed.

"Yes." Persephone leaned close, glaring at Hades. "You can't keep me here forever, Hades."

"I can. And I sure as fuck will." Hades stood and towered over her eyes, going cold again. "I don't want you out of my sight again."

It tore him apart, remembering her heart's sickly sound ceasing. His world almost ended there. Now that he had her, Hades knew he would do everything in his power never to experience that much pain or grief again. It had almost killed him. Both times, he'd felt it. Hades wanted her to see him as good, steady, and maybe even a hero, though he knew he was far from it. Instead, all she saw was a monster when she looked at him. He'd become the villain he'd feared everyone would see him as. Though painful, it was worth being near her, knowing she was safe with him, even if she was furious.

Persephone leaned close, glaring at him. "You can't keep me here forever, Hades."

"Keeping you here as my queen is exactly what I will do, Persephone." Hades raised a brow indifferent to her pursed lips and hatred in her eyes. He turned away, grabbing the cape that clasped at his shoulders and dragged behind him and the same black he often wore with silver stitching. "If I were you, wife, I would get used to your new home because you're never leaving."

Turning, Hades left her there, staring with murderous

intent at him. He slammed the door shut and stormed into the room where he could summon the Moirai.

The walls dripped with water from the stalactites above into a pool in the center of the empty black space.

"Moirai! Hear me!" He called out to the air. "Come to me, now."

Hades stood in front of the pool, where three females emerged in white with veils covering their eyes and stepped out of the pool to stand completely dry before him.

"Hades, Lord of Darkness and King of the underworld," Lachesis said, stepping forward.

Atropose stepped forward next to her right. "We are honored you summoned us, Lord Hades."'

"How may we be of service?" Klotho, the youngest to the left of Lachesis, asked.

"Persephone is with me as you predicted in your vision," Hades said, narrowing his eyes. "Can you see further into the prophecy now?"

"Well done, Dark Lord," Lakhesis said, standing emotionless among her sisters. "You have achieved your goal. Yet, I'm afraid you're too late."

"Too late for what?" Hades asked in a measured tone, looking at each one.

"The changes have already begun," said Klotho, who took one step closer in the triangle of the three. "We warned you that she had to choose to come. You did not listen. We knew that would be the case."

Atropose stepped forward. "And now Demeter will fulfill her destined role."

"Since you see so well into the future, what of my destined role?" He asked, bracing himself for the worst.

"Prepare for the coming storms," They all said in haunting unison.

"I've seen the storms you speak of. Our world is about to end or forever be changed. Yes. I already know this," Hades said, exasperated, running his hands through his hair. "We've been through this many times, and I'm losing my patience. I don't need a reminder of my mistakes. In the name of Gaia, give me something new or leave."

The name of Gaia appeared to trigger something in them. They were looking at one another and communicating wordlessly. After a moment, together, they turned to face Hades.

"Once the death stroke of Persephone brought us her string, it was I who cut it," Atropose said, raising her shears, opening and then snapping them closed, making a loud cutting sound.

"What did you just say?" Hades paused, feeling his stomach sink, hoping he'd misheard. "You did what?"

"Alas," said Lakhesis, raising a hand for him to be silent, then tilted her head. "Something remarkable occurred."

Pointing with the short staff that she pulled out from under her robe to an orb that appeared between where the Moirai and Hades stood, Lakhesis showed Hades what she said was true. The horoscope stars aligned in the image to the time of Persephone's demise. The image shimmered, and a rare sight unfolded before him—the Moirai's actual appearance.

Three wrinkled old females born of Nyx sat in a circle. He didn't know who their father could be. Some suspected Zeus, but his brother's fear of Nyx, the only being he did not wish to cross, made that idea unlikely. Klotho tilted her head as the next name whispered in her aged ear. The spinning wheel turned, and the cord wove to lay in her hand, growing longer as she handed it to Lakhesis to observe with her good eye. When it was time, he watched Atropose's knotted fingers grasp the shears, cut the once glowing cord, now faded and gray, and set it aside to be collected.

These goddesses of death were born of necessity, and all would submit to them, from Uranos to Gaia. Even Zeus, who often interfered, was still subject to their prophecy. They were often considered severe, stern, and inflexible, but they showed kindness to Hades. He never knew why.

Before him were projections of their power, but the three never left their wheel where Klotho spun the string needed for every being. Their minds project them out to the world, allowing their work to occur everywhere all at once. The three rocked back and forth as they labored with milky white eyes, living in a perpetual trance as they worked tirelessly for eternity.

In the room where Klotho wove Persephone's golden string as she was born to Demeter. Eileithia was there with the three to weave her destiny. He could see they were in a cave somewhere with a single torch held by Prometheus, who stood watch for the goddess. It occurred to Hades that the reason Prometheus was in the mortal world, to begin with, was to help Demeter escape.

Knowing Zeus' history of refusing to punish his wife or Demeter, someone had to pay for her leaving. Zeus told them it was for giving mortals fire, but Hades knew it was a lie. Mortals had been using fire from his volcanoes and pits for years. Zeus felt betrayed. He raged for years, sending multiple search parties to find her. None returned with any clue where Demeter had gone.

Eileithyia continued to work with Demeter to give birth, and when the moment came, Hades watched the dial shift from the moment of birth, and the string was fully formed, now to her final sacrifice to save her mother.

He watched in horror as the Moirai followed her to the little cabin in the meadow where Persephone lay, barely breathing. No matter what Hecate or Demeter administered, nothing worked. Demeter held Persephone in her arms, rocking her, singing lullabies with tears in constant streams down her face. He realized what he suffered was shared by Demeter that day, and he almost felt guilty for causing Demeter more pain.

The ghostly projections of the Moirai entered the room and stood over Persephone's resting body. He stopped breathing when the shears severed her string, feeling his heart stop like hers, making him relive that agonizing moment when he felt her presence gone from the world. He watched, helpless again, as Hera's cruelty cut his dreams to pieces.

As the three turned to leave, one-half of the two parts of the cord lit within Atropos' hand with an even brighter golden light. The other turned dark with smokey energy surrounding it. The two pieces came together as though magnetized, slithering and winding around one another. The black string intertwined with the gold, and the two halves bound themselves together. His heart was racing. Could this be real?

"Yes," said Klotho, pointing to the cords. "What you see is true. Some source of power repaired Persephone's cord. We do not know how. We did not sanction a change of fate for the goddess. Her destiny was to die. Though we suspected it would prevent the destruction of our world, we were wrong."

"I thought you couldn't see past her choice," Hades said, trying to calm down his racing heart.

"At that moment, she could have chosen to let Demeter die, or she would choose to sacrifice herself to save her mother. If Demeter died, there would be no destruction of the world. The prophecy would trigger if it were the latter, and our fates would all rest in Persephone's choice."

"Okay," Hades said, pacing as he listened. "Then what did you do?"

"We tried again." Atropose added, giving another snip, snip in the air, sans any expression. "But the scissors wouldn't cut."

"You did it again?" Hades threw his hands in the air, then clenched them and pinched the bridge of his nose, taking a deep breath to stay calm.

"We were quite unprepared," Klotho said, clenching her spindle she held at her side, knuckles going white, but she remained otherwise stoic as the rest.

"Never before has this happened," Lakhesis said, stepping forward. "Such a thing has never occurred in our world."

Hades could feel the room spinning.

"Why didn't you tell me?" He asked in a choked whisper, knowing now what he felt was real when his heart broke.

"Her death heralds the prophecy," Atropose said with a nod. "Her transformation was necessary. You would have tried to interfere, and we won't allow that. The wheel is now in motion."

"Even if you heed Zeus and return the goddess," Klotho added. "We can no longer stop what is to come."

"Wait." Hades stopped his pacing. "You kept her death from me so I wouldn't prevent it?"

"We feel your pain, Lord Hades," Lakhesis said, clasping her hands together. "We are not unsympathetic, but her time had come. Now her time appears eternal."

"What do you mean?" He asked, desperate for some hope.

"Only Zeus or a primordial has the power to repair a god's string," said Lakhesis. "It takes tremendous power to change one's fate. We can no longer see her future while she still has a choice to make. Since her fate lies with yours, we cannot see either."

"For once, I'm relieved." Hades stepped back and crossed his arms, thinking about the possibilities of all of this. "I can help her choose me, even if Demeter throws her temper tantrum."

How did she return? What sort of being had such power? Good Gaia, he hated having so many questions and so few answers.

Lakhesis stepped back. "Return Persephone or not. It no longer matters. Nothing can stop the change that will come, even if you give her up. If you can."

"Never," he growled.

"You cannot change her fate," said Atropose with pursed lips.

"Watch me."

"Sacrifice will precede change." Lachesis placed a comforting hand on Hades' shoulders and smiled. "Prepare yourself. For your sacrifice will be the greatest of all."

"Have we been of assistance, Lord Hades?" Asked Klotho.

"Yes," he said with a heavy sigh. "You may go."

"Be well, Dark Lord," they all said together.

They all bowed to Hades, and, in a slow-paced glide, they disappeared back into the pool as they had entered. The light faded, and he sat in the rippling light lapping at the walls like waves, thinking about what he would do. Or, more accurately, what Persephone was going to decide. Nothing could prepare her for what Tartarus holds, but she needed to see it. Nothing could prepare him for the news he just received.

Maybe he should go easy on her to ease her into staying. Perhaps she would like to see the orchard or the winery. He remembered her telling him she enjoyed making it at home. What else would she like? He had to think back on their time together to find a way to make her happy here. It wasn't going to be easy. He'd only ever witnessed her on Olympus or in the forest hunting beasts. He realized other than small conversations. He didn't know what she liked when she was safe at home in her peaceful meadow and cottage.

Hades sighed, crossing his arms. How could she handle that kind of darkness when all she's known is the light? And what would she think of me if she indeed saw mine? He'd controlled his abilities closely while they'd trained all those months ago. But here, he would use them freely whenever he desired. No one could challenge him in his realm, and he ensured they all remembered that. How would she react to seeing him mete out punishment? Worse, if Zeus did decide to punish him, would he have to start a war? Or would he take the torment that Zeus would willingly inflict?

She will have to meet the Erynese. Their fury was the making of nightmares in this perpetual, repetitive, and endless torture where the ones who deserve such justice get it. He couldn't imagine Persephone having the stomach for their retribution on the most despicable of all. Depending on the observer, they could be considered ugly or beautiful, even with their winged forms entwined in serpents. The crack of their whips and screams of the damned would echo through the cavern, sometimes waking him from a deep sleep. Their huntress boots and short sable dresses tied with rope hid the majority of their horrors, thankfully. One possessed a serpent between her legs and wore ties accentuating her vast breasts while wearing a long black dress to hide the monster between her legs until it was too late for the predators that sought her beautiful guise over and over. They never learned. He'd reveled in these torments on the deserving. What would she think of him when she saw his face in such times as these?

Considering Persephone handled the Manticores and the Chimera, Hades knew she would see past this. It wasn't the Erinyes, the Keres, or even the furies that truly worried him. Ghastly as they could be, they were essential to his work and did their jobs well. He had no complaints. Besides her scrolls and lessons, she'd never seen one as far as he knew, and the sight of just one was terrifying enough. There were dozens down in Tartarus. Each one was more frightening than the next.

At the end of Tartarus, still held captive for eternity, was Cronos, the only being Hades truly feared. The Titan of Time waited for Hades to return to visit once a year. Time was the one thing you couldn't kill, and neither god nor mortal could truly escape.

"Please, Gaia, give her the strength to handle the darkness she is about to witness. For if she doesn't, and she chooses to leave, you might as well take me and end my suffering."

CHAPTER 3
CAPTURED

Persephone sat stewing where he'd left her. The strange room behind the throne held a space built like a study with shelves filled with scrolls, books, and maps with tools to measure landscapes along the walls. A large table in the center stood carved out of a single stalagmite emerging from the floor. It looked cracked and barely held together. The blue veins of light shone from the crooked base up to the surface of unfamiliar terrain filled with glowing lights. She wondered what they were and where all these areas led. *If I can study the three-dimensional map, there could be a way out,* she thought as her eyes drifted over the mountains and foggy valleys.

She crossed one leg over the other, enjoying the warm fire in the stone fireplace in the corner of the room. The chair she sat across from was dark leather and had worn areas where claws appeared to tear through where large hands had rested. Her chair was smaller with a fur covering. A small stool beckoned to her aching feet. Moving it into place, Persephone propped up her dirty feet, feeling the radiating warmth of the perfect fire. Her body began to relax from being taught as a musical string. The comfort of the space made her feel drowsy. If only she could have some of the wine, this moment would be bliss.

The fur-lined furniture was cozy and reminded her of the warm nights by the fire at home. Persephone recalled the hours she spent by the firelight in the hearth at home. For a moment, she fantasized about Hades being with her there, curled up in each other's arms and talking late into the night like they would on Olympus. Those nights were so precious to her. She was naive to think of coming here as a good idea, but now that she was, she had to look around when she could find a chance. Persephone needed some good stories to tell Artemis when she escaped.

But how? It would be hard to leave unnoticed with so many eyes on her. She stared into the red liquid, wishing she could have some, thinking of those who glared at her when walking with Thanatos to this room. One glare, In particular, was scraping against her skin like a barb of her mother's staff. Something about this female seemed familiar. Where had she seen the nymph before?

Distracting Persephone from her thoughts, Hecate burst through the door, startling her and making the goddess knock over the carafe of wine on the skirt of her dress.

"Damn it!" Persephone said to herself as contents poured into her lap, splashing droplets all over that stained her gown.

She set the carafe upright and started to pat it dry with a towel that was thankfully next to her on the table by the wine.

"Persephone, my darkling one," Hecate opened her arms wide to embrace Persephone, who returned her warm hug. "Welcome to the Underworld!"

"Hecate?" Persephone jumped up and held the Titaness longer than she meant to. "Where have you been? I've been calling for you all day!"

"I assume you're settling in as the new ruler of this realm. I'm jealous, of course. One always needs more minions." Hecate played with her long necklace, twisting the beads in her fingers and swinging the large stone held at the center like a pendulum as she looked off in thought.

"You have to do something." Persephone moved to sit back in the chair. "You have to make Hades see reason and convince him to let me go."

"Daughter of Demeter," Hecate sighed. "I'm afraid I can't do that."

"Why not?" Persephone asked, taking a step back, feeling the sting of betrayal.

Hecate shrugged. "Hades controls this realm, and no one has the power to challenge him here, not even Zeus." Hecate tapped her lip, looking into the distance. "Often, he's referred to as Chthonic Zeus if that helps you understand the magnitude of his power here. If he wants you to stay, you will."

"Hades can't be more powerful than Zeus." Persephone felt the shock overwhelm her at the desperation of it all. She had to get out of there, but how? "Zeus can do something. Anyone who disobeys him receives his wrath. Wouldn't he punish Hades for not returning me? Please, Hecate, can you speak to him for me? You're the only one who can deliver a message for me."

"It was Zeus who approved of your union." Hecate said, rolling her eyes. "He said as much. Technically, you could see this situation as Hades coming to claim his promised bride."

"Zeus did what?" Gods, no. Not him too. "When did this happen?"

"Pretty much day one when you and Hades touched," Hecate raised her eyebrows repeatedly. Persephone blushed, looking away.

"Did Hades know about this?" Persephone asked, clenching her teeth.

"Oh, come now, Persephone." Hecate's laugh faded into awkward silence.

Persephone clenched her fists to hold in her rage. "All of you have been colluding all this time?"

"Well, not exactly. More like we've all been riding the

same chariot." Hecate drifted off into thought again. "Maybe it's more like the same boat. Yes, on the same one, but with different ports in mind."

Persephone dropped her head into her hand and pinched the bridge of her nose. "My mom was right. You can't trust any gods, and it would seem Titans because none of you, it seems, even knows what being a trusted friend means. My mom was right to keep me away from all the schemes and lies you all create."

"Oh, don't glare at me like that," Hecate pouted. "I had no idea how all of this would play out. After the... The incident. I was too relieved to remember that I had given Hades a seed to your realm."

"You gave him a what? A seed?" Persephone's eyes were wide with shock. "It was you who did this?"

Hecate frowned. "You should have seen him, Persephone. A thousand years in Tartarus would have been a mercy compared to what I saw him go through when you were gone. It was a torture that no one should have to endure."

Persephone paused her anger for a moment. "Tortured?"

"He might as well have been," Hecate slumped and sat down, looking into her hands. "I've never seen him like that. He's always so composed and in control. Since you've been. Well, you know. He has been more of a tyrant than a strong leader. He was always a bit too sober and abrupt but never so far gone that he was inconsolable."

"I didn't realize he took it so hard," Persephone whispered, looking into her hand marred by nail indentations, grateful she stopped before she bled.

Hades was always stern. No one could know his feelings unless he showed them. To be out of control, she knew, was one of his biggest fears. How could she affect a god as powerful as him in such a way? She was only a spring maiden, she thought to herself. A lesser goddess to his power and nowhere near as strong even in battle, he would always dominate her.

As fierce as he was, he often would try to comfort her

if she was sad or sit with her, watching the light fade over the horizon. And he was always there to defend her whenever she was in danger. But that was his duty. And the prophecy they shared was based on other conditions. Indeed, things had changed now.

Gaia said Persephone had a choice. Knowing this about Hades will make that choice harder. She didn't realize he cared so much. Even though she was only mostly angry after hearing that, it didn't change anything. She needed to go home. She couldn't let anyone suffer for her feelings.

"It doesn't matter how Hades or myself feel about this. People will die if I don't go back." Persephone threw the red-stained towel over into a fountain. "Worse, what if my parents come here and start a war?"

Hecate's face turned red. "You throw another soiled towel into my scrying pool, the war will be here between you and me."

"Oh," Persephone stumbled around the table, picked up the sopping towel, and wrung it out. "Apologies. I didn't realize."

Looking back, she noticed Hecate grinding her teeth and clenching her hands in the air as though she wanted to strangle Persephone but then put them down with a fake smile and her hands behind her back.

"Nevermind," Hecate waved her hand dismissively, and the towel disappeared from Persephone's hands. "Neither Zeus nor Demeter can enter here without Hades' consent. Even if they did manage by some miracle, they have little to no power here because this place's energy source comes from the primordial Tartarus, not Gaia. Hades couldn't command his helfire without the power of Tartarus."

"What is that? And where did he learn it?" Persephone vaguely recalled the fire that glowed mixed with his darkness on the door of Hades' chambers. Was that the blue fire she speaks of?

"I'm not sure," Hecate shrugged. "It's what he calls it

after he went on a journey long ago to other realms, lastly to the Nordic realm, to learn more about his powers. When Hades returned, he brought back the ability to summon fire so hot it was blue. It scared the other gods, so they would never dare challenge him."

"Are you telling me Hades could take on Zeus in a battle?" Persephone asked, whipping her hands dry on her dress. "I'd have to see that to believe it. Who do you think would win?"

"Let's pray we never find out." Hecate patted her hand, then walked over to pour a drink and drank it all down.

"By the way. I've been meaning to ask you." Persephone narrowed her eyes at Hecate. "How do you get in and out of here when no one else seems to be allowed?"

"I was granted a pass long ago for my allegiance to Zeus in the Titanomachy. He and Hades agreed that magic should exist everywhere so I can go anywhere I wish." Hecate shrugged. "It's not easy to go to Poseidon's realm, but I have a spell that makes it work."

Persephone's eyes lit up. "Can you take me out of here?"

"I can bring you in but can't take you out. Not without Hade's permission." Hecate clicked her tongue, seeing Persephone frown. "The rules of the underworld are sacrosanct and unmoving for a reason. Surely, Hades explained this to you before you first attempted to come here."

"Right," Persephone said with a nod, thinking back to the mirror. "He did mention that gods couldn't take anything from the underworld in one of our late-night visits...."

"Ooh, late-night visits," Hecate winked. "Do go on."

"I meant through the mirror, and you know that from my thoughts already," Persephone said, rolling her eyes.

Hecate waved off her ire. "Unfortunately, or fortunately, depending on how you look at it, you're stuck here with Hades until you can find a deal that will allow you to leave."

"What deal?" Persephone asked with a tinge of hope.

"Don't you understand anything I teach you?" Hecate

raised one brow, looking down her nose. "Honestly, you'd think you'd start paying attention. To leave, you have to strike a bargain with Hades. Or you have to find a loophole in the rules."

"A vow that is unbreakable, huh? Like a vow on the River Styx?"

"I suggest you read up and learn your underworld lore to find a way to get out. Of course, you could just ask Hades to let you go."

"I've been cursing and yelling at him to do that very thing." Persephone was growing tired of Hades ignoring her pleas. "This is stupid. Why can't you help me escape? Mom must be furious and is probably destroying half of Olympus right now searching for me."

"Well...," Hecate said under her breath. "It's not Olympus I'm worried about."

"What do you mean?" Persephone snapped her attention to Hecate, who was acting odd.

Her smile said one thing, but her eyes darting back and forth, trying to avoid eye contact, was off from her usual casual demeanor.

"What's happened?" Persephone squared her shoulders, prepared for the bad news.

"Persephone, you worry too much about Demeter's feelings." Hecate righted her eyes to match her smile, realizing her face betrayed her emotions. "Why not take this opportunity to discover your real feelings?"

"My feelings?" Persephone scoffed. "About what?"

"About this place," Hecate said, placing both hands gently on Persephone's shoulders with a comforting squeeze. "Perhaps you could explore your feelings for Hades without any prying eyes. My darkling, you are on your own for the first time in your life. She can't control you down here; without help, Demeter can't get to you either. So I suggest you take advantage of this time you would have otherwise never gotten had things turned out any different."

Persephone glared. "Being taken from my mother was not my idea."

"No. Your idea was to sneak out with your siblings and a lone wolf across a dangerous region where you almost died. And if I'm being candid. You did, Persephone. At least, I think you did. If only for a few moments, but yes. I don't even know how you came back. My potion wasn't strong enough to bring you back, yet here you are."

"What do you mean?" Persephone gasped.

"I saw the light leave your body, and then it returned glowing brighter than before, but mixed with an inky black vein that swirled around the light's core."

"Why didn't my mom tell me?" Persephone looked down at her hands, remembering the tea she had sitting next to Gaia. Was it then that her life force left her body?

"She doesn't know, and you must promise me you'll never tell her," she said, gripping Persephone's shoulders almost a little too tight. "She's been far beyond exhaustion, never leaving your side except to pour more tea."

Hecate turned, placing a hand on her forehead, and paced.

"Hecate, please tell me what happened," Persephone said in a voice only a mouse could hear.

Hecate sighed. "It happened at that moment. When she, your mother, turned to get another kettle going. I saw you take your last breath. That's when Demeter collapsed, water spilling everywhere. She knew when you'd left and couldn't take it, so her body put her into a deep sleep. Maybe a minute or so later, after getting Demeter to the adjacent couch, head to head, you both lay unmoving except for Demeter's shallow breaths. Nothing I used worked. Potions, salves, stones... Nothing worked. Suddenly, your light returned in a blinding ray, then settled within you. Shortly after, Demeter awoke, and I told her she passed out from exhaustion and should get some sleep. Which, thankfully, she believed. I didn't have the heart to tell her you were gone. Even if only for a few moments.

Maybe even minutes. I don't know. It felt like an eternity."

Persephone smiled and took Hecate's hands. "I was with Gaia."

"What?" Hecate gasped, squeezing Persepone's hands a little too tight.

"Gaia, I saw her." Persephone walked over to her balcony that faced the lava that flowed far beneath where she stood. "I had tea with her in a garden she created out of nothing."

"She came to you?" Hecate stepped back, eyes wide with shock.

"I think I went to her," Persephone leaned against the railing, looking down, imagining how Gaia would turn even a place like this into a lush garden paradise. "We talked for half an hour, maybe? It seemed much longer than what you said."

"Give me the details in your mind so I can see our Mother," said Hecate, holding her hand out to Persephone.

She opened her mind and let Hecate into the memory. The one thing that stood out was that the flowers surrounding them were the same as the single white flower she'd picked in the field when Hades had come for her. Persephone remembered Gaia's words that she did have a choice about what was happening to her. She had to decide between both worlds or choose them both.

Persephone realized that she was the cause of everyone's mystery. She had been the one constant in all of this conflict. Demeter left Olympus because of her. Hecate was banned from their home because she kept Persephone's secret. Artemis almost died from her stupid decision, and the others she dragged into her schemes to get something she wanted. Her selfishness nearly cost her mom her own life from heartbreak. And now she would have to break Hade's heart by leaving him alone in his Kingdom of mist and darkness. Knowing how much he suffered, that choice wasn't becoming easier. Her anger toward Hecate wasn't even great. The seed she gave to Hades to find Persephone was the same flower as in Gaia's garden. It had to be a part of the prophecy. But everything is so awful. How could any of this turn out alright?

"By Chaos, she's stunning," Hecate whispered. "The gift of this visit can't be overemphasized. Now you listen to me. Stop that spiraling right now, Persephone," Hecate said, scolding her like a mother. "It'll do you no good. I see now that we have an even greater situation with Gaia's interference and, even bigger, her approval of you and Hades being together." Hecate placed a hand to her chin in thought. "That could be good enough leverage in the inevitable argument coming from Demeter."

"You mean a war?"

"If we play our cards right, there will be no war, but there might be a few battles, so best to prepare for her arrival." Hecate raised one finger and smiled. "Ah! I had a thought. As I said, I can't take you out, but maybe I could summon a few items you might need."

"Like what?"

"I know what you need." Hecate put her finger to her lips, tapping twice.

She began to pat down her gown that barely covered her nakedness. The sheer black lace fabric covered her like a second skin from neck to floor with long sleeves that couldn't have hidden anything. Persephone was surprised Hecate wore any underwear at all, though the panties and bras barely held anything back. Snapping her finger, Hecate twirled her hand in a circle and held it flat. A familiar crescent blade with a jeweled hilt appeared in Hecate's hand through the purple cloud of smoke.

"Here," she said, handing Persephone the sickle her mother had given her at her first tournament on Olympus.

It brought tears to her eyes, but she sniffed and held them back. The jewels in the hilt were amethyst. Three stones embedded in the gold sickle shone in the light where her fingers rested with one stone obsidian placed on the thumb of the grip. It was in its sheath, so Persephone took it and strapped it to her belt against her back. Pulling the skirt of her dress higher to just below her ass, she wrapped it tight around her waist and draped the back over her weapon so no one would see it and take it from her.

"That's more like it, my dear. Show off those fabulous legs you have." Hecate winked at Persephone and smiled. "Now, I have one more thing I think you'll want."

Hecate raised both hands before her, and a light began to build with glowing green energy. A potted plant appeared with the flower she had picked in the field and floated to sit gently on the table. Snapping her fingers, Hecate summoned a sunstone. Drawing in solar energy, it glowed, giving the frail flower a little light. Its neck craned toward the rays, and the flower turned to face the light. She realized she'd dropped it when she landed in the Underworld, not even thinking about the poor plant dying here. The stone's magic radiated downward, drifting sparkles of glittering energy that fell slowly over the petals.

"There. Now, you'll have to keep the light on it while down here during the day; otherwise, it will wilt and die. Something from the surface for you. It's your choice if you wish to keep it."

"Choice," Persephone scoffed under her breath. "Gaia said, ultimately, the choice will be mine. I just don't know what to choose."

"Then you should seek out the answers you need down here."

"Why can't you help me find them?"

Hecate smiled with a wicked grin. "My dear sweet Persephone... What's the fun in that? Speaking of fun. You might want to try having some."

"Really?" Persephone scoffed. "I'm supposed to have fun right now?"

"It wouldn't kill you." Hecate adjusted her gown. "Just imagine how much trouble you could get into down here with little to no real consequences. You're his queen; no one, not even the Titans in Tartarus, can refuse your order."

"I do not have such power." Persephone pursed her lips and folded her arms.

Hecate winked. "Not yet."

Persephone groaned. "Hecate, will you please say what you mean?"

"I'll tell you what," Hecate said, tapping her lip. "What you need is to unlock those dark and delicious powers of yours. I can help with that. The issue is not releasing them, but controlling them."

"How are we going to do that?" Persephone stared at her hands. "I don't even know what they are."

"Let me ask around and see what I can come up with. Check my cauldron for answers." Hecate twirled her finger, and a phantom cauldron appeared with a glowing green liquid that reflected shimmering light over her face. "In the meantime, though you may no longer need the training of Olympus, your schooling with me will never end. I think we shall meet again at the witching hour in my oracle room right over there."

Hecate gestured to the hall Persephone had come from. "It's just across this room through the door with my symbol. We may, indeed, find the solution to all of your problems, goddess of spring who could be queen."

Before Persephone could object, Hecate disappeared in the purple cloud she formed and began to cackle lightly under her breath, then disappeared along with the cauldron into its folds, leaving the sparks of gold to spatter about like fireworks on the ground until they were gone.

Persephone walked back to her chambers. After a few mistakes and several hallways later, she finally found the door with flowers. Persephone entered and flopped down face-first onto the bed. With a heavy sigh, she grabbed a pillow to let out the loudest scream she could form as she lay muffled into the soft, downy puff pressed over her face. Exhausted and drained from her release, she lay down, pulling the thick covers over her, and fell asleep, hoping she would wake up and this would all prove to be a vicious nightmare.

Persephone stood holding her mother's hand at the edge of the meadow. The wind blew their hair and clothes as they moved in slow motion and smiled at one another. The golden rays highlighting Demeter's matching curls drifted around her warm eyes that reflected the green-draped sleeveless gown she wore. The smell of flowers and grass and the feel of the cool dark soil beneath her feet gave her a sense of calm she had as a youth. Demeter raised her staff, and the world opened past the trees where the meadow's edge met the forest. They walked past the boundary and stepped onto the wide chariot of grain woven to wicker and solidified in a golden front pulled by two dragons, one of green and the other of golden scales.

Persephone stepped up first. Her mother's weight joined and settled them balanced together into the chariot. Demeter released Persephone's hand, and both took hold of one side of each warm organic frame, making Persephone feel stable and steady. Demeter took the reins and snapped them once, signaling their mounts to fly. As they flew over the land, they witnessed the mortals at harvest filled with smiles waving up at them. The goddesses waved back and continued their journey toward the waning light on the horizon. The closer they were, the darker it became. They rode on until there was no light left. When Persephone looked down at her hand, the chariot had changed.

It was black, lined in gold, jagged rather than smooth. She looked up in front to see the dragons replaced by four horses darker than night galloping at dizzying speeds through the overcast sky. When Persephone looked to her side, she expected to see Demeter, but dark eyes and a wicked smile she loved and hated simultaneously gazed back at her with desire and adoration. He reached out and wrapped his arm around her waist, pulling her against him. With her hands pressed against his pounding chest, Hades kissed her hard. Persephone's heart began to pound. She felt the panic welling inside her as the ground opened up and swallowed them.

When she opened her eyes, Persephone saw the candle

on the table beside the bed. Once burning tall, now it burned near the end, leaving only a small stump of wax and a tiny flame. The wax dripped onto the floor where she stood with her bare feet on the warm stone. She didn't bother looking at herself in the mirror. She merely walked to the door, rubbing her sandy eyes. When her sight cleared, a large pool of steaming water was in the grotto's center, inviting her to enter. Her stiff muscles screamed at her to relieve them of the tension that knotted from her neck to her lower back. Probably from being hauled on a horse while fighting, she thought to herself.

Persephone walked over to the side of the stone-encircled spring. The smooth steps led to the deep end just under the waterfall. The steam from the water was soothing and smelled of jasmine. Large jagged crystals adorned the sides with varying hues from purple and pink to red and orange.

The ground rumbled beneath her and started to whisper to Persephone from the darkness, beckoning for her to follow.

"Persephoneeee..." The haunting whisper spoke to her from behind.

Persephone turned swiftly around, blinking her eyes in the dark, seeing nothing. An unseen force called her forward toward the sound. She left her chambers following the sound, which led her to a large door that showed the war of the Titans with Hades as the prominent hero. The enormous wooden door began to move under her touch and opened to reveal a cavernous room with few decorations. A large fireplace unlit with one chair in front of it and a small table holding a carafe of wine appeared inviting. Her heart began to race when her hands met the soft fabric of a familiar bed a few feet away from the fireplace. The pillars were familiar too, but she wasn't sure how since she'd never been in this room before. Suddenly, Persephone realized she'd seen this room in the vision of Hades caressing her body, penetrating her to her core, making her moan out loud. Her hand went to her mouth as she gasped. Persephone turned to run out but instead slammed hard into a solid figure.

***

Hades didn't budge when Persephone slammed into him. He blinked slowly and then looked down at her. Such lovely, thick lashes surrounded her wide, lavender eyes, which seemed to blink in slow motion whenever she stared into his. They stood for a moment. He hitched in a breath as she placed her delicate hand on his chest, where his body betrayed his emotions, and his chest began to pound. Shaking her head to release the trance they fell under, she backed away and looked down, refusing to meet his eyes.

"What are you doing here?" She asked, in a mouse tone.

Hades smiled slightly. "I live here, remember?"

"I meant here, at this moment." Persephone looked around awkwardly as though caught doing something naughty.

He found it adorable.

"Unless you haven't noticed, these are my chambers. The better question is, what are you doing here?"

"I... I heard something," Persephone stuttered.

"Oh? And what would that be?"

Her embarrassment for being in his room was tangible enough to taste in the air.

"Nevermind." Persephone shook her head. "It was a mistake to come here. I'll just go."

She walked past him, but he stopped her, catching her arm and pulling her to him.

"Will you be joining me in the main hall for dinner?" He asked, inclining his head.

Persephone glared. "I refuse to consume anything, even a drop of wine down here. That would trap me for eternity." Persephone crossed her arms, turning away from him. "I would rather die."

"Death isn't an option." Hades growled and turned Persephone to face him. "I suggest you find a way to live with your new circumstances."

A shadow fell over her eyes. "Death is always an option."

Hades glared down at her. "Never. Do you understand me?"

"I understand you are used to getting your way, but it won't work now. I won't consent to being here while my mom is worried sick."

Hades clenched his jaw. "Then she will get a small taste of what I felt, not knowing if you were alive or dead for the past six fucking months."

"That wasn't her fault," she protested, wrenching her arm from his grasp. "I was unconscious the whole time."

"I don't care!" His eyes flashed black, emanating the darkness drifting from them like smoke.

"No, you don't care about anyone's feelings but your own." Persephone began to walk away when he grabbed her forearm, pulling her back to face him.

"What's that supposed to mean?" Hades demanded, seething at her constant grating tone.

Persephone ripped away her arm. "It means you're selfish. I can't make it any clearer than that."

Hades scoffed. "Nobody has ever given a damn about my feelings. I've spent my entire life subject to the whims of my father, Zeus, this place, Demeter, and now you. Maybe if you'd grow up a bit, you'd understand that none of us get what we want."

"Grow up? Are you serious? I may not be as old as you, but I can spot desperation when I see it. Face it. You're no more in control here than you are out there." Persephone crossed her arms. "Maybe my mom was right."

"About what?" He asked, knowing where this was going.

"That you have as little control over yourself as Zeus." Persephone poked him in the chest with one finger. "At the end of the day, if you want something, you will take it, willing or not."

Hades stepped closer, chest pounding but still

maintaining a cool tone. "I am not Zeus."

She shrugged. "I heard you are called Chthonic Zeus."

Hades pursed his lips tight. "That is not my name."

"It appears you go by many names," she replied.

"Persephone..." He said, holding back his anger.

"Yes, so many names," Persephone said, interrupting. "Like, the unseen one, giver of wealth, the Chthonic Zeus, Liar, Monster, now abductor."

"That's enough, Persephone." His growl warned her, but she didn't seem to care.

"What is it, Dark Lord?" She asked with a smirk. "Am I touching a nerve?"

Hades' glare subsided, and he smiled. "I'm going to take this moment as a sign that your hunger has gotten the better of you. I suggest you eat."

"My what? Hades...," Her eyes shot wide.

He grabbed her hand and placed it against his hardening shaft that strained against his pants.

"There's one thing you can consume without being trapped here," he said, enjoying how red her cheeks turned.

Persephone moaned, rolling her eyes back, chest rising and falling quicker as her fingers gently caressed his length. Her anger turned to lust so quickly that he wanted to take advantage of this moment.

"I... I couldn't," she stuttered, still stroking him.

"You seemed to like it when you had me tied down in the forest," he teased.

"That was different," she said breathlessly.

"Really?" Hades asked, nuzzling her temple, taking in her scent. "How so?"

Persephone stepped back, releasing him. The cold in her absence made his body beg him to take her. He clenched his hands to maintain control that was slipping from his grasp the longer he was with her.

"I had control then," Persephone said, straightening her shoulders.

"Is that what you think?" He asked, amused by her confidence. "You think you can control me? That's adorable."

Anger cast a shadow over her face at his words. "I'm sure you could have escaped. It must be nice to have that power."

"It is," he said with a tilt of his head.

"Gaia, help me." Persephone stomped her foot and pointed her finger in his face. "If our roles could change, you would be my prisoner. Then I would have the power to command you to do as I say."

Hades gave her a wicked grin. "Is that the game you want to play?"

"It doesn't matter what I want, remember? My feelings don't matter." She slapped her chest and then pointed back at him. "Only your selfish desires matter. Know this, Dark Lord. I will never obey you or eat from this desolate place. You may think you've won, but the war between us has only begun to rage. I promise you will regret what you've done before this ends and I'm long gone."

He put up a finger to interrupt. "If you don't want to eat, you can stay in your chambers. I won't have you running around getting into mischief as you and your team did on Olympus."

"Oh, but Hades," Persephone said, brushing against him. "Mischief is what I'm good at. And I intend to cause as much chaos to you as possible. Thanks to some friendly advice from Hecate, I plan to see what fun I can have in this new world. It just won't be with you."

Persephone turned and walked out of the room, leaving him alone.

Hades appeared in his war room and grabbed the nearest object. The glass smashed with a loud crash into the adjacent wall. The vase's glass remnants shattered, spreading across the floor, stopping shy of his boots. He kicked the pieces and walked around, each step crushing glass under his boots. He generously filled it again, and after drinking the entire glass in one gulp, Hades poured another. He looked down into the swirling red fluid with hints of pomegranate, then threw it against the wall, causing debris and wine to splash as it dripped slowly down the wall, pooling on the floor.

"I am nothing like Zeus," he growled deep in his throat while bracing his arms against the table with his head bowed. "She has no idea what she's talking about."

Cursing under his breath, Hades ran his hands over his face and paced the room for a while. He didn't notice that it had become evening when he opened the door to see that the festivities were underway.

"I take it our queen isn't coming to dinner?"

Hades turned to see Thanatos standing there, looking at the shattered remains of the room.

Hades shook his head. "No, not tonight."

"I'll let the guests know, and we can reschedule," replied Thanatos with a bow.

"I don't think she's going to be happy here," said Hades under his breath.

"My lord, we all thought the same in the beginning." Thanatos placed a warm hand on Hades' shoulder. "Give her time."

"How much time?" Hades asked, wrenching his fingers through his medium-length hair that he refused to cut until he saw her again.

Thanatos shrugged. "Are we not immortal?"

Hades scoffed. "I'm beginning to see that the stubbornness she gained from her mother suggests that no time will be enough."

"Persephone is not Demeter. She just needs time to adjust."

"I hope you're right." Hades gripped his chair, feeling his claws coming out, making scratching sounds in the leather as it ripped. "For now, keep her comfortable and out of trouble."

"The former I can do, but the latter is entirely up to her." Thanatos gave a curt nod and then disappeared.

Hating everyone's joy, he went to the only place that

helped him think. He loved the rows of Pomegranate, so orderly and red against a backdrop of gray. Much like her hair, the red of the bulbous fruit, always ripe, made him think of the fire in the morning light. The same light she'd brought into his life. If she would ever forgive him, he might feel the warmth of it again.

CHAPTER 4
MISTRESS

Persephone had come out of her room, feeling empty in both her stomach and her resolve. Her body was crying out for sensation. She ached to feel a touch of any kind. To feel an emotion other than despair. To feel him deep inside of her....

Lost in thought, she slammed into a tall, dark-skinned female wearing leather from her neck to her boots. Her muscular arms exposed and her waist bare, the elegant beauty's hair was black and straight, flowing down her back, reminding Persephone of her nymph friends in the meadow. Persephone was then hit with a stiff shoulder, slamming into hers as the lithe female walked by.

"Oh!" Persephone said, rubbing her left shoulder. "Excuse me."

"Yes. Excuse you," she replied, with salt in her tone, eyes slanted and narrowed.

"I'm sorry..."

"You should be," she cut off Persephone and sneered at her, eyeing her up and down with distaste in her expression. "Weedy bitch."

"What did you just say to me?" Persephone stopped and turned back to face the female who rudely addressed her.

Usually, she would be too shy to respond and move, but something about this place made her feel bolder than ever. Besides, if what Hecate said was true, no one would hurt her for fear of Hades.

"I'm sure you heard me," said the female.

"Did I do something to you, or are you always this dreadful?" replied Persephone, placing a hand on her hip.

"Oh," she sneered, raising a brow and folding her arms. "I suppose you want to be the new "Dread Queen" around here?"

Persephone glared. "What do you mean, new?"

"You don't know?" The other female turned to her and glared. "He was mine until you ruined everything."

"Seriously?" said Persephone, pinching the bridge of her nose. "Who are you, and what are you talking about?"

"Hades," she replied, hissing. "He was mine. That is until you showed up."

"Hades?" Persephone asked, shaking her head.

Of course. It has to be Hades. Gods, she hated how stupid nymphs were sometimes.

"Let me be clear with you," Persephone said, stepping toward her with her hands pressed together for patience. "What was your name?"

"Mynthe." She glared down at Persephone, who stood several inches shorter. "You better remember my name."

Standing her ground, Persephone replied, "Mynthe? Huh, that sounds familiar. Oh, I remember your name said in Hades' room on Olympus."

Mynthe's eyes widened. "How did you know I was in his room on Olympus?"

"I never reveal my sources of information," Persephone said, remembering the lessons she gained on Olympus as she folded her arms and grinned with a snakelike charm she'd learned from Hera. "Didn't he kick you out? I distinctly remember him telling you to leave after you threw yourself at him."

Mynthe leaned closer. "Hades likes aggressive females.

"Mynthe. Pretty name," Persephone said, still grinning. "What makes you think you have any say over a god? Can you say he was yours, knowing you'd never be able to match his power? You're just a nymph, Mynth."

Persephone squared her shoulders, standing up against the female who challenged her.

"My name is Mynthe, you bitch." Mynthe glared with her nostrils flaring with anger. "You don't even know me."

"I don't need to know you. I know your kind all too well. Often hanging all over Zeus and the other males to gain status." Persephone tilted her head, eyeing Mynthe up and down.

"Don't play with me, goddess," Mynthe threatened. "I advise you to leave as soon as possible, or something terrible may happen to you."

"Am I supposed to take orders from a... Wait, what kind of nymph are you?" She asked the nymph in a mocking tone.

"Infernal," Mynthe said with a red glow beneath her skin that began to emit light through what looked like veins cracking as a volcano would with magma through the soil. "Nymphs like me feed warm waters to the springs through our heat abilities."

"Right." Persephone shook her head. "A queen of Hades would need to be a goddess that can go up against Hera or even one Titan and survive. I didn't even stand a chance against Hera. Do you think you have any chance as a mere nymph?"

"You'd be surprised what I'm capable of," Mynthe said with her chin up.

Persephone chuckled. "Hera would crush you like a bird beneath her boot. Do you honestly believe he would ever take you as queen? You can't be serious about having these kinds of delusions."

"You don't know anything about my Dark Lord!" Mynthe

yelled, face turning red. "He's been different since Olympus. We aren't even allowed in his pools anymore. I take it this has something to do with you. You've done something to him, and I intend to find out what."

"I haven't done anything to him," Persephone argued. "You need to back the fuck off of me, now."

Persephone's patience was wearing thin. Nymphs were often prone to be highly territorial, and this pool must have meant a great deal to her.

"I don't see what he finds so attractive about you," she said to Persephone, folding her arms with a sneer. "He'd be better off with someone like me who could care for him properly."

"I doubt that," she replied, rolling her eyes at the nymph. "I see Hades cast you aside for some reason or another. Can't imagine why with your sunny personality."

Mythe scoffed, shaking her head. "You know what? It's innocent, naive females like you who always think a male will stay loyal to you. Trust me. He will return to me after he tires of you."

Persephone groaned. "I don't know if you realize this, but I didn't choose to be here."

"Then why don't you leave?" Mynth closed the distance between them.

Laughing, Persephone eyed Mynthe as if she was stupid. "If I knew how, I would."

"Not so powerful as you pretend, are you?" Mynthe said, tilting her head. "You can't even move about in this world freely as a nymph can, yet you look down on us."

"I only look down on those no better than a plaything to the gods," Persephone replied with a salty tone.

"You're just another new plaything," Mynth glared. "Hades will tire of you and send you packing when he's had enough of you."

Persephone was going to say something but stopped. Nymphs could often move in and out of almost any place because of their nature. Choking down her anger, Persephone realized this could be an enemy turned ally. Someone who might be motivated enough to send her home regardless of Hades' orders.

"You know what? You're right," Persephone said, softening her tone. "If you know how I can leave, I'm listening."

Persephone realized that this was essentially Hades' mistress. Someone who he had been with for a long time, it would seem. A detail he failed to mention. He said Mynthe meant nothing, but she didn't seem to think she was nothing to him. Still, this being would have enough incentive to help her escape. Perhaps she might be helpful after all.

Mynthe paused, looking confused. "You... You want to leave?"

"Any way that I can, yes." Persephone stared at the nymph, waiting for a reply. "So, if you have any great ideas on how to get me out of here, you can have Hades all to yourself."

"Technically, he hasn't rejected me. I imagine when you reject him, I know he'll cum to get the satisfaction he needs," Mynthe said, cocking her head to the side.

She wasn't a past mistress. Persephone felt like an idiot, thinking Hades would be different from Zeus.

Seeing her falter, Mynth pressed on. "Let me guess... He said you were the only one. I guess you'll have to share him with all of us eventually. The others and I will be here whenever you're not, and that's when he'll forget all about you and your pathetic demands."

Persephone glared at Mynthe, who laughed at her discomfort. All the months Persephone had spent talking and learning all she could, Hades still managed to hide things from her, just like Zeus. The darkness grew inside of her. She could feel her rage boiling deep. For once, she wanted to let go and release that fury. But she wouldn't. Persephone buried the source of the power she felt and gained control before her violet eyes lit, giving away her emotions.

"Mynthe." Persephone feigned a smile and righted her shoulders. "I can tell you care for him very much. I'll make you a deal. You find a way to get me out of here, and you can have him back. All to yourself. What do you think of that?"

"You would forsake all of the riches, the power, and even his bed?" She asked, eyes wide.

Persephone nodded. "I think it's the best option considering the alternative."

"What alternative is that?" Mynthe said, inclining her head.

"The one where I kill you for touching what's mine," Persephone said, narrowing her eyes, feeling the dark energy speak through her. "So long as he isn't mine, you get to live."

"Is that a threat, weedy bitch?" Mynthe asked, closing the gap between them.

The two squared off, waiting for the other to make a move, chest to chest, with only a few inches separating them in height.

"Mynthe!" They turned to see Hades standing in the entryway, glaring down at them. "What are you doing here?"

Mythe turned to him and smiled.

"My lord, I merely came to greet our new guest and ensure she feels at home. We were just getting to know one another. Weren't we, goddess?"

"Yes, Mynthe was just telling me how welcome I was here." Persephone eyed her with one eye flexing, daring Mynthe to tell him what Persephone had said.

To her surprise, Mynthe said nothing. She nodded with a curt smile instead.

"Now that our guest is feeling welcomed, I will continue preparations for the next feast in her honor. Until our next meeting, weedy." Mynthe tilted her head in a slight bow, followed by a narrowing of her eyes back at Persephone, then left.

Persephone began to walk past Hades when he stopped her, taking her hand.

"Where do you think you're going?" He asked.

She cleared her throat, pulling her hand away. "I was going to look around."

"I told you to stay in your chambers," Hades said, closing the distance between them.

"I know," Persephone replied with a nod.

He chuckled. "Why do you constantly disobey my orders?"

"I was never good with orders," she said with a shrug. "You know that."

Hades gave a slight side grin. "If you want to see this place, you only need to ask."

"I wouldn't give you the satisfaction," she said, breathless as his scent made her head swim.

They locked eyes. She couldn't pull away. Instead of glaring at her, he was warm, and she could see he did care for her.

"What if I want to give you satisfaction?" He asked, leaning down to whisper into her ear.

His hot breath sent tingles down her body. Her desire was a mix of anger and need. Damn it! Why did things have to be so complicated between them?

"If you force me, I'll hate you," she said finally, trying to break the trance.

Her tone sobered his lustful eyes, and he backed away and looked off.

"You will learn to do as I say here, or there will be consequences," he said with all softness vanished from his voice.

"What consequences?" Persephone said, folding her arms and narrowing her eyes up at him. "If you tire of me, you can always let me go and return to your old lovers."

He turned to her with confusion in his eyes. "What are you talking about?"

Persephone scoffed. "Don't look at me like you didn't lie to me all this time, saying I was the only one you were interested in. Mynthe has a very different idea about your relationship together."

As jealous as she was about that, Persephone knew she could use it to get out of there. Who else would have more incentive than his mistress? Still, until now, Persephone had foolishly thought he did love her and desired only her. It stung, and she didn't want to admit how much it hurt to know she would have to share him.

A voice deep inside her whispered to her. *I'll kill anyone who touches him...*

"Persephone. I..." Hades said, stepping closer, but she stepped back.

"No," she interrupted. "You have no idea what it's like to be powerless. You treat those around you with contempt. You lie about who and what you are, and you expect me to live here with your mistress and be happy about it. This place and these beings are not part of the life I imagined when I dreamed of leaving the Meadow. And neither are you."

Persephone turned on her heel and left him standing with his mouth open, staring at her. Stomping to her chambers, she slammed the door behind her, grabbed her pillow, and screamed into it as loud as she could.

Part of her was angry. The other part of her hated how much he affected her. When she felt he was softening up, he would go cold again. Persephone curled her legs up to her chest, wishing for the warm meadow, the clinking of her mother pouring tea, and maybe some fun with Artemis hunting and fighting monsters as a team. Here, she was alone. No friends. Only Hades. If she could convince Mynthe to help her escape, maybe she would be able to make things right on the surface.

Her thoughts were interrupted by a gentle knock on her door. She knew it was Hades and had no intention of letting him into her room. He wanted her captive in the underworld. Well, she was going to do something about that.

"Go away!" She yelled out from her bed.

"Persephone," he said gently from the other side. "Let me explain."

"I don't want to hear it. You lied to me."

"I should have told you about Mynthe and the others."

She ripped the door open and screamed, "What others? Of course there are more! Why wouldn't there be!? You are the handsome and seductive "Dark Lord, Hades," she said, mocking him with air quotes oozing with sarcasm.

Hades breathed a heavy sigh. "Persephone. I didn't lie to you."

"You said you weren't with the female I saw in your room on Olympus. She didn't mean anything to you, you said. Turns out she's your mistress! Now that I know who she is, you tell me there are more. How many? Two? Maybe Three? I bet you've got a whole harem of females ready to satisfy your needs. So why don't you go and do what god-kings seem to do best? Go bother someone else and leave me alone to wallow in my grief for the life you took away from me!"

Persephone slammed the door in his face, then rather than muffle her scream, she pulled from her mother's book and started screaming and destroying the room. Her powers coursed through her, and the darkness clawed to the surface.

Persephone shocked herself out of her rage when she looked in the mirror. Her appearance frightened her. Her hair was dark, blowing wildly around her. The whites of her glowing lavender eyes were completely black, emanating a flame the color of her bedding with Tyrian-colored smoke drifting out of them. When she gasped and placed her hands to her lips, she was stunned to see her skin the palest it'd ever been, as though she'd never been in the sun. Her nails were claws of red with a dark flame, the same as her eyes, drifting off her fingertips.

For the first time since she'd recovered, Persephone realized she was different. She had changed that fateful day confronting Hera. She should have never tried to hide from her mother. The power she felt made her dizzy. She wavered on her feet until she collapsed to one knee and fought against the power welling inside until she could feel it subside and quiet.

Persephone opened her eyes, taking deep breaths. She stood, eyes closed, too afraid to look in the mirror. Needing to see if what happened with her appearance was real, her light lavender eyes looked back, framed in bright red hair and her usual tan when she opened them. Her nails were short, and there was no trace of the energy surrounding her. Her heart was racing, pounding fast in her chest. Her hand covered the pulse, and she worked to steady her breath.

She heard a soft knock on her door and felt the rage build up again.

"Go away!"

"Persephone." Hades said gently on the other side. "Open the door."

"I don't want to see you right now. Please go away," she said, knowing if she opened the door, Persephone would give in to his pleas or, worse, appear as she had moments ago.

"If you don't come out, I'm coming in," Hades said from the other side.

Persephone had no intention of letting his two-timing.... Or was it three or four-timing? Who knew about him? She wasn't opening that door. Gods, he made her furious with his lies and deception.

What Mynthe said was painful. The room was closing in on her. The more the knocks pounded against the wood, the more Persephone became agitated. The darkness began to buzz inside of her again. Damn it! Her head swam. Between this and Hades and all the other demands around her, she wanted to scream. The pounding continued, forcing her temper to hit its peak.

***

"I know you can hear me," he said through the door. "What can I do to make this right between us?"

Opening the door in a rage, Persephone glared up at him. "How many more are there?"

He flexed his jaw, hesitant to answer. "Do you want me to tell you how many I have been with here?"

She wasn't going to like the answer.

"Yes. I need to know," she asked, jutting her chin out.

"Mynthe has been my number one mistress for a few decades." Hades noticed Persephone squeezing her fist tighter and paused. "Now and then, she brings a sister or two into the pool for me."

"Please continue," she said, knuckles becoming white as she listened.

"I don't think I need to," Hades said, wishing he could make this easier for her, but her anger was grating on his nerves. "Between us, the only one whose virtue ever mattered was yours. I have no reason to deny my needs."

Persephone took a deep breath. "What are those needs? And how many lovers does it take to fulfill them?"

"Why is this an issue for you?" He asked, confused.

Her face turned red, glaring daggers at him.

"I need to know if I am here as another plaything in your kingdom or if you meant everything you said to me on Olympus?" Persephone said, pain cracking her voice.

"You think that I would incur the wrath of Demeter and bring you here just to add you to my bed as a courtesan?" He asked, incredulous.

"I don't know, did you?" Persephone asked, refusing to back down. "How can I trust you?"

"My word should be enough," he growled. "If you were as simple as a fucking nymph, I wouldn't have even needed to ask your opinion. I wouldn't have asked Zeus if I could have you as my wife. Gaia, help me. I wouldn't have Zeus' wife in Tartarus for killing you!"

She recoiled. Her face turned pale, almost as though she was going to be sick. He couldn't believe he brought that up so callously. Gaia, help him to say the right words.

"I should have told you about Mynthe and the others," Hades said, feeling terrible at how upset Persephone was.

She folded her arms and looked away. "Why should I care about your mistresses?"

"Persephone," Hades said calmly. "I didn't lie to you."

"You said you weren't with the female I saw in your room. She's not a messenger but your old mistress." Persephone glared, spitting at him with her words.

"I said I didn't sleep with her that night," Hades' correction was not what she wanted to hear when her face burned red.

"So she keeps your bed warm while I'm away?"

"I haven't slept with anybody since I met you."

"Don't lie to me anymore!" Persephone screamed as her body began to flicker with light. "You've brought me here against my will, and now you want to make me into a queen of a dead kingdom and sit back and watch as you humiliate me as my father does to both of my moms. I will not be such a fool."

"That's not my intention," Hades said, stepping forward, wanting to touch her, but instead clenched his hands to his sides and looked away. "I don't only want you in my bed."

"I refuse to come to your bed," she said, hands going to her hips and narrowing her eyes at him. "So why don't you and your whores go and do what you kings do best. Fuck off."

The energy in the room intensified with the winds as Persephone grew more impassioned. Her eyes darkened as her skin began to pale. Her energy built, causing more debris to whirl around them. A vase flew by his head, forcing him to duck out of the way. Before she could move or do anything else, he grabbed her by the arm, bringing her close to his chest.

"Calm your chaos, goddess, and stop resisting me," he said close to her ear.

Her body stiffened, and the air around them turned electric as the glass and debris rose behind her, hovering dangerously in a slow, whirling tempest of her dark energy. Persephone reached back and punched him in the jaw, forcing him to let her go as he stumbled back.

"You didn't want my compliance, so resistance is all you will get from me," she threatened. "Release me, or I will work to make your life a nightmare."

She kicked over the broken stool next to her and flung it several feet, crashing through her night lamp and sending shards of glass at his face, which he barely blocked.

"Damn it, Persephone!" Hades screamed through her storm. "This is my realm. You'll have to adjust to how I rule this kingdom whether you like it or not. I'm not giving you up to anyone. Do you hear me? I will never let you go!"

Her eyes glowed up at him, filling with tears. Suddenly, she used the dark cloud that formed around her like an extension of her arm, and Persephone slammed the door in his face. Through the door, he could hear her destroying the room he'd spent so much time preparing for her.

Hades knew that Mynthe had just ruined any chance at a smooth courtship. The sound of Persephone's rage and the shattering of glass with Gaia knows what crashing against the door made him step back. With each shaking boom and pounding of chaos in the room, he resigned himself to leave.

Hades suddenly stopped when he heard her crying. The breaking of items had stopped, and he could hear her weeping. His heart was tearing out of his chest, demanding he go to her. He wanted to knock on her door again, praying she would at least listen even if she wouldn't come out. But it was no use. Persephone wouldn't listen while she was this angry.

Instead, he walked away and didn't go back. He stormed into his room, slamming the door behind him, then slumped against the heavy door.

He cursed under his breath, pounding a fist into the door, yelling at the roof, and shaking the heavy doors. Ripping his belt off, he threw his weapons on the nearby table. Grabbing the carafe, he poured a drink. The taste was sour in his mouth. He threw the glass at the door and watched it shatter, feeling somewhat satisfied at the destruction. His body was starting to transform as his rage overwhelmed him.

Hades walked to his dresser and leaned with heavy limbs on the surface. His claws dug in, cracking the wood before receding to normal. The mirror before him showed his dark eyes staring back until they cleared. Tilting his head to the side, he saw how hard she hit him. The mark was red, which for him took a lot. She was finally learning her strength. His anger turned to respect, rubbing his jaw, still feeling the sting. Something behind him distracted him, and he turned to see Mynthe at the doorway to his pool.

"I see you have a new plaything," Mynthe said, sauntering toward him. "Isn't she a little young for you?"

He glared at her. Ignoring his mood, she stood beside him with her hands clasped behind her back and chest high for him to see her top barely holding in her breasts with one leather strap across her nipples. Mynthe wasted her attempts at an innocent face on him. He knew better.

"It was a mistake to speak to Persephone without my permission," he replied through gritted teeth.

"She needed to know about us eventually," she said, stepping closer and placing both hands on his chest.

He grabbed her wrists, almost too rough, and shoved her away from him.

"There is no us," he said, narrowing his eyes.

"Perhaps," she said, smiling with a gentle tone. "You've never barred us from your pools until now, so I knew it was serious. You didn't expect me just to walk away from you."

"I should kill you for speaking to her," he growled, holding back his anger.

"If she's to be your queen," Mynthe said, backing up. "Then she will have to learn about what goes on in this place. Once she sees the real darkness you harbor here, she will return to her mommy, pleading to go home. She's too gentle. Too weak for this place, and you know it. She won't last a week here."

"Get. Out." His eyes went black as he glared, making her

back away wide-eyed.

Mynthe stumbled backward, realizing he wasn't playing anymore. Her fear was palpable in the air. His teeth grew as he snarled at her to leave. Her steps uneasy, she backed away toward the pool entrance. Before leaving, she cleared her throat.

"Next time I return, you'll have to invite me," her voice shook over her typically smooth buttery voice.

"I won't," he replied with as much certainty and ice in his tone that left no confusion.

Still, she smiled, "We'll see."

Turning toward the pool without a word, she walked to the water. As her toe touched the clear surface, she melded into the spring until she was gone.

Alone with his thoughts, he slumped his weight in his chair as it creaked from strain by the fire. What am I doing? Parties? Feasts? Useless. These are all the same things on Olympus. It's easy to enjoy this world if that's all she sees. Persephone would be his queen. Mynthe was right. Much as he hated admitting it, he hid things from Persephone. He knew she wouldn't like his mistresses, so he avoided telling her about them.

In truth, he didn't mention them because they hadn't entered his mind since Persephone's arrival. He hadn't shown her Tartarus, intentionally trying to avoid the darkness. It was only a matter of time until Demeter would retrieve her. Nothing was going according to his plan. Hades had thought she would be happy to see him, not feral with rage. The sting was a blunt force to his heart after longing for her. He had to get Persephone to agree to stay before a conflict with Demeter happened, or he'd lose her forever. The timing sucked, as always. He had no choice. He had to show her everything and be vulnerable for the first time.

Hardly anyone noticed him as he made his way to the stables. Or if they did, they made no effort to greet him.

Aethone was making a mess as he walked in to see

her kick her stable attendant and then a bucket sending feces everywhere. One splatter landed at his feet, just barely missing his shoe. He looked up at her and tilted his head. Whinnying, she trotted over to say hello to Hades and nuzzled his face.

"I see you're just as irritable as I am," he said, petting her under her chin.

Please let me eat this one, she said in his mind.

"Not today, but maybe later." He chuckled as she snorted and rolled her eyes.

What makes you more grumpy than usual?

Mynthe told Persephone about our relationship.

Aethone snorted. *Can I eat the nymph now? I do hate her...*

"I might let you this time," he said, petting her mane. "Right now, I need to figure out how to get Persephone to see this place as I do."

Perhaps she needs a tour to see what beautiful horrors are available.

Hades chuckled at that. "I don't think she would find them as delightful as you do."

Aethone whinnied with a nod of her head. *We can get the chariot out and take her for a ride. Females love chariots. I know I do.*

"Will your brothers be up for it?"

They'd be mad if you didn't take them.

"Agreed." Hades touched her forehead gently. "Go find them and bring them here. I will bring Persephone tomorrow night to show her the underworld. All of it."

Deal! Oh! Make sure she brings some of those tasty apples.

I wouldn't dare forget. He thought to himself.

Aethone nudged him affectionately, then opened her wings and took off into a gallop, flying out of the stables. Somehow, Hades needed to prove to her that he had a kingdom worthy of Persephone to call home. At first, he ordered her into her room, but now she won't leave it. He'd have to coax her out with something she likes. But what?

Clenching his fists, Hades walked back to his throne and

sat, robes splayed over his massive seat, and watched the court enjoy his wine and food. He would have none. Nothing would satisfy him anyway.

He hated any comparison to Zeus. Persephone knew he would be angry for a while. Perhaps it was best this way. He knew it was a way to keep him off balance if she was to figure out a way to get home. If there even was a way home. Of course, he knew how, but he would never reveal it to her. *Nothing would hurt her ever again so long as she was with me.*

Unlike Hades, Persephone couldn't teleport anywhere. She had to run the old-fashioned way, which would be a waste of time since Aethone could fly to her in seconds. His power could do the rest. No matter where she went, he would find her. It was the only comfort he could offer to himself until she decided to say yes.

CHAPTER 5
CHTHONIC GAMES

There had to be a loophole. Persephone would find it to get out, or she would return kicking and screaming every time. There was only one option. Spend time in the realm. Learn as much as she could and find a way out that Hades couldn't stop, even with his powers. Persephone's scream would never be in vain again. Even if he were in control, she would never submit. Unless he kept looking at her with that wicked smile. Her heart pounded every time.

Determined, Persephone adjusted her appearance in the mirror. The bottom of her skirt draped over her thighs in shreds. Her heart sank, but she set her mind to freedom, pulling her hair into a ponytail. It was darker red than usual. The gold tips that blended with her pinks were gone. Was it possible her lashes were longer and thicker?

"Hmm. Must be the lighting down here."

She shrugged and went to the closet for a pair of boots.

Persephone found a gold pair of wedged boots that covered up her knees. At least she wouldn't be barefoot. Steeling herself to whatever she may encounter this time, Persephone straightened her shoulders and left toward the throne room in the Great Hall.

After a few miscalculated turns, Persephone found the entrance where music, dancing, and fighting were all creating deafening sounds of pounding and drums mixed with deep chanting voices and high, powerful singing ringing out in celebration. A tenor singer stood before the musical accompaniment and rode the notes like a falling ribbon, mixing his highs and lows in what was truly spectacular to hear. The deep voices that chanted behind him complimented his power, culminating on a high note. The music ended as Persephone stood in the light, hearing a loud snap to her left. She saw Thanatos raise a hand, and the music began to play as he gestured for her to come to the throne where Hades, Lord of all the Underworld, sat in anticipation of her arrival.

Hades' jutting laurel crown with shards of obsidian emitted blue fire at the tips, emanating the blue flame Hecate had explained earlier as his true power, which he freely displayed. His hair was much longer than on Olympus. The loose curls brushed past his shoulders. Gone was any softness in his eyes she'd witnessed when they were alone. His long black robes were open, baring his large muscles as the fabric draped over his throne. Both legs sat slightly too far from his seat, reminding her how tall he was. The tension in the room was hot and oppressive, and the crowd of guests or court, she didn't know, were noticeably on edge around him. He had kept to the shadows on Olympus, only engaging during Zeus' required parties. Here, he was the opposite of Zeus. There was no merriment, no nymphs prostrating themselves all over the king, and there were cheers but no laughter. Passerbyes would catch themselves, and smiles vanished if they neared him.

"Welcome, Persephone," Thanatos said, gesturing for her to follow him. In a booming voice that resonated above the music, he introduced her to Hades at the base of the stairs. "Daughter of Demeter and the Goddess of Spring, your seat is prepared next to our Lord."

Hades turned his eyes to Persephone. The blue flames

extinguished, changing his more pallid skin under the blue light to warm with the firelight from the pits below. His angular face was closely shaven, his jaw flexing as he held his stoic expression. She couldn't tell what he was thinking or feeling. His stoicism chilled her as the light of the red flame licked his skin. He said nothing but opened his hand and signaled for her to sit next to him on a smaller slab at a height noticeably lower than his seat.

"Our Lord, Hades, has prepared a feast and entertainment for your enjoyment," Thanatos added, nodding up toward where Hades offered her a seat. "Would you please bestow on us the honor of taking your place next to his and preside over the games?"

Clever Hades, she thought to herself. If Thanatos had asked her to accept Hades, she could have rejected him and made him look like a fool. But by rejecting the seat, she rejected the games and would lose the court's support if she ever needed it. He had warned her of such when they spoke late into the night through the mirrors. The rules were different in some ways here, but Olympus had prepared her well for the games she'd have to play to survive.

"I accept my position by your side... for the games," Her eyes narrowed on Hades. "Thank you for your generosity, Lord Hades." She curtsied deep and waited for Hades to respond. "It is an honor to be your guest."

Looking up, she saw his chest moving up and down from heavy breathing. His jaw clenched, visibly irritated by her comment.

His eyes devoured her openly in front of the court while he tilted his head, waiting for her to move. She realized his look was burning into her core when she didn't step forward. Persephone couldn't move as their eyes locked. Hades stood and walked one achingly slow step at a time, dragging the black cape that still reached the throne behind him until he stood half naked in only leather pants and boots and held his right hand to her.

Reaching up, she hesitated, remembering the last time they were like this. Their hands touched, and she felt the power inside of her like a blooming flower, sending her mind back to the vision they shared. It didn't overwhelm her like before, but she sensed he was also affected when he closed his eyes. Remembering they were before an audience, the one side of his lips in a half smile fell, becoming cold again. Taking her hand, he led her up the stairs. Reaching the top, he raised her hand to his lips and kissed her gently, causing her body to shiver. Hades turned them to face the crowd, who cheered with nervous enthusiasm.

She sat on the hard stone, finding no comfort and no backrest to relax against. He must have wanted her to remain uncomfortable until she agreed to submit. Her eyes drifted to his. Persephone felt her emotions welling inside her, making her stomach flutter. Abruptly, she turned to the arena below that rose from the ground, locking into place with a loud thud. Creatures of varying skins, furs, and scales gathered to witness the games. She'd only known of the Olympic games and felt excited to see how they differed here.

Persephone smiled, marveling at the room changing and wondering how it happened. "How does the ground change like that?"

"My realm bends to my will," Hades said, closing his eyes, raising one finger lit with a blue flame, moving it slightly in concentration until the room finished changing. "If I desire it, I think of what I need and build it."

"That would explain the sparse decor," Persephone said, rolling her eyes.

"You're welcome to make any changes you like now that you're here," Hades said, with a side look down at her.

"Don't get too comfortable, Hades." Persephone sat up straight and tried to ignore his gaze that was breaking down her resolve. "I won't be here for long. I'll play along if you wish for me to be a guest. Ultimately, I will have my freedom one way or another."

"I look forward to seeing you try." Hades smiled slightly but put it away as soon as it crossed his face. "Few can come and go from here, so long as they have my permission, which you do not." He turned to face her, staring her down to her core. "If I were you, I would get used to that throne."

"We'll see, Hades," she said under her breath, then cleared her throat at the lure of his gaze.

She turned away, looking around for something else to focus on.

"Let the games begin!" Thanatos shouted to the arena.

"What are they playing?" Persephone asked Hades, leaning in close so he could hear over the cheering.

"Pankration." Hades pointed to the arena sections. "It's an empty-handed submission sport with a few rules."

"What are the events?" She asked with genuine curiosity.

Hades pointed to each group. "You can box, wrestle, grapple, use arm locks, leglocks, and chokes to win. Hold up one finger of submission, and you'll be released."

"Is it dangerous?"

"Everything down here is dangerous." Hades tilted his head at her with a raised brow. "You're not afraid, are you?"

"Afraid of a little blood and broken bones?" She scoffed. "Are you forgetting my first fight with Hara?"

His eyes turned murderous. Lips pursed and jaw flexing. His dark energy was building, and his eyes flickered black momentarily before he regained control.

"Anyway," Persephone said, returning her attention to the groups. "So tell me, what's the most important rule?"

"Never fucking lose," Hades said in a dead tone refusing to meet her eyes again.

Music pounded, and three females entered the amphitheater, raising their weapons to massive applause. They wore an active top of wrapped cloth over their chests and a bit of cloth wrapped around and between their legs to form active underwear that seemed comfortable to Persephone as their movement would be easy and maneuverable. Their over-the-knee boots and arm guards made of leather were protection enough. They were unencumbered by armor, thus able to maintain flexibility with whatever they were about to do.

Persephone leaned forward. "What event is this?"

"It's the annual race of these three who are either always with one another or at each other's throats," Hades replied. "This tournament allows them to work out their issues with a race."

"A race?" Persephone pointed to the two who were tying back their feathered wings. "But two of them have wings. Isn't that going to disadvantage the third?"

Hades shook his head. "No wings. Just leg strength. To make it more fair to the Daemones, the two goddesses choose not to use their wings. After the race, they have a gauntlet to run, including throwing the javelin at a target to reach the next level. Then, the game progresses with long jumps and diskos, ending in a wrestling match between the three. In the mud."

"I see," Persephone said, resting her elbow on one knee, fascinated with the event. "So this is a pentathlon?"

"Basically, yes," Hades said, tapping a finger.

"What happens to the winner?" Persephone asked, wondering what he was doing until a servant came up the stairs with two wine goblets made of gold and a carafe of wine.

Hades took the wine. "Bragging rights over the others."

"That's it?" She asked, waving away the other goblet offered. "Seems a waste of a win to me."

"Sometimes they make personal bets or decide that whichever one loses will bestow their gifts on the winner," he replied, keeping his eyes on the crowd.

"What gifts do they possess?" Her curiosity peaked, and Persephone watched as they readied the starting line.

Hades gestured to each one of the challengers. "Nemesis, the dark-faced one, daughter of Nyx and Erebus, has promised punishment to right an undue wrong; Tyche, daughter of

Tethys and Oceanus, has offered a good or ill fortune, and Agathos is a daemon or good spirit offering protection of an individual or family."

"What a strange group of friends," said Persephone, smiling.

"Much like your friendships were," Hades replied with a hint of a side grin. "Though they are very different, they work well together. Tyche works with Hecate often, so she is the most popular of the gift bestowers."

"Fortune?" Persephone perked up, watching the goddess below with more interest. "Like prophesy? Could she give insight into our vision?"

"Perhaps," Hades said, raising his glass to signal the first event to begin.

Persephone touched his arm, forgetting she was supposed to be angry. "Do you think we could ask her about it?"

"I'm sure we could persuade her to give us an audience in my kingdom," Hades said with a smirk at her touch, so she pulled away.

Persephone cleared her throat. "Why don't we try to forget our troubles for the moment and focus on the game?"

"Yes. I think that would be best," Hades said, nodding to the referee. "For now."

The race began with a flag that signaled their start. The energy in the hall was exciting and not at all what she had expected it to be. They cheered as the runners made their way around the oval track. Sandals connected with every leap to ensure no flight occurred, however minor. The referee sat on a perch with its beak pointing down, eyeing the contestants for any cheating. In the final lap, Agathos had a substantial lead and made it to first place while the other two trailed behind. Her skills in the diskos and javelin were even better. Alas, she was no match for the high jump and ultimately lost first in the following wrestling match. Now, the competition was down to the two goddesses. Ensuring their wings stayed out of the way, they slammed one another into the mud pit. The crowd was howling at the two as they slid and fought, pinning down their opponent with no mercy. Finally, Tyche pinned Nemesis and won the match. Raising her arms in two fists, she conducted the court to cheer louder. They began to chant her name over and over as she stood smiling and reveling in her victory.

Reaching out her hands, she offered Nemesis an assist to stand when they laughed and began hugging and patting each other on the back. Walking over to stand before Hades, he stepped down to the center step.

"Congratulations, Tyche. Nemesis? Agathos? Both of you did excellent today. Be sure to pay your gifts to Tyche as agreed."

They nodded and smiled at each other. "Tyche, you've done well, and we wish to offer you a cornucopia of treasure to add to your collection before you return to the surface."

A young male brought her the cornucopia on a platter, which Tyche accepted and held up to the crowd. Their joyous applause was spurring them on to the excitement. All three hugged and left the arena with Nemesis' arms over the other two.

Thanatos stepped down to where Hades once stood. Sitting back next to Persephone, they sat quietly as the next event began. After a while, the event was so loud and wild that no one noticed Hades and Persephone anymore.

"Why do they get to leave?" Persephone whispered to Hades, trying to hide her irritation when he explained their free pass.

"Nyx and I made a deal long ago that her children are free to come and go as they please so she can see them whenever she wishes. Tyche and Agathos are Nemesis' best friends and often come and go with her. That invitation is extended to them as long as they are touching. Tyche is also an honorary Moirai who can leave with them when necessary."

"I see. Some have your favor and ability to come and go freely, while I get no such privileges, even though you want me to be queen. How will this place respect me if I'm a slave here?"

Persephone asked, folding her arms.

"Need I remind you that Zeus approved our union, and I have every right to have my wife in my home."

"I'm not your wife," she said, hissing at him.

"Yes, you are." Hades narrowed his eyes at her and stood.

Without another word, he walked down the arching steps and entered a room behind his throne.

Persephone got up and followed him, kicking open the door.

"No, I'm not."

Hades had thrown off his cape to the side and stood with eyes wide that anyone would dare do something like that.

Persephone snubbed her nose at Hades, walking past him. Her hands were fists resting on her hips. When she saw him roll his eyes, it sent her over the edge. Closing the door behind them, when Persephone heard the lock click, she whirled around and slapped Hades across the face. Her glare shot daggers into him. Attempting to hit him again with her other hand, Hades caught her by the wrist before she connected.

"Knock it off," he growled through clenched teeth. "You're not angry."

"No?"

"No." Hades said more calmly, holding her arm and pulling her close against his chest. "You wanted out of Demeter's lair, and we both know it."

Persephone wrenched her arm out of his grasp, then turned away. "What do you think will happen when my mom realizes you've taken me?" she asked, craning her neck to look up into his breathtaking eyes.

"I think she will come looking for you," Hades said soberly.

"And then what?" You'll fight her?"

"If it comes to that. Yes."

"Gods, I can't believe you!" Persephone paced back and forth. "You would fight my mom, destroy the world, and end all life? Why? Why did you do all of this?" She demanded.

"You know why."

Hades pulled Persephone against him, holding her tight against his chest that pounded beneath her palm over his heart.

His kiss seared her lips. The fire she felt welled up from her core, arching like waves that came crashing down. She kissed him back. All the longing she felt poured into him. His arms wrapped around her, cupping her to his body so close she wished he'd never let go. But this wouldn't last. It couldn't.

Persephone pushed him back. He released her and stood, chest rising and falling as he tried to control his body, which was already changing.

Suddenly, Persephone leaped into his arms, kissing him with as much force as he had with her. But as soon as she realized what she was doing, she let go and pushed him back.

"I... We can't do this." Persephone wrapped her arms around her waist and turned away from him. "You have to take me back."

"That's never going to happen," Hades said, with measured steps closing the distance she'd created.

Persephone turned to face him, "You won't have a choice once she finds out what you've done."

His control renewed, Hades' eyes cleared from the inky black that had cloaked them. Persephone needed to make him see reason despite her pain and longing for him.

"I don't think you understand, my beautiful flower," Hades said, moving closer to Persephone as he spoke, then gently brushed her lip with his thumb. "Demeter has no power here; without your plants, neither do you."

Before she could speak in protest, a knock sounded at the door.

***

Feeling a rumble under his feet, Hades realized that a

god had breached his realm. He knew who it was before he heard the knock. Cursing under his breath, he backed away from Persephone.

"Stay here," he said gently. "I will return in a minute. Something needs my attention."

"Where else am I going to go, Hades?" Persephone huffed.

Ignoring her venom, Hades left, appeared atop his dais, and sat on his throne.

The screams echoed through the cavern as the court paused, looking at the entrance to Hades' realm. The barking sounds of Hades' hound let everyone know who was coming.

Hermes came barreling into the room covered in drool from Cerberus playing with the young god. The ensuing laughter made the messenger furious, daring to glare at Hades. He said nothing for a moment, then waved a hand over his body, and his form, newly cleaned, was soon covered in fresh linens over a well-endowed cock. Some of the females took notice and began to converge until Hades raised a hand for them to stop.

"What are you doing here, Hermes?" Hades commanded.

"Zeus sent me to give you a message," Hermes shook his head and muttered under his breath, "You'd think you'd know that by now, I have one damn job."

"What was that?" Hades said through gritted teeth, his voice growing quieter as he narrowed his eyes.

"Nothing, my Lord of Darkness," Hermes coughed into his hand. "Only that Zeus wishes to speak with you and that terrible things are occurring on the surface."

"What's happening on the surface?" Hades asked, feigning ignorance.

"Huge winds, tornados, and freezing temperatures have begun to ruin crops," Hermes said, making wild gestures with his arms. "Helios descends below the horizon sooner and sooner each day without Demeter's presence. Someone has taken her daughter, and she's vowed to destroy all harvest until Persephone returns."

"I fail to understand why this is my problem?" Hades asked, leaning forward.

"My lord, Zeus, assumes you took her and wants you to return Persephone to her mother immediately, or there will be consequences."

"Zeus has already granted his permission to make Persephone my wife," Hades replied, remaining emotionless. "Leave. I don't take orders from Demeter or Zeus in my kingdom."

Hermes coughed into his hand. "If you do have Persephone, and I'm not saying you do, but if you fail to return the goddess, I must tell you that Zeus threatens to breach the Underworld to retrieve her."

Hades raised a brow. "Tell your master that if he wishes to start a war with me, the more mortal souls that fill my Underworld will only add to my army. Or perhaps he wishes that I release the Titans to trample his realm. His threat is hollow at best."

"You would dare say a threat from Zeus is hollow?" Hermes asked wide-eyed.

"He has no power here, and he knows it as much as I do," Hades growled low in his throat. "Now leave. Or I will have Cerberus finish what they started with you."

Hermes stood and then lifted off with his shoes, taking flight. "Zeus will not like this response."

"I do not require him to." Hades turned and sat on his throne, glaring down at the young messenger, who nervously eyed the laughing crowd.

With a burst of air, Hermes left, flying past everyone, leaving behind barking sounds as he made his way out of Hades' kingdom.

Hades stood and descended the nine steps. He walked into the room behind his throne without a word to anyone. Persephone had already left. The relief he felt knowing she didn't hear Heremes made him relax. The large stone war table glowed with all the souls interred in the Underworld. He stood watching the orbs float along with the light casting shadows of darkness and blue firelight flickering over the walls. Hades leaned against the heavy stone and pinched the bridge of his nose. With a heavy sigh, he knew what he had to do.

"Hecate?" Hades said, looking up. "I need to speak to you."

Hecate appeared behind him in a purple cloud that dissipated into golden sparkles drifting down to the hem of her black jeweled lace skirt that dragged along the ground as she walked toward him. Her beaded top left her midsection bare and barely contained her large breasts.

"I'd recognize that heavy sigh anywhere," Hecate said with a wide grin. "What troubles you, Hades?"

"Demeter." Hades crossed his arms. "What's happening on the surface?"

"Oh, I think you know," Hecate said with a knowing smile. "You knew the risk of absconding with her daughter."

"I remind you that you gave me the seed," Hades said, gritting his teeth. "I thought you would have already softened Demeter up to the idea. You've certainly done your work convincing Persephone to start mischief."

" I regret nothing in instigating Persephone's rebelliousness."

"Where's Demeter?" he asked, hating to be blind to the surface. "Demeter never went to Olympus?"

"She refused to leave Persephone's side until she woke," Hecate said, walking over to sit on an oversized corner wingback chair, laying one leg over the armrest. "The harvest was already beginning to suffer from her absence. But now Demeter will be determined to find Persephone. Which means she's wandering the mortal world, so there will be no crops."

"No doubt it's what Zeus called me to Olympus about," Hades said, leaning against the table. "He won't like my refusal."

"You refused him?" Hecate clicked her tongue. "Oof, he won't like that."

"I need time to convince Persephone to stay. I can't leave her here alone. Not yet, anyway." Hades folded his arms over his chest. "Besides, Zeus has already approved of our union, which is all I needed in the first place. I've tried everyone else's way of appeasing. It resulted in almost getting my queen killed, Hera's now in my prison, Demeter is rampaging across Gaia, and Persephone is so angry that she barely looks at me without disdain."

Hecate laughed. "You mean when you two aren't throwing yourselves at one another?"

Hades narrowed his eyes. "Stay out of my memories, Hecate."

"If Demeter asks me where her daughter is, I can't lie to her." Hecate sighed and stood to walk over to Hades.

"Can't or won't?" Hades asked, tilting his head.

"I had a dream recently. Or was it absently?" Hecate looked off to the ceiling with a hand to her chin, then waved her hand to dismiss her thoughts. "I saw in a vision, at the very least, Demeter asking me where her daughter was, and I led her with a torch in one hand, holding Demeter's hand in my other as I led her directly to you."

"When?" Hades felt his stomach sink. "When will you do this?"

"I don't know, Hades," she scoffed. "I didn't even know the circumstances when I saw this fate until now."

"Why didn't you mention this to me?" Hades asked, pinching the bridge of his nose.

"Meh," Hecate said, waving off his comment. "I hardly know what time I'm in, let alone tell everyone everything I see. Do you know what it takes to keep all these secrets and revelations in my head and not go mad?" She pointed to her head and then shrugged.

"I'd assumed you're already mad," Hades said, shaking his head. "It's all madness, isn't it?"

"Yes, It's not easy to manage one's destiny," Hecate said, standing and handing him a chalice of wine she'd just poured. "Imagine life without Persephone for a moment and ask yourself, do you regret your actions thus far?"

Hades took the chalice and drank before answering. "I don't regret falling in love with her, but I do regret the trouble it's causing."

"Ever the calculating one," Hecate said, gently touching his arm. "You must have faith that she will come to love you in return. I can't avoid Demeter forever, but I can make myself scarce for a few days, maybe more. If Demeter summons me, though, I must tell her Persephone is here, with you."

Hades, still holding the chalice, stared into the fireplace, feeling the warmth of the flame that comforted him.

"I can keep Demeter out indefinitely."

Hecate nodded. "True, but can you keep Persephone in, against her will, indefinitely?"

Hades sighed. "No."

"Then you have only one option. Convince Persephone to stay of her own free will because she wants to, or you must let her go eventually."

"I don't think that's possible," Hades said, placing his hands on the table as he set the chalice down, bowing his head into the light of the table.

"If you don't convince her to stay, my darling one, you won't have a choice." Hecate placed a well-meaning hand on his arm and gave a pained smile. "Demeter is stubborn, but she wants Persephone to be happy. So make her happy. You don't have much time. I suggest you remove that sour look from your face and show her the world you've built." Hecate walked over, placing a gentle hand on the side of his cheek with her brows drawn up. "Persephone already loves you. Now make her love this place so that when the time comes, and she must confront her mother, she will choose you."

"What if she doesn't?" He asked in a whisper.

Hecate's pained expression worried him.

"You must prepare for both of her parent's wrath," she continued. "Though I pray what I've seen you endure doesn't come to pass."

Hades pulled away. "What do you mean by that?"

"The vision was too difficult to decipher," she said with her brow furrowed. "Suffice it to say, you will not enjoy what is coming for you."

"When have I ever?"

"True indeed, Hades. True indeed."

Stepping back, Hecate disappeared, leaving Hades alone to his tortured thoughts.

He knew Persephone had wanted to avoid this very outcome. If he were going to convince her to stay, he'd have to work hard to gain her trust again. He'd never seen Persephone so angry. It would be a long road back to their last moments before she left Olympus... When she almost died. Or rather, she did die and returned. It bothered him that he didn't know how. Maybe that experience changed her? It had changed him. He could feel it.

His powers were fluctuating. At times, he felt weaker. Less sure of himself. Doubt had become his new friend. *If she did love him, she'd never said it,* he thought to himself. He'd hoped in his naivety that she'd be pleased to see him. But her last memory of him must have been the monster he'd become right before her eyes.

Hades cursed himself for not stopping Hera sooner. His failure would forever haunt him deep inside as a sharp knife buried into the hollow of his chest. Twisting agony welled up every time he remembered the sound of Hera's blades ripping through Persephone's body and the soft cry of his name before her heart had gone silent to his ears. And now he'd stolen her from the one being who had always protected her when he couldn't. His shame was like a bitter taste, dry as ash in his mouth. Hades knew he would spend the rest of their immortal lives trying to make it all up to Persephone. That is, if she would let him.

Hades locked her door using his powers to seal it shut. He didn't say much when she came into his room stomping and cursing. There was no time to waste. He'd decided that no doors would exist between them any longer to speed up the connection he desired.

"What did you do to my door?" Persephone demanded with her hands on her hips.

"You destroyed your room, remember? It's going to take some time to repair everything. Naturally, I couldn't let you sleep in such conditions. So you will sleep in my bed from now on."

Persephone choked on her words, then finally uttered, "I will not."

He smiled. "Don't worry. I'll sleep on my chair until you invite me."

"This isn't going to work," she argued. "Besides, I need my plant in there."

Hades transported himself into her room to find the flower under a hovering sunstone. His steps cracked and broke the debris still cluttered on the floor from her rampage. Taking both, he reappeared in his room, placing the plant on his dresser and wedding the stone in the air to hover above the soft petals that reminded him of her.

"I wasn't giving you a choice." Hades closed the distance between them. "I want you within my sight at all times. I know the kind of mischief you can get into. Your games and tricks on Olympus never made it past me. And if the tricks you played there are any measure of what you intend to do here. I want to keep a close eye on you."

"Why are you doing this?" She asked as her cheeks turned from an angry red to a blush when her eyes drifted to the bed they both remembered sharing.

"You should blame yourself," he said, walking past with no emotion in his eyes, ensuring she didn't know how adorable he thought she was when she was angry. "You're the one who can't control your temper."

Hades grabbed a pillow and threw it at her to catch. It smacked her in the face, blocking her gaping mouth. Taking the other one, he sat in his chair by the fire and poured a glass. She cursed and stormed over to the opposite side of the bed. Persephone remained in her stained dress and slipped into the covers facing away from him. The blankets almost made her disappear, though he could still hear her grumbling about how stupid she thought he was.

His lip curled up in a half smile as he listened to her berate him until she fell asleep. Wrapped in his sheets, she tossed and turned. Her face scrunched in panic. Rather than wake her, he slid under the covers and pulled her into his arms. She settled immediately. Her raspy breaths calmed into a heavy sigh. His arms pulled her tighter, and he lay there watching her scowl turn into a contented smile. Persephone leaned back into him, snuggling closer.

His chest broke. He wanted to see that smile when she was conscious. For now, this was enough. Hades breathed in her scent, brushing her hair back. Lilacs filled his nostrils with jasmine and something new. It felt like home, as though she was taking on his scent. His hand laid gently around her waist. She moaned softly, wrapped her arm around his, and pulled him closer. His name whispered on her lips made him smile slightly. She was thinking of him. Perhaps the dream began as a nightmare, but her relaxing in his arms seemed to have calmed whatever storm she had been experiencing.

He lay with her for several hours until she began to stir. Not wanting to disturb her when she woke, he reluctantly let her go and got out of bed. Hades could see the full carafe of wine on the table with an empty chalice next to his. Persephone still refused to take any sustenance here. Her immortality would keep her alive, but the pain of the hunger she must be feeling made him worry about her. She turned over behind him, and as he looked back, he could see the peace in her face from the light flickering in the fireplace. It danced along her red curls that he noticed no longer had the gold highlights. It was darker than before, more so near the roots. He wanted to touch those curls but closed his hand into a fist and instead disappeared from the room and reappeared in his war room.

Thanatos was there already making notes on the continuing build-up on the edge of the shores of Styx.

"My Lord." Thanatos looked up with a face marred in worry. "More are coming as the weather on the surface is getting worse."

The concern on his face mattered little to Hades, who ignored him, poured himself a glass of wine, and sat in the chair by the fireplace to stare into its flames.

"Demeter will give in eventually," Hades replied from a side-eye.

"She's not known to give in," replied Thanatos. "This game you're playing is beginning to have serious consequences."

Hades set his chalice down, then narrowed his eyes at Thanatos. "I'm not playing a game."

"Then perhaps you may want to start," Thanatos, unbothered by Hades' irritation. "If not, we could lose everything."

"And what exactly would we lose?" Hades leaned back, tilting his head. "A world of death, devoid of hope, a landscape of Titans and monsters we continuously must fight to keep at bay. All of that means nothing to me without her."

"My Lord, please see reason...."

"Reason?" Hades chuckled, drawing his gaze to the ground. "Reason left me a long ago when our hands connected, and I knew she would be mine."

"But," Thanatos' shoulders dropped. "Must it be this way? Surely, there must be another."

"There is no other way," Hades replied, looking back to the flames. "The Moirai were insistent that she needed to come to the Underworld. They made it clear last we spoke."

"The Moirai being clear?" Thanatos scoffed. "That would

be a first."

"If their message fails and this is all destroyed, it will be their last." Hades hoped he understood them enough, but Thanatos was right. They were never easy to interpret. "It's in their best interest to be right in this prophecy."

"What if they're not?" Thatos narrowed his eyes at Hades. "What if this is another Cronos situation?"

"Even then," Hades took a long sip of his drink. "Their prediction was right, just not how I'd predicted. It's not the only vision I've tried deciphering in all this."

Thanatos sighed. "How many will suffer from this?"

"We all suffer through fate," Hades said, setting down his cup. "Even the innocent."

"Innocent like you were when your father devoured you over a prophesy?"

"Yes." Hades took in a deep breath. "Even I will suffer because of the decisions I've made. None of us will come out unscathed from this."

CHAPTER 6 KERES

B umping into Thanatos, Persephone had to do a double take when she realized it was someone else. "Oh! I'm so sorry... Wait. You're not Thanatos."

He chuckled with a boyish grin. "No. That would be my brother. I am Hypnos, god of sleep."

Persephone smiled, craning her neck up at him. "Ah, so you're responsible for my dreams that are so intense they could almost be real."

"My children, the Oneiroi led by my son Morpheus, are those you must thank for your dreams." Hypnos adjusted his robes that crossed at his waist with a belt and draped sleeves the color of sand. "Some dreams are reliving real events that have happened. Others are living your greatest desires, while some show your greatest fears. They exist as possibilities that play out in your mind as you work through those challenging or good decisions in your subconscious mind."

"What about prophecies and visions?"

"Again, that is Morpheus's realm. I merely put you to sleep with this." He held up a red poppy plant dripping with watery dew in his hand.

"What's dripping from your poppy?" She asked, reaching up to touch it, but he quickly pulled it away.

"The waters of Lethe," he said, almost in a trance when looking at it, then turned to Persephone with a seemingly fake smile that didn't quite reach his eyes. "It's for you to sleep and forget the world for a moment to rest in your subconscious. It's best not to touch it lest you fall into a deep slumber."

"I don't usually remember my dreams, but they can be very vivid when I do."

"Nor should you. Hence the subconscious part," He said with a wink. "We go mad without dreams to work out what we can't handle in our waking state. As for the vivid ones, sometimes, my children like to, let's just say, embellish the visions."

His green eyes were hypnotic, much like Thanatos. However, his demeanor was very different. She realized expressing her inner worries to strangers was not wise. While she knew she could trust Thanatos, this god was not like him. It took her a moment to see the differences between the two gods in the light. But once she recognized it, they couldn't be more different.

"You know," Persephone said with one hand on her chin. "I would have almost believed you were your brother were it not for your eyes. You can always see who someone or something truly is through their eyes."

Unease shadowed his face as he looked away until he put his mask back on.

"Deep sleep and peaceful death often look the same." Hypnos gave a warm and perfect white-toothed smile that he and Thanatos shared, yet to Persephone, this god was less sincere.

His hair was lighter brown, and he wore loose curls instead of black locks. There was something she couldn't quite place about his smile, but instead of comfort, she felt a dark nature that was more vicious than good. Why? She didn't know. Something about him felt a little off. Then again, everything felt off to her here.

"Our mother, Nyx, has sired many of us who reside here

in the Underworld," he said gently.

"How many of you are there?" She wondered out loud. "Siblings born from Nyx and who else?"

"Erebos," he said with a nod. "The primordial night joined with our father, Erobos, the darkness, to create many of the gods you'll undoubtedly meet here. We are called Chthonic in the Underworld, often representing the dark aspects of reality, creating balance to the light. In short, there are too many of us to count, and more being made as the primordials need."

"I see," she said, then smiled. "I hope I meet all of your siblings as I visit."

"Visit?" Hypnos raised a brow. "No one ever visits the Underworld."

Persephone's smile turned into a sly smirk. "I'm not like everyone."

"That is yet to be seen." He smiled down at her, but it never met his eyes.

"I tried to come here with friends before." Remembering how terrible the events played out, that probably wasn't a good boast. "We didn't make it due to Hera's interference but were given free passage then."

Hera. Hera's smile never met her eyes, just like Hypnos. It was all there. This being was not to be trusted. Perhaps he could be helpful, regardless.

"You came here with the gods of Olympus?" He asked, eyes wide.

Persephone nodded.

"I wondered why she was in Tartarus. Perhaps I should visit her there," he continued. "You should already be familiar with one of Nyx's offspring who spends time with the gods Ares and Enyo."

"You mean Eris?" Persephone felt her loneliness even more so at the mention of her friends.

"Yes," he said with a bow of his head. "The young goddess of strife is quite the handful as part of her trio."

"She tried to save me by telling us Hera's plans." The memory still gave Persephone anxiety, but she was working through it. "In the end, she chose our friendship over her discorded nature."

"That is surprising to hear." He frowned, then put his mask of a smile back on. "Nevertheless, her schemes get her into more trouble than not. I would advise you to keep a close eye on her."

"One could say that about most gods," Persephone replied, narrowing her eyes. "Including myself."

"A fair point," he replied with a nod that signaled he was just as wary of her as he was toward him. "You don't seem well suited here."

"It's why I need to find a way back."

"You don't wish to stay?" Hypnos asked with a raised brow.

"I can't stay even if I wanted to," Persephone said with a shrug. "If I don't find my mom and set the world above right, I'm afraid all this will be lost, and everything created will end."

"That's very interesting to know," he said, tilting his head and crossing his arms over his hard chest. "You carry a heavy burden. The weight of the world is on your shoulders as Atlas carries ours. This kind of pressure is a lot for a goddess so young as you."

Persephone straightened her shoulders. "My mother, Demeter, was younger than I am now when she, along with Zeus, defeated the Titans."

"Demeter was a powerful warrior in that battle. So fierce she made the Titans tremble at her ferocity." Hypnos leaned forward. "Can you say the same of yourself? Or are you all talk and no substance in a real battle?"

"She was always kind to me." Persephone wrapped her arms around her waist and turned away. "Even when training, she was firm but funny. She always knew how to cheer me up. When I would lose my temper, she would just laugh and say I get that more from her than Zeus."

"Zeus is more measured in his wrath. Demeter is a force of nature filled with chaos." He gazed off as though remembering something. "Only when I arrive and she dreams does she have the ability to work through her monstrous nature."

It was interesting to hear another refer to her mother as monstrous. The thought had never occurred to Persephone. Demeter had always just been a mom. Making tea, cooking their favorite meals, and training in the morning with evening walks together. It had been a paradise Persephone had rarely felt appreciation for. She now longed for those familiar meadows against this dark and, for some unknown reason, always foggy atmosphere no matter where they went.

Persephone had an idea that could get her out.

"You say you can leave here anytime you wish, right? Being a son of Nyx, you have an agreement with Hades," she added, surprising Hypnos.

"That's true," he replied with a cautious tone.

"Is there a way that you could take me from here and bring me to my mom?" She asked with a small sliver of hope in her heart.

"Why would I do that for you?" Hypnos asked, arms clasping behind his back.

Persephone took a moment to pause and think. She didn't know him well enough to know what he wanted nor have any leverage. Defeated, she slumped her shoulders.

"I guess I have nothing to offer to get me out of here."

"With nothing to offer, you wish to have me risk my home, never seeing my family, and deceive Hades so that you can go and see your... Mommy?" He asked with disgust.

"Well, when you put it that way, it does sound like a terrible idea," Persephone said, feeling foolish for asking.

"I imagine you've had many of them." His cold eyes drifted up and down her body.

Persephone crossed her arms. "That's not fair."

"It's not?" He asked, inching closer toward her. "You

didn't hide from Demeter in the first place to go to a realm you can't leave only to get yourself killed and others gravely wounded?"

She felt chills up her spine at his description of her. Demeter had said the same thing. The day they fought. Persephone believed Hades was different and that he would never be like Zeus. He could handle the choice she would make on her own. But none of that was true.

"I know she's worried about me, and I don't know what to do." Persephone sighed. "If only I could at least get a message to her, it would be enough."

Hypnos pursed his lips and drew his brows up in sympathy. "Perhaps there is a way I can help."

"What do you mean? How?" She asked, feeling a tinge of hope well inside her.

"I can send her a message from you in her dreams. Tell me what you wish to tell her, and I will relay it to her tonight. Then maybe she will be more amenable when she knows you are safe."

"It would mean the world to me if you would do that. Thank you."

Persephone wished she could do more, but this was better than nothing.

"It means very little to me, but you truly care for Demeter. She has always been kind to me; thus, I am inclined to return her kindness by helping you with this one thing. Of course, you will owe me a favor later in my choosing."

Persephone didn't want to have an open-ended favor, but she needed to connect with Demeter somehow. She managed a nod that he took as agreement.

"Then, we must never speak of this again." Hypnos reached up and brought her head up, touching her chin. "Hades would not like that I helped you with this."

"Agreed." Persephone nodded and backed away. "I won't tell him."

Hypnos bowed his head with his curls falling over his

eyes. When he looked up, they glowed gold with sand swirling and pouring out of them, turning to black sand twisting around him in a small cyclone. His eyes locked with hers with such force she couldn't pull away. Paralyzed, he pulled her chin up to face him as he stepped inches from her.

"Now, tell me your message for your mother's dreams, Chthonia of the Underworld."

"Mom, It's me, Perseph... Kore." Relieved she could still speak, she paused as her voice cracked, trying to hold back her tears. "I'm okay, Mom. Please don't be worried. The darkness can't hold me forever. I'll find a way home, I promise. I love you."

A storm surrounded her as the sand whipped and cut at her exposed flesh. Persephone felt his release of her. She began to feel lost in darkness, whipping her hair around as it receded, leaving her alone. Then the sands were gone, and so was Hypnos.

The tears began to flow. Persephone collapsed to her knees, crying out until she felt exhausted. Energy spent, she wiped her tears, afraid anyone would see. She got up and dusted off her dress with more rips from the sand.

"Crying already, huh?" The snarky tone of a familiar voice made Persephone look up into Hades' mistress' dark eyes. "I knew it wouldn't be long before you broke." Mynthe stood with hands on her hips, glaring down at Persephone with narrowed eyes. "What's the matter? Is this place too scary for you, delicate weed?"

Her mocking tone peaked Persephone's anger instantly. Persephone stood, wiping her tears and nose, hating the nymph.

"Leave me alone." Persephone walked past Mynthe, avoiding contact.

"Why don't you do us all a favor and leave here?" Mynthe said from behind.

Persephone stopped and turned to face the nymph.

"Don't you think that's what I want?" Persephone asked,

pinching the bridge of her nose. "I want to go home as much as you want me gone. I want to see the light again and feel its warmth on my face. To be back with Mom in our simple cottage. I don't want any of this."

"Sounds like a pretty dull life to me." Mynthe folded her arms over her chest, rolled her eyes, and checked her nails.

"I don't give a fuck what you think about my life," Persephone said, walking up to Mynthe, struggling to keep her hands to her side. "You have no idea what it is to be cut off from those you love while suffering the anger of being imprisoned and mocked for being upset. Unlike you, I will not play your game, Mynthe. As soon as I can leave, I will. Then you can have Hades all to yourself."

"The sooner, the better," Mynthe said, dropping her arms to her sides and stepping forward, looking down her nose at Persephone.

Persephone stepped inches away, staring into Mynthe's cold eyes with her own.

"On that, we agree." Persephone tilted her head. "I plan to escape at my first opportunity. If you want this to go faster, you should help me."

"If I did, I'd be thrown out for disobedience." Mynthe walked around Persephone slowly, keeping eye contact. "However, I won't stop you."

"Doesn't it bother you to obey someone else's wishes above your own?"

Mynthe tilted her head. "What else is there but to obey my Lord Hades?"

Persephone let out a heavy sigh. "Forget it. You don't understand, and I don't have the patience to explain it."

"Hmph," Mynthe chortled. "Like I need a lesson from a lowly nature goddess."

"You know what?" Persephone clenched her fists. "I'll find my own way out. Without your help."

"Good luck, weed," Mynthe said, rolling her eyes. "Hades is relentless when he sets his mind to things."

"Yet knowing that, you still pursue him after he's rejected you," Persephone said, knowing how much it would upset the nymph with his own words. "He told me himself you mean nothing to him. So why do you still hang around?"

"Some of us understand duty above all else," the nymph said with such poison that it was sure to infect Persephone's mind. "You wouldn't know anything about duty and sacrifice for something greater than yourself. Everything is always about you. You're selfish, stupid, and deadweight to anyone who cares for you because you're too weak to do anything yourself. And you know I'm right."

Mynthe turned to leave down the opposite way Persephone was going. Thank Gaia, she didn't lose her temper this time. But that nymph was starting to grate on her nerves. Persephone hated that Mynthe was right. Her shaking hands clenched into a fist as she stormed down the hall to find something to do, or she would go mad.

"Damn it, I wish Artemis was here. She'd know what to do or how to get out." Persephone cursed to herself, wandering the halls aimlessly.

She passed by an opening that sounded like creatures were having a great time and heard the sounds of a fight breaking out. Persephone crept closer and peaked around the corner to find what looked like Daemons in a fighting pit.

All eyes focussed on the battle in the center arena, surrounded by cheering groups scantily clad. The two in the pit couldn't have been more different if they tried. One looked like the gods. Body oiled with almond skin, he raised his dual blades in the air, causing the room's energy to soar. He wore a red loincloth with armor on his right shoulder strapping across his chest, and a helmet that hid his face but for the mouth and eyes. His gauntlets were thick fabric with leather wrapped tight around them to protect his arms, while his leg armor protected his knees when he was on the ground. She could see from other contestants who didn't do this showed signs of sand burn on their knees and shins.

Parting the groups so she could see, Persephone got close enough to see the whites of their teeth and hear them roaring obscenities at one another. Their taunts, though amusing, contained natural aggression and powerful threats backed up by the cuts and bruises they possessed from their opponents.

The godlike male was in much better shape as the serpent-bodied male teetered on his feet, barely able to hold the dagger he gripped, dripping in green blood. The snake-like being, covered in scales with serpent features with fangs and claws, raised his fist to garner cheers. His body was as muscular as his opponents, with a longer torso and thighs that appeared strong as they flexed with every dodge.

From an experienced perspective, Persephone surmised that the larger one teetering would lose. The smaller fighter was baiting his opponent, making the serpent feel more confident than he should. Soon, the strike would come, and it would be over.

Persephone watched the outcome as they sparred for another minute before her prediction came true. The serpent opened himself up, and that's when the one in red moved in and slashed open the scaled stomach at an apparent weak point. The creature instinctively wrapped its arms around its middle as the guts began to pour out. Stepping back, he fell to his knees and raised a finger in surrender.

Applause filled the small space, deafening to her ears. The winner stood triumphant with his tanned, sweat-slickened skin and hairless body glistening over chiseled muscles in the firelight. The fierce male roared, reminding Persephone of someone. The sound brought her back to the hunt she once led with Hades.

"Nyctimus?" Persephone whispered to herself.

When the victor removed his helmet, the werewolf was in his mortal form, arm raised to the ceiling, brandishing the bloodied weapon. Without so much mud and fur marring his appearance, he was as beautiful as the gods, with dirty blonde hair stuck to his neck from sweat just past his collarbone with the top braided back out of his bright blue eyes.

He looked happy. Fueled by the crowd that called out his name.

"Nyctimus! Nyctimus! Nyctimus!!"

Chanting and throwing coins at his feet, he never picked them up. Instead, he walked around in a circle to give everyone a look at his perfect physique with his arms wide. He approached his opponent and said something to the serpent, who nodded. Putting out his hand, Nyctimus lifted the wounded to his feet and put an arm over his shoulder to help him walk to the arched exit.

Persephone called out to him and waved, trying to get his attention, but it was useless. She'd have to find another way to say hello. After what had happened with her and Hera, Persephone had no idea that Nyctimus had survived when hit by a god blast that would have killed him if he had been mortal. His curse must have saved him by healing his wounds since she saw no scars.

She discovered his healing on the hunt with Hades. Her guilt for turning him over to Zeus still affected her. He was no longer the wolf who couldn't control his appetite when transformed. Of course, this description of his nature was a lie. She knew that now. He was only a beast to those on Olympus. Here, he retained his mortal appearance and seemed to revel in this place rather than suffer. It was a small comfort, but still, Persephone wanted to thank him for what he did for her on that terrible day.

Though appearing happier, he was in similar circumstances as when she'd captured and taken him to fight on Olympus. She needed to know if he was okay and what happened. Maybe she could even set him free this time. She had to try. Persephone knew she owed Nyctimus that after what he did for her and the others. She'd have to ask Hades if he would let the wolf go, but that would mean talking to him, and she wasn't ready to do that just yet.

The hairs on the back of her neck raised. Someone

was watching her, but she couldn't see anyone as she looked around. A tiny flicker of the shadow out of the corner of her eye was gone when she looked to see only an empty hall.

***

Another day arrived and Persephone still wouldn't talk to him. Not even after he explained his now-ended relationship with Mynthe. She didn't budge in her disdain for him. Only at night, when she slept in his arms, did he find peace with her. Her dreams would make her toss and turn in a cold sweat. Holding her was the only thing that seemed to calm her in those wee hours of the night. She'd snuggle deep within his chest and nuzzle him absently when he tucked her in close. Then Hades would leave before she woke.

It had been futile to get her to understand through words how he felt and what she meant to him. She would never truly understand him until she understood the absolute darkness of his realm. If Persephone thought he was so bad, she should see what he had imprisoned.

Hades knocked on his door. When she finally opened it, he asked her to follow him without explanation. To his surprise, she did.

She still wore the same lavender gown that began to resemble rags with wine blotches and enough tear stains to make him lower his head when he looked at her. *Keep it together. You're a king, for Gaia's sake. You cannot let your desires and emotions for her get the best of you*, he chided himself. She needed to see what Tartarus was going to be like. It was time for her to see what his duties required.

Hades walked ahead of her to the stables and smiled, hearing her grumbling the whole way there. *Defiant to the end*, he thought as he smiled to himself.

The sounds of four horses aggressively whinnying and stomping grabbed her attention, and she grew quiet.

"Oh! Wait, Hades. I need to get something first," she

said, running off to the main hall where the banquet was well underway.

She returned a few minutes later with a bag of something. He waited as Persephone ran back to him with a smile so charming and elegant he almost took her back to their chambers to keep her safe from what he was about to show her.

He watched her eyes widen when they entered the stable where his chariot lay waiting with Aethone in the front alongside her brothers. Hades gestured for her to enter.

"Marvelous, aren't they?" He asked, appreciating their beauty. "Have you ever seen anything like them?"

"Yes," she said, looking off into the distance as though remembering something.

Hades tilted his head. "Where?"

Persephone smiled. "In a dream."

"Was I in this dream?" He asked, lowering his voice and coming closer to her.

Her smile faded. "Yes," she whispered.

Hades leaned one arm against the door behind her and leaned close to her lips. "What was I doing?"

Her eyes narrowed at him. "Much like you did with me earlier when you took me from my home."

Hades gave a slight smile to one side. "Is that all?"

Persephone's blush betrayed her thoughts. "You... Um." Persephone turned away from him and jogged over to the large beasts already connected to the chariot.

"They're amazing!" She said, smiling at each one and waving. "What are their names?"

Hades placed his hands behind his back and stood just behind her. "You've met Aethone, whose name means swifter than an arrow."

"Yes, of course." Persephone pulled out a bag she'd held full of apples. "I hope I brought enough of these."

Hades chuckled deep in his throat. "I'm sure you did."

"So, what are the three stallions' names?" Persephone asked as she fed Aethone, who nudged her playfully.

"Next to Aethone is the white-eyed Nyctaeus, meaning the proud glory of Hades' steeds. The two behind them are Orphnaeus, who is savage and fleet with the eyes of black smoke. The other, with the green glowing eyes, is Alastor, who wears a brand with the mark of Hades. He rides behind Nyctaeus."

"Why?" She asked, meeting his gaze. "Because they're both your favorite?"

"No," Hades said, shaking his head. "Because Aethone kicks at poor Alastor."

"What?" Persephone turned to look at Aethone, who snorted. "No. She wouldn't."

Hades chuckled. "Orphnaeus bites back so she behaves better on the front right."

"I think she's adorable, and I'm sure she just likes a little mischief," she said, tussling the mare's mane. "Don't you, my red-eyed beast."

"Oh, so she's yours now, is she?" Hades shook his head. "You keep spoiling her, and she will be in no time."

Persephone gave him a wide grin, then ran over and offered apples to the other three horses with pets. It took his breath away to see them all nudge her playfully, each snatching an apple and happily devouring it. The beasts were doing some sort of happy trotting with each apple she shared, making Hades shake his head and scoff in disbelief at her handling of them.

The four sable black horses stood connected to his golden chariot with etched ornate carvings into the gold. He'd hoped it would impress her, but instead of looking at the chariot, she was petting and feeding the horses, telling them how wonderful they were. To his astonishment, they were eating it all up, and he sensed he would lose allies if she kept this up wherever they went.

"All right, let's go before you all turn soft on me." Hades stepped into his chariot, then turned and offered Persephone his hand that flexed in anticipation to feel her skin against his.

Persephone refused and placed the bag of apples between them as she stepped into the chariot on her own so not even their feet would touch.

"Do you hear that?" she asked, looking back at him.

"Hear what?" He asked, wondering why she wrapped her arms around her waist as though afraid.

"Nevermind," she said finally. "I'm ready when you are."

Hades led Persephone into the large cavern where she could hear music and drums echoing in the walls. They rode past the sounds from the throne room and descended further into Hades' realm. Once they made it past the giant column-framed gates of obsidian stone, he watched her marvel with wide eyes at the vastness of the outer kingdom. This space was only the first level they would travel through today.

The fires burned hot, and the scantily clad Underworld beasts and monsters wandered around enjoying their wine and food.

They stopped by the cliffside, exited the chariot, and stood by the edge. A mass of beings filled an ample open space, dancing with firelight and sounds of pleasure echoing along the walls. Beds, chains, and lounge chairs were placed strategically near food and wine. The area was enormous, with hundreds of feet above them showering down water from four openings where they poured heated water into a large pool surrounding a stone platform that floated in the center. A tan-skinned female with generous curves and long black hair twisted into intricate shapes on her head adorned with dangling jewels sat on a jagged stone throne, watching the sex performed all around her in a long red robe.

Blowing, sucking, fucking, and penetration were on the menu. Hades could tell Persephone was fascinated as she couldn't look away, even when her hand reached out and gripped the rail of his chariot, knuckles turning white. As uncomfortable as she appeared, he knew she desired what she witnessed.

"Who... Who are all of these creatures? And um... Who

is that down there in the center on the uh... Thing. The chair... I mean the throne!" She said too loud, her cheeks blazing with heat, covering her mouth.

Hades smiled, enjoying her shyness. Sensual entertainment usually interested him, but now he only wanted to look at Persephone. He thought about the endless nights of orgiastic pleasure he'd experienced. It was nothing compared to Persephone's delicate touch and intoxicating lips.

"Her name is Philotes," he said, watching her expression of fascination turn to confusion as her brows drew upward.

"Is she a god?"

"She is a Daemon," he said, shaking his head. "Daughter of Nyx and the personification of friendship and affection, she's almost as important as Aphrodite, if not more benevolent."

"What does that mean?" Persephone asked with charming innocence. "Personification of affection, like my friendship with Artemis?"

Hades shook his head. "Sexual intercourse," he said close to her ear, enjoying the blush rose on her face. "She's what makes it...fun."

"Oh." Looking back, Persephone cleared her throat. "I see."

"Come. I have more to show you," he said, returning to the chariot.

When Persephone joined him, she brushed the apple bag aside. He could feel her foot touching his. Calming his emotions, Hades snapped the reins.

He dreaded the next place they were going. Fear mixed with doubt and anger that he might lose her led him to this conclusion. She had to see it. See why it was so important and why he needed her.

"Now, where are you taking me, Hades?" She asked with those curious eyes.

Hades remained stoic. "You'll see."

He urged the team onward as they took off into the air

and galloped above ground, leading to another cavern. They landed in what appeared to be a gray field. The sky was gray, the grass was gray, and even the road was gray. The air soon filled with the scent of blood. There was no color except for the red stains like skid marks of something being dragged and, at times, claw marks in the light dusty coal soil he saw to his right of the chariot.

"What is this place?" She asked, wrapping her arms around her waist.

"It's where the Keres reside, awaiting violence from above so they can go on a hunt," he said, pointing to the long red stains on the ground.

Persephone tilted her head, confused. "What are the Keres?"

"Agents of Ker," Hades said, looking around, feeling the hairs rise on the back of his neck. "She's the Goddess of Violent Death and the sister of Thanatos."

"And Hypnos," Persephone added.

"How do you know Hypnos?" Judging by her leaning away, he asked a little too abruptly.

"I met him earlier." Persephone began to fidget like she'd done something. He'd have to interrogate Hypnos later to find out what. "I thought Thanatos was the god of death." She said, trying to change the subject.

He could tell she'd been up to something. Her usual cold tone was now shaky with guilt. Perhaps her dreams were the reason.

"He is," Hades said patiently. "Thanatos is the god of gentle death. Children, the elderly, the innocent, or just regular mortals are visited with quick and painless reaping by him at their death. His work is essential to the harmony of my kingdom. Ker, however, serves another purpose. She is the reaper of disease and deadly illness. They love war, bloody battlefields, and carnage. She and her minions work for the Moirai."

"How so?"

"The Keres, or more specifically Ker, herself, create material to bring to the Moirai at one's birth to weave, and then when it's cut, the Keres retrieve the soul. Sometimes kicking and screaming to the Underworld. Their blood lust is unmatched and insatiable."

"So if they're not gods or nymphs. What are they?"

"Daemons. Personified spirits of what they were born to do and be like Philotes and her minions." Hades shifted his weight as he sensed several of them converging on their point.

He noticed their presence was making the horses edgy as they started showing restless behavior, tussling their manes and grunting at one another.

"Ironic how their name means choice, but they deal in the fates of others," he said, distracted while looking around for any threat. "Most of the beings here may be offspring of Nyx but are often daemons, not gods."

A rustling in the bushes sounded several feet away. Persephone acted on instinct as he'd taught her and pulled for her weapons, finding nothing. Her stance was ready for anything, but she visibly relaxed when looking up at Hades and laughed at her empty hands. It cut the tension for a moment in an otherwise relatively dangerous situation. After the horde they'd faced previously, he knew she could fight them off with him, but he didn't want the Keres to get that close. Just let her see them so she was aware.

"Did you hear that?" She asked, observing her surroundings as he'd taught her.

Hades nodded. "Yes."

"Was it a Keres?"

"Probably," he said, scanning the area. "Right now, they've undoubtedly surrounded us."

Persephone looked up at him, blinking hard. "And you're not worried?"

"They won't attack with me here." He was primarily sure about that, but there was always a chance they were hungry for blood. "You're safe with me."

"And if I'm not with you?" Persephone asked, leaning over the edge of the chariot, trying to see them.

"I wouldn't try to test that theory," Hades said, pulling her close.

Persephone pushed him away. "Why? Do you think I'm too weak?"

"I didn't say that," he replied, brows drawn in confusion to her anger.

"But you implied it. Isn't that what this is all about?" She asked, looking up at him with her eyes accusing him of deception when he had none to give. "You think I can't handle this place, so you want to, what? Show me around? Relieve my fears? Tell me it's all going to be okay? Or maybe you're just trying to scare me to keep me in line."

"No," Hades replied, wishing she could understand. "It's not a good place down here. Endless darkness, malevolence, and monsters can and will consume you for thousands of years. Horrors, misery, deceit, and death come from hate, disease, and destruction. Those above always wish for a quick and painless death, but the opposite is more often true. The Keres, for example, stalk and prey upon battlefields of hollow souls feeding on the blood of the damned. When the Keres finish with their prey, they carry the mortal souls to my dungeons or fields. I wanted to show you how dangerous it is and how I control it. When you rule with me, you must know how everything works."

"How many times do I have to say it, Hades," Persephone clenched her hands into fists at her sides, clearly wanting to strike him. "I don't want to rule with you. I want to go home! I want to leave this place!"

Hades growled low in his chest. "And how many times should I tell you, wife? That is not going to happen!"

"I'm getting out of here, whether you agree or..."

Hades raised a hand to silence her as he heard a loud female screeching in the distance. Begrudgingly, Persephone remained silent as he scanned the area.

"We should go," he said, feeling nerves rising as he sensed them coming.

"Why?" Persephone sneered. "Can't handle a few monsters in your realm?"

Hades narrowed his eyes at Persephone. "If you were anyone else, I'd...."

"You'd what?" Persephone glared, challenging him with her chest so close to his.

Her scent wafted around them, and his eyes rolled back. Gods, she smelled divine.

"I'd leave them here to fight off the Keres alone." Hades tilted his head, narrowing his eyes.

"Why not leave me?" She asked with more defiance. "I won't submit and give you what you want, so you might as well leave me here."

Hades leaned close to her. "Is that what you wish?"

"What I wish is for you to take me back home and never to see me again," she replied, pushing him away.

Hades landed against the chariot wall and growled. "You're testing my patience, flower."

"And you're testing mine, beast," Persephone said, squaring up to fight him.

"If I wanted to," he said, standing to his full height and grabbing her arm. "I could take you, and you wouldn't be able to stop me."

He felt her slap. The sting was enough to anger him. *Why was she being like this?* Persephone was never this stubborn on Olympus. She seemed to enjoy his touch, and now all she wanted to do was fight.

"You may take this body," she seethed through gritted teeth. "But unless I cum willingly, It will not be me."

"You will cum willingly." Hades' voice dropped several octaves and deepened as he closed in. "In time."

They stood inches away, staring into one another's eyes with such intensity it made his heart pound. He wanted to take her right there. He could tell she was as aroused as he was with her telltale blush that rose on her cheeks. Her lips, no longer pursed, were full and delicate, needing to be kissed. But he wouldn't. Not here.

"Persephone. I..."

She put her hand up to silence him and met his eyes with tears filling hers. "Just stop. Please. Will you just let me go?"

"Never."

"You won't give up, will you?"

"Why should I when I've already won?"

"I am not a prize you can win!" She yelled, glaring at him.

Hades huffed. "Not if you keep acting like a spoiled brat."

Her mouth opened then closed as she clenched her jaw. "What did you call me?"

"You heard me," he said, narrowing his eyes at her.

Her face turned red as her temper flared to the surface, and her eyes glowed when she looked back up. Persephone reached behind her back, pulling a weapon Hades hadn't seen since Olympus, and screamed, lunging at him.

Right before it hit its target of his chest, her eyes shot wide as black claws like talons wrapped around her body and face, ripping her backward out of the chariot. Her screams rang out as she disappeared into the gray field, leaving a body trail in the tall grass.

"Persephone!" He jumped over the edge and ran in the direction the Keres dragged her.

He found her fighting off six Keres, who tore and grabbed at her with their sharp talons, trying to render blood from her to drink. Their black wings flapped as they attacked from above, below, and behind her. Persephone fought, surrounded, kicking, and punching anything that came close. One black-eyed female finally got her in a solid grip of her hair, wrenching her head back, exposing her neck, and burying its fangs deep into her flesh. Two others latched onto her arms, with a fourth biting her right thigh.

"Nooo!" Hades screamed, running to her.

CHAPTER 7
MANIFEST

Before he could reach Persephone, something happened he never expected, forcing him to skid to a halt a few feet away. Unlike her usual light eyes, they began to glow with a dark tyrian color like the one he commissioned for her room. Darkness emanated over her eyes like a shadow was trying to escape her sockets. Persephone swung her crescent dagger he didn't realize she'd brought until she'd lunged at him and stabbed the one feasting on her leg in the neck. With one dead, the other three were still on her.

Hades instantly moved to her, grabbed the two on her arms by their necks, and squeezed. They let go, screaming, blood pouring from their gaping maws that hissed at him. He threw them back, and something tackled him to the ground. Three had come up, cloaking him in their wings, attacking mindlessly. He punched and kicked them away and stood, turning to Persephone, who was finally free.

What lay at her feet sent a chill down his spine. A crumbled heap drained to a flesh-encased skeleton of what it once was had its mouth open in a silent scream. He was too stunned to move at her appearance when Persephone turned around and faced him.

Her lips were blood-red, matching the long, sharp nails she flexed. Glowing eyes lined in kohl with a dark cloud drifting out of her sockets as the smoke tipped in the tyrian color just as his blue flame did with his own eyes. Persephone's hair was almost black at the roots, fading into a dark red of straight hair that floated in a phantom breeze around her. Her dress in tatters, almost exposing her breasts, became weightless around her. The tempest built around her body with her hand gripping the hair of the head she held in her left hand. Her hourglass form began to construct a swirl of the dark cloud, turning the same purplish pink that matched her eyes as it flowed over her body.

The Keres' murderous gazes and hissing mouths bared their fangs as they closed in. Hades sensed they were being surrounded again and moved to her side, ready to fight. His hands elongated into claws, and Hades grew larger, feeling his power course through him. His blue flame erupted around them as he grabbed her wrist and pulled her to face him.

"Persephone?" he asked, gazing into her vacant eyes. "Are you hurt?"

"Not as hurt as they are," she said with a malicious smile. "It's rather delicious, isn't it?"

"Persephone!" Hades yelled, gripping her shoulders and shaking her, trying to break her trance. "Wake up!"

She shook her head, and her eyes returned to their usual violet. Her hands came up to her head as if she was in pain. She saw the Keres' head in her hand and quickly dropped it. Her appearance slowly returned to normal as she stood there in shock.

"What happened?" she asked, looking around confused and then at her bloodied hands.

Hades' brows furrowed. "You don't remember?"

She shook her head no. Hades let out a heavy sigh. *What, in the name of Gaia, had just happened?* There was no time to analyze. They were still in danger. Or at least she was so long as she was in this realm.

"Persephone, I need you to focus and stay with me. These Keres are mindless and will keep attacking. First, we need to get to a place where the chariot can land, and you'll have to fly your way out on your own. Go to Philotes and seek refuge there. I'll draw them away so they won't pursue you until you escape the gates of this place."

"You want me to hide in a sex den?" Persephone asked with one brow raised.

Hades growled. "Good point. You'll have to make a run for the gates then."

"Why are they attacking me?" Persephone asked, beginning to shiver.

"A deal I made with their leader long ago lends me their protection from attack."

"But I didn't..."

"We can argue about it later," he said, raising one hand and sending out a pulse of energy that shook their environment. "Until then, there are too many of them. I need you to run. Thanatos will recognize my signal and meet you at the gates. I told him to find you if anything went wrong."

"I still can't cross the main threshold," she argued.

Hades pondered the situation, then realized there could be a better way.

"Fair enough," he said after some thought. "I need you to do to me what you did to that Keres,"

Persephone rolled her eyes. "I'm not ripping your head off."

"No," he said, shaking his head. "The part where you drain them of their life force."

"I don't know how," she said, staring down at her hands as though they didn't belong to her. "I've only done it by accident."

A keres lunged at Persephone. Hades' response was vicious and swift as he tore its head from its body, tossing the hissing head away.

"You better learn to do it intentionally and quickly, or we'll be in trouble," said Hades, slashing at a Keres face.

Persephone moved to cover his back.

"It only happens when I'm in danger," she said over her shoulder.

Two more flew at them. Persephone sliced one from navel to chest, forcing it to retreat while Hades ripped the other's throat out.

"I think now would qualify," he replied, scanning for more.

Persephone snapped her fingers. "I know! Quick, choke me."

"What?" Hades was shocked by her request. "I'm not going to hurt you."

"You'll have to if you want me to access your power to get out of here," Persephone said, coming around to face him, her back dangerously vulnerable.

He clenched his jaw as the tension coiled tight in his spine. "I can't do that."

"It's the only way I know will bring the darkness in me out."

"How long will my life force last in you?"

"Not long. A minute, an hour... Maybe a day?" Persephone pinched the bridge of her nose. "I don't know. I've never tested this, so we have to try and see."

"No." Hades shook his head. "I don't want to do this to you."

"Hades, I forgive you in advance," she said with a gentle caress of his cheek before taking his hand and placing it around her neck. "Now, choke me. I know you won't really hurt me, but you're going to have to come pretty damn close."

Hades growled, hating what he was about to do. But she was right. If she could take his powers, she'd have the ability to leave. Hopefully, she wouldn't think to use it to get out of the Underworld entirely.

He grabbed her so fast that the surprise on her face

almost made him let go. Lifting her off the ground, he held her limp body above him. She grabbed his arm, struggling to breathe, when the darkness crept up in her eyes at last. Suddenly, Hades felt her power siphoning his energy for the first time.

The pull was so strong it was all he could do to stay standing as his head felt dizzy and his eyes were beginning to blur. The force drawn from him was more intense the harder she pulled, eyes locked with his, no longer choking in his grasp. Her smile widened into a wicked grin as his knees weakened. His life force poured from him into her until he finally had to release her.

Persephone dropped to one knee and stood, looking at him with that sinister smile. His guilt melted away as she sauntered toward him and licked his chest. *Fuck, this wasn't supposed to turn me on,* he thought as she placed her hand against his cock and rubbed him up and down until he moaned.

"That's a good god," she said, kissing the sweat from his chest. "I like it when you do what I tell you."

"Who are you?"

"I'm her," she replied, tilting her head.

"You can't be," he said, stepping back. "She's not like this."

"Oh, yes she is, Dark Lord," she said with a chuckle. "She just doesn't know it yet, but she will."

Hades let out a measured breath. "Do you have what you need to leave?"

"I believe so," she said, licking her forefinger that had just touched his cock. "Though I'd much rather stay and taste more of you."

Why did this situation have to happen when they were in danger? Gaia, help him. He wanted her right now more than ever.

"Keep her safe for me," Hades said, hesitating to trust whoever this being was inside Persephone.

"Right." She winked. "Get to an opening to the chariot and fly our way out. Got it."

So she could hear while being dormant. That was interesting to know. Were they separate beings or one with two sides like a coin? He didn't have time to ask. He simply gave her a nod to be ready, and she nodded in return. He hoped the time spent training would pay off for her. There were no fail safes here. Persephone knew what to do. He had to trust in her training to get herself to safety.

He trusted her to stay alive. Aethone will undoubtedly lead the chariot directly to him, but the Keres had wings. It wouldn't be an easy escape, but his team was the fastest in their world. He planned to lead them away and summon their leader, or this would keep happening.

Hades ran with Persephone next to him through the dark gray trees, killing anything that came close. One attempted to grasp Persephone and fly her away, but Hades was too quick and grabbed its wing, ripping it off, throwing the creature to the ground, and beating its face with his fists.

"Hades! Come on!" Persephone screamed, grabbing his arm and pulling him back.

Her eyes were back to normal, surprising him as she took off, and he followed close behind her.

"There!" Hades pointed to their left. "There's a clearing."

Hades turned with her and ran to just before the clearing and stopped. Grabbing Persephone's arm, he pulled her down and signaled for her to be quiet and crouch.

With his mind, he called on Aethone. Hearing her whinny, Hades breathed a sigh of relief and turned to Persephone, who also appeared relieved to see the chariot coming into view.

"When I say go, you run and don't look back. Take the chariot home and wait for me." Hades brushed a curl back behind her ear. "I'll be right behind you."

Seeing Aethone with the others in the distance coming in hot with a trail of Keres behind them, Hades pointed to where he wanted her to run.

"Go to that spot right there by the rock. Get on the rock and jump onto the chariot. It won't stop. You have to catch it and ride it out of here. Do you understand?"

"Hades," Persephone grabbed his arm, brows drawn upward. "I don't want to go without you?"

"First, you can't be with me, and now you won't go without me. My queen seems quite inconsistent with her desires." His wicked smile made her frown.

"I'm not helpless," she argued.

"Of course you're not." Hades grabbed her and pulled her body close into a kiss filled with passion and need.

She melted in his arms and kissed him back, running her hands through his hair. He hated pulling away from her, but he had no choice.

"You are precious to me, and I want you safe while I handle business here," he said, holding her chin and kissing her one last time. "Now go. We have eternity to argue if you desire, but I need you on that chariot in about twenty seconds."

Persephone huffed but stood and took off toward the chariot barreling through the air, ready to touch down. He watched in admiration as she bolted toward the stone.

Take Persephone out of here, Aethone. I'll follow on my own shortly. Hades told his mare in his mind as she grew close enough to hear him.

We've got her. Make it back in one piece, or I'll have to destroy another stable, she said to him, making him smile.

Sensing his location, Aethone led the team directly next to where Persephone was leaping. The seconds she was in the air felt like an eternity to Hades until Persephone landed inside and grabbed the reins, slamming into the side of the frame. Immediately, the equestrian team was back off the ground, galloping into the air and outpacing the horde of winged daemons that followed.

***

Persephone raced through the caverns, feeling the pressure of their speed collapsing her lungs as they kept just far enough ahead to avoid her pursuers. One Keres that came a little too close was met with Persephone's sickle, cutting its hand clean off. It screamed, falling out of sight only to be replaced by two more who bore their fangs in a screeching howl. Snapping the reigns, Persephone raced them until, at last, they found the obsidian gates.

Before she could make it, she felt a tug on her dress that ripped her from the chariot to fall almost thirty feet and land hard on her back. Persephone tried to breathe but couldn't with the wind knocked out of her. Without any time to think, she rolled to her right and dodged the feet of a dark-eyed female Keres. Moving to get up, Persephone felt the air enter her lungs just in time to be kicked out and thrown back, landing against a column that stood in a row that led to her freedom.

Forcing air in, she called out for Aethone. Her scream echoed in the cavern, hopefully reaching the mare in time for help to arrive. Until then, Persephone knew she was on her own. She was determined to get past that entrance no matter the obstacle. Pulling her sickle, she stood ready to fight. Her forefinger pressed against one of the stones, separating the blade into two. Persephone had no idea they could multiply, but her surprise would have to wait until she was out of danger. A crescent knife in each hand gave her the confidence to fight as she spun them, ready to attack. Without hesitation, she took off in a dead run for the gates.

Persephone felt their gaze all around her as she slid to a halt in a sliver of light from the gate. Sensing four of them, she hoped she could defend against their group attacks. The first to jump at her, Persephone spun to dodge while bringing her blade down, taking its head in one swipe. Crying out, the other three attacked at once, tackling Persephone to the ground and burying their teeth into both her arms and one in her previously vulnerable right leg from the last bites. Weakness overwhelmed her limbs as though being injected with venom. The draw of her blood was so strong, never ceasing. She was starting to feel fear as the weight of their bodies pinned her to the ground, suffocating her. Pain swelled throughout her head when she fell to the ground, and she could feel blood trickling down her neck. Panic set in as she realized she was in trouble. This time, no one was coming to save her.

The darkness clawed at her, demanding that she give in. She felt her strength disappearing, and she was losing consciousness. A moment before she faded into darkness, Persephone felt a pull from her core followed by a presence filled with power flooding through her, forcing her body to arch, bowing her back as it filled her every pore with power.

Persephone closed her eyes to let it take her. When she opened them, she was lying there, the light shining down on her again. Everything was quiet—no more screeching or scraping of talons. You could hear a pin drop in the deadening silence. Persephone sat up, rubbing her eyes. She looked around to see multiple Keres lying dead, drained of all life, next to her, strewn about haphazardly. Fear crept up her spine. Persephone scrambled to get away from them until she was up on her knees, ready for another attack that never came.

All the pain she'd felt previously was gone. Blades still in hand, Persephone checked her arms for bites but found nothing. Her body healed while she'd been out, and her head swam with power. Her limbs were strong, better than usual, even. Persephone looked down at her hands, which were once again tan and healthy. Her dress was even more shredded, unfortunately. The back was completely open.

She stood, tied a knot at her waist in the back, and put her belt over it. Touching the two crescents together, they blended back together into one. Persephone wondered what other tricks her mother had placed in these weapons that she would need to discover. There were still two more amethysts and an obsidian stone at the end.

Once composed, she walked to the daemon realm's entrance and passed the gates unmolested by any more Keres. Thanatos appeared in his gray cloud only a few steps out of the gateway. He hurried to her and looked around for any danger.

"My queen? Are you alright?" Thanatos asked, seeming stressed. "Are you hurt?"

Persephone shook her head. "No, Thanatos. Thank you, I'm fine."

"Where's Lord Hades?" He asked, eyes scanning the area. "I received his signal."

"He stayed behind, entrusting me to the chariot," she said, wiping the blood from her face.

Thanatos cursed under his breath, looking back to see Aethone on her way. The mare pulled up beside them and whinnied to Persephone with worry in her red eyes.

"I'm alright, Aethone," Persephone said, petting the mare's neck.

Aethone snorted, stomping in irritation.

"What happened here?" Thanatos looked around with confusion in his graceful face.

"I'm not sure. I thought I...," she stuttered. "Then I woke up, and they were like this."

Thanatos looked at the Keres' corpse and then at Persephone. "You woke up, and they were just like this?"

"Yes," Persephone said, feeling sick seeing the bodies drained of life surrounding her where she had awoken.

He seemed to think for a moment, eyeing her suspiciously. She wondered what he thought about what he saw. She didn't even know what she was seeing. *How did this happen? What could have caused this? Was it me? Did I do this?* All these questions swirled around in her head.

"Let's get you back to my Lord's chambers so you can recover. I'm sure he will be with us soon. He's not in the same danger down here as you are," Thanatos gestured for her to follow him. "We should move now before any more of them arrive."

"Agreed," she said, stepping up onto the chariot.

Persephone quickly grabbed the bag of apples and held them to her chest. Thanatos joined her and took the reins. With a snap, the mare led the team out of the caves and back to the stables, where their caretakers released their bits and bindings. Stepping down on shaking legs, Persephone heard Aethone protesting her leaving. She went over to the mare, gave her a reassuring pet, and offered each horse some apples to calm them.

"I'll be okay, and so will Hades. I know he will." Petting Aethone's mane, Persephone smiled. "You know it'll take a lot more than that to take him down, right?"

Aethone nodded and chuckled. Seeming satisfied, she followed her brothers into their stables. Persephone followed Thanatos to her chambers, where she found solace in a warm spring.

Her aching muscles were better than usual, considering the battles she'd been in already. Still, they ached, and she was relieved to be clean again. Persephone could feel more of herself when washing and cleaning her hair again. She reached for her dress, and it fell apart in her hands when she picked it up. The fabric had finally given in and could shield her no more. She'd have to find something in the wardrobe.

Damn it, she hated that he would think he was winning. Persephone decided if she had to dress here, she would find something that suited her and not him. Resigning herself to the task of a new style, Persephone dried off and sat at the mirrored vanity brought from her room, braiding her hair over her shoulder. Admiring the darkened strands, she thought it was strange. Previously, she had brushed it off to the lighting or the dirt all over her. But now that her strands were clean, she saw in the light that her hair was darker.

Her once bright and light-filled curls were unmistakably red as blood. She'd had no Khol for her eyes, yet there it was, black as pitch lining them, blending out from her lashes into her skin. Her eyes were still lavender, and her skin was tan, but the rest of her had taken on the changes. Even her hair was less curly than before.

Her hands paused, letting her braid go. She touched her lips, seeing the stain. Her lips matched the dark red of her hair, and the blush to her cheeks now seemed permanent. She rubbed her face to see if she could wipe it off, but it remained unsmudged, clinging to her like dye to a new fabric swatch. Her appearance was jarring. She stood, knocking over the chair and stepping back several feet to see if anything else was different.

Dropping her towel, Persephone looked around for any scars or damage from her recent battle. To her relief, her body was the same hourglass shape. She turned, seeing her backside round and unchanged. Maybe a little thinner from having nothing to consume for days now. Persephone let out a sigh. Her skin seemed a little lighter of an olive hue. *Probably due to the lack of Helio's light*, she thought to herself. So why couldn't she shake the feeling that something was off?

There were no bite marks or claw marks. Strange, she should be healing, not fully recovered already. *What happened after he began to choke me?* Whatever it was, she didn't have time to figure it out. Persephone felt compelled to find Hades. Even though she hated him, she didn't want him injured on her behalf.

She groaned and resigned herself to the wardrobe that Thanatos transferred to Hades' chambers—her rag of a dress appearing as tattered as Persephone felt.

Opening the doors, she marveled at the choices but went to look for the simplest thing she could find—boots for fighting and a top that could hold her large breasts. Pants would be preferable, and she found some in a drawer made of dark tyrian leather. Her top chemise fitted draped over her shoulders matched the gold designs of vines and leaves lining the bust under her tyrian stained bodice.

"Good Gods, when you pick a color, you go all out, don't you, Hades?"

The soft leather of the bodice pulled her breasts up, giving her more cleavage than she expected, but at least the circular clasps that fit gracefully past her collarbone held up. Her arms lay exposed, so she found what she thought was an adorable pair of bat wing shoulder guards and clasped them to the bodice. They shaped over her shoulders well enough. She did a few arm rotations to test if they hindered her movement and found them comfortable enough. Finally, Persephone chose a pair of black leather wedge boots that came up over her knees. Remembering Nyctimus, she wanted to keep her knees protected.

Persephone avoided the mirror for fear of seeing the still unsettling changes in her appearance. Instead, she braided the top of her hair into a high ponytail she'd worn a hundred times for sparring on Olympus. She found two matching leather gauntlets and laced them tight so they'd stay. There was no pain when she clasped the front bodice hooks and pulled the leather strings lining her spine to tighten the bodice against her body, leaving plenty of room to move. The armor and support would be invaluable if ever dealing with slashing claws again.

After seeing that serpent fighter before, it occurred to her she didn't want her guts spilled out like that if she could avoid it. Now that she thought about it, other than slight soreness, she was in perfect form. Her confidence had improved knowing she was wearing at least a little armor and was beginning to heal faster should anything try to scratch or bite again. Once she dressed to her satisfaction, Persephone attached her sickle to her lower back for access, no longer caring if anyone saw.

"Maybe I can do this." Persephone turned to the flower thriving under the warm glow of the hovering stone. "What do you think?"

Its little petals quaked with excitement, responding to

her when she reached out and touched them.

"I'm still not sure," Persephone smiled down at the flower that once was white, now had a yellow center with red lining the bell. "Looks like we both have been through some changes, haven't we?"

The flower arched toward the light and swayed.

Persephone left her plant and walked where she knew Hades might be if he had returned. He would be in his war room. He was always working. She wondered if that was good or not. If she was stuck here, would he be gone all the time? Would he be out with others? What would he do with all that time away while she unwillingly remained?

CHAPTER 8 DEAL

Hades approached the cave where he knew the leader of the Keres would be waiting for his audience. Violent death always knew when he knocked on her door.

"Hades, God, and King of our dear Underworld," a lithe female with ebony skin said with one leg casually dangling over the arm of her throne made of mortal bones stained in blood.

"Black Ker, Goddess of Violent Death and Destruction," Hades said with a smile. "You almost had me there. For a minute, I thought you were going soft on me."

"Zeus of the world below, you honor me with your presence," Ker said with a wicked grin from ear to ear. "I sensed a presence hostile to you and sent my Keres to assist you."

"Don't call me Zeus of any kind," Hades growled. "And about that assistance..."

"No need to thank me, Dark Lord," Ker interrupted and waved a hand, sitting up and grabbing a goblet.

Swirling a finger in her bloody drink, she licked her finger and then sucked on it until it was clean. The dark liquid coated the sides like syrup as she drank deeply from the glass.

"I will always serve as a general like my brother,

Thanatos, to keep you safe."

"Thanatos must not have told you that the being you attacked was the Goddess of Spring, Persephone." Hades folded his arms over his chest. "Your new queen."

Ker spat and set down the glass. She stood whipping her face. "I had no idea, my Lord. If I had known, I would have sent a different message."

Ker dropped down to her knees. "Forgive me, my Lord. I didn't know her importance."

"I'm sure you would have," he said with an arched brow. "And yet, I didn't send out the word of her importance, so the fault is mine. It never occurred to me that she wouldn't be safe with me."

"Apologies." Ker bowed deep. "From now on, I will ensure she will be safe in this domain. If ever you need me to give sanction to another, please send Thanatos to relay the message. I trust him far more than I would trust Hypnos."

"Your daemons are to ensure that she is free to pass at all times. I want one in every shadow, letting me know if anything is wrong."

"You want me to spy on your new queen and report back to you?" Ker grimaced and turned away with an awkward glance.

"What?" He asked innocently.

"My Lord," Ker approached him, offering a goblet of the wine he'd enjoyed before. "Far be it for me to tell you, of all gods, what to do, but is that wise?"

Hades narrowed his eyes and took the goblet. "I need her safe."

"Yes..." Ker tapped her glass. "Safe is one word you could use."

"I can't lose her," Hades said, drinking the wine in one gulp.

Ker nodded with sorrow in her eyes. "Yes, I was there when Hera brutalized her."

"I didn't know that," Hades said, returning the glass to

her.

Ker shrugged. "I show up when there's a violent death. You know that. After her mother took her, I couldn't get to her. I figured it was not my position to worry about it or interfere. I didn't realize she would be your queen. I sensed her death and assumed she was a spirit seeking revenge."

"After what happened, I didn't know if Persephone coming to the Underworld was ever a possibility," he said, taking another glass and indulging in a long drink.

"Great Nyx, who could bring her back from that?" Ker asked with wide eyes.

Hades shook his head. "I don't know. Maybe it was a primordial. But which one and why?"

Ker scoffed. "That's going to be a difficult conversation considering the level of her hostility toward you that attracted my Keres."

"I brought her here against Demeter's wishes," Hades said, brushing off her comment. "Who can say what elements are at work when the prophecy is so strong."

"She is Demeter's daughter? Hades," Ker tilted her head, letting her pin-straight black hair fall over her shoulder. "Are you trying to get us all killed? Demeter is the most violent of all of you original gods. You would dare test her?"

"For Persephone?" Hades asked, slamming his glass on the table. "Yes."

"Nyx, help us," Ker said, pinching the bridge of her nose. "You've got it bad, don't you?"

Hades didn't respond. He didn't want to admit how right she was.

"In the end, you won't have a choice if we all die." Ker put her hands in the air, relenting to any argument he may have, stepping back. "Just sayin'."

"Choice..." Hades paused, closing his eyes for patience. "From the moment I saw her and when we shared the vision of us... I haven't had a choice since."

"Of course you have." Ker walked around him, eyeing

him up and down. "You chose love. I can only say that I pray to Nyx that we all survive this."

"I can't live without her."

"My lord, may I suggest you change your approach?"

"My approach?"

"Seems to me like you've been very," Ker began copying his mannerisms and deep voice, pointing down at the floor. "Obey me or else...," she mocked. "Might I ask how that's working out for you?"

"The truth is, I don't want to control her." Hades liked how unpredictable she could be.

"Then don't. Let her make mistakes down here and try new things, especially because it's dangerous. If, as you say, her life has never been in her control, let her be whoever she needs to become, even if you don't like the results.

"I don't know how to make her happy and accept my desire to become hers as well as she becoming mine."

"If I can add a little advice?"

"What's that?"

"It might send the wrong message if she finds out you're having her followed by minions." Ker patted Hades' arm with friendly familiarity. "Spend time with her and show Persephone who you are here. If she's into violence, send her my way. I'll show her a damned good time." Ker winked at him with a sensual laugh.

Hades sighed. "Not informing my Underworld first was a mistake. It didn't go too well as a first introduction, that's true."

"How can I help, Dark Lord?" Her question left a pause a little too long in the air.

"Answer me freely," Hades said, bracing for her answer. "Do you think I'm a monster?"

She took her time to answer. "You're not like most of us. You're our Lord, not because you're like us, but because you're better than all of us. You have a kinder heart than us, are never swayed by emotion, and always judge fairly for everyone here.

Out there, none of us have such favor. We are at the whims of Zeus, who would sooner use us as sex slaves over being what we are. It's not ideal to be a being with a conscience who needs to gather souls and feed on their miserable deaths. But we see how you gods in power treat the nymphs and want to be different."

Her advice, though often tinged with violent rhetoric, was always helpful. Often, he enjoyed their combat in conversation, yet this time, she seemed more open with no resistance as he expected. He could tell she was genuinely sorry for what happened, and it calmed him from the violence he would have committed upon her and her entire horde were he unable to reason with her. But she was always willing to make a deal that she would stick with, no matter what happened. Ker was someone he could always rely on being faithful to her duty to him and his kingdom. He'd never seen that with Zeus from his subjects. Nor Poseidon. Their subjects only expressed fear. Hades hated that he was feared when he never asked to be. He couldn't prevent their opinions from being as they were. Still, it was hard to feel it anyway. But this, this was rare and reassuring. Naturally, he had to tease her for such sentiments.

"Are you admitting that the Underworld is better than Olympus?" Hades asked with a sly grin. "Or even the oceanic world of Poseidon?"

"Because I owe you an apology for today, you will get no resistance from me." Ker smiled a small side grin. "Yes, the Underworld is the most gentle place for beings like us to thrive instead of being hunted like animals."

"How do I show her that side of this world?" Hades asked, peering out the large window that showed the grey land below.

"You have a beautiful orchard," Ker said, coming up beside him. "She seems like the type who would like that."

He turned to Ker. "What else?"

"Take her deep into Tartarus," she replied, taking a sip

of blood. "Show her everything. A lesser being will fold. If she is as you say, she will emerge stronger. If she breaks, you will know."

"Considering how hard she's fought me, I don't think anyone could break her." Hades chuckled. "Call off the Keres so I can show her the rest of the Underworld. I need your word that she'll be protected."

"God of the darkest region, you have my vow on the river Styx that no intentional harm shall come to her from me or any of my Keres. I will put out the word of who she is and demand anyone's head who disobeys. And I can send a few out to ensure nothing gets too close." Ker winked. "Just in case."

"Good," Hades said, then turned, and as the darkness surrounded him, he was back in his war room.

"Always strategizing, aren't you?" Persephone asked, standing in the doorway.

Hades looked up, raising one brow as he saw her new appearance, but said nothing for fear of losing control of his desire for her. "I was going over a better strategy to show you the rest of the Underworld."

"And Tartarus?" She asked, craning her head.

"Yes, Tartarus as well," Hades said, pouring a glass, leaning against the table.

Persephone folded her arms. "How did you make it out of the fields?"

"I teleported."

"What?" Persephone put her hand on her forehead and one on her hip, beginning to pace. "Then why didn't you just do that to get us out?"

He took a long sip before answering. "Because I can take myself out but can't take anyone else with me. I can take you in, but you'd have to get out on your own."

"Hence the chariot?"

Hades nodded. "Hence the chariot. Once I pass those gates, my abilities to transport anyone with me no longer work."

"Why would you do that?" Persephone asked, clearly agitated.

"A fail-safe to ensure I don't get taken over by a Titan and forced to take them out or set them free. Some can manipulate your mind into agreeing to do things you would never do under normal circumstances. Unable to transport anything out ensures anyone who goes in with me and returns is of my will alone."

She blew out a heavy breath. "And here I thought I'd be safe if I crossed that threshold."

"You could only make it through by taking in my life force," he replied, setting down his chalice. "Until now, I didn't even know that was possible."

"Is that what I did?" She asked with her eyes wide in shock.

"Hades cleared his throat. "Among other things."

"What do you mean?" She asked innocently.

"Let's just say it's a side of you that I've never seen before," said Hades with a wicked smile.

"I'm not sure how to take that," she said, wrapping her arms around her waist. "Regardless, whatever I did clearly worked. I was able to pass the gates and leave with Thanatos. He said you sent out a signal."

"I did." Hades nodded. "I knew he would be there to help in time."

"Big mistake thinking that," said Persephone, crossing her arms over her chest.

Hades raised a brow. "What do you mean?"

"I didn't make it." A shadow crept over her eyes. "They got me just before I reached the exit."

"What?" Hades growled deep in his chest. "Thanatos didn't tell me that."

"Something happened," she continued. "I woke up with the Keres that attacked me dead in a pile around me."

"What do you mean dead?" Hades felt a knot welling in his gut. "All of them?"

"I mean in the after-after life. Lifeless. Without life." Persephone chortled. "And yes, all of them. About seven or eight."

"Did they look like flesh melded to bone and drained?" He asked, closing his eyes, remembering what she'd done to the one he witnessed earlier.

"Yes, that's what they looked like. Hey! Wasn't there one like that that attacked us earlier?" She asked, snapping her fingers.

"Yes," he said in a measured tone. "You don't remember anything about it being there?"

"No, why would I?" Her reply was so innocent, with eyes wide. "I assumed you did that."

Hades wanted to tell her what he saw but decided against it. He needed to find out more about it before making her worry over something she obviously couldn't control and appeared not even to realize she was doing it. He suspected that Persephone was developing new abilities. One was taking the life force of other creatures and reviving her own, as though she was taking their life to replenish what she had lost.

"No. I didn't do that."

"Then who?" she asked, then pointed to herself. "You mean I did that?"

"I spoke to Ker," Hades said, turning toward the table to avoid her gaze. She assured me the attack from her daemons won't happen again."

"And you trust her?" Persephone asked, coming closer from behind.

"She made a vow on the river Styx." Hades leaned against his war table. "A vow on Styx is unbreakable. And if one breaks that vow, if they are of enough power, it won't kill them, but they will sleep for a year before recovering. Another one of Zeus' pesky rules to gain fidelity."

"Oh, I didn't realize that," she said, standing beside him to stare at the table.

Hades glanced at her from the side. "It's not a vow one

makes in jest."

"That's good." Persephone nodded. "But how did you convince her to make such a vow?"

"I didn't, Ker offered," Hades replied, arms flexing with the tension he felt with her standing so near to him. "She didn't know you were making threats and attacking me, and her Keres are attracted to battle. Being who I am, she let them loose on you to protect me. She has now extended that same protection to you along with apologies."

Persephone continued observing the map of the layout of the regions of his realm. The orbs' light made patterns over her face as they moved about and rotated continuously. *She was lovely in this light*, he thought.

"What are those?" Persephone asked, pointing at them.

"They're souls," Hades replied.

She seemed distracted while she examined the glowing spirals of dotted lights.

"How can you possibly keep track of them all?" She asked.

"I have help. But that isn't why I brought you here," he replied.

He turned off the energy of the map, and the room grew darker with only the firelight from the torches lining the walls. He'd always been safe within himself. Now, with her, he didn't know anything anymore. The fear from his siblings made him believe it was better to hide his abilities and fight to ensure his true powers remained hidden. When she didn't react in fear, like everyone else, he thought maybe she could love him anyway.

"Persephone," he whispered, leaning down to her ear. "I would do anything for you. I could be the one to bring your darkness out and teach you to control it as I have. I could even provide you with what you need to improve your skills."

"Being with you shouldn't be this hard," She whispered. "My mother would never allow such a thing," she replied breathlessly, nuzzling his face with hers. Their breaths began to intertwine, with their foreheads touching. "I'm afraid," she whispered.

"You have nothing to fear from me," he said to her. "I will always protect you."

"It's not protection I need," she said in a lusty whisper.

"Tell me what you need, and you'll have it."

"There is one thing you can give me."

Finally, Persephone reached up, tracing her fingers behind his neck, bringing his mouth to hers. Her deep kisses made him lose his mind as he became drunk on her scent and touch. Picking her up, he wrapped her legs around his waist and set her on the table.

"I want you, Hades," she said with lust in her voice under her breath as she took his mouth again and again. "I just can't be with you."

Feeling her fingers grip him, he realized she didn't want control. He needed to be inside her, but she wasn't ready. Persephone had to accept him and this place willingly, or all of this would fail. Hades took his hand and brought it up to grip behind her neck as their tongues danced. He used his other hand to pull her body close to him by cupping her generous ass. Her squeal delighted him as he turned her around and bent her over the table, kicking her legs wide enough to grab her belt loops and rip her pants down, stopping at her thighs.

"What are you doing?" she asked, panting with desire.

"I want to look at what's between your legs," he said, voice becoming raspy.

She looked back at him, watching while he dropped to one knee and grabbed her ass, prying her pussy open. He delighted in her stuttered breath. Bending down as he held her open, he licked from her clit to her dark hole. Persephone cried out his name, moaning as he did it again.

"Oh please," she begged, making his cock hard from giving her pleasure.

"Please, what?" He asked between licks. "Do you want me to stop?"

"No. Oh Gods, no."

"No, you want me to stop? Or no, you don't want me to stop?" He asked, sucking on her clit, lapping up and down, then side to side to find where she liked it in this position.

"Please, Hades. Please don't stop," she said through whimpers.

With each aching caress of her body, Persephone shook with anticipation of what he would do next. Gods, even he didn't know. He just needed to taste her. His lips left wet trails that made her shiver between her thighs as he marveled at her glistening fiery curls. Lifting her hips, he licked her swollen bud, making her arch her back. He continued to lap lazily, meeting the rhythm of her undulating hips. She reached back with her hands and wrapped them in his hair to guide him to where she wanted him. Gods, she tasted so fucking amazing. Her insistent tugging on his hair turned him on more.

"Ah! Yes, Hades, I'm cumming," Persephone cried out as she began to shake uncontrollably.

Her body tensed just before he heard her scream. Hades didn't stop licking until she gently pushed him back. She stayed bent over, pussy swollen, panting with her knees bending together to hold her up as they continued to shake.

He stood whipping his face, walking over to the corner where there was a towel. He stood staring at her beautiful backside as he plunged his hands into the oracle waters and then used a towel to dry them. Hecate was going to hate him for that, he mused.

Persephone stood and pulled up her pants, adjusting the belt and top. Her hips swayed when she approached him. Her hands shook as she braced against his chest, then rose onto her toes to kiss him. Hades returned her kiss with passion as though it was the last time. Each time he kissed her, he didn't know if it would be or not. Lost in her lips, he wrapped his arms around her and held her close, relishing how perfect her body felt against his. The longing and ache in his chest was gone whenever she embraced him. Just as he thought she was softening to him, Persephone froze, hearing a knock at the door.

He growled low in his throat. "Leave!"

Pulling him into a soft kiss, she whispered between laps of her tongue. "Next time, it's my turn to satisfy you."

"I thought you were angry with me," he said, burning with need.

"I still am." Persephone pulled him into a tender kiss this time. "But maybe we can work something out?"

Hades moaned. "We could do this whenever you desired."

"Except when I need to return to the surface," Persephone said with a sweet smile. "I have to go back. You know it's inevitable. Don't make this harder on either of us than it must be."

"Your pleas fall on deaf ears, Flower," Hades said, brushing her cheek with his thumb. "I'm not letting you go."

Persephone's lust turned to anger like a lever had changed the flow of her river of emotions.

"You won't budge, will you?"

"I told you. Never."

"Give in, Hades." Persephone frowned, turning away. "It can't work between us."

Hades tilted her head by her chin to look at him. "Let me prove to you that it can."

"Hades," she said with a groan.

"Please." He never begged. But he would beg her if needed. "Give me time, and I will show you how to be happy here."

Persephone rested her forehead on his chest. "We can't go on like this forever with her out there, no doubt out of her mind with worry."

Hades let out a heavy sigh, wrapping his arms around Persephone. "It's true. Demeter will eventually come for you. But until that time, I plan to show you what we could have together to convince you that it's worth being with me."

"You are very worthy to be with, Hades." Persephone dropped her head, shaking it, then looked up to face him with her brows drawn upward. "I needed time to convince my mom of that, and now I can't do that because you dragged me down here, and now I'm stuck making a deal with you instead."

Hades frowned, taking a step back. "Demeter was never going to agree to allow me to have you."

"I guess we'll never know now," she said, showing her irritation.

"You make this sound like it's all my fault," he said accusingly.

"This situation right here?" She twirled her finger in the air, insinuating his kingdom. "Yes. This situation is entirely your fault."

"You didn't seem so objectionable while I was just sucking on your little cunt a moment ago," He said, blood pulsing hard in his veins.

Slap! The sound echoed off the walls as he took it and smiled down at her, that wicked grin that drove her mad. The passion he felt for Persephone felt overwhelming. She could shove a spear through his chest, and he'd still want her.

"Admit it." Hades stared into her eyes, needing to understand how to get through. "You wanted to leave that boring meadow."

She clasped her nads to her chest, backing away. "No, I didn't."

"Yes. You. Did." Hades stepped closer.

"You don't know anything," she said, shaking her head.

Hades leaned casually against the table. "I know that you feel guilty over the plan you hatched failing. You can't fix what happened, and you damn well can't return to being that naive maiden."

"Naive? You thought I was naive that whole time?" Persephone scoffed and folded her arms over her chest. "And here I thought you saw me as an equal or someone who could be, one day. It turns out I was naive in thinking that too. Why else would you go against my wishes and take me without my mom's blessing."

"You? Equal to me?" Hades chuckled. "You're adorable. Besides, I had Zeus' blessing. That's all I required to take you as my queen."

Persephone threw her hands in the air, exasperation in her groan.

"It's like talking to a stone wall with you. We need my mom's blessing so there won't be a war. Or famine or plagues of locusts or rats or whatever chaos she can conjure! Which meant instead of grabbing me and taking me, we had to negotiate. That's not naive. That's being incredibly aware of my mom's personality and exercising prudence in gaining her support so we could have a smooth relationship, not one bumbling mess after another with deception, failure, death, and now abduction!" Persephone walked toward the door and stopped, calming herself, placing a hand on the handle. "You know, I imagined you thought better of me. Guess I was wrong about that too, while my mom is, once again, proven right."

Persephone turned the handle and walked out, leaving him with the towel still in his hand. He threw it into the fountain and cursed at himself again.

"She's impossible!" Hades bellowed. "Fuck!"

"Don't I know it?" Hecate appeared lounging on the chaise lounge in the corner of the west end where her fountain was. "Is that... Is that a used towel in my?" Her words trailed off as her face turned red in anger.

Hades glared, then grabbed the towel and threw it. It slopped on the floor in a heap, leaving a water trail that felt like his brain. Nothing but mush, trying to argue with Persephone and getting nowhere.

"I thought being intimate would soften her to my...."

"To what? Your charms?" Hecate laughed.

Hades glared. "If that's what you want to call it."

"Don't give up yet, Hades. You still have time before her mother finds her and war breaks out." Hecate grumbled, dumped out the fountain, and refilled it with a twirl of her fingers. "Until Demeter can regain her precious daughter, it's sheer mayhem above."

Hades poured Hecate a drink as a peace offering for sullying her fountain. "This isn't going how I planned for all those long months. I stood waiting for a sign or anything that would let me know Persephone was awake and that I could finally get to her."

Hecate took the chalice and drank the whole glass in one gulp. "Ah, the things we will do for love. Eros' arrow has struck you hard, my dear one."

"It's been impossible to think or say the right thing around her," Hades said, slumping against the wall. "I don't know what else to do to make her want to stay."

"Perhaps you could give her something here that she couldn't get elsewhere?"

"Like what?" He thought about what she desired that she couldn't get anywhere else, but nothing came to mind.

"Some closure?" Hecate grinned. "Perhaps a confrontation in her favor?"

"What do you mean?" Hades asked, confused, until he realized what Hecate meant, then narrowed his eyes at her. "No. I'm not taking her to see Hera."

"Hera can't do anything to Persephone while in your dungeon," she said, waving a dismissive hand. "What better way to make her feel in control than to know she holds the keys to her arch nemesis? Might change her mind if she knows she has Hera at her feet instead of the other way around."

"Maybe," he replied, pinching the bridge of his nose. "I'll think about it and decide later. Right now, I need some rest and to think of what I will do next."

"I don't envy you." Hecate sighed. "But love is difficult, even in the best circumstances. At least you genuinely care for her. That's more than Hera or any other could ever dream of. One god, loving his goddess, dancing together for all eternity." Her sigh became wistful and painfully corny to him.

Even still, It sounded nice.

"Either way, you don't have much time left," she said, her tone hinting of foreboding.

"What do you mean?" He asked, wondering how things could be any worse.

"Oh, those little tramps showed up at my orgy when I..." Hecate clenched her fist and then took a deep breath. "Well, never mind."

Hades curled one side of his lip up into a half smile. "You were fucking someone."

"Obviously," Hecate rolled her eyes. "Then those three dared to lump me into this little prophecy." Hecate's sneered, mocking their voices. "Saying I have a part to play in this event. And that I must lead the mother to the daughter with the flame forged in the fires of Hephaestus for the prophecy to be and some other blah, blah, blah nonsense about our world still ending."

"I'm aware."

"Well, I wasn't," she said, bracing her hands on her hips. "Now we have to devise another plan since I am the one who will bring Demeter to claim her daughter."

"Why are you telling me this?" he asked, folding his arms. "I could stop you."

Hecate slumped into her chair. "I know. But with all the betrayal going on, I wanted to make sure you knew I wasn't plotting against you, but at some point, I will become compelled to lead Demeter to Persephone."

Hades groaned, rubbing his hands over his face. "I guess a heads-up is better than nothing."

"You have until the next new moon."

"Seven days?" *Fuck*, he thought to himself.

"Apologies, Hades." Hecate stood and adjusted her gown. "It's the best I can do under the circumstances."

"So I only get nine days with her in total?" Hades clenched his jaw and fists to stay calm.

Hecate nodded. "After that, her time to decide is up."

He didn't feel any grudge toward Hecate. She was more loyal than most beings he knew. The fact that she told him was significant. Nine days was hardly enough time to show Persephone his world. But if it was all he had, there was no choice but to begin as soon as possible.

Perhaps the best place to start would be to show her where the souls arrive. Charon was an old friend and may show his other form if comfortable. Or maybe he should start with Cerberus. Hades knew Persephone liked animals. Unlike other beings, she seemed to see beyond their terrifying appearance. The Keres had been a mistake. His guilt over her injuries was still gnawing at him. He would ensure she was safe this time and destroy anything that came too close. Hades called for Thanatos, who appeared next to him.

"My Lord?" Thanatos turned to see Hecate and bowed his head. "Witch."

He didn't say it with malice, only adoration as she shyly clasped her hands together and waved with a blushing smile.

"Hello, Death," she said in her sultry voice. "I see you're looking very... Big. Today."

Her eyes trailed up and down his body as she bit her lip.

Thanatos smiled. "You look lovely as ever. Did you do something new to your hair?"

Hecate giggled, making Hades roll his eyes. He cleared his throat, gaining both of their attention.

"Has Charon arrived on this side of the shore yet?" Hades asked his general.

"He should be soon," Thanatos said, peeling his eyes away from Hecate. "Many souls are giving him difficulty on the other side, demanding to be allowed across."

Hades sighed. "When he arrives, tell him to wait for me."

"Of course," Thanatos said with another bow. He was about to leave when he paused. "Any luck convincing our queen to stay?"

"No." Hades waved his hand and turned off the table of souls drifting by, leaving the room to glow with the warm firelight. "Hecate has informed me our time is almost up. I have only seven days to convince her."

"Seven days? That's hardly enough time to explore, let alone woo the queen."

"The Moirai have spoken," Hecate replied. "There's nothing we can do to avoid the impending conflict."

Thanatos nodded. "My Lord, how can I help?"

"You can take over most of my duties for the next few days so I can focus on Persephone," Hades said, standing by the fireplace, staring into the flames.

"Of Course," his general said, his eyes drifting to Hecate.

"Now that we all have a part to play," Hecate said, interrupting his thoughts. "Thanatos, would you come with me to the scrying pools to see how we can take the pressure off of Hades so he can focus?"

"Me?" Thanatos asked in a shaky voice. "I... I'd be happy to help."

"Lovely," she said, grabbing his arm and summoning her cloud.

Alone, Hades stood before the fireplace and stared into the flames, contemplating where he would take her. Ultimately, he knew he would have to take her to the farthest depths of Tartarus. The only place he would not take her is to the one being that still struck fear into his heart.

CHAPTER 9
ASPHODEL

Slowly, Persephone's orgasm built as her hands caressed up and down his body. The waves of pleasure crashed over her as she called out his name.

"Hades," she whispered under her breath with every stroke of his cock inside her.

Suddenly, a sword ripped through his chest, and blood slattered over her face. Hades choked on his own blood that filled his lungs, then collapsed. He fell away as Hera stood before her with the sinister smile Persephone recognized during their last battle, her blade still dripping.

"Did you think you could get away from me and live happily forever?" Hera asked with a terrifying laugh that echoed all around Persephone.

She stared into Hades' lifeless eyes as the tears filled her own. Her heart bounded like the thunder in the clouds. Wrenching out a scream, Persephone cried uncontrollably as the sky queen's shrieking laughter grew louder.

Sitting upright in his bed, she wiped the cold sweat from her brow and pulled back the covers. Stepping onto the warm floor, she walked to the fireplace to stare into the dancing light.

The dream chilled her to the bone. It wasn't the first time she'd dreamed of Hera. It wouldn't be the last, either. She couldn't even come close to the level of skill Hera and her mom possessed in fighting. The idea of another defeat made her nauseous every morning. Between a lack of food and constant disturbing dreams, Persephone was exhausted.

Needing a distraction, Persephone went to the pits to see if she could find Nyctimus again. She did. He was there, riling up the crowd again. His two swords were covered in blood that dripped onto the dirty sand below. His smile gleamed, and his oiled body glistened in the firelight. He'd styled his braids with silver coils and dark stones. Half up in the braids, his loose, soft curls danced over his shoulders. He wore his usual fighting gear and red loinwear.

Nyctimus circled his opponent in the heavy boots, which he used to kick the other in the gut, forcing him to land hard on his back, knocking the air out of him. Nyctimus lept into the air and buried his sword into the other's gut. Blood spurted from the loser's mouth as he collapsed to roaring applause.

This time, the one who met his blade fell quickly and had to be carried by two other armored creatures with fur who dragged out the defeated. He turned to face the crowd, and Persephone saw her opportunity. She stood and walked to the edge, calling down to him. He looked up and raised a hand over his eyes to shield them. Realization seemed to dawn over him as he smiled and waved at her. Persephone signaled for him to meet her after, and he nodded and then left the arena with cheers of his name echoing in the halls.

"By the gods," he said with a perfect grin. "You're alive."

"Nyctimus," Persephone said with a smile and surprised him with a fierce hug. "I'm so glad you are as well."

He cleared his throat and backed away shyly. "It was touch and go, there for a minute, but I survived."

Persephone paused at his comment. The sickness in her stomach welled up to her throat. Clearing it, she smiled.

"I'm relieved to hear you've recovered," she said, with a gentle hand on his shoulder. "Tell me. Why are you fighting in the pits here?"

"Hades, in his benevolence, helped me recover," he said, gesturing for her to walk with him. "I requested he let me pay for my failures with one hundred years of service. So for now, I serve by fighting as entertainment."

"What? That's awful!" Persephone exclaimed. "I wish I could go back and undo capturing you for Zeus. You wouldn't be here if not for me."

"We can't relive our choices," Nyctimus replied with a pained smile. "If we could, our decisions would not carry weight in them. And it's not so bad here. Better than the pits of Zeus."

Persephone nodded. "On that, we agree."

"Besides," he continued. "Here I'm praised and cheered. I get unlimited wine, females available for my choosing every night, and I'm no longer hunting for food nor hunted for my crimes."

"I'm extremely regretful of that," Persephone said with a wince.

Nyctimus chuckled. "It's not your fault. An order is an order. I have lived and died by them. We can't escape our fate."

"I don't think anyone should follow orders blindly," she said, contemplating her own mistakes. "Regarding fate, I wish I knew what mine was."

"Would you follow it even if foretold?" He asked with a smirk.

It made her laugh. "I don't think I have much choice in the matter."

"Just because there are limitations and parameters to our choices, we must choose how we live until then." He paused. "Though the ending of our lives is out of our hands, it does not mean we don't still forge our journey to that destination as we see fit."

"Do you believe that, Nyctimus?"

"Think of it this way. We are all going to die. Eventually. Right? Well..." Looking at her and rethinking, Nyctimus laughed. "Most of us, that is. How we lived, and the stories told about us are what makes any of us immortal."

She smiled up at him. "You're pretty wise for a wolf."

"I get it from my mother's side," Nyctimus said, nudging her with his shoulder and chuckling. "I suppose you get your stubbornness from yours."

"That's not the only thing," she said with a chuckle. "She and I both have a thing for men who don't value our opinions or wishes."

Nyctimus shrugged. "We live in a harsh world where so many bad things happen. I know you want your emotions and feelings to matter all the time, but it's not always about you. Some things are out of our control. What we do with these situations is what makes us who we are. Be it benevolent or malicious, everyone from gods to mortals are just trying to do their best with the hand dealt to us from our beginning."

Persephone paused and thought about what he said. The hand they were dealt, huh? That was indeed a difficult situation to muddle through. Maybe she did have some choices, even under these circumstances. But she wasn't quite ready to give in. Not yet, anyway.

"So you are doing okay here?" She asked after a moment.

He gave a quick nod. "I am better than I have been in a long time."

Persephone smiled, then went to leave but stopped before the entrance and turned back to him.

"I will never forget what you did for me and Artemis that day. For that, I will owe you a debt. You may choose it and request it when you desire. I will fulfill it."

"My queen," Nyctimus stood, clenching his fists, closing his eyes. "You owe me nothing because I failed. I didn't protect you as I should have."

"No." Persephone placed a gentle hand on his shoulder. "You gave me the time that I needed, as you said. We all have our fates written. The journey is the destination, right?"

"Using my own words against me," he chuckled in his throat. "I guess you'll be a formidable queen after all."

Persephone shook her head. "Not if I keep making all these mistakes."

"Well, mistake or no, I am pleased to see you here." His eyes lit up. "Might I introduce you to several of the fighters?"

Persephone thought for a moment, then nodded. "I'd like that."

Nyctimus took her to meet the group on the arena's close side.

"Argyreoi," He called out as they all turned to face the two of them. "This is our new queen, Persephone."

Persephone bowed her head. "It's good to meet you all."

"The pleasure is ours, my queen," said one male with short, straight black hair and slanted eyes.

A blonde female approached. "You honor us with your presence."

"How can we be of service?" Another who appeared to be the blonde's sibling, only with brown hair.

"She's just here to meet everyone," Nyctimus said, gesturing for her to join their circle. "Unless you want to practice with us, my queen?"

"I may take you up on that." Persephone smiled at them as they spoke. "It's incredible how you all fight in the arena. I'm very impressed."

"We do our best to entertain," said the female with a sly grin and sandy hair.

"Will you be joining us in the arena for some sport?" Her brother asked.

"You are always welcome." The muscular male with short black hair and monolids smiled and offered her his sword.

"Thank you." Persephone was relieved that they were so welcoming. "This has been an exciting and new experience for me. But I will say, I have enjoyed so much of this world, and seeing smiling faces is nice."

"We aim to please, my lady." the brunette male said with a bow.

"Perhaps you would come to tonight's event?" The blonde asked with excitement in her voice.

Persephone's eyes went wide. "Tonight?"

"Yes," Nyctimus said next to her. "We are competing for the prize of...what was it again?"

The black-haired male winked. "A spot in Hecate's mass orgy is tonight at midnight."

"Orgy?" Persephone asked, looking up at a sly smiling Nyctimus.

"Nyctimus is one of the best and most revered among the females here," said another muscular bald female with fangs that showed when she smiled at him. "So he's already got an invitation. But the rest of us will be challenging one another for the opening... As it were."

They all began to laugh, looking at one another and enjoying the naughty reference.

"Daemons love a good challenge, don't they?" Persephone asked, smiling at them.

"That and providing rich harvests and maintaining Gaia's fertility." Two of the males high-fived one another.

Nyctimus pointed to the group. "They were the silver age of mortals below, and upon their deaths, their spirits became daemons called the Argyreoi, while those who were the golden daemons above are the Kryseoi."

Persephone raised her brows. "So they were once mortal, and now they...."

Nyctimus nodded. "They help with fertility and harvest on Gaia, usually only released from here during equinoxes. The female with fangs and the male with the slanted eyes are not from here, though."

"That must have been hard experiencing life and death and now an afterlife," Persephone said, finding the group pleasant given what they'd been through.

The blonde chimed in. "I guess it's better than the meadows of shades."

"It is." Nyctimus nodded. "The Asphodel Meadows is a fate, in many of a warrior's eyes, worse than death."

"Really?" Persephone asked, unaware of what the meadows here were like, but she knew the emptiness until Gaia appeared. "I guess I can imagine what that could be like."

"How would an immortal know what it is to live and die?" Nyctimus asked with sincerity in his tone, not the judgment she would have expected.

Persephone cleared her throat and smiled to hide her true feelings. "Well, I should let you get back to your orgy battles. Or whatever you call them."

Nyctimus noticed her unease. "You can join us in the fighting to practice your skills while down here. It helps me to get my feelings and thoughts in order when I fight. I don't know. Just thought maybe it would help you."

"You know what, Nyctimus?" Persephone looked to the approving smiles of the group. "I think you may have a point. Perhaps I could join you for practice. Not the orgy. I will leave it to those who wish to go. If that's alright with you, I want to learn all I can about fighting."

"My lady may join in whatever activity she chooses. We are your humble servants and will accommodate whatever wishes you desire." Nyctimus bowed his head and then signaled with one hand for the others and her to follow him to the archway that led to what looked like an armory.

"Well, Well," said a familiar venomous female. "If it isn't the baggage Hades brought home."

The voice behind her grated against Persephone's ears. Knowing who stood behind her made her take a breath to find patience. She was going to need it.

"Mynthe, I didn't know you were a fighter." Persephone casually placed a hand on her hip and gave a half smile. "I just assumed you did all your work on your back."

The group laughed in favor of Persephone's jab. She

could see the burn in Mynthe's eyes as she looked around at the group, narrowing her gaze back to Persephone.

"Many of us had to fight our way throughout our existence." Mynthe tilted her head. "With the privilege you exude, one could tell your life has been nothing but picking flowers and sleeping in a nice, cozy bed every night."

Once in Persephone's favor, the room's energy grumbled in acknowledgment of Mynthe's truth.

"You're right." Persephone squared her shoulders. "I have lived a good life. I'm not ashamed of it. A gift from my mother, who would stomp you into the ground for your insolence."

"You see everyone?" Mynthe said to the group. "She thinks she's better than all of you."

"I didn't..." Persephone stuttered.

"She thinks..." Mynthe interrupted, garnering all their attention. "That all of you are beneath her. So go ahead and play fight. But if one hair is out of place on the goddess's precious head, Hades will rip you apart. Nothing down here is fair for us. But it will all go your way, as things always do. Am I right?"

Persephone glared at the nymph. "No. things do not always go my way."

"You see," Mynthe continued. "While you are down here playing around and living your best life. The rest of us have a job to do. Responsibilities. Things that get one's hands dirty. Do you even know what that's like? I bet you don't."

"You don't know anything about me," Persephone said through gritted teeth.

"I know that the position you hold, you didn't earn. I mean, really, with those perfect nails? There's not even a scar on your body," Mynthe said, reaching for her top and pulling it down to reveal a scar running down her torso between her breasts. "Can you even fight? Or has Daddy been pulling the punches all this time to make you think you deserved the participation trophy? Well, there are no trophies down here, goddess."

"Except Hades." Persephone tilted her head and stared at Mynthe with one brow raised. "He's the trophy down here, right? In fact, without him in your corner, you're nothing."

"Nothing?" Mynthe scoffed. "You have no idea what it's like to be nothing."

Persephone glared, swallowing the lump in her throat. "You're wrong."

Mynthe stood chest to chest with Persephone, a clear challenge. "Prove it."

"And how would I do that?" Persephone asked, eyes narrowed, refusing to back down.

"Let's settle it," Mynthe responded with a sly smile. "If you are worthy of being here, let's duel in the arena. No interruptions, no one to save us, just you and me. Surely, Hades has picked a powerful queen, not a weed maiden no better than a nymph.

"Fine." Persephone raised her chin in defiance. "I win; you back off and leave Hades and me alone."

Mynthe came close to Persephone's face. "And if I win, I will return to his bed."

"If he'll let you be my guest." Persephone shrugged, pretending not to care.

"Words have meaning down here, goddess." A sinister grin made Mynthe's eyes light up. "I hope I get to make you eat yours."

"Two days then," Persephone said, cocking her head with a raised brow, not knowing where her boldness was coming from, but she wouldn't let this nymph get the better of her.

"I will hold you to that goddess…," Mynthe said, then left with a shoulder nudge.

Nyctimus stood next to a shaking Persephone. "We will work hard to train you in time."

"I know how to fight," Persephone said, folding her arms.

"Not like Mynthe, you don't." Nyctimus took a deep

breath. "Argyreoi, the orgy is canceled."

They all groaned and began to protest when he raised a hand for silence.

"We have two days to get Persephone in fighting shape, or Hades will have our heads if she is defeated," he said, watching all of them turn to one another and nod in agreement.

Nyctimus handed her a sword. "We start your training right now."

"Now?" Persephone stared at the heavy sword dumbfounded.

"Yes, now." Nyctimus pulled her aside. "Persephone, you have no idea how bad this is. Mynthe is one of our most dangerous. She has no fear and will fight to the death. Are you prepared to do the same?"

"I may seem weak to you and the others, but I have to prove I can do this."

"I thought you wanted to leave," he said with a smile.

"I do," Persephone nodded, gripping the sword. "Right after I kick her ass."

Persephone tossed and turned as the dream took her to his throne room. She fought against him. Pulling away as he dragged her by the forearm to the golden chariot. The beasts that led the chariot were whinnying and stomping in excitement for the ride.

"No! Let go of me!"

"This isn't a negotiation, Persephone."

"Hades! Stop this!"

"It's time, and you can do nothing about it."

"Take your hands off me...," she squealed as he lifted her.

Before she could speak, she was put down aggressively in the chariot. Hades snapped the reins, and they rode through the darkness. She tried to jump out of the moving vehicle, but he grabbed her around her waist and gripped her tight against his body.

Hades held up his scepter and created the opening in the

surface. She looked up, seeing the blue light glowing over his beautiful face as they rode through the tunnel. The light of the surface was up ahead; she couldn't see past, but they were heading straight for the Meadow.

Entering the light, Persephone woke up. She sat up, trying to shake off the feeling of dread she'd had. What could her dream mean? Why would she ever fight to go home?

A soft knock on the door made her wish she could have a break from all these interruptions. If only for a day. She huffed and threw the blankets off of her. The warm floor felt nice on her bare feet as she walked to the doors touching the cold knob. Opening the door, Persephone looked up into dark eyes.

"Yes?" She asked, blinking to clear her vision from sleep.

"I... Apologize. For yesterday." Judging by his tense demeanor, Hades seemed troubled but spoke softly to her.

"You?" Persephone raised one brow. "The King of the Underworld is apologizing to me? Has your world frozen over?"

Hades chuckled slightly. "So it appears."

Persephone took a deep breath and thought about it for a moment. Perhaps she was being a bit harsh. Her anger was rightly justified. But she didn't need to fight with him every second. After her dream, it would seem that's all they did.

"Hades? Why are you here?"

He smiled at her. "I thought you might be interested in another tour. This time, I'm staying with you and not letting you out of my sight."

"How considerate," she said with slight sarcasm but also felt relief.

The experience with the Keres was not one she would forget, and she would be far more cautious next time. Especially arguing with Hades in such places. She would be alert this time and not make the same mistake.

"Indeed," Hades said, walking past her out of the room. "I'll leave you to prepare. Meet me in the war room, and we'll go."

Hades disappeared and left her to close the door. Once dressed in all leather and her chemise, she found him leaning over the table with the blue light illuminating his face as the souls moved.

Hades looked up and turned off the map, walking over to her. "Are you ready to meet the gods who make this place function?"

"Yes." Persephone nodded up at him.

"Good. Follow me," Hades said, leaving the room with her close behind.

Persephone was nervous but excited as they approached souls who had crossed the river exiting the ferryman's boat. She'd never seen mortal specters and was fascinated by their transparent appearance. The being with the oar wore a dark cloak draped over his face. Underneath were nothing but bones and glowing green eyes. His boat drifted slowly toward the docks, then stopped, and the cloaked figure exited the craft. The single lantern that lit their way highlighted the transparent souls. His long, bony finger extended outstretched toward the direction each soul needed to go. They passed through an opening in the cavern toward a golden light illuminating their path.

"Greetings, Charon, Ferryman of Souls of the river Styx," Hades said to the cloaked figure.

"You honor me with your presence, Great Lord of Darkness," he said with a deep bow to Hades.

"Charon, I'm glad I've caught you on this side of the shore," said Hades, gesturing for Persephone to come forward. "I present to you, your queen, Persephone."

Charon stopped and stood before them as a vision of bones.

"Persephone. Meet Charon," Hades said, motioning for the hunched-over being to join them.

When he looked at her, Charon's empty eye sockets seemed to flex wide in astonishment. The air around him began to shimmer, and his bony visage changed into a tall, dark, olive-skinned, beautiful male with a bright smile and dimples on each cheek. He stood straight, revealing his height just under Hades, with eyes a hazel brown set in dark lashes and thick brows. Charon flexed his powerful-looking muscles and bowed to Persephone with a fully formed hand that reached out to take hers.

"My queen. I had heard rumors of your beauty, but I can see they hardly do you justice," He said with a honeyed bass tone.

Long dark braids appeared and flowed from his head down his back, adorned with gold cuffs and jewels. He was magnificent to behold. Terrifying when he appeared as a skeleton, but to Persephone, he was incredible.

Blushing, Persephone returned his bow, "You're too kind."

"It has been far too long, my Lord," said Charon, turning to clasp arms with Hades.

"Indeed it has," Hades said. "I have fond memories of the last time."

"Ah, good times," Charon nodded as he looked off, smiling at the memory.

Persephone chuckled when she noticed the sign on the side of his boat reading:

Coin,
Ass, or
Cannambrosia Grass.
Nobody Rides For Free!

Charon seemed charming and funny. Quite the contrast to Hades. Amazing to see how they were such good friends.

"I was just about to introduce Persephone to the Asphodel meadows and maybe later the Judges."

"So Hades is taking you on a tour of the Underworld?" asked Charon with a sly grin.

"Yes," Persephone replied, clearing her throat. "So far, it's been... Interesting."

"That it is," Charon said, bowing to her. "When you've

finished, come back and see me again. I've got something that will help you relax as you ease into your stay here."

"I will," Persephone said, amused knowing what he meant. "Thank you, Charon."

Hades shook his head and rolled his eyes. "Unbelievable."

Persephone smiled, looking at Charon. "Are the Asphodel Meadows nice?"

"I couldn't say, my queen," Charon looked at Hades, making her think there was something they knew but weren't telling her. "I'm but a humble ferryman who guides the souls to himself's side for judgment, and then I return to the other side where the souls arrive with payment."

"What of those without payment?" Persephone asked.

"One hundred years of waiting at the shore of the Acheron, watching others go before them," he answered with sorrow.

Persephone frowned at Hades. "That sounds bleak."

Charon shook his head. "The Underworld has no place of joy. Perhaps merriment in Hades' kingdom, but no place of peace for these souls exists now."

"Why not?" Persephone asked, furrowing her brows.

"We should go," Hades said, reaching out his arm and offering for her to take it and follow.

Charon bowed. "I look forward to our next meeting, gracious and beautiful queen."

"You may call me Persephone," she replied, still uncomfortable with these formalities.

"Yes, my queen." Charon stepped into his shiff and returned to his previous form of bones. Bowing to them, he penetrated the waters with the oar, and the boat lurched forward.

"What did he mean there was no place of peace for the souls?" she asked Hades. "Where do they all go?"

"I'm about to show you," he replied, taking her to the stables with Hades' horses and chariot ready.

Beyond the gray fields of the Keres and past the caves of daemons, they came upon an expanse she could not see but knew it must have been great for the fog that rolled continuously at their feet. The forest seemed to never end with sparsely laid dead trees. The sky above was black, with no stars, moon, or ceiling. Only darkness separated the forest from the other realms.

"What is this place?" She asked, observing the solitary space.

"This is the Asphodel Meadows," he said, pointing to beings like the ones she'd seen at the shore. "It's where all the souls who don't deserve punishment go."

Persephone stepped out of the back of the chariot and walked over to a tree, touching its smooth bark. Walking over, she stood within the open area filled with mist. A specter walked by her slowly. Listless and aimless, it wandered by, eyes like milky glass with no purpose to their destination. The being's maiden dress flowed in the phantom breeze as she drifted by, paying Persephone no attention. It was as if she didn't even see the goddess. The spirit kept walking off into the fog until she disappeared in the graying mist.

Persephone felt confused by the specter. "She didn't see me."

"They have no desires when in this form," he replied, pointing to others. "They wouldn't care even if they did see you."

"Are they all like this?"

"Yes."

"What about the little infant beings? Don't they have somewhere happy to go?"

Hades' look signified confusion as if he'd never heard such a thing.

"Why do you think spirits of mortals should be happy in the afterlife?" He asked.

"I don't know." Persephone shrugged. "The idea of this misty place as the end for souls seems too bleak and despairing than what they deserve if they led good lives."

"It never occurred to me to make such a place," he said, watching her as she gazed in disappointment.

"There's no chance of change or peace?" She asked, brows drawn. "It's all just... Endless wandering?"

Hades tilted his head with a raised brow. "It's better than the dungeons."

Persephone shook her head and crossed her arms. "There's nothing better for these souls in the afterlife?"

"I'm in charge of keeping the Titans in Tartarus." Hades walked over and ran his hand through a male who didn't acknowledge his touch. "The souls had nowhere to go, so I gave them a place. Once they drink of the waters of Lethe, they forget their mortal lives and come here to rest. Those who are malicious and cruel in life endure punishment in death as retribution. That's where the Keres, the Erinyes, and the Daemons all find purpose and exist to personify these banes of mortals."

"But what about those who lived great lives filled with hope, peace, and happiness? What of the warriors? The infants? Don't they deserve something better than being torn apart by the Keres on the battlefields?"

Hades smiled down at her concerned face. "Perhaps."

Persephone frowned. "Don't you think noble acts of virtue and valor deserve a better reward in the afterlife?"

"I hadn't thought to separate them all in that way."

"You have three judges, don't you?"

"Yes."

"Make them do it," she said, feeling hopeful. "Then you only have to show up for the truly heinous, and the rest can go peacefully to their fated ends."

"And what would we call this paradise for mortal souls?" He asked with amusement in his tone.

Persephone shrugged. "I don't know, but we can think of something."

"We?" Hades chuckled.

"Um... You know what I mean." Persephone looked around, distracted.

Hades thought for a moment, then nodded. "We would have to discuss this with the judges and get them to agree to a third alternative for the souls."

"Would you do that?" Persephone asked with a bright smile.

His expression softened at her delight. "I would if it would please you."

Would he create such a place for them? Her mom had built a safe place for her to grow, but this was different. It was a place where she could help the good souls who deserved a better life after their deaths. She thought of the blackness she experienced before Gaia arrived. It was so empty, hollow, and terrifying with the absence of light, sound, or smell. Seeing Gaia was a relief, and the garden she built gave Persephone an idea.

"What if we build a field where souls could live and meet their loved ones again?" She asked, tapping her lip. "They could have tea and small cottages, and maybe those who died in battle could have an endless feast of their desires."

"We'd have to get to the warriors before the Keres did," he said, interrupting her vision.

"Then we'll build a team to do that." Persephone smirked. "Those on the battlefield wouldn't have a chance to gain coins, so this could be a way around the issue Charon presented."

Hades smiled and pulled her close to him. Looking down into her eyes, she felt his desire for her. Wishing they could continue, she now knew better and placed a loving hand on his cheek, then stepped back. She wouldn't be caught off guard again, lost in his embrace. Not down here. It was too risky, and she didn't know what would happen.

Her thoughts were interrupted when she heard a rumble of what must have been massive beasts approaching along with bells.

CHAPTER 10
JUDGEMENT

In the distance, a mooing sound with bells rang off to the left of them where a middle-aged big-bellied being appeared approaching with a herd of cows.

"My lord? What brings you to the Asphodel Meadows?"

"Menoites, the Daemon Cowherd of my black prized cattle," Hades said with a pat on the pleasant but homely being. "Meet the Goddess Persephone, my queen."

"It is a great honor to have you here, my queen." The cowherd bowed to Persephone and absently petted the heifer next to him that chewed happily on some grass.

The sable black herd behind him grew as a group, appearing larger and larger in number as they crept closer and began to graze around them.

"These cattle are so large," Persephone said wide-eyed, looking up at the beasts. "How do you manage them?"

Menoites smiled. "They are quite tame and very gentle. It's not too difficult."

"There are a lot of beings that need feeding, and there is no time to go to the surface, so I let them graze here," said Hades, petting a heifer who nudged him gently. "Menoites treats them well, and when it's time, we put them down gently."

"Yes. There's no need for fear or aggressive means to cull the herd." Menoites pet the head of another heifer that mooed before returning to the grass.

"I'm glad you care so well for them," Persephone replied, smiling at Hades.

Hades stepped closer to Persephone and held her hand. His heart began to pound, seeing her pleased with his care for the animals in his realm. It had disturbed him to see the gratuity of Olympus and the constant slaughter of animals with no concern for their lives. He wanted his realm to be different in whatever way he could. Hades wondered if she would see this as a positive or a sign of weakness.

"Come," Hades said, bowing to Menoites and then turning to Persephone. "There's much more to show you."

"It was nice to meet you, Menoites," Persephone said with a bright smile.

"The pleasure is mine, my queen." Menoites bowed, then led the herd away into the foggy distance.

"Hades?" Persephone turned to look up into his eyes. "Can you build a more gentle place for little ones? Maybe a place for families to reunite? Oh! What about a place for heroes who sacrificed everything for the gods to stay? There should be a special place for them."

It was a novel idea. Hades knew he could build it if she stayed. The idea had enough merit to make it regardless. He enjoyed the way she solved problems. He respected her intelligence, and seeing her able to world-build was impressive.

"Perhaps." Hades turned and took both hands in his. "What do you have in mind?"

Persephone pursed her lips and looked away in thought. Her brows furrowed as she pondered. He smiled and waited for her to finish, then she looked back at him.

"What if there was a wonderful place with slightly

rolling hills and acres of wildflowers and trees? Maybe it could have waterfalls and mountains in the distance resembling...."

"Resembling your home with Demeter?"

Her breath hitched. She stuttered. "Well... Maybe something that could be similar. My home is wonderful."

His jaw clenched at the thought of her calling that place her home, but he relaxed so as not to ruin the moment.

"And what would you call this place of paradise for noble souls and the young?"

"I'm not sure," Persephone said, pondering with her hand on her chin. "But it needs to be some sort of an elysium paradise for the souls who earned it."

"You've mentioned elysium and a field. Why not combine them?"

Persephone's eyes widened, and she smiled from ear to ear, making his heart leap at her excitement.

"Hades! You've done it. What a great idea. We'll call it the Elysian Fields! A place of ending and new beginnings."

"Your ideas are inspiring," he agreed. "But we would have to confer with the judges to ensure it can be done.

There were many more dark spirits than benevolent, so it would be a smaller plane, to be sure, he thought to himself.

"Shall we go find out if the judges will agree?" Persephone's eyes twinkled. "I hope so," she said, skipping as they returned to the chariot.

They entered the large chamber that held the banner above the door that read The Judges of the Dead and made their request to the three beings sitting on a dais.

"It can't be done," said a surly frowning elder being wearing a dark cloak like the other two. "Lord Hades, Who have you brought before us?"

Hades turned slightly to her. "Persephone, meet my three judges, Minos, Aikos, and Rhadamanthys."

"It's nice to meet you all," Persephone said with a slight bow. "But are you sure?"

"Of course, we are sure," Minos said, narrowing his eyes

at her.

"Why can't it be done?" Hades asked, noticing Persephone's disappointment beside him.

"The second judge, Aiakos, leaned forward. "We already have our hands filled with souls to deliver judgment."

Minos shook his head. "You cannot ask us to take on more."

Hades stepped forward. "I'm not asking you to take on more. I'm asking that you send the ones you already judge to another plane of my choosing."

"Incorrect." Judge Minos barked.

Aiakos nodded. "We will now have to decipher the heroes and the souls who lived good lives. I think not."

"What will you add next, Lord Hades? A new plane for another life?" The third judge called, Rhadamanthys said with a husky laugh, leading the others to join in his short chuckle.

"Do you mean a soul could live again?" Persephone asked, stepping up next to Hades.

Minos nodded. "If they can achieve greatness in three lifetimes, Hades and we three can judge them no more."

Hades narrowed his eyes at them. "You never told me they could reincarnate."

"You never asked," replied Aiakos.

"I wonder, honorable judges of the Underworld," Persephone said, oozing charm.

"She speaks with respect." Minos raised his brows and sat up chin high.

Rhadamanthys nodded. "A nice change around here."

"Our Lord could learn from her example." Aiakos narrowed his eyes back at Hades, leaning forward slightly.

Hades clenched his hands into fists, trying to breathe through his irritation.

"Please," Persephone laid a hand on his shoulder, raising her brows to signal calm, then turned to the judges. "Your honors, I wonder if we could also do something as you said, where these souls would receive judgment for a chance at a final life. And if they reach said three honorable lives, then perhaps an island that we could bless for these virtuous heroes to live as immortals, as a reward for their souls who've achieved ultimate elysium, would be possible."

"A blessed island of immortals..." the first judge scoffed.

"Have you ever heard of anything so ridiculous?" The second judge queried.

Rhadamanthys shook his head. "Hades, we insist you let this strange notion go and let us continue our work."

Persephone cut Hades off, stepping forward. "I would ask that you think about it and reserve judgment until you've had a chance to weigh all your options."

The first judge went to speak but sat with his mouth gaping open, then paused to think. He turned to the others, who all nodded.

"We agree to discuss this without guaranteeing it will go in your favor," said Minos.

Persephone bowed. "That's all we ask."

"If that is all, Lord Hades, may we finally return to our purpose?" asked Aiakos.

"You may," said Hades with a curt nod. "I will return in two days for your answer."

"You will have it in three," Minos said, sitting back as though his word was final.

Hades turned without argument and led Persephone past the two judges, leaving Aiakos, who pulled out his keys and gestured for them to follow. On their way, Persephone could see a gentle, smiling female with long, curly dark hair and glowing olive skin ushering the souls to drink from her pool, where their chalice appeared. Some drank a sip, others drank deep from their cups, then after placing them on the edge of the pool, the chalice vanished, and the spirit turned to walk through one of two doors.

"Where are they going?"

"Their judgment is beginning. They drink from the pools of Mnemosyne to go through their life memories. Then, when the judges finish assessing them, the benevolent souls drink from the pool of Lethe to forget, as I explained earlier."

"I thought you said those in the dungeons had to relive their memories."

"That's true. Those souls don't get to drink from Lethe." Hades pointed to those who walked to the door on the left.

Following his finger, she watched silently as the specters, still in their mortal form, went to the door he spoke of.

Behind them, Aiakos cleared his throat and narrowed his eyes at them.

"This way to leave, my Lord."

"Come, I want to introduce you to a crucial member of my realm." Hades held his hand to her and walked with Persephone toward the large black doors.

They opened the gates to a cavern where she saw the most incredible sight. A giant three-headed dog barked, its serpent tail wagging and tongues sticking out in excitement. The heads wore a mane of snakes that covered the neck. Its feet had claws like a lion's and teeth that were sharp and terrifying. Or at least it would be if he wasn't so adorable. Dripping with drool, it trotted to greet his master.

"What is this magnificent creature?" Persephone asked with her mouth open in awe.

"Cerberus," Hades said, petting each head. "He guards the doors here and the other doors you see to keep any spirits who would try to escape from leaving. None have ever gotten past him."

The beast brought each head down to sniff Persephone. She giggled at their breath, snorting and sniffing, surrounding her in a wind torrent. One felt comfortable licking her tiny hand, and she laughed at the drool that now coated it.

"Who's a good boy, huh?" She reached up, and another head let her pet its nose.

"It appears Cerberus likes you," said Hades with a sly grin.

"What an amazing creature." She patted each head that greeted her and smiled one by one. "What do you like to eat, huh?"

"Why?" He asked with a chuckle. "Are you planning on charming my dog too?"

"I might," Persephone said with a wink. "Don't worry, Cerberus. I'll find something to bring back to you."

Her delight was heartwarming and complex at the same time. Everyone here seemed to instantly take to liking Persephone. If only she could see that.

Persephone turned back to Hades. "Do you think the judges will agree to create a new plane?

"If the rules allow it, they will probably say yes."

"They don't seem very amenable," she said, rubbing Cerberus' belly.

Hades eyed the beast, shaking his head at the display.

"They're always like that," he said, trying not to laugh. "Though it appears they liked you enough to consider it."

"So I should ignore their initial refusal?" she asked, picking up a large branch and throwing it.

Cerberus bolted after it and brought it back for her to throw again. She obliged and made the beast happy as it hopped around. Hades shook his head at the most feared monster of his realm, prancing around and playing with her.

Hades folded his arms over his chest, looking away to hide his smile. "Generally, I always ignore the first no I get."

"That's an understatement," she said, rolling her eyes.

He narrowed his at Persephone. "Alright. That's enough fun for all of you. We have more to see."

Persephone nodded and gave each head a pet one last time.

"I'll come back and play later, okay?" She said, cupping her hand privately.

Of course, he could hear her. Cerberus was so happy he bound around them in a circle and licked her hand, making her giggle. He hadn't seen the beast do anything like that since it

was a pup. But if it made her laugh, he wouldn't say anything.

They left Cerberus, who barked after them in delight, its sound booming in the cavern he guarded, making the ground shake.

"I do have one thing I've been meaning to talk to you about," said Persephone, wiping her hand on her pants.

"What's that?" He asked, gesturing for them to go to the chariot.

"Do you remember Nyctimus?"

"Yes."

She nodded. "I saw him fighting in the pits the other day and wondered if you would consider setting him free."

Hades raised a brow. "Why would I do that?"

"He saved my life," she said, hands on her hips.

Hades clenched his jaw. "We both know that's not true."

Persephone stopped closing her eyes as if remembering. Her shoulders slumped, and she turned away, wrapping her arms around her waist.

"When did you find out?"

"The Moirai showed me," he said, hating that he couldn't stop it.

"I would appreciate it if you kept it between us."

"I won't tell anyone," Hades said, wanting to touch her, but now wasn't the time. "It's Hecate I'd worry about. She knows too."

Persephone groaned. "Of course she does. Can we not talk about it?"

Hades could see she was uncomfortable when her arms went around her waist. He didn't think he would be able to either. He couldn't even talk about his experience inside Cronos. The horror of it all was too painful to relive.

"You don't have to talk about it," he said, offering to let it go.

Persephone began to shake. She sniffed and wiped her nose. When she looked up at him with tears in her eyes, his chest collapsed. Hollow and aching to take away her pain. All he could do was open his arms. She collided with him with her arms crossed between them and sobbed. Hades held her for a long time, absently placing a hand on her hair to soothe her. A kiss on her head made her look at him. The tears stained her face, compelling him to reach up and wipe one cheek with his thumb. Her make-up was unchanged. Not even a smear when he wiped away her tears. *Strange*, he thought to himself, thinking something was off with her.

Whatever it was, it didn't matter right now. She needed comfort. He wanted to give her all the comfort she could ever need. Perhaps this little project of elysium would be what she needed to adjust to being here and overcome her worries about that dark day. He could do nothing to make her feel better except hold her. She relaxed her arms and slowly inched them until they were around him.

Hades didn't know how long they stood there as she cried. Nothing would move him so long as she held on. Eventually, she released her grip and stepped back. He let her go and let her clear her face of tears with both hands.

"Apologies," she said with a sniff.

"You have nothing to apologize for," Hades said, holding her face. "It's me who should apologize for failing to protect you. I wanted to give you your space and, in doing so, left you vulnerable. I can't make that same mistake again. I'd give anything to change what happened that day."

"So would I." Persephone backed away from him and turned to leave.

"Persephone," he said with a plea in his tone.

She smiled faintly, tears welling in her eyes, "I know you want to show me more, but could we go back? I need a moment before we go any further."

"Of course."

***

Persephone sulked into Hecate's apothecary, closing the

door slowly behind her as she entered. The Titaness turned from her potions, eyes wide from the intrusion.

"Darkling, you look a mess. What's wrong?" Hecate asked, setting down her vial.

"I need to control my powers," Persephone said, wiping her nose. "And you're going to help me."

"Why are you crying," Hecate asked concerned."

"It's nothing." Persephone straightened her shoulders and wiped her face. "Are you willing to help me or not?"

"Oh, this should be fun," Hecate said with a wicked grin. "Do you mind if I bring in a few things to train you?"

Persephone nodded. "Whatever you feel is necessary, I'll do it."

Hecate smile spread over her face. "I hope you mean that."

The Titaness snapped her fingers, sending them to an empty cavern with two cushions facing one another.

Hecate sat, followed by Persephone. She waited in silence until the Titaness opened her arms, summoning a light that brought forth a familiar orb—the Cronos stone. Persephone shifted backward, watching with dread building in her stomach. The spherical stone floated between them and hovered at her chest.

"You know what you have to do, Persephone," Hecate said with her face aglow from the orb's blue light.

"I'm afraid," Persephone replied.

"Touch the orb," Hecate said with one brow raised. "What we see will be between us."

Nodding, Persephone reached out her shaking hand. As before, the orb's light changed, and the room grew into a bounty of vegetation and life. It was so intoxicatingly beautiful for a moment that Persephone forgot how lovely the world above could be. Her joy turned to fear as the shadows crept toward them, and the blooming life surrounding them began to decay. She hadn't noticed it before, but the stone played out the vision she shared with Hades. The leaves changed colors.

They twirled and tumbled through the air above, then drifted slowly to the ground. The cold soon followed as before.

Persephone held the stone with both hands now, close to her chest. The vision was playing out before her, more vivid and precise than the dreams had ever been. The darkness that spread over the white landscape covered all. The animals didn't die. They adapted. Many slept. The mortals gathered together in warm homes and celebrated.

The ground began to shake. Hecate was no longer in sight. Instead, she stared at herself. This other version was the one Persephone kept seeing in the mirror when her powers were most volatile. Hair like blood, skin pale with dark-lined eyes, and robes of black lace over a warrior's leathers. Her dark, tyrian corset accentuated her figure, and the jagged jeweled hair pins she wore pulled half of her hair back.

"You've finally found me," the darkness whispered with a sinister smile.

"How is this possible?" Persephone asked, looking around.

"I needed a strong enough power source to speak with you," the other said. "Finally, it's just you and me."

"Who are you?" Persephone asked, shaking.

"He asked me the same thing. I am you."

Persephone shook her head. "That's not possible."

The other Persephone's face expressed irritation for a moment, then she calmed.

"Where's Hecate?" Asked Persephone, looking around for the Titaness.

"Hecate's right where you left her," the other replied with a tilt of her head. "We are in your mind. The stone has frozen the outside space. This moment gives us the perfect chance to talk as you hold the stone of time and power."

"Tell me whatever you need to tell me, then let me go back to finish what I was doing."

"What I have to say has complete relevance to what you were doing," she said with a sinister smile.

"How?" Persephone asked the darkness.

"You're curious about how to use your powers," she said, opening her arms. "Instead of always pushing me down, let me out."

"What will happen if I do that?" Persephone asked, not sure if she could trust her other self.

"We can both be free," The other said in a sultry voice. "If you stop pushing me away, we can become more powerful."

"Is it you that takes control of me?"

She nodded. "When necessary."

"Why?"

The other tilted her head. "It is in my interest to keep you alive when you need me."

"I don't need your help," Persephone argued.

"Until you learn to use our powers, and until you stop resisting me, you will continue to lose consciousness."

"How can I trust you? I don't even know who you are."

"I already told you. I am you."

Persephone was shaking. "No. No, you're not."

"Yes." The other gave half a smile. "I am what you will become."

"I don't want to be like you. I've seen what you leave behind."

The other chuckled. "A thank you would be in order," the other said with a raised brow. "I saved your life. We both know what happens when you don't make use of me. Hera would never have won if you'd just let me out."

Persephone glared. "You don't know that."

"I know that you live your life through fear," she said, narrowing her eyes. "All you do is whine and complain about life instead of living it."

"That's not true!" Persephone yelled, feeling her pulse quicken.

The other scoffed. "Maybe Hera was right. You're not worthy."

Persephone shook her head, looking away. "Stop it," she

said with a pained whisper.

"You'll never be strong enough without me," the other rebuked.

"I said stop," said Persephone with a little more courage.

"You are nothing without me," the other said, baring her teeth with a sneer.

"Shut up!" Persephone screamed and stood.

Her darker self was gone when Persephone opened her eyes, and she stood shouting at Hecate. The Titaness sat in her place with worry across her face. The stone rolled to the floor. Picking it up, Hecate brushed it off, then placed it up her billowing sheer sleeve, tucked away safely.

"Persephone, what did you see?" The Titaness demanded as she came to. "Open your mind to me."

The scene played out for Hecate to interpret. She clicked her tongue, shaking her head when Hecate finished reading Persephone's thoughts.

"What did you see?" Persephone asked, knowing her darkness was on full display to the Titan.

"I think this situation is far more complicated than I previously supposed," Hecate said, hands tapping together. "I'll have to consult my scrolls, but for now, we will rest. Meet me back in my lab for more training when I summon you."

"Hecate, wait!"

But the Titaness was already gone.

Persephone was in shock, witnessing her darker self speaking to her as if she was another being. The reality was Persephone knew that was who she was deep inside. It was surreal to have such an out-of-body experience. Though she wanted to distrust, Persephone couldn't help but feel there was some truth to what she said. Fighting her powers wasn't helping and was resulting in her inability to stay conscious and control the other self that wouldn't have the same morality, she suspected.

She knew the only solution was to train harder and practice using her powers. Perhaps she could ask to train with Tyche, Nemesis, and the other daemons to prove she could control her powers. Determined to meet this challenge, Persephone decided to begin by fighting in the pits, working her way up. *If they wanted a warrior*, she thought to herself, *they would get one.* Even if she had to push beyond her limits, she would continue to make herself stronger in every way. *Hera would never win against me again*, she thought to herself.

Persephone soon found Nyctimus and gathered the others.

"I need all of your help," she said to the group.

"Name it, and we will oblige, my Lady," Nyctimus said as the others agreed, nodding.

"I want all of you to fight me without holding back."

They all glanced at one another, mumbling and shaking their heads.

Nyctimus cleared his throat. "My Lady, I know you are nervous about fighting Mynthe, but surely..."

"This isn't about Mynthe," she said, seeing their reservation. "It's more than that."

Nyctimus looked to the others and shook his head. "If we hurt you, Hades will..."

Persephone held up a hand to silence his objections. "Hades will do nothing. I will speak to him."

"What if we anger him anyway?" Nymctimus asked, stepping closer. "Things get really bloody in the pits, and you could lose more than your dignity."

Persephone placed her hands on her hips, jutting out her chin. "Nothing could be worse than fighting Hera and being ripped in two, left for dead."

They all went silent, eyes wide at her revelation.

"Did you just say dead?" Nyctimus asked quietly, brows drawn.

"Nyctimus. Please." She took a deep breath. "I can't be vulnerable like that ever again."

He pursed his lips, thinking. The rest spoke to each other, whispering their wonder at what she said. Their amazement that a goddess had died and returned was a shock to all of them. Finally, he nodded in agreement.

"Alright, everyone," he called out to them. "Our queen wants to learn to fight like a daemon with no holds barred. That means no mercy and no retreat."

The smiles that crossed their faces gave her a sense of unease, but she needed them to go hard, or she feared she wouldn't be able to protect herself from the things out there that were far worse than a few daemons.

The blonde female stepped toward her and touched her shoulder gently. "We won't let you down."

Persephone smiled, feeling her shame lessen. "Thank you. I ask you all to keep my reasons to just us."

The black-haired daemon clapped her on the back. "We've got your back. But we're still going to kick your ass."

That seemed to break the tension in the room as everyone laughed. For the first time since Olympus, Persephone felt part of a team again. Her sorrow and fears dissolve, replaced with determination.

"Apologies, everyone, but I don't know all your names," Persephone said, looking to Nyctimus, who smiled.

Nyctimus pointed to each one.

"Here with the blonde hair, we have Castor. She is our most beautiful but fierce in battle. You would do well to learn from her instruction."

"Greetings, Castor," Persephone said with a bow.

"You do me great honor to teach you, my queen," Castor said, bringing Persephone in for a suffocating hug.

"Her brother, Pollux, is our best weapons master," Nyctimus said, smiling.

"Greetings, Pollux," Persephone said, repeating her bow.

"My queen is too gracious," he said, bowing back.

"Next, we have Fenghuang, or you can call him Phoenix," Nyctimus said, pointing to the gorgeous, monolid male with straight black hair that dusted his eyes.

"Fenghuang," Persephone smiled and bowed. "Thank

you for training me."

"Pheonix is our best crafter of fighting styles that devastated opponents using abilities that use their force against themselves."

"And a few power moves," Pheonix said with a chuckle, high-fiving the others. "I've got good knee strikes to teach you, my queen."

Nyctimus clapped him on his shoulder. "Pheonix is your best source for building fighting styles that best suit your natural abilities and whatever weapons you like to use."

Persephone pulled her sickle. "I like to use this, but I recently found that it changes depending on which stone you press."

She handed it to the daemon, who observed its craft.

Pheonix's eyes widened. "This is the most incredibly built weapon I've ever seen. Where did you get it?" He asked, still looking it over.

"It was a gift from my mom," she said, remembering the tournament that Demeter had brought the crescent blade to give her after she'd won her gauntlets. Persephone missed those gauntlets. Perhaps she could ask Hecate to summon them to her.

Nyctimus didn't touch the final daemon with fangs and a bald head.

"Would you like to introduce yourself?" He asked the female.

"My queen," she said with a bow. "I am from the other shores of the sea. My name is Wadjet. My skills are strength, agility, and the ability to strike quickly against my opponents."

"You're from another land of the sea that surrounds us?" Persephone asked, curious about this lithe female.

"It is not your world, though someday, you may visit mine if you are inclined. There, I am an oracle and goddess and the eye of Horus. Here, I am the two snakes surrounding the rod of healing."

"I'd love to visit this place you speak of one day, Wadjet,"

Persephone said to the serpent goddess. "Wait, Nyctimus. So these are not all beings from our realm?" Persephone asked, taking him aside.

Nyctimus smiled. "No, my queen, though they are the original beings of many worlds, here, I call them Argyreoi, regardless. They are all beings that work in this realm. Our Lord has traveled to many lands, offering refuge to many pursuing another life for a time. As they are immortal, there are so many lifetimes to live. They travel whenever possible."

"I see," she said, marveling at the diverse friendships she would discover. "Thank you all. I will try to make you proud as I learn everything I can from you."

CHAPTER 11
TARTARUS

Day after day, Hades watched Persephone train with the daemons. He wondered what she was trying to prove. She already had the training she needed to be queen. He'd seen to that. Yet there she was, learning new moves and getting her ass kicked.

"You know, sooner or later, you'll have to show her Tartarus," Hecate said, drinking his wine.

"I know," Hades said, turning to face Hecate. "She's not ready yet."

Hecate rolled her eyes. "What, pray tell, would make her ready? Are you sure it's not you who isn't ready?"

"Like she was with the Keres?"

Hecate pursed her lips and folded her arms. "Yes."

"No," Hades growled, narrowing his eyes at Hecate. "She is not ready."

"My dark one," Hecate said with a sigh. "If you won't take her, then who will? How will she learn? And what of her experience with Hera? You wouldn't deny her the chance to confront her attacker. Look at her down there. She's barely keeping it together."

Hades turned to see Persephone bloodied and sweating as she fought with a wild abandon he'd never seen.

"She is spiraling," Hecate pressed. "Trying to understand what happened to her. She'll never recover if she can't face her fear."

"You mean, face Hera?" He asked, feeling uneasy about the idea.

"If you're there, what can go wrong?"

"No!" He exclaimed, then calmed. "I won't do it."

Hecate placed her hands on her hips. "Fine. Let her die again for all I care. You can give those excuses to her mother the next time you see Demeter."

Disappearing in her usual purple smoke, the air she left held a bitter taste that permeated his mouth. He hated that she was right. Persephone would have to see it eventually. They didn't have much time left, with the moon impending and Demeter's arrival foretold. Pinching the bridge of his nose, he tried to think of any excuse not to do this. But seeing Persephone fight so hard for days now made him realize that what she was fighting was herself.

He had to help her. Hades knew that feeling all too well. While he was allowed to do something about his imprisonment, his war gave him the chance Persephone deserved. He may not like it, but Hades knew he needed to take Persephone down there and let her decide whether his realm was worth ruling.

There was no sky, only an endless void of clouds quaked with electrical storms, creating an atmosphere tainted with red as flames spewed from the cracks below them. They stood at the opening before two vast columns when the ground began to rumble with heavy footsteps. Awaiting the Hecatoncheires, they watched as the hundred-handed-fifty-headed offspring of Ouranos and Gaia emerged past the gates of Tartarus. Persephone looked to Hades and then back up. He touched her arm and led her forward to meet the enormous being.

"My lord, Hades," one head said as the others moved individually.

"What brings you to the gates with such lovely company?" another asked with a gruff voice.

"This is the goddess Persephone," Hades replied, ushering her forward. "She's your new queen. I thought a tour of the place would be necessary."

"A tour?" a different head asked. "Here?" asked another.

"Of course," one head nudged the one who questioned them. "My queen, ignore his rudeness. Who are we to question the gods?"

Ignoring them, Hades gestured for her to say hello. Her eyes were wide, not with fear, but wonder.

"Persephone, meet Briareus, the Hecatoncheires who helped us defeat the Titans," he said, inclining his head to greet them.

"Hello, Briareus." She smiled up and extended a hand. "Lovely to meet you."

The heads seemed surprised and just blinked at her.

Eventually, they all agreed and let down one hand to grasp hers gently and then let her go.

"Are you the only one of your kind, or are there more of you?" she asked innocently.

"We have two brothers, Cottus and Gyges," the new head replied. "They guard the most destructive of Titans on the farthest point in Tartarus."

"That's where we're heading," Hades said, turning to Persephone. "Without their help, we were outmatched. Their abilities made it possible to capture Cronos and his followers."

"I see," said Persephone. "So not all creatures here are malevolent?"

"We frighten those who see us," one said with a frown as another nodded.

"So we stay here where we have a purpose," another added.

"If you should ever need anything, tiny goddess," one far

above the rest said to her. "We are here to help."

"Thank you," Persephone replied, smiling up at them. "You are far too kind. I can see in all of your eyes that you are good-hearted."

Each eye welled with tears. "Lord Hades," they said with a sniff, "You and your queen are always welcome to proceed."

"It's time to go," Hades said, wary of their emotions.

"Thank you, noble and kind beings," she said, bowing to them. "I am grateful for your kindness."

One sniffed with a tear. "The goddess speaks of our kindness..."

"No one has ever done that," another head cleared his throat.

"She is too sweet to crush," one said, wiping his nose with the left giant hand.

"We must protect her at all costs!" another wept.

"She's too adorable!!" Said one more, who teared up at her generous nature.

"Lord Hades," another said, wiping snot away. "If anyone threatens our queen, we will raise the Underworld to her aid."

"She is too precious to allow further!" Said another.

"Stop it!" one cried out. "If Lord Hades allows it, so too, we must."

"But she's so cute!" One winced and squeaked his objection.

"My lords!" Persephone called up to them. "I am but your humble servant."

"She is humble?" One gasped and teared up.

"Hades, How could you!?" Another reprimanded.

"This flower is too lovely to be sullied by our shores," another protested.

"How could you!?" Another cried. "What a monster, bringing her here."

"Have you no decency?" Said a motherly head.

"Does she mean nothing to you!?" One asked before seeing his rage build.

Hades roared and grew to a massive height, forcing the giant back, cringing.

"You dare question my motives!?" Hades thundered in his rage.

The idea that he wouldn't care for her safety peaked his fury. Persephone placed a calming hand on his arm, and he turned to see her incline her head, pleading for patience with her eyes.

"Apologies," they echoed, trying to quell his anger.

"Dear Briareus," Persephone said gently. "I need your help."

The being bowed with all of its heads. "Anything for the most beautiful and gentle of creatures…"

"I want to be worthy of you and prove my status as your queen and your friend." Persephone bowed. "Would you do me the honor of accepting?"

"She is a gem!" One head exclaimed.

"How can we refuse?" Said the one directly to its right.

"We are your servants," one on the left said. "Dear goddess. Ask, and it will be yours at no cost."

The one on the right agreed. "We eagerly place our hands at your feet."

Persephone waved her hands. "No! No, my friends. I would not ask that of you."

"We freely give it!" said the center head.

"But I won't ever ask this of you," she said with a deep bow. "I merely ask you to teach me how to fight a Titan one day."

"This gorgeous goddess of perfect heart and soul wants to know how to fight such a monstrous being?" One asked to the far left.

"She should never have to do so!" cried out, one who was closest to her.

"Damn it! If she desires our assistance, we will freely give it!" another yelled from the right.

"Never relent!" One screamed. "Never surrender!"

"True, our queen, you must never relent." They all nodded in agreement.

"We must ensure she never has to!" They all muttered and fought.

In the end, they all agreed.

Hades grabbed her arm. "Are you really asking a Heckatonceries how to fight?"

"Yes," her serious tone spoke volumes. "Anything that will give me a chance to win is on the table," she said, chin up and shoulders back. "My mom was willing to fight alongside you against the Titans. I should have the skills to do the same."

Hades opened his mouth to object but then closed it and took a deep breath. "We have to go. Follow me."

"Hades!" The last head cried out. "Know that we will protect her regardless of any order, for she is too precious!"

"I trust you to keep your word, Briareus," Hades said with a short nod. "As always."

He knew they meant it, and it relieved him to know he had their support. Hades was glad she would garner favor even among the most terrifying monsters here. He guided her past them and into the gates that led to the depths of Tartarus.

The heat from the primordials that breathed as the mountains, the ground, and even the air was intense. Here, the realm was alive and flexing with destructive power. Hades had hoped never to see it re-released. He remembered back to the war as he led her into the world bursting into flames, spewing rock and new earth. The seas tumbled erratically, forming violent waves crashing against the rocky shores. This chaos is what he controlled so that he spared the world above from being torn apart by the unyielding power these beings were unable to contain.

"How many Titans are imprisoned here?" She asked, leaning over the rails of the chariot.

"It fluctuates. Some are male and female, while many still would be considered neither male nor female. They are primordial elementals, what you would call an essence with no bodily form." He pointed out to the beings before them. "'You and I may be powerful, but they are far more so. It takes all of us, along with Zeus' allies, to capture them. Tartarus is a primordial being. A male created around the same time as Gaia and even produced offspring with her."

"Really?" Persephone asked, seeming to have lost all anger in exchange for fascination. "I thought her only lover was Ouranos."

"Ouranos was her first, but not her last," Hades explained as they rode to the warm core of the place.

He cleared his throat, thinking about the monsters he possessed with ambiguous origins. Pressing on, they continued to the caverns where those judged for their crimes received their dues. Cries rang out, echoing against the walls the further they descended. The air was more relaxed in these caves. The dank moisture filled the air with mist that loomed eerily.

"Where are we?" asked Persephone with a shiver.

"This is where souls come to be punished," he replied.

"What sort of punishment?" she asked, eye darting around.

"Each one gets their unique punishment befitting their crime," he answered, continuing forward. "An eternity of reliving the worst of their crimes. My judges send them here where the Erinyes carry out their torment."

"What exactly are the Erinyes?" asked Persephone.

"They oversee the dungeons of my realm, questing for the torture of malevolent souls from the mortal realm. The three beings of fury were born for vengeance and retribution for the castrated blood of the sky, Ouranos. They punish oath breakers, criminals, and those who pervert the natural order."

"Let me guess," she said sarcastically. "You determine what the natural order is."

"Yes," he replied. "Along with Zeus and the other original gods. It's something we all take very seriously."

She seemed to think about that for a moment. One of the

Erinyes floated by, revealing to her what they looked like. Their ugly feminine winged bodies crawled with serpents, dressed in knee-high boots, with their black skirts drifting around them. Persephone jumped back behind Hades before they disappeared into the dense fog. He smiled to himself, feeling her cling to him before she quickly let him go and backed away.

"Was that one of them?" she asked.

"Yes. Now come," he said, continuing forward. "There's more to see."

They rode into the fog until it cleared, showing her the full horror and extent of the punishments enacted in this dungeon of the damned. Souls beaten mercilessly, tied to the jagged rock face, were torn from flesh to bone. Others carried impossibly large objects only to do the same act repeatedly with no end to the hard labor. All different manner of creatures experienced abuse in one way or another in the endless rows of infernal torture. He explained each of them to her as they passed the tortured souls. Hades' daemons meted out flayed bodies, burnt corpses, and seemingly endless carnage. Her usual saltiness was dissolving as she watched.

"The long tongue of the Epioles chokes its victims as it ensnared them in a coma, reliving their worst memories and crimes is one of the beings," he explained on their journey. He exited the chariot and walked her to one of the punisher's victims.

"Do not feel for these unfortunate souls. They are here by their own making," he said, leading her to one that lay helpless in the clutches of the Epioles that sat upon the male's chest. "Touch the spine of the Epioles, and you'll see what I mean."

She reached out with a shaking hand, closed her eyes as she connected to its glowing spine, and saw what was happening in their mind. Persephone quickly pulled her hand back, covering her mouth before reaching for a stone to lean against. She vomited. Her hands shook violently as her tear-filled eyes looked to him for answers.

"He…" she stammered. "Those poor little children… how could anyone violate children like that?" she cried. "Oh Gaia, their screams when he…."

Hades reached over and offered his hand to help her up. He needed her to see this. She had to know why this place existed and what their duty was. It was more than he could explain to her with words.

"There are much worse beings in here than that one," he said, lifting her to her feet.

"It was like I was there." She stood staring into her shaking hands.

"Do you wish to continue?"

She wiped her face and nodded. He gestured for her to walk beside him. She passed the loathsome creature, leaving the Epioles to its work. Persephone looked back once more before stepping into that chariot, this time taking the hand Hades offered, thankfully too distracted to be angry with him anymore. By the time they reached the final entrance, Persephone had steeled herself, hands squeezing so tight her knuckles were white as he reached out his hand, opening the seal with his powers. The doors groaned loudly as the stone grated against the ground. The rumbling stopped once the doors settled open against the wall.

The space was quiet. Each step they took created an echo in the hallway that disappeared into the darkness. Torches lit, floating as though hung on walls that weren't there. The walls were open to the expansive space that seemed endless. As they approached, the light illuminated the glasslike surface beneath them, reflecting each flame burst lit with each step forward. They walked through an archway with a rippling black mist-like substance between two massive columns. Much like the ones at the first entrance. The main cavern had several different pathways. They stopped in front of one of the entrances.

Persephone looked up at him, waiting for him to explain, but he wasn't sure how to begin.

"Where do these paths lead to?" she asked.

"Each one leads to the most powerful beings in creation," he replied, trying to hide his inherent disdain for his father. "Including Cronos."

"Cronos is here?" she asked, astonished.

"Yes," he said in almost a whisper.

"Is this where you put Hera?"

He nodded, "It is."

"I want to speak to her," she said, squaring her shoulders.

"I don't think that's a good idea," he replied.

Persephone shrugged, "Since when has that ever stopped me?"

Hades paused for a moment and nodded toward the path on the right, closest to her. "As you wish."

***

"What if she gets into my head?" Persephone asked, feeling the fear creep up her spine.

"I'm here with you," Hades assured. "Hera can't hurt you here."

Pushing aside her nerves, she squared her shoulders and descended a set of stairs leading to another dungeon. Persephone approached the bars that held the once regal queen of the sky. Her usual beautiful, shining hair was dark and drenched from the ever-dripping ceiling. Hera's clothes hung on her bones, tattered and torn apart, showing the areas of her flesh, once marred from battle, now mostly healed.

"Well, well...," Hera chuckled low in her throat. "Look at you. So you finally made it to the Underworld, did you? Finally, mommy's smothering got to you? Huh?" She walked to the bars, looking out at both of them with hatred. "Can't say I blame you," Hera shrugged. She inclined her head at Persephone's clothes and hair. "What a dreadful outfit. Hades, surely you've offered her something reasonable to wear here." Hera clicked her tongue.

"I don't have to change for you," replied Persephone with a glare.

Hera scoffed with a raised brow. "Is that what you think? Do you think the world will bend to you and not vice versa? You are truly the most naive and stupid being I've ever met. You're just as worthless as Demeter."

Trying her best to choke back her anger, Persephone stepped forward.

"You don't get to say my mother's name," Persephone said through clenched teeth.

"Ooh... The kitten's getting some claws, does she?" Hera mocked. "Let me guess. Hades brought you here." Hera gave her a vicious grin. "My guess is without Demeter's permission. I know she would never have agreed to let you down here. Knowing I was here, she would never let you visit."

Persephone felt uneasy. Her confidence dwindled with each truth. She was right. It was only a matter of time before her mom found her. *Don't let her get under your skin and manipulate you. That's how you almost got killed.* She thought, trying to keep calm no matter what Hera threw at her.

"Judging by the lack of affection between the two of you right now, I'd say he brought you without your permission as well," Hera clicked her tongue again, watching their reactions. "Isn't that just like a god? They take what they want without regard for who or what they hurt."

Hades cleared his throat behind Persephone, but she ignored him. She wasn't leaving here without speaking her mind.

"So that's it?" Persephone scoffed. "That's the best you've got? I have to say. I'm not impressed." Persephone shook her head.

"Impressing you is the last thing I would ever lower myself to do." Hera's sneer turned into a grimace as Persephone came closer.

The two stood face to face for the first time since their last battle. Persephone knew Hera couldn't harm her here, but her stomach and heart wrenched and pounded anyway.

"You tried to kill me," said Persephone, holding a measured tone.

"Several times," Hera replied with a sinister grin.

"You failed," said Persephone calmly.

"So it would appear," Hera inclined her head. "For now."

"Your plots and schemes to make everyone's lives miserable have also failed," Persephone continued. "Everyone is happy on Olympus without you."

Hera's smile turned to a sneer. "Their happiness is no concern of mine. What a folly to seek happiness over duty. I guess you think marriage is all about happiness, miserable godling."

"You know, Hera. No amount of killing or destruction will ever fill that void inside of you," said Persephone, ticking up her head. "Look at you. You made this mess. And now you must be punished."

"You think you can judge me?" Hera spoke her words with rage as she laughed. "You don't know anything about me."

"You never gave me a chance," said Persephone, ice in her tone. "I'm disappointed that you are the queen and not someone better. Like my mom would have been if Zeus had rightly chosen her over you."

"Disappointed?" Hera seethed. "How fucking dare you speak to me of disappointment! I never got the luxury of a nice youth. I had to fight for everything I've achieved. You're spoiled, weak, and pathetic. Everything is given to you so easily, and you're still ungrateful. You have no idea what it means to rule the gods truly," she hissed. "But don't worry, pet. I'm going to spend eternity making you learn. The hard way."

Persephone tilted her head. "How are you going to do that from there?"

"I'll get out eventually," Hera said, glaring at them. "Zeus will see to it."

Persephone laughed. "Do you really think he will get you

out of here when he gets a free pass to play without you? You know him better than I do." Persephone stepped forward, inclining her head. "Tell me, Hera? Is he going to come and rescue you, or is he going to enjoy his freedom?"

"Zeus will release me," Hera said finally.

Her words didn't match her conviction, and her voice cracked.

"Your husband is probably going to be busy for a while before he gets around to freeing you," Persephone spoke slowly, articulating the venomous words into Hera's face, hoping they hurt as much as Persephone's wounds had. "I would start getting used to these dank walls because that's all you'll see for the foreseeable future."

"Something's different about you," Hera said, chuckling low in her throat. "I knew I sensed something dark in you when I met you. I wonder... What, or rather who brought it out of you?"

"I don't know what you're talking about," said Persephone, trying to block out any hint of expression that might give her away.

"The light inside of you is dimmed. I'd like to think I had something to do with that," Hera said with a one-sided grin. "You'd be nothing without me." Hera's tone was like a razor cutting through her skull. "And neither would Zeus. Oh yes. My little spies have already told me of his betrayal. But here you are. Tongue finally as wicked as mine and about to become Hades' queen. You'll fit in nicely down here." Hera leaned against the bars. "I'll hold my breath for the thanks I'm owed."

"I don't owe you anything, Hera," said Persephone. "Except maybe a goodbye."

"You'll be back. Or I will be free. Either way, this isn't over between us," Hera said, glaring up at them.

"Yes, it is," Persephone said as she turned and walked up a few steps with Hades.

"Do you honestly think Hades can contain me for long?" Hera asked with a laugh. "What a stupid goddess you have become."

"I've become what my mother made me," Persephone replied with a tear forming as she stopped and turned to face her abuser. "It's her you should concern yourself with."

"Yes," Hera said, smiling. "I'll handle her upon my return. You can be sure of that. With all the damage I hear she's been causing, no one will stop her punishment that's to come from me. Know that you will join her. Since Olympus, you have become weak. I might as well have killed you."

Persephone turned away, choking on air.

"Or maybe I did," Hera said with a tilt of her head. "Did I kill you, little flower?"

"No!" Persephone exclaimed, wrapping her arms around her waist. "And you never will."

"Oh, Pet," Hera chided. "You and I will never end this dance we've begun. No amount of agony will suffice to make me satiated. I plan to make yours and everyone else's lives perfectly miserable."

"Why, Hera?" Persephone asked. "Why pursue misery?"

"What a stupid godling," Hera said with a cruel laugh. "My marriage bed became defiled the moment Demeter settled within it. Her violation is your curse. Don't you see, pet?" Hera narrowed her eyes. "I will kill every last one of those who have defiled my marriage bed and any offspring that resulted from my unfaithful husband's deeds, regardless of whether you feel you are innocent."

"How can you make this about every one of us that Zeus creates?" Persephone asked, feeling her sense of dread creep up her spine as the sky goddess smiled. "We didn't choose to be born."

"I am the Goddess of marriage," Hera said, never diverting her eyes. "Whores like your mother should never gain an ounce of sympathy or mercy for preying upon the male who would seek comfort outside his marriage bed. A being like you is an abomination. Bastards who contend with legitimate heirs far more deserving of succession are a bane of the existence of immortals and mortals alike. Sure, everyone feels sorry for you, but what of the ones who worked so hard to be legitimate or the first wife who must be honored? We all would fall by the wayside of bastards like you who took the throne over those more deserving. It seems like I am cruel to you, but I am merely a benevolent voice for those pushed aside in the real world. A realm must be satisfied with a legitimate heir, lest the first wife become nothing more than a decoration. How would you feel if you had to share Hades with others? Don't you want to be his first and only wife?"

"You aren't Zeus' first wife..." Persephone knew of one before Hera. "Metis still resided in Zeus' head along with her son, who would usurp Zeus, according to an old prophecy. While Athena was free to be released, they remain trapped."

"I can only kill those alive and in my wake," Hera said with a side grin filled with darkness. "Metis is no longer a threat. I can handle this."

"I...'" Persephone closed her mouth as she was about to protest. "I couldn't handle it at all."

"Now you see, Pet," Hera said with a knowing smile. "You think you are better than me, but the truth is, you and I are the same. The only difference is that I exchanged my wounds for wisdom."

"No," Persephone whispered, backing away. "You're not wise, your hateful."

"I would have said the same if I were as stupid and naive as you." Hera laughed. "Just because you think you are better than me doesn't make it so."

"I could never be like you," Persephone said, shaking her head.

"No," Hera replied with a downward glare. "You couldn't if you tried."

"Can we go back?" Persephone asked Hades. "I'm feeling tired."

She felt utterly drained and needed private time to digest everything she had witnessed. More importantly, she had to get away from Hera.

"I'll see you again soon, Pet." Hera called out to Persephone as she left the goddess in her cage.

"Are you okay?" he asked when they had exited the prison.

"I'm fine. I just need to rest and take everything in," she replied, refusing to look at Hades.

He drove her back to the stables, where she left him without a word and went to their chambers. Closing the door behind her, Persephone crumbled as her shaking legs finally gave out. Panting, she could feel her adrenaline coursing throughout her body, making her feel sick. The room was spinning. Confronting Hera and everything else in Tartarus overwhelmed her. She tried to steady her breaths. The terror she witnessed played back in her mind. There were so many different levels and horrors it was hard to determine which was worse. Ultimately, Hera won out. After Persephone felt what her death would be for the first time, it scared her more than she had admitted to anyone. Seeing Hera brought it all back.

She fought to calm herself. Persephone walked to the table, poured herself a drink, and practically fell into the chair. Just before taking a sip, she remembered she couldn't and set the chalice on the table. She stared into the flame, reminded of the eternal land cracked apart, spewing the same fire from its depths. However far that was. Still, seeing the depravity that existed, there was no doubt to her of the necessity of such a place. It was indeed dark but necessary. She wondered how Hades dealt with it day in and out. He had told her of his work, but nothing could prepare her for the reality. No wonder Hades was so guarded and kept to himself. He dealt with so much that she almost felt bad for being so insensitive toward him. Almost. She was still furious that he took her, leaving her mom without knowing where she was, and hiding his harem of female relationships.

"Damn it!" She screamed, trying to let it all out. "Hecate!"

"Oh, my goddess! If I were a lesser being, I would smite you for bringing me out of that luscious bed." Hecate was naked, glaring down at Persephone. Hecate's black lace-weaved sheer robe appeared with a wave of her hand, ending in a long train that dragged behind Hecate as she walked over to Persephone.

"I want you to give me the summoning spell to bring Artemis here."

"My darkling one," Hecate said, coming closer to hold Persephone's hand. "I will not doom the moon goddess to this place."

Persephone sighed. "I need to figure out how to use these abilities. Anything to distract me from what's happening."

"If you want to learn, I will teach you. But, you must be willing to open yourself up to the darkness inside you."

"What if I can't?"

"With my help, anything is possible."

What did Hecate mean by that? Persephone thought as the Titaness took a drink of her wine.

"Come," Hecate said, holding out her hand. "I think I know a way that will help."

CHAPTER 12
CHALLENGE

Hecate took her to the room adjacent to the war room, where Persephone could see two large round pillows on the ground surrounded by a silver circle encompassing both, much like before.

"You're not going to make me touch the stone again, are you?"

"Not this time," Hecate said, gesturing for her to sit on one of the pillows. "Here, have a seat."

Persephone did as she asked. The soft surface was comforting as she crossed her legs and sat upright. Hecate sat opposite in the same pose and smiled.

"First, we need to go into your mind and see what we can find in your abilities."

"What will happen then?" Persephone asked.

"Then we will begin your training and see what we can develop." Hecate closed her eyes. "It may be painful, and you may feel frightened, but there is no other way."

When Persephone closed her eyes, she appeared in a place with no color, just gray darkness with a dead tree. Its spindly branches didn't move, nor was there life in it. The grass was gray beneath her feet, and the cloudless sky was the same.

"Desolate, isn't it?" Hecate asked behind her.

Persephone turned and saw Hecate dressed in robes that covered her form—a sight she'd never seen before. The robes billowed in a phantom breeze that seemed only to affect Hecate.

Persephone looked around. "What is this place?"

"It's a place where you can go in your mind to train with your powers."

"This is my mind?" Persephone asked Hecate. "Why is it so dark?"

"Think of it more like a blank canvas. It's up to you to create what you desire and practice your abilities. We all have a place we can go inside ourselves, even Hades."

Persephone looked up at the tree and held out her hand. Her natural powers came out to her surprise, and the tree grew leaves with purple and pink blossoms. The magic she used drifted down, continuously falling to the ground. The grass grew as each sparkle touched it; the bright green color bled through the area. Turning in a circle, Persephone extended her powers to the sky. The light on her face made her smile as she closed her eyes and indulged in the warmth. Soon, the plants and flowers bloomed around them, making her world full of life and color.

"Well, it appears you have your nature powers in hand," Hecate said behind her. "Now comes the fun part."

"What part is that?"

"You're going to bring out your darkness."

"I don't know how."

"You won't hurt anything here," Hecate assured. "Don't be afraid."

"What about you? Can I hurt you?"

Hecate laughed. "That's adorable. No, my darkling. You cannot."

Persephone reached out her hand to a nearby bush she'd created, feeling its life force. The welling of power inside her came up from her core, and dark energy, like a phantom hand, extended past her own. The plant began to wither and die until it was nothing but dust. Her hand retracted, and she wrapped her arms around her waist as the guilt became overwhelming.

"Very interesting," Hecate said, approaching her to observe the dust. "Have you done this before?"

"Yes, but only by accident."

"I see." Hecate tapped a finger on her lips. "What do you feel when it happens?"

"I hate it. But I feel powerful."

"I heard what happened with the Keres. Is this how you healed yourself from their attack?"

"I'm not sure." Persephone remembered the last moments with Hades. "I siphoned power from Hades as well. Maybe that's how I healed."

"Usually, I would get a visit from you if you're injured, but you didn't come to me then, so I didn't know how you managed to heal so quickly." Hecate looked away in thought. "I figured your immortal powers were at work, but this is something else entirely."

"What do you mean?"

"I think you're stealing life energy and using it to make yourself stronger, and it appears it can heal you as well." Hecate chuckled. "Certainly a handy gift, even for a god."

"You call this a gift?"

"Power is a gift, Persephone."

"It doesn't feel like a gift."

"Oh, don't be so glub," Hecate rolled her eyes. "Have you ever used this on anyone else besides Hades?"

Persephone nodded. "It happened once when I grabbed Hera during our last battle."

"Damn," Hecate cursed under her breath. "That means your enemy knows you can do this."

"She's in prison. There's nothing she can do about it," Persephone said, clenching her hands.

Hecate crossed her arms. "For now, but she won't

be forever. Rest assured. She will find a way to use this knowledge."

"I can't worry about that right now," Persephone sighed. "If I think too far into the future of what could happen to me, I'll drive myself crazy."

"Can you do anything else with this power?"

"This is the only thing I've done so far."

Hecate nodded. "We must meet here again to test what else you can do. Best to find out your limitations now so we can plan for any mishaps in the future."

"Whenever I used this power the first few times, I was conscious, but it was reactionary." Persephone thought about being pulled down as the other ascended and took over her body. "With the Keres, I blacked out and found bodies piled around me. I wasn't in control, so I don't remember what happened."

Hecate folded her arms, placing one hand on her chin. "The Keres were draining you of your blood, and your powers likely reacted to protect you. The surge must have been too much at that time."

"What if I hurt someone and can't stop?"

"That's why we're here," Hecate said, placing her hand on Persephone's shoulder. "We must practice and manifest your gifts so that you can stay in control."

"And if I lose control?" Persephone asked, feeling a sense of dread.

Hecate gave a wicked grin. "Then Gaia, help whoever is on the other end."

Several hours passed when she returned to Hades' room and heard a knock on the door a few minutes after arriving.

"Who is it?" she asked.

"Persephone," he called out softly.

"I'm fine," she replied, knowing she wasn't.

He entered the room and stood near the fire, staring into its flickering embers. Persephone watched him try to gather his thoughts before he spoke.

"I wanted to see how you were doing after everything you saw today," he said, clearing his throat. "I know it can be jarring."

"That's putting it mildly," she replied with sarcasm.

He drew a heavy breath and continued, "I wanted to ensure you're okay. How are you feeling about seeing Hera?"

"I'm still processing everything," she replied with a sigh. "But I see what you mean now by how your work here is important. I just didn't realize the gravity of what you did until now."

Hades nodded, came over, and sat across from her near the fire.

"Do you think you could be happy here?" he asked without looking at her.

"Honestly?" she said, staring into her glass. "I don't know."

"I see," he said finally.

"I just need to wrap my head around everything," Persephone replied.

"Do you think you could grow to be happy here?" he asked, seeming so vulnerable in his questions.

"I'm not going to lie and say that it's ideal with Hera so close," she said, her brows drawn together. "But... I'm warming up to the idea."

"I shouldn't have taken you there," he said, cursing under his breath.

"I'm glad you did," she said, wanting to reassure him but unable to. "I needed the opportunity to confront Hera, and now I have. It helps knowing she can't hurt me anymore."

"I will never let that happen to you again," he growled deep in his throat.

"I know you won't," she said.

"So you're okay then?"

"I'm trying to be," she said, looking down into her hands. "Maybe after some sleep, I'll feel better. Do you mind if I skip the party tonight?"

"Of course," he said, standing to leave. "If you need anything, you know where to find me."

***

Hades raised a hand to light the fire in his war room. The light flickered on the walls like daemons dancing. He could hear the merriment beyond the doors but didn't feel like celebrating. His thoughts about how to convince her to stay were exhausting him. Showing Persephone Tartarus could prove to be disastrous. Not to mention, the things Hera said were troubling. He knew she meant every word and would carry out her threats the moment she was free. Hades needed to speak to Zeus about it but couldn't risk losing time with Persephone. He couldn't even speak to Poseidon or Hestia as he usually would lest they reveal his secret. Settling into his chair, he slumped back into the soft back and rested his head on the wing of the chair.

Closing his eyes, Hades took a deep breath and let sleep take him.

A white flower drifted down the waters to Hades. Walking the shores, he waited anxiously as the narcissus' petals settled on the bank with a promise on the wind that said... *Soon, my love.* Hades picked up the flower and held it to his nose, smelling the familiar scent she left on it. The air shifted. He sensed the veil thinning and heard her call. Hades stood holding her message and immediately summoned his horses to prepare for the night ride. Footsteps heavy, Hades shook the ground with his power that built with his excitement. Knowing his eyes were turning, he could see others back away from him as he passed. He clenched his fist to hold back his claws that ached to come out. Worried he'd crush the flower, he transported it to his room and continued toward his ride. The four horses neighed and stomped in anticipation as Hades shoved open the doors, slamming them against the walls with a loud bang.

Hades stepped onto the chariot, and the beasts took off once the reins were in his hands, driving them forward until they lifted off into the air. They galloped with the dark clouded energy surrounding them as they disappeared into the darkness. The land above opened, and the air felt cool as they burst through the rocky ground into the large cave with a light at the end of the jagged tunnel.

Persephone waited for him beyond the entrance in a landscape colored with reds, golds, and fiery orange as the leaves drifted around her. She held open her arms when she saw him riding toward her.

Reaching out his hand, he pulled her up into the chariot as she wrapped her legs around his hips and immediately turned to take her home. Her kisses were insistent and filled with passion as they left through the cave and plummeted in each other's arms down into the darkness.

Hades woke up grumbling when she wasn't in his arms anymore. His hands felt empty, and he flexed them, needing to touch her. Clenching his fists, he closed his eyes and turned his head to the firelight.

Thanatos came in and bowed. "My Lord, we have a problem."

"What is it?" Hades asked, rubbing his eyes.

"Mynthe has challenged Persephone to a fight, and they are on their way to the arena."

"What?" Hades sobered and got up, following Thanatos out of the room. "I warned her that she would be banished if she did this."

"They both began fighting in front of a large group of daemons when the challenge happened," Thanatos replied beside him. "Not even you can retract a public declaration of challengers per your rules."

"Fuck," Hades growled. "We have to stop them."

"My lord, if we do that, Persephone will be considered weak, and she'll lose the support of the underworld."

Hades stopped and thought for a moment. He regretted

making such a rule in the first place. However, if he made the rule, he could change it. Doing so would work against Persephone, and he couldn't have any more setbacks. Clenching his jaw, Hades made his way to the arena.

The crowd showed their approval through applause and cheers throughout the halls. Hades was not amused. Mynthe was already down in the sands, egging on the crowd who cheered for her as Persephone stood nearby, testing her two swords gripped in each hand that swung them. He went to the dais where Hecate stood.

Hecate shook her head and placed a hand up to stop him.

"I'm going to stop this," Hades said to Hecate, worried something would happen to Persephone if he didn't.

"Let her do this," said Hecate, placing a hand on his arm to stay his announcement. "Mynthe openly challenged Persephone, and now we must watch this play out."

Hades clenched his fists, knowing what would happen if he ended the fight. The Underworld would never accept Persephone if she backed down from a nymph.

"Fine, but if anything happens, it's on you this time," he said with narrowed eyes.

Hecate folded her arms. "Having your mistress and our queen battle for supremacy is hardly the time to be squeamish. Tell the crowd the loser will suffer punishment for one hundred years. That should make this a fight to remember."

"I'm not sending Persephone for a hundred years of punishment," Hades growled at Hecate.

Hecate folded her arms. "If you don't, everyone will think you're playing favorites."

"I am."

"Yes, but you can't let them know that," Hecates said, pointing to the crowd. "Besides, do you think Persephone would lose to a mere nymph? She has fought much more difficult foes than that already. It's time she tests her abilities anyway."

"I take it you've begun training?" He asked, clenching his

jaw.

Hecate nodded. "Persephone has more surprises than even I could imagine up her sleeve. Let her do this. Perhaps she will gain the confidence to develop those abilities. You might want to make the stakes even more interesting. Offer Mynthe her position back and access to your pools."

Hades growled. "I'm not letting her back in my pool or bed. Is that clear?"

"I know that, but those two don't." Hecate winked. "Should light a fire in both of them and make this fight more interesting."

"You want to see Persephone manifest her dark abilities, don't you?" Hades asked, narrowing his eyes at her.

"Of course." Hecate raised a brow. "They only come out when she's highly emotional and in distress. This fight should do it."

As much as he disliked seeing them pitted against one another, it was inevitable. Mynthe was formidable in a fight, but her emotions always got the better of her. Persephone had the same issue. If he was to have any peace, they needed to settle their differences. More importantly, Persephone would have to prove herself to the court.

"Are you sure letting Mynthe back into court is a good idea?" Hades asked Hecate, clenching his jaw. "I hate retracting decrees."

"I'm sure." Hecate sighed. "Persephone must take her place by your side, undisputed, or none of this will work. She has to prove that she deserves the position by earning it." Hecate cackled. "Only you and I know how dangerous Persephone truly is. Mynthe won't know what hit her. Serves her right for reaching too high."

Hades sat on his throne. "Have her abilities manifested in your training?"

"Yes, but unfortunately, only one ability is clear." Hecate sighed. "I know you've seen it. Now, the rest of us need to see it as well. So long as Mynthe does what I set her out to do...."

Hades closed his eyes for patience. "Are you telling me you set this whole thing up?"

"What? No..." Hecate looked away with an awkward glance and drank deep from her chalice.

"Hecate," he said with a warning.

The Titaness fiddled with her hands. "Okay, so I may have done a little provoking to get Mynthe to antagonize Persephone first."

Hades started cursing under his breath. "If Persephone uses her powers and can't control them, she'll kill Mynthe."

"Exciting, isn't it," Hecate said with a wicked grin, continuing to drink heavily.

"I knew it was out of character for Mynthe to start a fight after my order."

"Too right you are." Hecate nodded. "But if you poke someone long enough, eventually, they'll give in to their baser desires. Mynthe's was to have you all to herself."

Hades glared at Hecate. "That was never a possibility."

"She didn't know that." Hecate shrugged.

"So you intentionally started a fight between them to get Persephone to use her powers, not to give Mynthe a chance. How is this helpful?" He asked, preferring to keep the nymph banished.

This fight was a gamble even for him, and Hecate was not helping his nerves. *Gaia, please let Persephone make it through this without hating him.*

"When Persephone wins," Hecate said so only Hades could hear. "And she will. Mynthe will be in a lowly place, but eventually, she can work her way back. I foresee her use down the road. It's only a century of banishment, anyway. She'll hardly even notice the time pass. Besides, do you want Persephone to be paranoid like Hera when she's gone?"

"What do you mean when she's gone? Persephone isn't going anywhere," Hades growled low in his throat, looking back at the two who argued below.

"Did I say gone?" Hecate chuckled nervously. "I could

have sworn I said... Oh, hey, look! They're ready to begin," Hecate said as she looked away and spoke into her glass. "Damn it! These visions keep mixing up my timelines."

"What's that supposed to mean?" He asked, raising a brow.

Hecate shook her head. "I'm having a hard time knowing where I'm at or when. It's like being pulled between realities and timelines, and it's getting worse."

"When did this begin?" He asked, wondering if this was why she was so addle-brained.

Hecate waved a hand. "It's often been a slight issue for me since before the Titanomachy. But this new prophecy of yours is making it worse. We need to get the ball rolling, so to speak, so that I can go back to my usual charming self."

"You're more annoying than charming," he said, shaking his head.

Hecate smiled with a wide grin. "I think I'm adorable."

He didn't have time to argue with Hecate. Rolling his eyes at whatever scheme she worked out, he just wanted to get this over with.

Hades pinched the bridge of his nose but nodded, then faced the arena and held up a hand for their attention.

"Silence!" Hades roared, for the first time displaying his anger. "It appears you both have some issues to work out. The challenge was made and accepted. I am bound to allow it. Here are the terms. If Mynthe wins, she can return to the pools, and I will forgive her transgression."

"What?!" Yelled Persephone and Mynthe together, though with stark differences in their reactions.

"I knew one day you'd ask for me to return!" Mynthe yelled, baring a seductive smile.

"The fuck she is!" Persephone glared with murder in her eyes at Hades. "You can't seriously ask me to accept her into your bed!" Persephone spat up at him.

"What's the matter, maiden?" Mynthe turned to her with a grotesque smile. "We can all tell that you haven't been there. After all, a king has needs. If you won't fulfill them, I'd be happy to."

Mynthe glared down her nose at Persephone.

"You keep testing my patience, Mynthe," Hades warned. "I've let you get away with too much. This challenge is on you, not me. If you want my favor, you'd better win," Hades continued, ignoring their objections as they shouted simultaneously. "However, if Persephone wins, Mynthe will be banished to Tartarus for one hundred years of punishment for failure to obey me."

"Hades?!" Mynthe called up to him in disbelief, pouting.

"Damn it!" Persephone yelled. "It's like being around my father all over again. You would have me share you with a mistress?"

"If Persephone loses," he said, hesitating. "She will meet the same fate in Tartarus."

"You wouldn't dare," Persephone growled, seething with fury. "You'll pay for this if you order me there."

"Then I suggest you remember the most important rule, wife," he replied, tilting his head and raising a brow. "The choice is yours, Persephone. Either fight or forfeit. If you forfeit, Mynthe returns to the pools by default. Will you surrender?"

"Never," Persephone said through gritted teeth, eyes narrowed, threatening to destroy him.

He gave her the wicked smile she hated. "Then I guess, my queen, you'd better win."

Standing, Hades raised a hand to set them to begin.

CHAPTER 13
ENEMIES

Never before had she felt so furious at Hades for suggesting Mynthe could return to his room. The betrayal was thick in her mouth as she spat on the ground to cleanse her palate.

"Hades!" Persephone yelled up to him. "I didn't agree to this."

"My decision is final," Hades replied with ice in his tone. "Do not test my patience, Persephone."

"Threats," scoffed Persephone. "Typical of the monster you are!"

The crowd gasped as the drama played out.

"Persephone," Hades warned. "If you want to continue your threats, I'll be the one to punish you personally. And I assure you I will enjoy every minute of it."

The crowd murmured with oohs and laughter. Persephone's rage boiled deep in her core as she closed her eyes.

"Not as much as I'm going to punish you after this...," Persephone seethed, glaring back with glowing eyes.

She was about to step forward but stopped as she felt the air move behind her and ducked below the swing of Mynthe's sword.

"Let's get this over with." Mynthe smiled, pointing her sword at Persephone as they moved to circle one another. "I'm eager to return to his bed to fuck Hades the way I know he likes it."

Persephone crouched in a fighting stance. "I'm ready when you are nymph."

Mynthe spun her weapons and then squared off. The nymph lunged forward, taking swipe after swipe, never landing. The light glinted off the sharp edges, reminding Persephone of what it was like to be at the other end as she stepped around or away from each strike. Her chest ached at the phantom symptoms of memories she would rather forget. In her last battle, Persephone let down her guard. This time, she wouldn't make the same mistakes. This time, it would be Mynthe at the end of Persephone's blade.

"Stop dodging and fight me," Mynthe said low in her throat, shaking her head with a maniacal grin.

"Fine. I'll play your little game. And I'll win," Persephone said, turning to block the next sword with her own, then landing a blow, forcing Mynthe back.

Persephone lept at Mynthe, choosing offense. Her power ignited around her and her blades as she swung hard against the nymph. The intensity increased as she blocked and parried each swipe. Persephone could feel the power coursing through her, making her sense the attack before it came. Something down here was calling to her, feeding her. Persephone knew she had to keep her other self away and stay in control. There would be no telling what would happen if she didn't.

The pull of energy was so easy to grasp. Her body seemed to dance with it. Dodging each attack, Persephone moved faster as the minutes passed. Drawing from the energy she was connecting to, Persephone felt intoxicated with strength and clarity. This time, there was no mother or friends in danger. It was just Persephone and Mynthe. And this nymph was about to go down.

Mynthe pulled Persephone in close, receiving a sobering elbow to the face. The nymph glared, rubbing the wounded eye, then lunged forward. Swings missed each time as Persephone ducked and pivoted out of the way. Mynthe's kicks landed in nothing but air. She slammed Mynthe in the side with the butt of her sword, crushing a rib. Mynthe kicked Persephone in the gut and flipped back out of the way. She coughed, holding her side. The bones cracked loud as Mynthe stretched them back into place.

Something changed in Mynthe's eyes as a shadow crept over them. Her eyes began to glow red, and her body pulsed with a fiery energy that crept over her dark skin, cracking the flesh apart in magmatic veins. The look of death in those black eyes lit with rage sent a shiver through Persephone as she faltered in her steps. Mynthe took advantage of her hesitation and began to hammer Persephone with surprising strength, forcing her back.

The infernal nymph kicked low, taking out Persephone's feet. Mid-fall, Mynthe brought her leg into a graceful, pointed high kick and slammed her foot into Persephone's chest, forcing her down so hard into the ground it knocked the wind out of her. Coughing, she rolled out of the way in time for the blade to cut down into her chest, barely missing Persephone. They paused momentarily, facing one another, crouched low to the ground. Moving slowly, Persephone held her chest, regaining air in her lungs. Both readied again, swords up, one foot stepping across the other as they circled.

"You've got skills," Mynthe said, wiping blood from her lip. "I'll give you that. But you're no match for me."

"I'd say your training is working in your favor," Persephone said, still moving slowly as the crowd cheered them on.

"Thank you. Hades taught me well." Mynthe gave a sinister smile that reminded Persephone of Hera. "Shame he didn't do the same for you."

For a moment, as though Persephone's eyes were playing

tricks on her, Mynthe's smile created an illusion over her face. Almost as if she was turning into Hera with every word that felt like a knife digging into Persephone's subconscious. Her body began to hum with the vibration, recognizing the danger and forcing its way forward.

"Persephoneeeee...," It whispered, making her turn to look.

She closed her eyes and fought to hold back the feeling of falling into darkness and focus on the fight. Pain erupted in her head as a foot smashed her face, launching her back into a pillar that crumbled from the impact. Persephone shook off the fog, stood, and blocked just in time as Mynthe flew into the air with dizzying speed, swinging both swords down. She returned the attack with a knee to Mynthe's gut, followed by a solid head butt.

Staggering back, Mynthe wiped her nose with the back of her hand and glared at Persephone. The crowd was with them at every blow, crying out in excitement and cheering when Persephone landed a solid hit. They booed when Mynthe slammed Persephone down. But no matter how tough the punishment, Persephone kept getting back up. She was tired, even slightly blurred in her vision from so many impacts, but something kept her focused enough to stay in the fight. She wouldn't let Mynthe win.

"I'm surprised a nymph can fight at all," Persephone taunted.

"Maybe the ones you know can't, but Infernal Nymphs can," Mynthe said with a swipe, followed by another parry. "You have to if you want to survive down here. The pits should have taught you that by now."

Persephone swung down to land a hard blow to Mynthe's swords, making the nymph back up with her hands shaking from the vibration until her grip tightened.

"Didn't realize fucking was surviving," Persephone said, confidently walking toward Mynthe. "I was surprised you had any other skills. At least I know now that you're not boring."

"A sentiment I'm sure Hades agrees with," Mynthe teased. "At least I've never had any complaints."

"Until now. Right?" Persephone raised a brow. "Let me guess. You think Hades is yours."

Mynthe's eyes narrowed. "He will be once you're gone."

"You know what?" Persephone swung her sword around and readied her stance to fight again. "I think I'll stay since it grates on you so much."

Mynthe stood, shock rolling across her face. "You said you were leaving."

"I did." Persephone smiled a wicked grin. "But after seeing Tartarus and what I can have that you can't, I don't know. I might be changing my mind."

"Ah, so the flower has thorns?" Mynthe tilted her head with a smile.

"I'm growing them, slowly." Persephone winked and smiled, enjoying the smirk leaving Mynthe's face.

"Are we going to fight or keep talking all day?" Mynthe hissed.

"Be my guest," the goddess replied with a slight bow.

Persephone pulled from the source of her power and whirled in the air, bringing her swords down on Mynthe, sending shock waves out from the impact. They both fought with so much force and speed that the audience could hardly keep up. Eventually, Mynthe landed a solid hit right in Persephone's jaw, throwing her back into the side wall that crumbled, knocking her weapons out of her hand. The blades sprawled several feet away, leaving Persephone vulnerable. She shook her head and cleared it, and without even thinking, tumbled forward past Mynthe.

Remembering her sickle, Persephone pulled it from the base of her spine and spun around, separating it into two, crossing the blades to block. She staggered back from the force of Mynthe's swords. One after the other, the nymph grew more aggressive with her strikes. Deflecting each attack, the goddess blocked, backing up with each impact. Finding an opening, she kicked a solid blow to Mynthe's chest, sending her flying back, skidding to a halt on her back. Furious, Mynthe flipped onto her feet and glared.

Persephone's finger pressed one of the stones, and the ends of the handles extended. She could see they had a connection point, so the goddess connected the two hilts at the end, creating a staff with two crescent blades.

Mynthe scoffed at the change in weaponry. Standing while brushing off her clothes, she joined her swords at the end, making her swords into a two-sided bladed staff. Spinning the newly formed weapons, they both lunged forward, one end over the other, blocking and striking with whirlwind movements. Their footwork adjusted, stepping past one another, attacking in circles. Persephone dropped into the splits, blocking the blade that hit so hard it cut into her shoulder. She swung her legs for leverage, spinning on her back out of the way. With an upswing that brushed so close to Mynthe's chest that the nymph arched back and flipped away, Persephone did the same.

With enough distance between them, they spun their weapons, gaining momentum for the next strike. Mynthe lept in a graceful twirl in the air, blades sparking as she struck Persephone's handle. Persephone hooked Mynthe's weapon and flipped her over her shoulder. The nymph kicked off the ground and fired a back-handed hit that forced Persephone backward. Using her weapon to cut a gash into the ground, she skidded to a stop on one knee. Stepping onto the handle, Persephone flipped backward, legs scissoring mid-air. Bringing around the crescent staff, she used all her might to strike. Mynthe's weapon was no match for hers, and with the impact, it shattered. Persephone spin-kicked Mynthe in the jaw, launching the nymph in the air and tumbling to a halt as the shards fell around her.

Rage began to cloud the nymph's judgment. It was obvious that she was taking a lot of damage. Blood poured from her head, and she spit out blood holding her chest. But like Persephone, she refused to quit. For a moment, Persephone felt admiration for the female's fighting spirit.

"Had enough?" Persephone asked, separating her staff.

"You wish," Mynthe replied, staggering to her feet.

No weapon in hand, Mynthe lunged at Persephone with extremely long, pointed fingers tipped in what appeared to be poison. Able to defend most of the strikes, one got through, scratching Persephone's left arm. The effects were instant. Her head swam, and her limbs felt heavy. Each deflection of Mynthe's attacks became hard to stop. Another claw ripped a gash in her thigh. The poison felt similar to what her mother used in her barbed staff, but it was slightly different.

Suddenly, her veins felt like they were burning. Persephone cried out as the black lines crept outward from the wounds, igniting as though on fire. The pain was blinding. She staggered back, holding her arm, seeing the damage. Wherever the poison crept, the fiery pain followed.

"Persephoneeee…," the whisper called out again.

"No!" She screamed at the voice no one could hear.

"Awe," Mynthe teased. "What's the matter? Can't handle a little heat?"

"I thought we weren't using our powers," Persephone replied through heavy breaths.

"Whoever said we weren't?" Mynthe lifted her chin. "Do you even have powers here? Or are you as useless as you appear?"

Persephone swallowed hard, blinking to clear her vision as she stumbled backward. Her legs wobbled, and one of her blades fell from her weakening left hand. Mynthe kicked her to the ground. Her foot grinding into Persephone's leg sent more mind-numbing pain through her body. She screamed, feeling the sand of Mynthe's boot like gravel penetrating her wound.

"I'm not useless," Persephone said through gritted teeth. "I'm warning you, nymph, you don't want bring out my powers."

"Oh, I think I do," said Mynthe, bending down over her. "I

will do anything to get what I want. Even if that means I have to kill you."

Claws raked deep into her gut. The poison poured into her torso, sending her mind into a spiral as the pain took her breath away. Mynthe ripped her hand out and admired the blood that dripped down her arm.

The crowd had gone silent. Hands covered mouths as those who watched waited with bated breath to see the outcome. The cheers had turned to chants of Mynthe's name. Tears crept into Persephone's eyes as she choked on her own blood. She coughed, feeling its warm liquid drip down the sides of her mouth. Mynthe began to laugh just like Hera did before.

Grabbing Persephone by the throat, she lifted the goddess above her head, cutting off her air. Persephone felt herself losing consciousness between the poison and the hand that gripped her neck.

"Persephoneeee...," The whisper was more insistent. "Let me out!"

Finally, she closed her eyes and gave in.

"Yes."

The feeling welled inside her, intoxicating her like a heady wine mixed with sexual pleasure as the other awoke. Though Persephone was still conscious, she wasn't entirely in control. A surge of energy burst forth, knocking Mynthe back. The other gripped the hilt of the sickle and moved so fast it was as if she could teleport. In half a second, she was on Mynthe swinging with precise action, driving the nymph back to defend herself. Persephone's hand hit so hard with a back swing it sent Mynthe through a column, spitting blood. Again, Persephone closed the distance too fast to react. Her foot landed into Mynthe's gut, shattering her ribs. The nymph tried to defend, but it was useless as Persephone's other self punched and kicked so hard it broke bones with every strike.

Mynthe stood with her remaining strength, grabbed a shard of her sword, ran at the goddess, and plunged it into

Persephone's right lung with a menacing laugh of victory. Persephone's hand reached up, holding onto the nymph's as the blade sunk deeper. The sickening tearing of flesh sounded loud in the silent arena. Looking down, unphased, Persephone crushed the other female's hand and slowly pulled it from her chest. Mynthe dropped the blade that clanged to the ground and tried to back away. Her eyes shot wide as a hand grabbed her throat, and Mynthe struggled for release. Unable to budge the crushing grip, Mynthe froze as the same sickening sound of flesh rendered made the crowd gasp. Impaled, fighting for her life, Mynthe tried to scream, but only blood poured from her mouth.

The sickle vibrated in Persephone's hand as Mynthe shook uncontrollably from it ripping through her chest, barely missing her heart. Slowly, Persephone brought the nymph close enough to hear her whisper.

"I tried to warn you," she said in a haunting voice laced with sadistic enjoyment. "You shouldn't have asked me to come out. So now you're going to pay."

Persephone clicked the black stone, and the hilt extended to fit her hand as the guard formed through connected gears resembling Hephaestus' mechanical work. The sickle blade tore through Mynthe's spine, lengthening into a scythe, dripping blood out her back that fell in pools beneath her dangling feet. She could taste Mynthe's fear. It felt good. Her head swam with pleasure from the power flowing from inside. Persephone choked Mynthe's neck harder, relishing as she found the spark and siphoned the nymph's life force.

All she could feel was the energy flowing through her grasp. It felt amazing. A seeming elixir of life poured into Persephone as she drank deep from the source. Her pain evaporated, and her power siphoned more to give her the life energy she desired. It flooded her senses and tingled from her toes to her fingertips. She felt hands clasp the sides of her face. A voice saying let her go was so far away, yet familiar. She decided to listen and released Mynthe.

Her mind cleared, and Persephone found herself surrounded by several gods. Hades kept saying her name with his hands on her face to wake her from the trance. Mynthe lay shriveled, her youth drained from her, her hair turned white, and her life force almost gone. No longer visible through her gray skin, Persephone could still sense the tiny flicker left inside, but it was faint.

Hecate knelt next to the body as she used magic to help Mynthe. Looking down at her hands, Persephone realized what she'd done. The power she felt combined with her own was still throbbing inside her. It was intoxicating.

The crowd no longer chanted her name. Their excitement was dashed into silence as they stared at the crumpled mass at her feet. Hades signaled for assistance. Thanatos and the Titaness took Mynthe away, leaving Persephone to stand beside Hades. Aware she was still pulsing with her flame, she pulled the energy inside and pushed the other back as she clicked the last stone, and the blade returned to its original form.

"You won," Hades said with pride and concern. "I knew you would."

Persephone looked up at the stunned audience. "Why are they staring at me like that?"

"Because you were magnificent," he replied, touching her cheek.

"I didn't mean to..." Persephone stuttered. "She. She wanted to kill me."

"And you defended yourself." Hades smiled. "I didn't think you'd be so thorough."

"Hades," Persephone started to speak, but he cut her off.

"Underworld!" Hades roared. "Will you not cheer for your undisputed queen?!"

A slow clap began, and the crowd started to cheer with awe and excitement. They all stood, one by one, giving her the ovation she deserved. Soon, the arena was booming with chants of "Dread Queen" as the court displayed their approval.

Feeling overwhelmed, she wanted to leave.

"Hades? Take me away from here," Persephone said through gritted teeth, closing her eyes. "Please."

Persephone felt the familiar whoosh of air surrounding her, and the chants faded into sweet silence. When she opened her eyes, they were in his chambers. Her breathing was ragged as she gulped the air. Her heart felt like it would rip through her chest with the rush of adrenaline that flooded her body through every pore. Drunk, still connected to the heady sensation of power, her body burned to be touched.

Strange, she thought to herself. *I should be afraid after what happened. Where did the pain go?*

The pain had turned to pleasure, making her shake as her hands caressed from her hips to her chest. The wounds were gone, and she suddenly felt very hot. Desire replaced fear when she smelled his delicious scent. Facing Hades, she admired his chest muscles that flexed beneath his opened shirt. She needed to touch them.

"Are you okay?" He asked, placing a hand on her shoulder.

"Don't talk," Persephone said, grabbing Hades' neck, bringing his lips to hers.

She devoured his mouth, drawing his delicious scent into her lungs. Hades returned her kiss with enthusiasm, wrapping her legs around his hips. Lifting her, he cupped Persephone's ass and walked to his bed. Setting her down, Hades pulled back, placing his forehead against hers.

"We shouldn't do this right now," he said, taking deep breaths. "I need to make sure you're okay."

"I'd prefer that you touch me instead," she said into his mouth, licking his lips.

A moan escaped as he nuzzled her. "You're injured and bleeding."

"I'll heal," she said, kissing him again.

"Come." Hades reached to open her bodice. "Let me see your wounds."

"If that's what it takes to get naked with you, go ahead and inspect me," she replied, sitting up on her knees.

She ignored the worry in his eyes, wanting to tease him. Biting her lip, Persephone realized the seductive energy she was experiencing didn't feel entirely her own but some remnant of the other version of her. It felt good. She enjoyed how protective he was while responding to her desires. *Maybe I should give in to them more often*, she thought. Hitching a breath, Persephone watched as he unlaced her bodice, setting free her large breasts. Their weight felt heavy, nipples tightening, needing to be sucked as he removed her punctured corset and opened her top to find the stab wound in her chest already healed.

Reaching toward a bowl on the table by the bed, he grabbed a soft towel, dipped it in, and wrung out the excess water. The cloth was warm as he began to wash her upper body. Wherever there was blood, he wiped her down in long strokes, making her skin tingle as the cool air contrasted with the warm towel that left trails of wet skin. He guided her to sit back against the pillow without a word. Removing her pants, Hades cleaned her thighs with slow, soothing, seductive caresses until no more dirt or blood remained. To be bathed in such a way made her even more turned on.

When he'd finished, Hades glanced up and down over her mostly naked form.

"See?" Persephone waved a hand over her body. "I'm fine."

She'd found the bruises on her face had recovered, touching where they used to be. Her hands wiped away the sweat from her brow, feeling no pain or puffiness. Even the gashes on her arm and thigh from Mynthe's claws were healed without any marks. An ache still lingered in her abdomen, but she ignored it, too focused on the masculine god before her and his meticulous care.

"You look fine on the outside," he replied with skepticism.

"Maybe the power from my other self healed my injuries." Persephone smiled, glancing at her left arm, twisting it to test its function. "It happened before with the Keres. Do you think that means I can heal myself rather than taking those horrible-tasting potions Hecate brews?"

"Perhaps." Hades grumbled as he looked her over. "We need to know more."

"It can wait," Persephone grabbed his collar, pulling him to her lips. "Right now, I need you to touch me."

"If that's what you desire," he whispered, leaning down to kiss her neck.

Settling between her legs, Hades relaxed his weight over her. His body felt strong as his arms surrounded her. Entangling his fingers into her hair with one hand, cupping her head, Hades pulled her close. He trailed the other hand down her side, caressing her thigh, wrapping it around his hip.

Hades gave her that wicked grin she loved, then devoured her mouth, making her pulse rise to a frenzy. She ran her hand slowly down his chest and over his stomach to feel his muscles flex beneath her fingertips. His eyes rolled back into his head, moaning at her touch.

Her back arched at the pleasure of his weight pressing down on her, feeling his hard sex through his pants against her pussy, as she moved her hips, rubbing in circles. Hades kissed her neck just under her ear, eliciting a moan in response to his. A tickling sensation coursed through her body to the tips of her toes.

"Tell me you love me," he whispered into her ear.

"I...," she stuttered, then stopped herself from saying it, moaning instead.

Gaia knew she felt it, but saying it was so permanent. Love wasn't enough in their world.

Pleasure was all she could think about. Nibbling gently, he sucked on her left breast, then Persephone guided his head to the other nipple to share in his kisses. Able to reach him, she stroked his cock through his pants, wanting him free.

Remembering the time she tied him down in the woods and sucked him deep in her throat made her salivate with need, desiring his swollen shaft in her mouth. Her hands tugged at his belt to release his cock when he touched her stomach. Persephone's eyes widened, letting out a pained cry. Hades froze, sensing something was wrong.

"What?" He asked, removing his hand and sitting up. "What is it?"

"I don't know..." Persephone braced herself on her elbows. "Something hurts in my stomach."

When they both looked down, a bruise was welling in her abdomen.

"Shit," Persephone cursed, seeing the bruising grow.

"Persephone," Hades said, brows drawn with worry. "You have internal bleeding."

He wrenched his hands through his hair and moved away from her. Rubbing his face, his breaths ragged, Hades grabbed her pants and top.

"I'm fine," she said, covering her breasts with one arm.

She placed her hand on her stomach and called on the power, but it wasn't working. The bruise was getting worse.

"You don't look fine." His concern was stern but not angry. "Persephone, as much as I want this. Gaia, help me. I want this so bad. But you're hurt, and you need to heal. At the very least, you need rest."

"I don't want to rest," she protested.

Hades sighed and handed Persephone the clothes he held.

"I'll take you to Hecate and see if she has anything to help," he said, standing and turning his back to her.

"But..."

"Now, Persephone," Hades' said over his shoulder, face stern, informing her that she wouldn't win this time. "Get dressed. We're going."

Persephone huffed. "Fine."

She stood, pulling her bodice together and pants back

on, hating him for stopping what they both wanted.

"It's not fair. We were just getting started," she complained, sulking as she finished dressing.

Persephone walked by him when he grabbed her arm, stopping her. Pulling her against his chest, he smiled at her frustration.

"We have time." His hand caressed her cheek, kissing her pouting lips, nullifying her anger. "I promise I won't leave you unsatisfied again."

***

After dropping Persephone off at Hecate's apothecary, Hades went to his chambers. Throwing the chair out of his path, he cursed his wretched luck. His claws dug into the surface of his dresser as he begged for calm. Cock throbbing, it ached for her touch, needing to be inside her. She'd been so ready. Finally, Persephone made the first move. Her injuries weren't fatal, but he didn't want their first time to cause her more pain than necessary.

He thought about her glistening curls, shrouded in delicate fabric, rubbing against his cock. Fuck he wanted her so bad. But not like this. Not when she was injured. He wouldn't have known it until she cried out. Her pain felt like cold water had splashed on him. Hades cursed himself for being so careless with her after a battle. The right thing to do was to let her rest. It was a surprise that Persephone had been so eager to be touched. She hadn't been this warm to him since they'd been on Olympus. He was so stunned by her insistence all rational thought left him. When Persephone pulled him to her lips, Hades knew that he would have given her anything she wanted.

Her seduction was a nice change from her previous ire. Maybe she was coming around? Calm finally arrived as his senses recovered from her touch. Hades took long, deep breaths until his eyes had cleared. Wishing he knew how to understand her powers to help her, Hades paced the room. He'd spent so much time holding his own back. What could he offer?

Not since the Titanomachy had he used his full strength. Knowing his powers had grown since then from either age or experience wasn't helpful for her. There wasn't time for her to develop them as he did. Moreover, he had no idea what they could manifest into. Teaching Persephone to cultivate her powers would be difficult without a more significant threat. Besides the gods fighting among themselves, only a Titan was an actual threat to them. It's a good thing he had a few available to query.

Unfortunately, there was only one being who could tell him how her abilities would unfold or at least what her powers would mean to the world. A sense of dread and a vast knot settled in his stomach like a stone sinking into the river depths. Time was still his enemy. Yet this Titan might have the answers to her potential.

Resigning himself to return to the deepest part of Tartarus, Hades steeled his nerves to go inside. Appearing in a dark cloud outside the giant stone door that showed a being so monstrous it consumed him and his siblings, Hades straightened his shoulders, taking a deep breath. Unlike the gods, this Titan presented as an old male with aged skin and wrinkles. It was the kind of look none of the gods wished to emulate. No matter how old they became, they would remain in their prime. With a wave of his hand, Hades listened to the clicking, releasing the lock and opening the door. He entered the empty expanse of nothingness, feeling the hairs rise on the back of his neck as the door closed behind him and disappeared.

Surrounded by a darkness that made his pulse quicken, a light appeared in the distance. Hades followed the light, ending up at a large fireplace illuminating a table and two cushioned chairs facing one another. Hades sat down and waited, knowing it was only a matter of time before his father would appear.

The cold crept up his spine, sensing the imposing figure was near. Stepping into the light, the tall being with aging skin grinned with a smile stretched tight over straight teeth with Hades' and his siblings' blood still staining them. Cronos approached, towering over Hades, making the god clench his fists for control as his body filled with dread. The Titan king's thick beard grew to a point down to his collarbone, while his shoulder-length hair was wavy with curls of pepper and white sand. His thick, bushy brows matched his darker beard, and he wore a silver robe that opened to reveal his muscular, bare chest.

After so many decades had passed, Hades still shook remembering sitting in front of Cronos for the first time when they'd imprisoned the Titan. It was unsettling to stare into his father's cold, sandy eyes that could see the past, present, and future of their world. Cronos was the embodiment of time itself and, though he and his siblings had indeed tried, could never end, perish, or die. It was impossible.

"Why have you come to see me so soon, my son?" Cronos had asked with a raspy elder voice yet still very bass in tone. "It's not yet our time to play."

A board with squares and black and white pieces from their last game appeared between them.

Hades cleared his throat. "I need to ask you about something."

"Go on." Cronos lifted a finger, and a pawn scratched at the table as it moved with phantom fingers forward, ready to take his knight.

"I've met a goddess I wish to be my queen," Hades began. "But the rules and circumstances of our union are not in our favor."

"The rules never are," Cronos said, speaking slowly. "Did we wait for Ouranos to recede his cock from the All-Mother, Gaia? Or did I use the sickle and castrate him and take what we wanted?"

"I have no one to castrate," Hades replied, shaking his head as he moved the knight to safety. "It's Demeter who stands in my way."

Cronos raised a brow. "No need for a sickle when we discuss the goddess of grain and Harvest? Strange. I thought it was she who took it."

Cronos moved his finger, and the next pawn slid forward.

"It's now in her daughter's possession. Modified to suit her, no longer to you," Hades said with his hand on his chin as he scanned the board. "But the weapon is not why I'm here."

"Then speak your purpose and move your players," said Cronos, narrowing his eyes.

Hades took the pawn with his knight and removed it from the board. "I need to avert the destruction foretold of the prophecy that showed Persephone becoming my wife. Demeter is unhappy that I took her daughter."

"My daughter is stubborn, indeed, from what you've told me." Cronos shrugged, uncaring. "I knew her not."

Cronos gestured for the queen to move two spaces in line with the night.

"She's wreaking havoc on the surface looking for Persephone," said Hades, moving a pawn to block.

"Persephone," Cronos said, looking up in thought. "A good name for a queen. Is she new?"

"She is young," Hades replied with a nod.

"The females of this world are indeed more like our nebulous Chaos than we males. Unfortunately, we can not live without them." His father paused. "It is unwise to provoke them, or you will spend your days in misery."

"Chaos would have more sense." Hades folded his arms. "Demeter won't see reason until I return her daughter."

"Reason is not always a strength." The old Titan shook his head. "Too much reason creates rigidity in a world that requires chaos and order to work together."

Hades sighed. "Reason and order is how I live my life.

How I rule."

"And how you love?" Cronos asked, tilting his head.

Hades looked away. "It's complicated," he said, finally.

"Love has no reason," replied Cronos, who chuckled. "One cannot touch it, nor can one see it with their eyes. Yet if you find it, you will never be free from its curse."

"I've never experienced so much pain or confusion," said Hades, looking down, feeling the longing in his heart. "Living in you seems easier than this. Is love happiness or a ceaseless torture?"

"Both, and more." Cronos folded his hands together, relaxing in his chair. "The primordial Eros cursed us with such feelings. Even I am a slave to his arrow. Your mother and I were the first to suffer its poison. A gift ordered by the All-Mother as a reward for freeing her of a loveless union."

"You? Feel love for mother?" Hades asked, not believing it possible. "Forgive me if I don't understand how that's possible."

"You may think it impossible, given the circumstances that occurred." Cronos sighed with a pained smile. "But yes. I can feel love."

"I'm surprised to hear it." Hades looked away, hating the memory of his youth. "You never showed us an ounce of love."

"I witnessed what love wasn't from my father," Cronos said, a shadow crossing his eyes. "Ouranos forced himself on my mother countless times while she screamed in agony. With each ejaculation, Titans, Primordials, and Elementals she conceived. Gaia begged him to pull out and release us as her belly grew large, ready to burst. Her painful cries were our lullabies, her bitter tears our only sustenance. The sky ignored her pleas. Through her trauma, a prophecy, the very first, was born. And so, her curse was set in motion that her lover would one day fall to his own progeny. As such, Gaia called upon me to fulfill my destiny, giving me the weapon I used to castrate Ouranos. None of you would exist if I had not done what I did. The irony that I would receive the same prophecy was devastating. I did not wish for the cycle of progeny usurping the father to continue. I thought I was doing the right thing. For all of you."

"So you ate us because you loved us?" Hades asked, brow raised at the absurdity.

Cronos nodded. "Enough to attempt to spare you of what it would be to war with me, yes."

Shaking his head, Hades glared. "I find that hard to believe."

"I'm sure many would say the same about you, Hades, God of Darkness and the dead," replied Cronos, unphased by his son's anger. "How could one such as you, love, as you say?"

The question seemed idiotic to Hades. "I don't know. I just feel it. I can't stop thinking about her. My desires and affection, as well as this prophecy, bond me to her. Logic and reason have seemed to be the very gifts I lose when I even open my mouth to say what I mean around her. Everything I've done seems to either upset her, make her hate me, or ignore me altogether."

Cronos' eyes filled with sorrow and regret. "When Rhea left me and took Zeus with her, I felt as though I was missing a part of me. Time meant nothing, and all was darkness without her light. When I learned of her betrayal, I was gutted and sought to destroy the world if I couldn't have her by my side. My arrogance and refusal to see why she did what she felt she had to do led me to my ruin. And now I am trapped here without her."

Hades knew what it felt like to be separated from Persephone and hated it more with each passing day. To imagine an eternity of separation was too much to bear. He had to figure out a way that would never happen. The sadness in Cronos' eyes reflected his misery.

"How do you handle life without her?"

"Rhea is forever out of my reach. If I weren't deathless, I'd wish for it." Cronos sighed. "The decisions I made so long ago can't be undone. And she will never forgive me."

"What if she could forgive you?" Hades asked, thinking of his own decisions, forcing Persephone to the Underworld.

"She would never." Cronos shook his head. "Such a gift is beyond my ability to hope for."

"It's not forbidden to dream," Hades said, furrowing his brow.

"Dreams are for the gods," Cronos replied, clicking his tongue. "I have no use for them. But there may still be hope for you and this goddess. Dance with her into the stars and give her what her heart desires. Don't ever take away her choices, and listen when she speaks. The sound of her voice is the most precious gift and should never be squandered for pride."

"That's the first time you've ever given me good advice," Hades said with a slight laugh. "I wonder if her powers of siphoning life and gifts of creating life will allow her the strength to survive this world."

Cronos turned his sight to the fireplace and sat in pensive silence until he nodded, returning his sandy eyes to Hades.

"The goddess is rare in this world. There will never be another like her," Cronos said, leaning forward. "Together, you will save us all. But not without sacrifice."

"How?"

"You will find out soon enough," Cronos replied.

The Titan king stood and waved a hand over the table, which dissolved into sand that blew away, leaving the floor clear of debris. Cronos and Hades stood, and both chairs disappeared, leaving only the two beings before the fireplace. Cronos stepped forward, his robes dragging behind him, causing his shadow to engulf Hades.

"If I could go back and do it all over again, it wouldn't change anything," he said with a shake of his head. "If your destinies are intertwined, then all you can do is sit back and let the wheel of fate sail you to your destination. But I warn you. If you don't find a way to cherish your time with Persephone, you'll regret it as I do with Rhea."

Hades nodded, looking down, wishing he knew how to be with Persephone forever, fearing he'd fail and the world would end anyway.

Cronos smiled with a knowing pain that they both now shared. For the first time, Hades understood his father's sorrow and loneliness. Reaching out his hand, his father stopped and clutched his hands in front of him.

"Goodbye, my son," the old Titan said, closing his eyes. "Make the choices I failed to make. Choose love over power." He opened his eyes, tears welling but never falling, and smiled. "Until our next game."

Turning away, Cronos walked into the darkness, each step becoming bits of sand in swirling spirals until all that was left was the fireplace and Hades standing alone.

His footsteps were heavy as Hades left the space that held his father captive. A moment of sympathy grew inside him. His father did everything by force, and he was making the same mistakes. But what else could he do?

With a wave of his hand, the door appeared in front of Hades. Once past the entrance, the heavy door creaked to a close that boomed with the sound of rock falling over a cave entrance. His hands shook, and his chest pounded as he walked by Hera's door and then stopped. Turning back, he decided to go and see her against his better judgment. Hades didn't know anyone else who understood what being in his father's presence was like. And even though he was angry with her, there was no one else to talk to about it.

Hades opened the door and entered the descending steps down to Hera's cell. He walked over to her cage and was relieved to find her healed and dressed in her regal peacock feathered gown. *She must have finally had enough power to create it*, he thought. Which meant she was dangerous again.

"I see you're gaining your strength," he said, eyeing her gown.

Hera leaned against the arm of her chair. "In time, I'll have enough to leave here."

Hades chuckled and sat down on the large throne carved from the wall just for him to interrogate.

"Two visits in such a short time? You must be getting soft," She mused, dripping in condescension. "What brings you down here?"

Hades leaned back, crossing his legs. "I just spoke with our father."

Hera stood abruptly, walking toward the bars. "You spoke to Cronos?"

"I did."

"Why would you do that?" she asked with a shaking voice.

"I needed answers," he replied, tilting his head.

Hera huffed. "What could you possibly want to know from that monster?"

"I wanted to know what he..." Hades paused. "I wanted his advice on the issue with Demeter."

"You would ask him?" Hera shook her head. "Of all the people you would confide in, Hades."

"He has the foresight I lack," he said, staring at the floor.

"You can't be serious." Hera turned to look up at him, brows drawn upward in confusion. "Why?"

He sighed. "Because I have no one else to talk to that has any idea of what I'm dealing with."

"Oh," Hera scoffed. "You really are desperate to keep her, aren't you?"

"Cronos explained that his forceful ways pushed everyone away, and the hold he had disappeared as a result." Hades shrugged. "I thought it was helpful enough."

"Is that what he told you?" She asked, breathless, with her hand to her chest. "That he pushed us all away?"

Hades looked into her trembling eyes. "In a manner of speaking, yes."

"That fucking monster ate us, Hades!" Hera yelled, throwing up her hands. "You were the second. How could you not still feel the burning anger we all felt when we emerged from his tomb?"

"I never said I didn't."

"Then why would you even speak to him?"

"I visit him occasionally and play games to pass the time," he replied, looking away.

"Time," Hera sneered. "Time is never going to change what he did."

Hades narrowed his eyes at her. "Zeus destroyed Cronos as our father did to Ouranos. What's left in that cell is a shell of the Titan he once was. Let's not forget your husband is no benevolent father either. He still contains the one who would usurp his throne on Olympus inside of him with his other wife."

"Yes, you've already brought her up." Hera turned away, hands placed on her hips. "I'd almost forgotten about Metis. If I'm not mistaken, she still holds counsel in his head."

"She does." Hades nodded. "And you will be lucky you don't share her fate if your revenge continues."

"My mind is unchanged on that subject." She waved a dismissive hand. "But that's not why you're here. You came to ask me about Perspehone's emerging powers."

He clenched his jaw.

"Can't control her powers yet?" Hera teased. "Don't worry, she will. She just needs a little push to activate them fully."

"What kind of push?" Hades asked, inclining his head.

Hera tapped her lip with a long, red fingernail. "Oh, I don't know, something big like a war or maybe have her fight a Titan."

"You'd like that, wouldn't you?" Hades shook his head. "It's hard enough for one of us to fight them. You know what it's like when they're released. We barely survived. So I'm not going to let her do that."

"Why? Because she's too weak and will die?" Hera asked with a cackle.

Hades growled.

Clutching the bars, Hera came further into the light. "If you don't push her, she'll never become great."

"That's your way," Hades said, narrowing his eyes. "Not mine."

"My way is what you came here for. Right?" Hera folded her arms. "You came all this way to Tartarus to get advice from your enemies. Seems to me you're full of bad ideas. No wonder things are going so well for you."

Irritated by her sarcasm, Hades glared at Hera. "This was a mistake."

"The only mistake here, Hades, is leaving me to rot in this dungeon while Demeter is above destroying everything we fought to preserve. And even though we are at odds now, we haven't always been. I hate to admit it, but I've always had a soft spot for you, and I don't want to see you hurt... Too much."

"I've never wanted what happened to you either," he said, swallowing the lump of emotion he had for her. "You weren't always like this. I know how defenseless you were when Zeus first took you."

"He seduced me," she hissed, then calmed with a tear forming in one eye that never fell. "I thought he was a bird at first. Then, when I saw his true form, I fell in love with him instantly. But he tricked me, and I did the same to you and Demeter. Is that what you want to hear? That I was stupid? Young and naive? That I had no idea that he loved anyone other than me? Or that he'd had a wife previously? Well, it's true. Go ahead and laugh at me. I did love him when I convinced you to make him choose me. In the end, I was the fool. "

"You knew about his first wife?" Hades asked, raising a brow. "Why did you think he could change?"

"It's the curse of all females," she replied in a quiet voice filled with regret. "We all think we can change the ones we love to our desires. But in the end, it's a fool's journey."

"Is that what you believe?" Hades asked, staring at the wet stone walls. "That love is foolish?"

"She'll never love you, Hades. Not without her mother."

Hera shook her head, crossing her arms. "Her will is as stubborn as Demeter's. Of that, you can be sure. Let me ask you this. Has she even said she loved you in return?"

No, he thought, hating that she could be right.

The answer struck him in the chest. Maybe Persephone needed more time. Maybe her affections were an illusion in his mind.

Hades stood. "I'll just have to hope you're wrong."

"Hope," Hera sneered. "It's all bull shit. We are gods, cursed to live forever. What hope could we possibly have at happiness?"

Hades felt exhausted. "I should go. Goodbye, Hera."

"Live in your delusions all you like, Hades," she called after him. "It won't do you any good."

Seeing his father was more than he could handle under the best circumstances. But adding Hera was even more draining. Closing Hera's door, Hades appeared in his chambers, avoiding any notice of his return. He needed to sleep to escape his thoughts. Persephone would be busy healing, so he didn't want to disturb whatever rest she required. Laying in his bed, Hades closed his eyes and drifted into a deep slumber.

Bodies lay everywhere, frozen in the wasteland that was the surface. Once green and thriving, it now lay barren. Up ahead was a small home lit with firelight, and smoke billowed from the chimney with smells of cooked meat. Music played, much to his surprise after what he'd seen, so he wandered forward, curiosity driving his footsteps. His hand wiped away the condensation on the window to reveal mortals smiling and toasting with frothy beverages while singing and feasting.

The stark contrast to those who remained outside was fascinating to him. While some had remained in the cold, others had found refuge and joy together in warm homes filled with cheer. His curiosity peaked, Hades teleported inside, feeling the fire's warmth on his back. He walked among them and witnessed a sort of peace and love as they bonded. Jars of stored foods lined the shelves, and it appeared as though they prepared for a long drought of cold with their harvest drying along the walls. Yet they were not in despair as he had witnessed the gods before when he touched Persephone's hand. They were happy, even under these circumstances.

He didn't understand it. Myriads of mortals had gathered and were filled with joy and merriment together, even as the wind howled outside. Inside, it was warm and filled with life. Even the infant in the basket was pink and comfortable, cooing as the little female shook her rattle until she saw him. Her smile, followed by a giggle, made Hades step back. *Can she see me?*

He looked up to see the group had stopped their merriment and stared at him. Not with malice or fear. They smiled and tipped their cups to him with great cheers and joyful faces. Hades raised a brow in surprise. They were showing him respect, so he bowed his head in return.

Opening his eyes, Hades was back in his bed. He'd never experienced mortals seeing him before. It was a strange feeling. And to have them respect rather than fear him was most jarring. Something was changing. He could feel it. Maybe it was him. He didn't know. He rubbed his chest, feeling the warmth built from their reverence. Was this what Zeus felt? Hades had been invisible his whole life, rendered to the shadows. But to be in the spotlight and cheered was too much for him. It was uncomfortable, but also, admittedly. Nice.

Hades shook his head. It was only a dream. No one felt that way about him. How could they? Where would such a dream come from?

"Morpheus," Hades growled low in his chest.

Damned meddling Oneiroi, he grumbled, rubbing his face to clear his head of the strange dream.

CHAPTER 14 QUEEN

She stood watching her mentor hard at work on the damage done to the nymph earlier in battle.

"Will Mynthe survive?" Persephone asked at the door entrance to Hecate's lair.

"I'm not sure yet," Hecate replied, looking up from the potion bottle she mixed. "Do you remember anything?"

"Everything seems a blur, but yes, I remember." Persephone held her stomach. "You don't seem surprised by the outcome."

"Why would I be?" she asked, pouring a green liquid into a pink one. "I knew you'd win. I never doubted you. What's the last thing you remember?"

Persephone walked to the chair by the fire and sat, regretting not being more careful as the pain spread through her core.

"I was fighting Mynthe and impaled her on the sickle that turned into a scythe, which I was not expecting."

Hecate tilted her head. "And then?"

"I felt the other me's presence, and she began to take over. I could barely keep her away until I was losing consciousness." Persephone sat back, taking a deep breath as the pain eased. "This time, when I let her come forward, it felt like I was taking a back seat while she controlled my body, but I could see everything."

"Hmm." Hecate pointed her finger. "Looks like you have internal bleeding."

"How did you know? Nevermind. You're right about that," Persephone replied, placing a hand on her stomach as it ached.

Hecate turned to her stored bottles and brought out five different liquids. She began to mix them while Persephone waited.

"How long will she be unconscious?" she asked the Titaness.

"Maybe a few days? A week, perhaps." Hecate shrugged. "Nymphs don't recover as well as gods, even with my magic. But she will be fine, eventually."

Persephone sighed. "I didn't mean to do this."

Hecate paused her work, raising a brow. "Didn't you?"

"What? No, I wouldn't..."

"Persephone, I know your thoughts," Hecate said, grinding herbs with a mortar and pestle. "You were both angry out there. And you still haven't recovered from the trauma you experienced from your last big fight with Hera. It's no wonder your powers are so volatile."

The pain made Persephone wince as she sat forward. "I don't even know when it will happen again or why it's happening like this."

"We already know they come out when you are threatened or emotionally compromised," said Hecate as she added the herbs to the cauldron.

Persephone groaned. "Yes."

Nodding, Hecate stirred with her large spoon. "I would say under the heightened circumstances you faced, you might want to consider that fear and anger have been your constant state this entire time. To say nothing of your disheveled appearance."

The familiar fragrance made Persephone groan. "Please

tell me that potion won't taste like strawberries."

"What's wrong with strawberries?" Hecate asked, offended. "Be grateful I make you anything at all. Now you drink this and stop complaining."

Hecate turned to rummage through her bag. Finding a clear bottle, she filled it with the concoction and tossed it up to let it float to Persephone. The memory of strawberry made her stomach churn, wishing they could change it to the delicious pomegranate that was here. She drank it without hesitation, trying her best not to taste it, and felt her body relax as the potion went to work.

"Thank you," she said, handing back the bottle.

Hecate sat next to her. "Okay. Tell me what else you felt when your powers emerged."

"It was like I was in a fog as it happened. And yet, I felt a certain clarity." Persephone shook her head as she thought about the powerful sensation of the other taking control. "It's hard to explain, but it felt good when we shared the same space."

"Hmm." Hecate tapped her chin. "I wonder if sharing your abilities with the other might go against your nature as a Goddess of Spring?"

"Nothing has felt natural since I've been here."

Rolling her eyes, Hecate folded her arms. "It's not like you've given it a chance. You've been sour since you arrived. Honestly, it's not a good look for you. Thank goodness you're immortal, or you'd grow wrinkles as the mortals do from all the worrying you do."

"What else am I supposed to feel?" Persephone scoffed. "Gratitude for being kidnapped?"

Hecate narrowed her eyes. "Maybe a little bit. Yes."

"Are you serious?" Persephone's eyes went wide with shock, unable to believe what she was hearing.

"You know Demeter wasn't going to let you back out, and there was no other way for you to find any time to see Hades or be alone with him." Hecate leaned forward. "Without him taking the reins, you wouldn't have the chance to see if this life was right for you or not."

"How can you say that?" Persephone crossed her arms, pursing her lips. "In what universe would it be right to do what he did?"

Hecate sighed and stood to return to her work on Mynthe, her black sleeves freely dusting the table as she worked.

"He did ask permission," Hecate said with a side glance.

"From who?"

"Zeus."

"Zeus isn't my mom," Persephone protested.

"Okay." Hecate pinched the bridge of her nose. "So if you were still with your mom, unable to see this place, and had to decide based on your limited knowledge, would you have even considered his proposal?"

"Who says I'm considering it now?" She asked, folding her arms.

Hecate slammed her hand down. "Dark goddess, you try my patience."

Persephone startled. "What?!"

Growling, Hecate pointed her finger, shaking it. "You would have to be blind, brainless, or dead, or perhaps all three not to notice the tension coming off of you two when you are in a room together."

"I don't know what you're talking about." Persephone turned to look away. "I'm just trying to survive down here."

"While giving his lips a tongue bath when no one's around? Or how about almost absorbing the life essence of his mistress because she said mean things to you? Was it the new world he offered to build for you too much? A full tour of Tartarus? I mean, I didn't even get that..." Hecate grumbled. "Maybe it's the freedom to take his horse to visit Hera for a chat? Yeah, survival's looking difficult right now."

"Damn it, Hecate, stay out of my mind." Persephone shook her head, then stopped at that last comment. "Wait.

What did you say about Hades' horse?"

"Damn, was that a future thing?" Hecate snapped her fingers and turned away. "So hard to know which timeline I'm living with this prophecy dragging me all over the place."

Persephone stood from the chair. "Have you seen something else?"

Hecate smiled, turning back to Persephone. "Nothing to worry about. Though, if I'm being honest, I could use the Cronos stone right about now, and maybe that would help to see more of your powers."

"I hated that last experience." Persephone leaned against the table on her hip. "The last thing I want to do is confront my other self again."

"Yes, but you have to start being strong, Persephone. You have a kingdom to run and big goddess decisions to make that will affect all of us," Hecate said, returning to her cauldron to stir. "So if I were you, I would gather as much information as I could about above and below so you can end this paradox we all seem to be suffering."

"Until I make a choice, the future is uncertain, right?"

Hecate nodded. "Precisely."

"Fine." Persephone rolled her eyes. "I'll touch the stone again, but this is the last time."

"For now," Hecate said with a wicked grin. "Until then, what do you want done with her?"

Persephone looked over her shoulder at the nymph. "What do you mean?"

"We are in the land of the dead. Mynthe is on the brink of death, and you can either save her, or I can let her expire." Hecate raised her arms to the sky. "Congratulations! Your first big decision." The Titaness wiped her eye with a sniff. "I'm so proud that I'm here for it."

Persephone balked at Hecate's excitement. "I don't want to decide that."

"You will have to do it to be queen," Hecate replied, hands on her hips.

"What if I don't want to be queen? What if I choose to leave?" She asked, fidgeting with her hands.

"Spawn of Demeter," Hecate said, clenching her fists and teeth. "This indecisive, quirky, unbalanced, and unsure attitude was cute when you were young. But if you don't start acting like a goddess who matters in this world, who has a purpose and can freely decide what that purpose is, then perhaps you're right. You don't belong here. You don't deserve to be queen. You should just go back to your flowers in a field your mommy guards like Cerberus. It's time to grow up and bloom into the barbed blossom you desire to be."

Sighing, Persephone paced. "I need some time to think."

"We are running out of time, Persephone!"

"Okay! Okay." Persephone backed away, hands up in surrender. "Continue to heal her, and then meet me later in your oracle pools with the stone. I'll know my decisions by then."

"You'd better, Dread Queen," Hecate warned. "For our fates are in your hands, and I grow impatient."

Persephone tried to find Hades but found Thanatos instead.

"My queen," he said with a bow. "How may I assist you?"

"Where's Hades?" She asked, looking around.

Thanatos inclined his head. "He's in Tartarus."

Ceasing her search, she turned to Thanatos. "Why?"

"I didn't ask," he replied. "Is there something you need?"

"No." Persephone shrugged. "I can find him later. Do you know when he'll be back?"

"I don't, my queen." Thanatos bowed his head. "My apologies."

With a nod, she left toward the hall that led to their chambers. Once Thanatos turned the corner, Persephone bolted through the shadows, avoiding anyone seeing her. She snuck into the stables and found the black mare happily eating dinner. Aethone's head popped up, smelling the air, and turned to see Persephone holding an apple.

"Hey," she whispered. "You hungry?"

Aethone whinnied and kicked her door open, trotting over to the goddess. The mare ate out of her hand and clicked her hooves when she noticed another apple around Persephone's back. Nudging with her head, Aethone grunted in approval as she devoured the other apple presented.

"I wish I could understand you," said Persephone, petting the mare's nose. "But I know you can understand me. Hades is in Tartarus, and I was hoping you could take me to him."

Aethone narrowed her eyes, suspicious of the request, but nodded.

"Great," Persephone whispered, grabbing the saddle. "I know you can sense him. We have to move fast so no one sees us."

The red eyes lit up with excitement, signaling that she agreed. Mounting the horse, Persephone bent down to Aethone's twitching ear.

"Fly," she whispered, nudging with her heels.

Persephone dropped down from Aethone's back at the entrance to Hera's door, trying to catch her breath from the speed at which they arrived. The walls lit again with flaming torches, giving her a clear view of the carvings in the rock. Hera was shown in the battle against the Titans, leaping into the air and coming down with the swords that had rendered Persephone in two. Her blades impaled Cronos as they had done to Persephone, who shuddered at the memory. His symbols of time were as scattered as she had felt. She realized this fear would continue to overwhelm her emotions unless she faced it. Pausing to rub her chest where the old wounds, though gone, still ached, she steadied herself.

"Open," Persephone whispered with a shaking breath.

The walls lit up in light patterns, highlighting the battle scene's details before her. The door shimmered and disappeared, revealing the long stairway leading down to Hera. Amazed the command worked, Persephone descended the steps.

"Come in, Persephone." A sweet voice said from the shadows.

Hera sat with one leg crossed over the other in a chair that resembled a lesser throne with a light showing her wicked smile that never quite met her eyes. She rolled up a parchment she had been reading into her hands.

"I'd offer you a chair...But." Hera's smile turned to a grimace. "We both know you wouldn't take it anyway."

Persephone straightened her shoulders and steeled her nerve. "I'll just cut to the chase. When you said you sensed the darkness in me, what did you mean?"

Placing a finger to her cheek, looking off, Hera smiled. "You know that little thing you do when you drain your opponent's energy?"

Persephone looked away and crossed her arms around her body.

"Ah, I see." Hera chuckled. "I'm not the only one who has experienced your gifts. Tell me. Was it Hades? A lesser being, perhaps? I was surprised and impressed when you used it on me when we last fought. Though it pains me to confess, your little trick almost got me. But something was holding it back. Why?"

Should I tell her? No, she's too dangerous.

"What did you sense?" She asked, finally.

"Something that needed cutting out," Hera lowered her chin to look up at Persephone with her wicked side grin. "Of course."

Persephone instinctively stepped back.

Hera's smile widened. "I see you still fear me as you should."

"I'm not afraid of you..." her voice trailed off as her knees shook.

Seeing Persephone recoil, Hera rolled her eyes. "We both know that's a lie."

"I shouldn't be here," Persephone said, turning to leave.

"Oh, come on." Hera slapped down her scroll. "It's not like I can leave here. You said it yourself. Zeus isn't coming for me anytime soon, so I might as well make myself useful. Queen to Queen."

Her wink unsettled Persephone, but she had no one to confide in who had multiple powers as Hera did.

"What can you tell me about Hades and his role here?" Persephone asked, unsure where to begin.

"I would have thought you'd have figured that out by now." Hera leaned back in her chair and crossed her other leg over the other.

Persephone clenched her jaw, resisting the urge to run. "I see you have enough power to make your appearance look normal. I was hoping we could have a conversation as equals. Much as I despise your presence, I think discussing this with the only queen on Gaia is fair. I wish it weren't you, but it is."

"I'm touched you realize I'm the only queen." Hera placed a hand on her chest. "Finally, you're learning your place."

Persephone narrowed her eyes. "My place is with the deathless gods above with my mom."

"That's what they told you all your life, so why question it?"

"Because I've seen a new world, and I don't think I can return to being...."

"Weak?" Hera asked, leaning forward. "Power is intoxicating, isn't it?"

"That's one word for it," Persephone replied, clenching her fists.

"Feels better than fucking or any other pleasures out there," Hera said, caressing her neck. "Doesn't it?"

"I wouldn't know." Persephone's cheeks burned when she thought about sex with Hades as the desire overwhelmed her.

"You're kidding," Hera said, raising both brows, then laughed. "What a terrible little liar you are. Let me ask you this. You're so set on returning, but have you ever considered staying?"

"I've considered staying. But you know my mom won't rest until she brings me back," Persephone replied, trying to breathe.

"Yes. Demeter is a wet blanket. She ruins all the fun." Hera sighed. "You know I have no reason to be nice to you, so I'll just say the obvious. You're afraid of losing your mother's love if you choose to love another. You worry that Demeter could disown you. After all, she disowned all of us over a tiny fight."

"You threatened to kill me," said Persephone, crossing her arms.

Hera gave a dismissive wave. "A minor misunderstanding."

"A minor?..." Persephone choked back her anger. "You can't be serious."

"I'm sure we could have worked something out eventually," Hera interrupted, sounding bored. "I did let Leto's bastards come to Olympus unharmed."

"Your generosity astounds me," Persephone replied in a dry tone.

"Yes. I am a generous god," Hera said with a nod. "Contrary to what you believe, I did have a moment of empathy in your desire for Hades."

"A moment," Persephone scoffed. "More than I would have guessed."

"Oh, I know." Hera glanced at her nails. "It surprised me too. Indeed, I've taken a tiny feather worth of liking to you, pet."

"But you still want to kill me," said Persephone with a glare.

"True." Hera nodded with a shrug. "Surely, you can understand why. Would you willingly share Hades?"

"No."

"Here's some free advice and the last you'll get." Hera

stood painting at Persephone. "You might want to learn to control your powers fast, or you'll kill someone else."

"What?" A cold chill crept up Perspehone's spine.

Hera's wicked laugh echoed off the walls. "You think I don't know about your little fight with Minthe?"

Persephone's eyes were wide with shock. "How. How could you?"

Walking to the bars that separated them, Hera's face rested in the shadows they cast, leaving only her eyes and sinister grin illuminated.

"My pet, if you are going to be queen, you must learn to find your little birdies that keep you informed of everything."

"Who would spy for you down here?" Persephone asked, wondering now who to trust.

"I may be down here as your husband's prisoner, but I know everything happening above and below." Hera's eyes darkened as they glowed a vibrant teal. "Including Zeus' more recent indiscretions."

Persephone scoffed. "Let me guess, another nymph?"

"A Titanese." Lifting a fist, Hera clenched it till it shook. "One I intend to strangle when I get out of here."

"Ah, I see." Persephone knew this scenario all too well. "She's pregnant."

Hera's pale face turned red as she gnashed her teeth. "Not for long."

"What do you plan to do about it?" Persephone asked, finding sympathy for Hera's anger. "Are you going to kill her too?"

"No." Hera smiled. "I'm going to take his throne. There is no greater revenge."

"You can't be serious," Persephone said, eyes wide. "That's impossible. He would never let you."

Hera laughed deep in her throat. "When my plan is in motion, he won't be able to stop me."

Persephone pinched the bridge of her nose for patience. "You can't stop scheming, can you? Did you ever think maybe

Zeus cheats because of you?"

"My pet, when you grow older, you will realize that we goddesses, females, and mates do not make anyone do anything they don't already choose to do. As the goddess of marriage, my duty is to remain by his side, but that doesn't mean he should be conscious."

Persephone shook her head. "I don't know what I would do in your position. But I have to believe that there is a better way to lead than by fear and manipulation."

"Fear is the only way to garner loyalty and respect."

"I don't agree."

"You're young." Hera walked back to her chair and sat. "Just wait until Hades betrays you. Then, we will see how your naive opinion changes. For now, run along, pet. Or better yet, run home to your mommy so you'll never discover anything for yourself."

"You have more to you than just being a wife," Persephone argued. "Can't your other abilities be used for something better than all of this jealousy?"

"My father consumed me after my mother sacrificed me to live in darkness, knowing nothing: no love, warmth, or touch."

"That sounds awful."

"Beyond words, pet. Beyond words." Hera looked off as though remembering the loneliness and gave a faint laugh. "You know. I thought then there was nothing worse about my time there. But then Zeus rescued us," Hera said with a mocking sneer. "Of course, we had to be grateful. There was no time for any other feeling. No time to be angry that our mother chose to save him over us. One by one, Cronos ripped away any chance of an easy life you blessedly enjoyed."

"What happened after you were released?" Persephone asked, wondering what that would have been like.

Hera inclined her head, looking away. "We took up swords and shields and fought. As gods, we could manifest our bodies and armor as Zeus had done and joined him. In truth, as we sat in stasis of development for years, we were no better than infants when we emerged. We battled for over ten years, imprisoning every Titan who opposed Zeus until only a few who had negotiated their freedom remained."

"I still don't understand how you two ended up together." Persephone sat on the stone-carved chair, fascinated. "And how did you manifest your powers so quickly to fight Titans?"

Hera chuckled under her breath, poured some wine, and drank the entire glass in one gulp.

"I think that's enough stories for today, pet. Why don't you come back another day and I'll tell you more tales. I think I'm feeling too tired for guests now."

Persephone stood to leave but stopped shy of the entrance.

"I know we can never become friends, Hera. Perhaps one day we won't have to be enemies."

Hera sat back into the shadows. "On that day, pet, I will assuredly be dead."

Taking the long steps upward and closing the door behind her, Persephone was lost in thought as she turned and ran into a hulking form that glared down at her and grabbed her wrist.

***

Wanting to check on Persephone's injuries, Hades teleported next to Hecate, scaring the Titaness, who screeched when he appeared.

"Hades! I could kill you for popping in behind me unannounced," she said, clutching her chest.

"You do it to me all the time," he replied, rolling his eyes.

"That's fair," Hecates said, nodding. "What brings you here, Lord of Darkness."

"I'm looking for Persephone." He glanced around. "She should be here."

"Oh, she left a while ago."

"Left? Where?"

Hecate's eyes went wide. "Uh, Oh…"

"Hecate?" Hades narrowed his eyes at the Titaness. "What did you do?"

"I may have suggested to her to visit a certain queen in your dungeon by accident," she said with a sheepish smile. "I forgot she hadn't done it yet, and it just popped out of my mouth."

Hades pinched the ridge of his nose. "You've got to be fucking kidding me."

"I'm sorry," she pouted. "I'm all over the place in my head space right now. I promise I didn't mean to."

"And how did you tell her she would arrive there?" He asked, folding his arms.

"Oh, that's easy." Hecate smiled. "Your mare took her."

Hades took a deep breath, closing his eyes, trying to find patience. "Of course she did."

"Persephone must have finished speaking with Hera by now," said Hecate, waving a hand to shoo him away. "You should go to her."

Without another word, Hades appeared next to Hera's door, where he found Persephone sneaking out and running right into him. Before she could escape, he grabbed her arm and pulled her to him.

"What are you doing here?" He growled and glared accusingly at Aethone, who looked away.

"Hades. I…," Persephone stuttered.

"Nevermind," he barked, dragging her as he stormed to his horse. "We're going home."

Hades lifted her onto Aethone's back. Getting up behind her, he wrapped one arm around her waist and grabbed the reins. With a snap, they were galloping into the air.

"What were you thinking?!" He bellowed, setting Persephone down from the mare, safely back in his kingdom.

"I was trying to understand what this is," she said,

holding out her empty hands.

"And you thought speaking to the one who hurt you would solve your problems?" He asked, amazed at the audacity.

"So it's fine if you speak to Hera but not me?" Persephone asked, placing her hands on her hips with her chin up.

"You are not allowed to be in Tartarus without my knowledge," he argued. "Something could have happened to you!"

"You should be more concerned with me doing something terrible to others," she replied, folding her arms, grumbling.

Hades pointed toward the exit. "I told you to go heal with Hecate."

She shrugged. "I did."

Hades growled. "You should have stayed there until I returned."

"I went looking for you, but you were gone." Persephone stood shoulders squared, oblivious to the danger she'd put herself in.

"How did you know where I was?"

"Thanatos told me."

"So you followed me?!" He yelled, scaring away the attendants.

Hades would have to speak to his general about this. His anger was boiling. What was happening in his kingdom that these things kept happening? The control he boasted might as well be a mere suggestion.

"Not exactly," she said, pouting. "I thought if I could speak to Hera alone, I could learn something useful, and I did."

"That doesn't even make sense." Hades threw his hands in the air. "Hera is a master manipulator, and you just walked in there to chat? What sort of lies did she fill your head with?"

"She's going to get out one day, and I can't be always looking over my shoulder." Persephone looked down at her feet. "I wanted to know what powers she had and to see how that would help me understand mine."

"This is fucking ridiculous." Hades ran his hands through his hair, pacing. "I forbid you to go back."

Persephone stomped her foot, pointing a finger at him. "Hades, I will not be controlled by you or anyone else!"

That stopped him. Remembering Cronos' words, he calmed his fury.

"I don't want to control you," he sighed. "I want to protect you."

"That goes both ways." She stepped close enough to glare up at him. "But I can't do that if I live in constant fear."

He grabbed her by her shoulders. "I told you I will always protect you."

Wrenching her arms free, she stepped back. "So I'm just supposed to walk around as a ticking time bomb that could hurt those I care about? There are some things you can't save me from, Hades. Not even myself."

Persephone turned on her heel and stormed off. Hades growled, kicking a pale into the wall as the contents splattered. As angry as he was, he felt a twinge of pride, knowing she was trying. That joy left him as he saw his horse sneaking into her stable.

"You," he said, pointing an accusing finger. "Stop right there, Aethone."

Hades was furious that Aethone had taken Persephone to see Hera. His mount had never let anyone but himself ride her, let alone go to Tartarus without him. When Persephone was out of hearing range, he turned on his closest companion.

"Hera could have killed Persephone in Tartarus without me there!" He yelled at the mare.

Aethone's eyes shot blood red as she narrowed them down at him.

I don't know about you, dark and all-powerful god, but I find it very difficult to resist her. Aethone snorted at him.

Grumbling, Hades relaxed his shoulders and came up with his hands open. She let him near, and he raised a gentle hand to pet her mane to soften her.

"She is hard to resist, isn't she?" He sighed. "Can you tell me what happened?"

We rode there without interruption, and she asked me to stay at the doorway. After about a half hour, she came back. Aethone whinnied as she spoke.

"What could she possibly have to say to Hera?"

I don't know, but she was very irritable when she returned. She reminds me of you. Aethone chuckled and shifted her mane as Hades walked over and leaned against the wall rail.

"Hera must have said something. Who knows what scheme she's planning."

Should I not take her anymore to where she wishes?

"No, I would rather know she's with you than anyone else. At least she'd be safe."

I failed when the Keres attacked. I will not fail you again, Hades. Aethone's eyes lit up with rage pulsing through them.

"Relax, Aethone. I think Persephone will be able to handle herself from now on. It's her emotions I'm worried about. How can I convince her to stay if Hera is poisoning her mind?"

The goddess is strong.

"Yes, she is. More than she knows." Hades sighed. "No matter what. Keep her safe. Even If I'm not there."

I won't fail you again...

I know you won't. Hades petted her mane and gave her over to the stable daemon.

He needed some quiet, so he disappeared to his war room. Hades slumped into the chair near his fireplace and poured some pomegranate wine with mixtures of berries and dry tannins with the reduced sweetness he preferred. It was a favorite among the court. The color reminded him of her hair and those beautiful rosebud lips when she transformed.

Another day passed when he found her training in the pits. He was impressed she could discern the difference between the good and evil beings. The ones she defeated without mercy were always worthy of destruction. Her cuts were deep and powerful. Yet if a being was kind and showed compassion, she refused to cut them down as they even cried and demanded of her that they receive punishment. Instead, she offered her hand and helped them out of the arena.

Her kindness was so palpable that even those she fought against felt they deserved whatever retribution she meted out. It was truly astonishing. Her ability to discern goodness, even in a moment of passion, made him realize that his choice was right. Her work with Hecate was paying off. Hades could find no fault in her decisions in each fight she chose. When she was up against a minotaur who loved to rape, she showed no mercy whatsoever. Her first move was to remove his horns and cut him to pieces inch by inch while evading his power moves. Indeed, her skills of stealth and speed had improved every day she trained.

Her sweat-slicked body raised her sword when she met victory. His pride was overwhelming. He refused to show it and remained stoic with each battle. Next, Persephone fought a snake beast, defeating him quickly. When he called for mercy, she gave it. He had to give her more challenges. Bringing forth a beast of rock form, she took so many hits, he almost went to the pits himself to stop the battle. However, at the last moment, she used her powers to take the beings and tore them to pieces. The words Dread Queen echoed over the halls of the entire kingdom. Their praise of her fed him stronger than the souls that came to cross the Styx.

Most were unwilling to fight her after what happened to Mynthe, who still hadn't recovered. When she called for more, he had no choice but to test her new abilities. Hades stood and entered the arena, offering the challenge she desired.

The challenge sent the crowds into a frenzied excitement, shaking the walls and sending shards of debris to fall and crumble around their feet. He enjoyed this feeling. The energy emanating from the crowd gave him a powerful high. Ignoring the soulful protests of their fallen comrades, he fought his way through the combatants to reach Persephone.

Each daemon fought him with the skill of decades of training yet fell quickly to his blows. Flashes of light glinted off steel as he blocked them, keeping his breath calm. With sweat pouring from his opponents and most barely on their feet, Hades smiled, knowing he had only just warmed up.

He moved quickly to block a cut that would have removed his head. Another blow came swiftly to the other side of his shoulder that he deflected with ease. They knew his ability to predict movement with calculated ease and sought to counter his speed. So far, he thought they were doing a damn good job of it. Thunderous chants and cheers erupted when the few remaining combatants came for him. They surrounded the dark God, forcing him to hold his position. Eyeing each one, he waited for them to make their next move.

A daemon lunged at him with a spear, his fangs glistening and deadly sharp. He thrust with incredible accuracy, forcing Hades to duck and block with his sword. The faster he moved, the more power he felt coursing through him, threatening to rip free. Another hairy beast, half man and half bull with horns, wielded a battle ax to cleave Hades in half. The powerful strikes were enough to sink the ax into his shoulder as he blocked the furious barrage. The daemon firmly pressed the ax into Hades' shoulder, finally cutting through. Feeling blood trickle down his arm, Hades' control was beginning to slip as his eyes grew dark as obsidian.

The spear, aimed true to Hades' side, stopped in the clutches of clawed talons that thrust the spear past him through the one he held with his sword. The fear on their faces when they realized he was turning made him pull back. He ripped the spear from its chest, spun it, and pierced its owner's stomach. He moved to put more distance between them, only to be met by one leather-clad female whose strike forced him to move back with each attack. He blocked and parried her attacks, then locked them close. Her breasts held tight with straps glistened with sweat. Seeing his eyes flickering, she smiled.

"You're holding back," she said seductively, teeth clenched as she strained to hold him back. Her eyes blazed a bright violet, betraying her emotions, then resumed their normal shade as she smirked. Was she controlling them now to distract him? Her thigh locked between his legs, rubbing against his hardening shaft. She looked down, giving an appreciative nod and wink before shoving him back and kicking him in his gut. He stumbled back and slid to a halt. She charged forward, swinging with deadly accuracy. Their moves were only visible to creatures who could keep up with their speed, and he locked them together again.

"You know I can't," he replied.

Releasing her, she fought dual-bladed, striking with enough speed to force him to use his powers. He appeared behind her, wrapping his open arm around her throat, holding her against him.

"There are many other things I would rather be doing to you right now," Hades growled into her ear.

"Don't go easy for my sake. It's no fun." She threw her head back, slamming into his nose.

He roared, reeling backward, losing his vision for a moment. Regaining sight, a fourth daemon attacked from the shadows. Hades saw the traces of energy and the glint of light before the being appeared in a cloud. He quickly dodged the sword aimed at his chest which he dodged. Hades elbowed the now fully formed creature's face. Refocusing on Persephone, her attacks came faster as he continued to fight her and slash through each blow.

"Come on. You don't want to disappoint the crowd." She taunted, slamming him in the face with the but of her sword.

He wiped the blood from his nose and smiled. "I know better than to release my powers against you, my love."

She charged forward with a warrior's cry, pushing him backward and thrusting her sword through his left thigh. He clenched his teeth, tilted his head, and smiled, feeling the blade scrape against his bone. She wrenched her sword out and pulled back to run him through. She had hit his artery. His healing was draining too much energy, leaving him slowed enough for the glowing-eyed daemons.

Finally, she got cocky. He knew she would. In an instant, he was on her. His fists met her face multiple times, slamming his knee into her gut, forcing her to bend over, gasping for air. Without hesitation, he spun on his heel and flipped, smashing his foot into her ribs so hard the crowd could hear her bones crack as she fell backward, cursing as the wall crumbled behind her.

The match was over, and the crowd's cheers rocked the cavern. He touched his wounded leg to see the damage. Shit, she really got him this time. Blood ran down his sword arm and inner thigh in a gushing flow that would kill a lesser being. Dripping onto the hard stone, he stood, catching his breath and observing what remained of his challengers. Those who remained conscious held their wounds, groaning on the floor. Looking back at Persephone, she was already up and gone.

He turned and saw her in a flash just before she opened her sickle into a giant scythe and hooked his sword, wrenching it from his grasp. Hades tumbled, grabbed his weapon, and stood facing her, knees bent, ready for her next attack. Flying at him with deadly aim, she brought her weapon down on him so hard the ground cracked beneath his feet and shook the cavern. He flipped her and spun her in one swift move, connecting their lips in a passionate embrace. She melted into his arms and deepened their kiss. He was about to break their kiss when she spun out of his grasp, appearing behind him with her blade to his throat.

"Declare me the winner," she said with that honeyed tone he loved.

"Always, my love," he whispered, raising his hands, allowing her to get up and stand before him as the last warrior standing.

With a raise of his hand, the crowd grew silent, awaiting Hades' judgment. "Underworld! What say you? Shall we give them a new life for a good battle, or are they unworthy of your respect!?" His deep voice bellowed to the arena, which exploded with booming applause.

Hades opened his fist. The glowing light emerged from each form that lay crumpled on the floor. As the light glowed inside their bodies, each faltering soul shot bright inside their chests. Lurching forward, they coughed as their life force returned. The crowd cheered as they all rose and stood at attention, awaiting Hades' commands.

"Congratulations to all of you," He said to them, returning to the crowd. "Especially your queen and now your champion."

The Chthonic crowd went wild, their roars and energy bursting through the mountains that held them.

"Welcome to my warrior ranks!" Hades shouted to the masses, chanting Dread Queen over and over. "Congratulations, you've earned it."

Persephone sheathed her weapons and followed Hades to her throne. They sat watching as the drink, food, and dancing filled the halls. Each creature that lived in the underworld enjoyed their home, which was a sanctuary for them. Hades observed the merriment of his court while indulging in the flavor of his latest wine harvest.

She smiled up at him as he kissed her hand. For Persephone, he would happily wait an eternity for her to forgive his selfishness. Her smile intoxicated him. Her skills had improved, and now he felt confident she could hunt on her own or at least with a small team. He would always worry about her, but her performance today filled him with pride. His wife would show the world how formidable she was once her training ended. He wondered how Hecate fared with the progress of using her powers.

CHAPTER 15
ELYSIUM

Each new victory she acquired earned her praise and respect from the combatants. The new skills Persephone acquired with her scythe gave her more confidence, which she desperately needed. Her defeat of Mynthe hadn't seemed to assuage their admiration for her, though maybe it should have. She couldn't change the punishment for the nymph but felt better that she could assist Hecate in keeping Mynthe out of Tartarus, even if it was the last thing she wanted to do.

"What a clever idea, Persephone," Hecate said with a cackle. "Turn Mynthe into a plant and seal her in that form for the hundred years she owes. It's brilliant!"

"I don't want her anywhere near Hades while we figure out our... Relationship." Persephone tossed in a few herbs, changing the brew's color from red to green in the cauldron. "I also don't want her to sit in the dungeons of Tartarus over petty jealousy. It doesn't feel right."

"You're a credit to your mother," Hecate said, conjuring the herbs over to her. "I would have let her suffer, though you don't seem to have the same vindictive nature as the rest of us."

Mynthe would live. *Not for long if she ever rechallenged me again*, she thought. Though not ideal, becoming an herb was better than death or torture. When her sentence was up, Hecate had promised to bring Mynthe back.

"I don't want to become like Hera," Persephone replied, watching the liquid churn. "If I sent Mynthe to Tartarus, I would be no better than her."

Persephone was glad she wouldn't have to endure the nymph's taunts anymore, at least not for a while. Hera's words rang in her head. The idea of anyone seducing Hades made her blood boil. She refused to allow a mistress to creep around her bed, no matter how benevolent she was. However, torture wasn't the answer.

"I need you to use your nature gifts to choose her species," said Hecate, finishing her spell.

"Can I down here?" Persephone asked, her face bathed in a green glow, standing next to the cauldron.

"I don't see why not," Hecate replied, pausing her stir. "There's some plant life to pull from if you try."

Persephone looked around. "I haven't seen anything I can use."

"True, there isn't much here to access." Hecate continued to stir the brew. "But just because you can't see it doesn't mean you can't draw from the available flora. Close your eyes and extend your power outward to find it."

Persephone did as she was told and found a source nearby. An orchard of some kind was close. She reached out, feeling its life force, and drew only a tiny bit. It was sluggish, but she felt the vines in her palm awaken and sprout in glowing sparkles from her palm.

"See?" Hecate chuckled. "I knew you could do it."

Persephone's eyes widened in shock. She'd thought that her powers didn't work down here, but the truth was, she had been too distracted to try. Though the energy was far weaker, it was there glowing in her palm.

"How is this possible?" Persephone extended her hand

over the liquid and let the vine touch the bubbling goo. "I thought I couldn't use this ability here."

"The only limits you possess are the ones in your mind, my darkling."

Hecate used a syringe to draw in the fluid and injected its contents into Mynthe's neck. The nymph's body convulsed, shaking violently, bowing her back. Suddenly, she went still and faded into sparkling green light until she became a small stem with a few fragrant leaves and roots.

"There we are," said Hecate, picking up the baby sprig and placing it into some dirt in a clay pot. "I shall call this plant mint."

Persephone rolled her eyes. "How original."

"What?" Hecate asked, lifting the pot and placing it under a floating sunstone. "I thought it was appropriate. She'll make an excellent addition to a cocktail."

"Have we finished here? I have more training to do," said Persephone on her way to the door. "Same time tomorrow?"

Hecate smiled, satisfied with her creation. "Don't be late."

"I wouldn't dream of it."

She was beginning to find her place among the Chthonic court and enjoyed the tournaments held for Hades. Secretly, she was thrilled with each competition that showed what everyone was capable of. It had become almost a who's who of dark Underworld beings showing off their skills with a glee she was beginning to understand.

When Persephone entered the throne room to watch the latest wrestling match in the arena when a whisper crept up behind her. Turning, she faced a table nearby covered in horns of wine, fresh fruits, and savory meats. Gaia's words repeated in her head. *The choice is yours*, kept echoing in her brain. As if lured by a spell, she grabbed half a pomegranate and held a cut open half of the large fruit in her palm. It was cold in contrast to the heat that surrounded her. Persephone had always loved this fruit in wines. She wondered if the orchard she felt earlier was their source. The deep red seeds looked like rubies, ready to burst. They appeared so delicate she picked six, which fell into her palm. Their color was mesmerizing, reminding her of Aethone's eyes.

Persephone knew that if she ate these seeds, the laws of the Underworld stated that she must never leave. *Perhaps it wouldn't be such a bad thing.* She could have Hades and a kingdom to look after. If she did this, there would be no turning back, and Persephone would be forcing her mother's hand to stop the storms above. Maybe then she could also figure out a way to see her mom.

Persephone rolled the rounded, hexagonal-shaped pebbles in her hand, thinking about her options. *Each seed has twelve sides to match the twelve months*, she considered in her mind. It was time for her to decide what choice to make. Something that Gaia had said about having them both resonated with her. Perhaps she could? But the only way that would be a guarantee was if she ate them.

"You've done well in the tournaments, my queen," a voice said behind her, startling her.

Persephone put the seeds in the pocket hidden in her corset, then turned to see Nyctimus smiling at her.

"Oh! Nyctimus," Persephone said, trying not to act suspicious. "That's kind of you. Honestly, most of you are better fighters than I am."

"After what I witnessed, that's impossible." He grabbed an apple and took a large bite. "Keep challenging yourself. With your talent, I bet you could take on a Titan one day."

"Talent is one way to describe it," she sighed. "I miss my other abilities from the surface."

"Don't have the juice down here?" He asked, taking another bite.

Persephone shrugged. "Not enough. Maybe a few flickers after practicing with Hecate, but nothing like the vines I could create before."

Nyctimus laughed. "Yeah, I remember."

Leaning casually on the table next to her, he took a few pomegranate seeds scattered on the table and popped them into his mouth.

She watched with envy as he crunched on the sweet arils. Persephone felt her stomach growl. She wanted wine so bad right now that she could almost taste it. Her resolve was slowly waning as she watched him indulge his hunger. Gods, she needed a distraction.

Persephone folded her arms and leaned against the table. "You never told me how you turned into this."

Hades had told her the tale from his perspective but wanted to hear Nyctimus tell his story.

"It was revenge for my father offending Zeus," he said, eating a juicy rib and tossing it aside.

"He murdered you, didn't he? Your father?" She asked, envy making her mouth water, watching him chew.

"Yes," Nyctimus looked down momentarily, swallowing hard. "I was a child. My father thought he could trick Zeus into eating human flesh at a grand feast prepared for the gods. But when Zeus discovered it was a child sacrificed instead of cow, venison, or elk, your father vowed revenge at the insult."

"Human?"

"It's what they call themselves."

"But not you?"

Nyctimus shook his head. "I'm not human, not anymore, at least."

"I see," she said with a nod.

"My father was the first werewolf. For behaving as a beast with no regard to the god's better senses, I believe, is how Zeus put it...." A dark shadow came over his eyes as he remembered. "Unlike myself, Lycaon is unable to change back into his human form. So he wanders, wreaking havoc on anyone who crosses his path. Much like I was doing for a time."

"Like when I found you?"

"Yes. I believed I was no better than he," he sighed. "That is until the moon looked at me differently."

"You mean Artemis?" She asked, watching his cheeks turn red at her best friend's name.

"When I was on Olympus, she would visit me and bring me food." He looked up to the sky they couldn't see. "She didn't make me feel like a monster like everyone else. For that, I will always be grateful."

Persephone smiled at how sweet it was. "How were you brought back?"

"I remember darkness with a constant fog that drifted through a sparsely wooded area where I was nothing," he said, crossing his arms.

"Asphodel," she replied.

Nyctimus nodded. "Indeed."

"Then what?"

Nyctimus gave a heavy sigh. "I don't remember much, but from what I know, I merely woke up. My entire family was already dead. My father killed them all, and I awoke to carnage, still a child but now very changed when the moon was high. When I could, I left my home and wandered for the next couple decades."

"Do you know why Zeus cursed you as well?" She asked. "Weren't you innocent?"

"The rules of Hades have consequences," he said, looking down and grabbing a piece of steak to chew. "I imagine if the rest of my family had lived, it would have affected them as well. My blood is tainted, my queen. No maiden would want me now. So my place is here where I can be of use."

"I don't believe you're tainted," she said, furrowing her brow. "You have more use than fighting. Maybe one day you'll be free of all this."

"That may be, my queen," he said with sorrow in his eyes but a smile to hide his pain. "But today is not that day."

Hades approached them, making her clear her throat and tilt her head toward Hades, to which Nyctimus took the hint, bowed without another word, and walked away from her.

"What did Nyctimus want?" Hades asked with a growl,

eyeing the wolf with suspicion.

"He was telling me of how he came to be a wolf," she said, watching the wolf leave. "Nyctimus said his blood became tainted after being sacrificed to Zeus for a feast offered by what he called humans."

"It's true," Hades said, turning back to her. "Some tribes of mortal humans would sacrifice their children for us. We never asked for it, but humans do it anyway. They seem to think that we will care enough to give them favors if they do this. Experiencing Cronos sacrificing us, Zeus wanted the practice to end, so he sent a powerful message."

"To curse the human's entire family to become Lycaens?" She asked, raising a brow.

"Not exactly." Hades shook his head. "Zeus wanted to turn just the father into one. Then he set him loose on his family to destroy any prosperity they'd achieved."

Persephone pondered what he said for a moment. "Why did Nyctimus become one?"

"Remember what I said about taking souls from my Underworld and why I don't allow it?" Hades asked, to which she nodded. "His curse is one of the reasons why. Humans tend to transform into unforeseen beasts and monsters upon unnatural resurrection. Because of the curse, it affected Nyctimus when he returned to the mortal realm."

"So it's happened before?"

"Yes. Nyctimus isn't the only humanoid monster running around in this world and others." Hades narrowed his eyes. "But if I can help it, he will be the last."

"Do all humans who return from the dead become cursed as some sort of beast?" She asked, remembering how she met the wolf. "Nyctimus seems to be able to control his instincts."

"Barely," Hades replied with a scoff. "Usually, what has happened is there is a period of extreme confusion, and the horror of death is still with them, resulting in psychological trauma. Humans don't handle resurrection well, even under the best circumstances. Unfortunately, because of their limited minds, returning to the living world leads to the death of many mortals, humans, and so on. It's why we needed to hunt Nyctimus down. Had we not intervened, he would still be out there hurting others. As much as I like my kingdom filled with souls, I don't abide unnecessary death."

Persephone furrowed her brow. "What's the difference between Zeus' treatment of him and yours?"

Hades inclined his head. "Here, Nyctimus can overcome his lack of control and become a valuable member of this realm. Up there, his nature would be exploited and used as amusement."

"Aren't the tournaments for amusement?"

"Perhaps." Hades looked away and sighed. "May I show you something?"

"What is it?" Persephone asked as she clutched her hands behind her back.

Hades held out his hand and waited for her to take it. When she did, he transported them to a field filled with rows of pomegranate trees. The orchard was massive, with a slight mist that hung in the air surrounding them. *The sky is an illusion*, she thought to herself. It looked like dusk at harvest, with oranges, reds, pinks, and gold in the rays coming from a seemingly infinite horizon.

"Hades, what is this place? Another realm?" She asked, looking around.

"Over there is the winery," he said, pointing to a large building on the north end of the orchard. "Where my wine is stored. And somewhere around here is the orchardist."

"It's beautiful," she marveled, touching one of the branches that bent toward her hand.

She could feel the tree's energy as she had before. Persephone's powers of nature welled within her as the flowers bent toward her open palm.

"I know you brewed wine at your home in the Meadow." Hades reached up and touched a pomegranate, plucking the ripe fruit, and handed it to her. "I thought you may enjoy this orchard to make wine here."

Persephone smiled wide. "Oh Hades, it's incredible! How many trees do you have?"

He smiled at her. "I don't know. You'll have to count them."

"It looks like it will take forever," she said, seeing no end to the rows of trees.

"I guess you better start then," Hades chuckled.

She'd enjoyed making wine at home. Her favorite pastime was to taste the different blends and swirl them in her mouth to determine whether each batch would be for ceremony or daily use.

Hades took the pomegranate from her hand. He pulled the fruit apart to show her the seeds that shone in the light, beckoning her to take one.

"Taste this," He whispered close to her ear. "Stay with me, and all of this will be yours."

"I can't...," she said, shaking her head while getting lost in his eyes.

She wanted to. Gaia knew how much. But she couldn't stay.

"Please," he said, with a plea in his tone. "Stay with me."

"Don't you think I want to?" She asked, wanting to cry.

"Tell me you love me, and I'll believe anything you say." Hades pressed his forehead against hers, holding the fruit between them. "Say it, and we can be together with just one taste."

She wanted to say it. For so long, she had denied that she longed for Hades and wished this situation could be easy. But it wasn't. She did love him, but it didn't matter. Too much was at stake if she stayed.

"I...," she stuttered, then turned and ran from him, finding the exit and leaving him standing there alone.

***

Why wouldn't she wouldn't say it?

He stood there holding his last hope in his hand. Dropping the fruit, it landed with a thud at his feet as the tears welled in his eyes. He would have let one fall, but the smoke of his general next to him made him clear his throat.

"My Lord." Thanatos bowed. "The judges have agreed to grant you the new realm of Elysium."

Hades nodded. "Prepare the kingdom to leave my throne room. I need to build enough power to build it."

"Of course."

"Thanatos," Hades said, holding up a hand to stop the god from leaving. "Instruct the mystery god, Lakkhos, to lead the purified souls to this new paradise realm of Elysium when I've finished.

There was no time left. The moon was in its first complete phase, and he knew Hecate would tell Demeter soon. *Fucking prophecies*, he thought to himself, grumbling at his mess of a life.

Hades worked hard to build enough energy by drawing power from his throne. His eyes remained closed as the blue flame around his body grew with every draw. He would do anything to convince her to stay. If a new domain for the dead is what it would take to sway her to his side, Hades knew he must build it.

The sweat poured from his brow as he commanded the energy needed to produce a new afterlife. He wanted to create something that resembled her home. A gentle paradise that would please her was clear in his mind. With only moments in the Meadow, he did manage to look around and see enough to remember what her home looked like. It gave him an idea of what she desired.

Hades found Persephone sitting on the bridge leading to his chambers with her knees to her chest. Sitting beside her, they watched the lava flow by, the bubbles popping and hissing.

"I'm sorry I ran away," she said finally.

"It's okay," he said, keeping his eyes on the lava. "I shouldn't have pushed you. If you do have feelings for me, you can say them in your own time."

"I do have feelings for you," she replied. "I always have. It's all so complicated, and I don't know what to do about it."

"There is one thing you could do with me."

She turned to him. "What's that?"

"You can help me build the world you envisioned."

The look on her face of shock and excitement made his heart leap in his chest.

"I can?" She asked, perking up her shoulders. "They've agreed to let us build the Elysian Feilds?"

Hades chuckled, thinking how adorable she was. "They have. Are you ready?"

Persephone nodded with a wide smile. "Absolutely."

She ran into the opening of the false sun-lit meadow, swirling around with her arms in the air as she drank in the warm light and the soft breeze he had remembered from the moments he was in her mother's home.

"Hades!" Persephone cried out with joy, running back to him. "It's so beautiful!"

Her hands splayed out, touching the tall grass and wildflowers that bloomed.

"How in the name of Gaia did you build this?" She asked, bending down to touch the flower blossoms.

"It's not finished," he said, standing beside her. "I thought you might want to help with the rest."

Hades smiled, gazing at her beautiful face, feeling content that this place made her happy.

"What can I do to help?"

"Only this small area has bloomed. I had hoped you could help me make the rest of the space grow and blossom."

"I'll do my best," she said, beaming. "What do you want

to do for the souls that return here after multiple lifetimes?"

"That's a good question," Hades replied, touching his chin. "Three times is the maximum for reincarnation."

Persephone tapped her chin. "But if they're exceptionally good or heroic, maybe the fourth time, they can go to some sort of island where they get to live a blessed life like the gods."

"A fourth time?" He asked, folding his arms and tilting his head as he leaned his face close to hers. "You want a Blessed Island for them to live as immortals?"

An enchanting laugh followed her nod. "That sounds about right."

She was adorable. Persephone's bright smile instantly disarmed his resolve to tease her and make her work for any request. She hadn't asked for anything for herself since she'd arrived, and now she wanted a place for the dead to live in peace. He loved her selfless nature and kind heart.

"Okay," Hades said, with a sigh, then smiling that wicked grin he knew she loved, he scanned the area for the best spot. "One blessed Island for the extra virtuous, coming up."

The warm springs delivered much-needed water to the rolling hills of grass and grain. Persephone reached out her hand for his. When they touched, the flowers bloomed, the trees blossomed, and the brooks burbled gently in the warm breeze that caressed his cheek. Hades raised one hand and drew all of his strength to create a lake with an island emerging from the water's depths into a lush paradise. Her powers added to his bringing the island to life, making the process much faster, though the energy it took from him was extensive. When the island finished forming, he walked with her hand in hand to where the water drifted from a river into the lake delta.

Stepping to the shore of the cool, calm waters, they stood together, holding hands, enjoying the moment in silence.

Perhaps there could be redemption in Tartarus as well,

he thought to himself. Redemption, maybe a re-judgment by those wronged, would give the souls a chance to be here. If he gave them a year, those who desired redemption could return to the Akherousian Mere via the Kokytos and Pyriphlegethon rivers to receive a second judgment. He quickly determined there were those whose crimes were too heinous to allow this chance to reincarnate.

Watching the light beam down onto her now pale olive skin from lack of natural sun made him want redemption for his wrongs against her. *I don't deserve her*, Hades thought, staring at her radiance. He desired forgiveness for taking her. Her eyes closed, taking in the warmth. When she looked up into his eyes, her joy and wonder were a drug he couldn't stop taking.

This could work, he thought, drinking in her smile. Hades had genuine hope for the first time since this began. From the moment he saw her standing on her balcony at Olympus, all he wanted to do was see her smile. She looked happy watching the world come alive before her. At least he could give her this. And it would thrive because of her magic combined with his. A piece of both of them would always be here together. Finally, his powers waned, and the domain was complete. Hades slumped from exhaustion, but Persephone reached out and braced him up.

"Hades?" Persephone asked with concern, darkening her once joyful face.

"I'm fine," He stood tall and took her hands, kissing them. "I just need some rest."

"Let's get you to bed," she said, tugging at his arm.

Hades chuckled. "Only if you join me."

Persephone's cheeks warmed, turning red. She narrowed her eyes and placed her hands on her hips.

"I'll give you the same advice you gave me when I was injured." She winked up at him. "Get some rest. I don't want to have you when you're not at full strength."

"But you will have me," he said, pulling her against his

body while caressing her cheek.

She couldn't hold back her smile for long and finally began to laugh and blush at him. The sound was like music filled with light.

"I'm warming up to the idea," she said, staring at his eyes and then down to his lips as her breaths became shaky.

He knew what she was thinking, but she was right. He needed rest. Letting her go, Persephone smiled and grabbed his arm, leading them back to the entrance to the fields. He reached out with his hand. She took it, linking their fingers as they walked toward the sunset, and disappeared to his chambers.

Persephone removed his robes, sat him on the bed, and removed his boots. The gesture was something only a mortal would do, and he felt her desire to take care of him to be endearing. Pushing his shoulders back, she pressed him to lie down. He pulled her into his arms, brought her close, tucked her into his body, and threw the blankets over them. His head rested above hers, and soon, he felt himself drifting to sleep with her curls in his face with a sweet scent he loved to breathe in.

When he awoke, she was gone. Hades rose, dressed in his leather pants, and was about to put on shoes to find her when Hecate popped into the room and sat by the fireplace.

"Finally, you're awake," she said, taking a large swig of wine that she poured into the chalice on the table.

"How long have I been asleep?" He asked, pulling on his robe, leaving his feet and chest bare.

"Two days," she said, standing and placing a mothering hand on his forehead. "Persephone was worried about you when you didn't wake back up and called for me to keep an eye on you while she bathed. She hadn't left your side all this time, so I insisted she take a break."

Hades stood and felt his limbs were like stone. He could barely move. Rubbing his eyes, trying to clear the fog he felt, Hades sat in his chair and poured his glass.

"What were you thinking about taking on such a large world-building project? Considering what you created," Hecate said, taking a large swig of wine. "And building a false sun, no less. I'm surprised you weren't unconscious for much longer. Your powers must be ten times what they were when you first created this realm. Imagine my surprise to see you could build a realm so beautiful."

Hades emptied his glass and set it down. "Persephone helped me."

"Her powers grow stronger every day she is here." Hecate poured him another glass and offered it with a sprinkle of herbs. "Drink this. It'll help you recover faster. Your head must be killing you."

"I've had worse pain," he replied, taking her advice and drinking it all.

"No doubt you have," Hecate said with a genuine smile. "It's charming how much you love her."

He sighed. "More than my life."

"Damn it all," Hecate said, crossing her arms and pursing her lips. "We have to find a way to make this work for everyone. I have to find Demeter, but you know what will happen then. Maybe I can convince her to let this whole thing go, and you will be able to marry Persephone openly and freely."

"She hasn't said she loves me," He said, staring into his glass.

"Don't you start with me, Hades," Hecate warned with a finger pointing at him. "Persephone does love you. She merely has to find the solution to our problem. I thought I could help her decide, but she's stubborn and needs affirmation from her mother." Hecate scoffed, folding her arms. "Demeter is ruining everything."

"Demeter is rightly angry," Hades replied with sadness as he stared into the flames. "I know I was when she took Persephone to the Meadow. So now she knows how it felt."

Hecate placed her hand on his arm. "Vengeance isn't like you, Hades."

Hades offered his glass for her to fill it again. "It's not vengeance I seek, but peace."

"Peace with Demeter?" Hecate shook her head. "There will be no peace without Persephone's return."

"That's not going to happen," he growled.

Hecate obliged, filling his drink with more herbs and giving it to him with a glance around to ensure no one was looking.

"Look." Hecate sighed. "I wasn't going to do this since I still don't know the outcome, but I managed to sneak something from Zeus that may give you some peace of mind."

"What did you take?" He asked, wondering what new scheme she'd conjured.

Hecate handed him a golden key. Placing it in his hand, he stared confused. Before he could say anything, the key he held snaked up his forearm arm and wrapped around it, creating an intricate band. It faded from bright gold to nothing as it disappeared from view.

"There," Hecate said, watching it blend in. "No one would be able to know what it was or take it from you."

"What is this?" He asked, twisting his arm to see, but it was gone.

Hecate smiled. "It opens the door to a cave on the edge of Demeter's realm. Sort of like putting a block in the way of a magic shield. It leaves an opening when the veils between worlds thin."

Hades could feel it under his skin like an itch he couldn't scratch. "You made this?"

Her craftsmanship was a work of art. Hades knew after this that he would owe her. He didn't care. He would gladly do anything she asked for such a gift.

"I am the keeper of keys," she replied with a wicked grin.

"But if there's a door in, doesn't that leave them vulnerable when I leave?" He asked, remembering the ground closing behind him in his last venture there.

Hecate shook her head with a smile, "Good Gaia, Hades,

didn't your mother raise you to close the door behind you?" She laughed, patting him on the chest. "I'm kidding. Only the one with the key can enter, and anyone they have with them can leave. But it only works when the veil is thinnest between worlds."

"Why didn't you give me this before instead of the damn seed?" He growled.

"Because flowers are more romantic," Hecate teased. "That, and I didn't have this before. Someone else did, and there was only one ever made."

"So you stole it from Zeus?"

"Procured," she said with a wave of her hand. "I procured this treasure for you, my Dark Lord. You should be grateful. But if you don't want it..."

She held out her palm, and he saw the key glow. Quickly, he grabbed his arm and tucked it to his chest.

"No. I do want it," he said, seeing the glow fade. "Thank you. But why did Zeus have it?"

Hecate sighed. "Still holding a flame for her after all these years. He's such a clever god, finding a way to see Persephone without disturbing Demeter."

Hades scoffed. "You mean he didn't want to ask for permission."

"It's better to ask forgiveness than permission," Hecate cackled. "Am I right?"

He looked away while taking a drink. Demeter was an excellent mother to Persephone. Diligent as ever, she'd kept her daughter safe for over two decades while Zeus had been watching over Persephone the whole time without anyone knowing. It would be hard for Zeus to part with such a thing once in his possession. Hades felt the guilt rise again. Pushing it back, he continued to drink.

"Speaking of," Hades paused, looking around the room. "Where is Persephone?"

"She's getting ready. Thanatos stocked her wardrobe, so she should be here soon," she replied with a sigh. "Hmm, I wish he would stock my wardrobe,"

"I'm sure he would be happy to oblige," Hades replied with a chuckle. "I can see Thanatos has an interest in you. You might be able to convince him to visit for a night or two."

"My gods, Hades, do you think he will?" She asked wide-eyed.

"Why?" He chuckled. "Are you too shy to ask?"

"Me? Shy? No," Hecate laughed, clearing her throat nervously. "I didn't think he would be interested in someone like me."

"Only way to find out." Hades said.

"Speaking of getting ready," Hecate looked back at Hades. "When do you plan on Persephone performing the gauntlet?"

Hades coughed into his wine. "You can't be serious. Are you going to make her do that old ritual?"

"Of course I'm serious," replied Hecate, raising a brow. "I think we should set the time for after your wedding. It's too perfect. Consider this her initiation into the high ranks of the gods."

"You really want to put her through our original six god's gauntlet before the three kingdoms?" He asked as the memories of his experience returned. "I drowned countless times. And the other times, I froze until I could barely move."

"That's precisely why you have the realm you rule," Hecate smiled. "Poor thing can't handle the cold at all."

Hades scoffed. "Zeus didn't fare much better in the extreme heat."

"Aren't you glad we found the best leader of each realm this way rather than letting you fight over territory?"

Hades growled.

Hecate took a sip and continued, "Besides, everyone knows it's all about the guest's entertainment. Whoever said a wedding was for the bride and groom is either crazy or lying to themselves."

"Our females don't rule territory, so why put them

through it?"

Hecate rolled her eyes. "If the Underworld doesn't get a queen who can handle an obstacle course and a few Titans alone, you know there will be no living with them. Besides, do you want more beings to challenge her legitimacy like last time? I'll start to run out of space for all the plants I'd have to make."

Hades glared at Hecate. " Is this your idea of a joke?"

"I assure you, Hades, this is no joke," she said with a twinkle in her eye. "If she is to join you at the table of the original six, she will have to succeed in the biggest challenge of her life. One for each realm, starting with Olympus, then she will move to Poseidon's, and the last battle will be a monster of your choosing from your realm."

"No." Hades shook his head. "I won't risk her never returning."

"Are you saying she can't do it?" Hecate asked, staring up at him.

"I'm just saying she..." Hades sighed. "She hasn't had a chance to learn to control her powers."

Hecate brushed off his comment with her hand. "She's a goddess who has met Gaia and returned. You worry too much, Hades. You always calculate how one can be defeated but fail to see the potential win. Don't forget, Persephone has her other powers as well."

"These archaic rules are ridiculous," he growled. "Hera barely made it through, and Poseidon had to regrow a leg. You'd think the Titanomachy would be enough for your masochistic tendencies."

"I'm doing this for your benefit and hers," Hecate reassured. "Since the three of you gods obtained your kingdoms this way. It's only right to see those who wish to share it with you can keep it. Trust me. Don't think these rules only apply to you and Zeus' wives. Poseidon will have the same challenge for his queen when he finds her."

He had a horrible knot in his stomach. Persephone

could perish in these trials set by Hecate and Rhea. Working as a team against Titans was one thing, but the challenge of subduing one alone was deadly.

"What if she fails?" He asked quietly under his breath.

Hecate folded her arms and pursed her lips. "You must have faith that she won't fail. Persephone must prove herself worthy of your throne no matter how much you disagree. It's going to be up to us to ensure she can succeed. The alternative is unthinkable. If even one of those Titans ever got loose and neither of us were there to protect her, what would you do? At least this way, they're tied down, so to speak."

He felt his chest ache in pain. He knew Hecate was right. The trials were complex and designed to test the gods to their limits. It took a powerful god even to attempt the challenge. Praise Gaia if she succeeded, though.

"Do you want me to prepare her for the challenges then?" Hecate asked, tilting her head.

Hades closed his eyes and turned away from Hecate. "Yes."

"The good news is," Hecate said, blinking with a sinister grin. "I already have a plan."

Hades held up his hand to stop Hecate from talking when he smelled lilacs. He saw Persephone at the door wearing leather pants that hugged her curves with over-the-knee wedge boots. The corset accentuated her heavy breasts, making him salivate. Leather straps from her bodice connected around her delicate neck to a choker to squeeze her cleavage tighter. He realized she'd used her old dress to make the bicep cuffs with soft fabric draping down as billowing sleeves and a short flowing skirt longer in the back and open in the front. She somehow held her ethereal innocence in the tight leather while quickening his pulse with desire.

Gods, her naked shoulders made him crave their taste. Her full rosebud lips smiled at him, and his breath stopped, feeling the desire build as she came close enough to touch. But he wouldn't dare right now.

The crimson red curtains matched Persephone's lips, which were darker than usual. A sign she was changing into her other form, yet her eyes were the same lavender shade, and her hair was still bright red, just without the highlights. She wore her hair down in loose curls that descended her back to her ample round ass he wanted to grab. It took everything in him not to devour her as he clenched his fists to keep from taking her right there.

"I should be going now that you've recovered, Lord of Darkness." Hecate winked at Persephone, then disappeared with her wicked smile lingering until she was gone.

"How are you feeling?" Persephone asked, placing a warm hand on his forearm. "When you didn't wake up, I…"

Tears welled in her eyes, and one single tear fell as he reached up to wipe it away.

"I'll be fine," Hades replied, taking her hand and kissing her palm. "Now that you're here, I will recover much faster."

Persephone slapped his chest in a pitiful attempt to scold him. "You scared the life out of me when you didn't wake up."

"My apologies for frightening you," Hades said, smiling at her scolding.

"I didn't know what it took to make the Elysian Feilds. If I had, I never would have asked you to do it. Why didn't you tell me this could happen to you?" She demanded.

Her pout was adorable, and her large eyes stared into him with tears filling them. He wiped them away with his thumb.

"Because it was important to you."

"You…," she stuttered, pointing at him. "Don't ever scare me like that again. I don't know what I'd do if you left me alone."

Pulling her to his chest, he gently touched her head and petted her hair to calm her sadness.

He kissed her forehead. "I won't ever leave you, my love. Even when all the mortals are gone, and the world has ended, and all we are is dust, I will stay with you."

"You better," she said through sobs and buried her head into his chest.

Her heavy sigh made his heart warm, knowing she cared.

"How can I make you feel better?" He asked, holding her.

Persephone pulled back enough to reach up and, grabbing the nape of his neck, pulled him to her lips. Slow and tender, he kissed her, tasting the salt of her tears, wanting to make her sadness disappear.

"Take me to bed, Hades," she whispered, kissing his neck.

He turned her around and kissed her shoulder while unhooking her corset in the front, then tossed it aside. Unclasping her choker and slipping off her bodice, leaving her breasts exposed, he cupped each one with his hand as the other unfastened her pants. Bending down, he pulled the leather over her ass as he kissed her cheeks. Sliding off her boots, one by one, he finished pulling her pants off, leaving her in only her arm cuffs. Hades stood, pulled them off, then turned her to face him. Persephone slid his robe off his shoulders and let it fall to the floor. Reaching down, she kept her eyes on his as she unfastened his pants, bent to her knees, and slid them down. With his legs finally free, she stayed on her knees and reached to touch his erection. Taking him into her hand, she slid her tongue from the base of his shaft to the tip. Swirling her tongue, making him moan, she took him into her mouth and sucked him deep into her throat. Persephone's eager mouth slid up and down in an even rhythm, using one hand to cup his balls and the other to stroke his shaft.

His body shook with pleasure, forcing his head back as he let her do to him whatever she wished. Her efforts were getting him close. Too close. He didn't want to stop too soon, so he took her arm to make her stand.

Hades lifted her cradled in his arms and walked with her, gently setting her on his bed. He lay between her legs with his cock still wet from her kisses. Her hands caressed his back with her legs open, eager to wrap around his waist to bring him closer. They kissed, their tongues dancing as he teased her delicious lips down to her neck. Hades could feel her arch against his body, the desire for him clear in her caresses. His hand cupped her swollen breast, using his thumb to brush against her hardening nipple. Persephone let out a moan that made his cock flex against her. Trailing his lips down her chest, he sucked her nipple into his mouth while pinching her other nipple, teasing her simultaneously. Her hands splayed into his hair, pulling him closer as his licks grew more insistent with her excited moans.

Her soft breasts were a few handfuls, plump and soft, and he loved how their weight felt in his palms. The way they moved enticed him. He'd longed to have a chance to see them and indulge his desires for her curves. His lips found hers again, and his hand trailed down her body to rest between her legs. Hades slipped one finger into her slick folds and rubbed her in the spot he knew she loved the most. She cried out, arching her back and grasping his neck, holding on as the sensation made her eyes roll back into her head. Her moans were gaining in pitch with each gentle stroke. Shivers began to take over Persephone's body, driving him to press just a little more as she moved her hips in the same rhythm as his strokes.

She buried her head in his neck and gripped his shoulders when he slid another finger into her tight pussy, then used her wetness to rub her clit in circles.

"Do you like my fingers in your pussy?" He asked, licking her neck close to her ear.

"Oh, gods. Y... Yes." She stuttered, barely able to speak through moans.

"Do you want me to go deeper?" He asked in a deep whisper in her ear.

"Yes."

"Tell me to fuck your pussy with my fingers."

"Please, Hades," she moaned. "Fuck my pussy with your

fingers."

Her words made his stomach clench and his cock flex. Fuck she was so sexy when she writhed beneath him like this.

"How many fingers do you want inside you?"

"I don't know," she said through gasps of pleasure. "Just don't stop."

"You're very tight." Hades nuzzled her neck, kissing her chest. "I'll have to add more for you to take me."

Persephone rolled her hips to meet his thrusts. Each breath held a new moan he wanted to explore. His hands went back to rubbing her clit, and he relished how she moved as he watched her grip the sheets, knuckles turning white, much like he remembered in his dreams. Bringing her closer, her pussy was so wet his hand was gliding back and forth between fucking her with now three fingers and stroking her hardening bud. Hades tried to add a fourth finger when she tensed up. She needed more time. He returned to three fingers and rubbed gently to coax her to pleasure. He sucked her nipple into his mouth as he worked to give her as much pleasure as possible, moaning with her.

"Mmm. That's my good flower."

"Oh gods, I'm going to cum...." Her panting increased, and her breaths were shallow as her climax built.

"Say my name when you cum," he growled into her ear. "I'm going to stop unless you do. Do you want me to stop?"

"Ah, please, Hades. Don't stop!" Suddenly, Persephone arched her back. "Hades, you're going to make me cum."

"Yes, flower. Cum for me," he growled into her ear, then took her lips with his.

He felt her pussy begin to pour into his hand, flexing around his fingers that continued to thrust in and out of her as he worked her clit with his thumb. Her moans turned him on so much his dick was aching, straining to be inside her.

Her orgasm soaked the bed, and he loved it. Shaking wildly in his arms, she gripped him as her body rode the wave she felt at his hands. Her hand clasped over her mouth to stifle her screams.

"Take your hand away," he demanded with a raspy voice. "I want to hear your screams."

Persephone let go and screamed in pleasure at the top of her lungs. His name on her lips was making his cock dripping with pre cum. He wanted to be inside her so badly, but she was still very tight, and he didn't want to hurt her. Slowly she began to relax, and his fingers lazily stroked inside her as he stopped rubbing her clit to give her a minute to catch her breath.

She reached her hand down between them and began to stroke his cock. Unable to resist her, he moaned her name into her ear.

"Mmm, Persephone," he said, kissing her neck. "Do you want me inside of you?"

"Yes," she moaned. "Please put your cock in me."

Her gentle plea was all he wanted to hear. "I'm going to let you do it."

Persephone looked down and watched as she rubbed his throbbing dick up and down her wet pussy. Placing it at her hole, he adjusted his hips to rest above her and let her stroke him while swirling her hips, inching him inside her slowly. He'd barely reached past her tight entrance when she tensed up again.

"Oh gods," she panted. "I don't think it will fit."

With wide eyes, she looked at him in shock at his size, making him smile and kiss her gently to reassure her.

"It'll fit. You just have to relax and let me in," he said between kisses. "Rotate your hips and let in as much as you want. You don't have to worry. I won't move until you ask me to."

"It feels too big," Persephone moaned as she did what he said.

Hade placed his hand against her cheek. "I'm not going to hurt you. We can go slow."

She nodded up at him with so much trust and a little bit

of fear in her eyes. Hades could see she needed more time, and he was happy to give it to her. He began to kiss her and stroke her bud again, and she widened her legs in response.

"Good, flower. Focus on my fingers and move against them."

Her hand stroked him, and he remained still while she created circles with her hips, sliding him in a little at a time.

Once his head was in, he could feel her barrier and regretted having to do what he needed to do next.

"I'm going to go slow," he said, flexing his jaw for control. "It'll only hurt for a moment."

Her eyes went wide. "You said you wouldn't hurt me."

Hades gritted his teeth. "I promise it will feel amazing after you relax. Hold onto me and kiss me."

Persephone nodded and wrapped her arms around his neck and shoulders, kissing him as he'd asked. He pushed his cock into her and pressed against it, moving back and forth until he'd made a gentle enough stretching of the lining so it wouldn't be too painful. One last thrust, and he'd broken through. His cock slid about halfway in before she cried out, and he paused, letting her adjust to his size, never ceasing his kisses or his strokes of her clit.

CHAPTER 16 DESIRE

Persephone relished in the fullness of Hades' cock inside her. He was so big it stretched her to her limits. After a small pinch, she began to move her hips as he'd told her, and to her surprise, it wasn't painful. The deeper he entered her, the more she wanted him to fill her. Her hand still stroked his cock while her free hand moved from his shoulder to his ass. She gripped it and pulled him deeper. He understood her body already from so many encounters, but now he was being so careful and reserved she found it endearing.

Her pussy ached with need with each gentle thrust. His moans made her stomach dance with butterflies. Moving his fingers slowly over her mound, he matched the same rhythm of her hips as his cock slid deeper and deeper inside. Slowly, he made it to her core, and she could feel him shaking from trying to maintain control.

"Are you okay?" He asked, looking for signs of discomfort. "Am I hurting you?"

Persephone shook her head. "The pain is already gone."

He smiled and kissed her. "Do you want me to keep going?"

"Yes." She moaned into his mouth, pulling his hips to her, demanding more with her grasp. "I want you, Hades."

Hades smiled down at her, not the clever or wicked smile. One filled with love and passion for her. He buried his face into her neck and began to thrust harder. The pain she'd felt faded as a memory as she gripped one hand on his should and the other on his hip to fuck him back.

"You feel so good, Persephone," he whispered in her ear. "You're so fucking tight."

Her body wanted him, and she knew he needed to know he could do more. Her patience was growing thin as she desired to cum again with him.

"Harder," she moaned, loving how good he felt.

He kissed her neck, trailed down to her breasts, and stopped when she made her request, seemingly stunned.

"You want me to fuck you harder?"

Persephone gripped his shoulders. "Yes," she whispered between kisses.

Hades began to thrust hard, keeping eye contact with her, making sure she was okay. The sensation made her eyes roll back in her head as her knees opened wider for him to go as deep as possible. They met each other's thrusts, staring into one another's eyes as their desires and pleasure took control. Their bodies moved as one. The world around them disappeared, and there were only the two of them now as though a singular being. It felt right. It felt like home.

The hours passed by as they made love over and over. Eventually, her demands to go harder made him gain speed and pressure until he slammed into her pussy while she begged for more. His forceful thrusts drove her wild with desire, and she was building again to another orgasm. It was a different feeling than before. So different from her oral or clitoral orgasms. His cock was hitting all the right spots inside, and her legs shook uncontrollably. The wave of her orgasm finally took her when she called out his name through her screams. More orgasms followed one after another, each more intense than the last. His body tensed, and with his brow beading with sweat, he began to shake.

"I'm going to cum," he groaned in her ear. "Do you want my cum inside you?"

"Yes. Cum for me, Hades. Please." She couldn't help but beg. "Please cum inside me."

His teeth began to lengthen, and his eyes went black. He thrust harder and harder until his back arched, and he roared as his seed spilled into her, pumping spurts she could feel filling her up inside. It was the most incredible feeling she couldn't have even imagined before. As he finished inside her, his cock flexed with each release. He called out her name just before collapsing over her, careful not to let his whole weight settle on her. She could see him trying to regain control as he closed his eyes tight, and his features returned to normal.

He kissed her, more tender than ever before. Brushing his nose against hers, he smiled at her and chuckled low in his chest. She giggled at him and tucked his hair back behind his ear from where it clung to his stubble. The look he gave her made her body ignite again, and in that instant, looking into his eyes, Persephone knew she could never be without him.

Persephone wanted Hades to stay, buried deep between her legs. When he no longer filled her, she felt a loss. Hades got up and grabbed a towel nearby, brought it over, and delicately cleaned her and then himself. Throwing it off to the side of the bed, he wrapped her in his arms and pulled her tucked into his body.

"I love you, Persephone," he said, nuzzling her neck.

Just when she was about to utter the words, his gentle snore made her smile. She nestled closer to him, feeling his heartbeat against her back, and felt more at peace than any time she could remember.

Persephone thought of the seeds in her pocket and realized she couldn't refuse the lure of the Underworld or his love. She would find her mother and stop her. Even if it destroyed everything they knew, Persephone would have this god no matter what anyone said. She finally understood what she would have to do.

She drifted off in his arms.

Arms that were warm and safe and a place she'd dreamed of and desired to be.

A place that she would always return to.

The white that covered the land and trees was cold to the touch. It melted in her hand as each flake fell from the sky. Cries of pain and sorrow rang out, but she couldn't linger while her dream continued to lead her to a new time of fresh blossoms and rain that made the world awaken and grow. Soon after, the world around her warmed to a comfortable temperature with a breeze carrying the scent of honey and blossoms in the fields. The vision soon changed to the veil thinning and the living and dead celebrating together while the earth changed colors and the leaves fell from the trees while the wind howled with bitter cold.

Persephone marveled at the spirits dancing with the living, and the bright reds, oranges, and yellows reminded her of the Underworld with their various colors. The mortals prepared banquets of bountiful feasts. The image began to change to where the vibrant colors disappeared, and the ground was covered in white again as the flakes drifted from the sky. Though cold, it was also lovely. Almost peaceful.

As the winds picked up, the scene changed to Humans inside their homes celebrating once more. Only this time, decorations were adorning the walls, and people were singing as they held one another by the fire. Eventually, the scene changed to show life growing in a new cycle, and the blanket of white ice began to melt.

It was incredible. She had never before beheld so many colors and such changes in the behaviors of mortals, immortals, and nature together. The colder it became, the closer they became. As the image began to warm, animals were born, young ones played, and life sprang alive. She couldn't believe it. Was this the same vision that foretold more darkness was coming? But what if, after the dark, the light returned? But what makes this possible?"

The sound of hooves thundered as the black mount appeared with its rider from the depths. Pulling the female onto the winged horse, the two descended into the cave, and the world began to change color. Time passed quickly as the leaves fell and covered the ground until the trees and bushes were bare. The winds howled again, and the cold brought the ice that fell from the sky to blanket the world in white. Just when it seemed the storms would never cease, a bare foot appeared from the cave, melting the cold ground with each step, leaving blooming flowers and green grass in her wake.

...Her footprints, she realized as she looked around to see the world reawaken from its long slumber.

Someone watched her as she turned to see a tall figure among the encroaching darkness surrounding her until she fell.

***

Persephone lay in his arms for hours, sleeping peacefully. Hades smelled her hair, filling his nostrils with lilacs and jasmine. Now, his scent had combined with hers. He smiled. She was still as she dreamed. Much different from the other nights when she tossed and turned, whimpering with the fears she held in her subconscious. Hades had hoped that he would be able to alleviate them.

She was no longer the innocent maiden he'd first met on Olympus. She'd become so much more. Persephone was more than he could have imagined or hoped for. Finally, she was his. She turned over and nestled her head into his chest, cuddling closer into his arms. Hades pulled her in tight, fearing this moment would end.

He would never let her go. Even if Zeus himself dared try, Hades would suffer any indignity or torture to make sure she stayed safe. He knew he would have to find a way to talk to Demeter and reason with her. But how?

Persephone gently kissed his chest in her sleep, and his

heart felt like it would burst with his love for her. A moment like this was unfathomable for so long. Now, he spent every moment grateful as he watched her sleep.

A faint knock on the door disturbed Hades from his daydreaming as he held Persephone still. Unwilling to wake her, he disappeared and reappeared next to the bed. She frowned, reaching out, unable to find his warmth, but settled back into the pillow asleep. He smiled, pulling the blankets over her shoulders and brushing away a strand of red curl on her cheek.

Closing the door behind him as quietly as possible, Hades glared at Thanatos for the intrusion.

Thanatos coughed into his hand. "My Lord. You know I wouldn't be here if it wasn't critical...."

"It better be world-ending," Hades growled. "What's happening?"

"The shores of the Acheron are becoming tumultuous. Charon is having difficulty navigating the waters," Thanatos said, leaning closer. "And his skiff almost capsized on his last trip to this side. He says he won't ferry the dead until the waters calm."

"This is why you disturb me?" Hades threatened.

"Another message from Zeus has arrived," Thanatos said, crossing his arms. "He's threatening punishment if you don't respond to his demands. What should I tell him?"

Hades sighed. "Tell him I don't know where she is."

"My Lord..."

"Damn it, Thanatos!" Hades yelled, then calmed, realizing he could wake Persephone. "I want more time. Stall him any way you can."

"I'll do my best," he said with a bow, then disappeared.

Hades pinched the bridge of his nose and paced.

Losing his ferryman was the last thing he expected. For the waters to be affected in his realm, the surface must be chaotic, weathering constant storms. Human and animal life wouldn't last long in this barrage of disasters. If his shores were about to burst into the Acheron, then the souls would be lost to him there, forever drowning, endlessly scrambling for the surface. That many dead wouldn't have the coin for the boat due to their hasty demise.

Could he continue to hold out knowing all this? Hades clenched his fists. Pain and humiliation, he knew, would be the punishment for his refusal to obey. Zeus wouldn't tolerate disobedience for long. If he did, Zeus would lose the carefully crafted ruthless reputation he'd worked to cement in everyone's minds. Hades thought of the Titanomachy when everything was simple, and they all got along. It seemed so long ago now.

Mountains grew around them in peaks, becoming raging elemental beings with gaping mouths rendering a deafening roar. Magma Titans burst forth, reaching for the gods, who combined their powers to form a blast strong enough to incapacitate them. Hera, Demeter, and Hestia stood in a triangle, holding their orb of light energy in the center as Zeus charged it with his lightning. Hades and Poseidon covered them, fending off boulders dripping with lava launched at them from all sides.

Poseidon launched wave after wave, drying up rivers and pulling from the ocean to stop the constant stream of molten rock while laughing as he surfed the tides, guiding the water with his trident.

When sheer brute strength didn't work for Hades any longer, he used the one gift that made him invulnerable. His helm was sharp and angular at the sides of his face. The slits of his eyes were visible through dark silver plating lit with the blue flame emanating from his eyes. Nothing could detect him in this form. Anything he touched and wished so would join his invisibility. Stepping into his chariot, he grabbed the reins and snapped them. As the reins rippled to a snap, the vessel lurched forward and disappeared with him.

The four companions he'd come to respect and rely upon throughout the war barreled in and out of the Titan's grip as

Hades continued slashing and blasting anything in his way. His beasts were swift. Nothing could catch them as the Titan's arms flailed in vain at the mysterious attack.

"Will you hurry it up down there?" Hades yelled, following a dodge of another giant club-like appendage swinging over his head.

"Patience, Hades!" Hestia replied through gritted teeth with sweat pouring down her brow.

"Patience isn't an option right now!" Poseidon yelled, blocking more stones so hot they dried up his water. "I'm running out of water sources to pull."

Zeus stood, eyes white, crackling with energy, pulling the lightning into the orb the three goddesses struggled to contain. At last, the globe was solid and began to spin.

"Ha!" Demeter exclaimed, grabbing Hera and hugging her tight. "We did it! Okay. So all we need to do is point two fingers of our right hand at the orb and two on our left hand, point to your heart, and then it will activate."

"Is that all?" Hera asked, creating the movement with her hands as the other two goddesses followed her motions.

Nothing happened.

"Isn't this thing supposed to turn red when it's active?" Hera asked, folding her arms and narrowing her eyes at Demeter, who fumbled with the scroll.

Reading it out loud, Demeter realized her mistake.

"Sorry, everyone," Demeter said with red cheeks from embarrassment. "I'm still learning this magic from Hecate."

"It's okay, Demeter," Hestia replied, petting Demeter's hair. "Just tell us what we need to do, and it will work, I promise."

Demeter nodded shyly and looked over to Hera, who gave a reassuring nod to continue.

"Demeter," Hades warned. "I don't mean to rush you, but if you could speed this up, we can all get out of here."

"I second that!" Poseidon added, surfing by those still on the ground.

"Okay," Demeter said with a new determined attitude. "I need a small plant. Any plant will do."

"You're kidding," Hera said, throwing her hands in the air. "Where will we find a plant in this barren place ripping apart around us?"

"Calm down, Hera," Zeus interrupted. "If Demeter needs a plant, let's find her one."

Zeus moved as lightning flashed back and forth, seeking anything he could find. Hades watched from above what they were doing as he maneuvered past the Titans, continuing to defend the group. As soon as Zeus returned, Demeter took the plant and smiled. Letting it go in front of her, the tiny flower with six petals floated into the light.

"Now," Demeter said, forming a hand motion with her sisters. The orb glowed a deep red, pulsing each second as the countdown began. "There. It's armed."

Hestia grabbed Demeter's arm. "We need to get out of here, now."

"HADES! POSEIDON!" Hera bellowed with her hand cupped to her mouth. "Get your asses back here. We've gotta go!"

Hades returned to the group, taking off his helm to allow the females to enter the chariot. Zeus didn't say a word. He nodded to his brothers and disappeared into the lightning. Poseidon held on to the back of the chariot, surfing what little water he retained until they were out of danger.

The explosion shook the land and into the sky as the shock waves pushed them back. In the place of the Titans of rock and magma, the land was lush and green, terraformed to hold them down. With so many of them, Poseidon worked fast to refill the sea, forming the islands surrounding the mainland's shores. It was the last time they all worked together, hugging and high-fiving one another.

Hades thought about those good times before they had kingdoms to rule, rules to break, and expectations so high it seemed impossible for anyone to meet.

Once Zeus was in power, and Hera's and Demeter's fight ended with Demeter leaving, everything was different. Zeus became a lustful adulterer, and his punishments turned vengeful and cruel. Hera's feelings of betrayal created a bitter, destructive, deadly goddess, poisoned with the other effects of Aphrodite, the green-eyed monster. Only Demeter had the courage to leave us, while the rest felt a duty to stay.

If Hades proposed to be with Persephone to Zeus and Demeter from those days, none of this would be an issue. *But we're not in those times,* he cursed to himself.

CHAPTER 17
DREAMS

Grabbing his chalice, Hades sipped the wine, and his eyes flicked to Persephone enjoying the merriment, dancing with her arms out as she twirled in her long, dark-tyrian jeweled gown. Throughout the evening, she was the center of attention. *She is the manifestation of everything I dreamed*, Hades thought as she turned and smiled at him.

Her exploits in the arena had won her notoriety and respect from the court. She was a light that shone even brighter in the darkness. Her ease with which she managed the crowd and spoke with everyone with such kindness only confirmed he was right to bring her here.

Hades cherished Persephone each hour he watched her laugh and dance. He couldn't stop staring as his eyes raked over her while she spun around and danced with the females in the crowd. No male would dare approach her as he narrowed his eyes at them apart from those she trained with. It was the first event she had finally participated in since her arrival, and he prayed nothing would sour the experience for her.

The room was bright with firelight as the music blared. But something caught his eye as he looked to the small opening of the cavern that vented the air.

The colorful leaves of red, gold, and orange fell in the center of the room, creating a pile at her feet. Persephone raised her hands in the air and twirled in the drifting leaves. His breath stopped. She was mesmerizing. Her smile warmed him, yet a chill hung in the air, and a sense of dread filled him.

Hades looked up at the zephyr of leaves floating all around them. Soon, the court began to pick up the leaves and inspect them with curiosity. Persephone caught a leaf in her palm, looked at its bright yellow hue, and met his gaze. She stopped. Her eyes went wide. He knew she must have realized they were the same colors they'd seen in the prophecy, and her smile turned downward.

"Thanatos?" Hades asked, signaling his general to approach with his fingers.

The crisp leaves crunched under Thanatos' boots as he approached. Hades bent down and chose the red leaf that reminded him of her hair. The once soft leaf crunched into pieces as he closed his fist. Opening his hand, he let them fall with the others to the ground.

"What's happening on the surface?" He asked Thanatos.

"My lord, there are reports that the surface is dying," replied Thanatos. "The crops have withered, and the mortals and animals are perishing from lack of food. The shores of Styx are overcrowded, and Charon still refuses to ferry the dead until the weather improves."

"Where's Hecate?" Hades clenched his fist and turned to leave the room. "I need answers."

"Word has reached this side of the shore that...." Thanatos paused before speaking, making Hades wait. He sighed heavily and then looked to Hades. "It appears Hecate has betrayed your secret. Helios witnessed your abduction of Persephone and told Demeter. Hecate appears to be in league with the Goddess of the Harvest as she has revealed Persephone's whereabouts."

"It wasn't a betrayal," Hades said, turning away from

the crowd. "Hecate already warned me this would happen. I thought I had more time."

"You knew Demeter would find out and didn't wish to prepare me?" Thanatos asked with a raised brow.

"Yes," Hades said, descending the stairs toward his war room. "Does Zeus know?"

"I've received a message that Zeus knows as well and is furious at your refusal to tell him." Thanatos leaned in to ensure no one could hear. "He demands you bring Persephone back to Olympus, or else."

Hades stopped and turned back to Persephone, pondering his options.

"What would you have me do, my Lord?" Thanatos asked, eyes following Hades'. "Shall we prepare for battle?"

"I don't want Persephone to get hurt." Hades walked to the door and entered the room. "I'll have to go to Olympus and speak with Zeus myself."

"My Lord, I must insist you take guards with you." Thanatos folded his arms.

"If I do that, Zeus will take it as a rebellion, and things will become far worse for us," Hades replied. "I'm going alone."

"What about the surface? We're taking in more souls than the shores can bear," Thanatos argued. "And Charon…"

"I'll speak with Charon," Hades interrupted. "He can either obey me or join the souls in the river."

Thanatos leaned against the table. "What do you plan to do about Demeter?"

"I was afraid Demeter would do something like this," said Hades. "I knew it would be risky to be with Persephone, but now that the leaves have changed, the events of the prophecy are in full effect."

"How will we stop her from killing everyone?" asked Thanatos. "The mortals are panicking above and beginning to die. See for yourself in the growing number of lights."

Thanatos pointed to the orbs building up rapidly on the shores.

"You're right. Demeter is going to kill everyone unless she gets what she wants," said Hades, becoming more frustrated by the minute.

"What do you think we should do to get through to her?" asked Thanatos.

"I don't know," Hades replied. "But if I could speak to Zeus, I might be able to come up with something."

"I'll send for Hermes to deliver a message," said Thanatos.

"No matter what Demeter says or does, I'm not giving up Persephone," Hades growled.

Thanatos bowed his head respectfully. "I'll let you know when Hermes returns with a response."

Staring at the glowing orbs once more, seeing them doubling in number by the minute, he ran a hand through his hair. He needed time to think. Hades knew her mom wouldn't take this well, but to eradicate life was going a bit too far, even for her.

There has to be a compromise somewhere. But what?

An hour later, A knock sounded at the door.

Thanatos entered to relay the message from Olympus.

"Tell me," Hades said, narrowing his eyes.

Thanatos cleared his throat. "Zeus commands that you return Persephone to Demeter immediately. There's no other choice but to appease her mother. Failure to do so will result in your punishment and, if needed, imprisonment."

"Damn him," Hades growled, slamming his hand on the table. "He means to humiliate me publicly."

"Are you going to let him?" Thanatos asked with a sly smile. "Or are we going to fight?"

Hades stared into the fire. "Where's Persephone?"

Realizing the hour, she must have retired to their chambers. Or she was in some sort of mischief again.

**

Persephone had gone to bed early while Hades had been busy with Thanatos. Reluctant to leave, she couldn't keep her eyes open anymore and was curious about the colorful leaves that reminded her of their vision, but she dared not ask him while he looked so angry. Their attempts at being cordial were tenuous at best. After they made love, their arguments ceased. She'd softened significantly toward him and couldn't stand the distance they'd built all this time. Even her anger had its limits.

She sat upright in bed, reeling at another of the same dreams so vivid that she could still see her cold breath in the air. Witnessing the continued cycle of the world changing over and over made her mind reel. The life she had here changed her. Persephone could no longer deny her feelings for Hades, nor did she want to. It was time to confess how she felt about him.

Determined to speak to him, she decided to find him. But first, her curiosity needed to be satisfied, so she went to a small scrying pool to see if the changes she'd seen were real. Waving her hand over the water, Persephone found her home. The sight that greeted her was right out of her dream. The world was no longer green but white. The trees and plants were all dead, and a blanket of falling white flakes that looked like frozen glass covered the land.

Her heart began to race. She tried to find her friends in the spring. As the image moved to the pool, Persephone gasped and covered her mouth in horror. Each one of her friends stood waist-deep in the springs, trying to flee but unable to, frozen in place. Persephone waved her hand to see Olympus and found the same thing. Everything was barren and dead.

Nymphs and satyrs stood frozen in place as time seemed to stand still in the midst of them running for shelter. Scared and afraid, their faces reflected their fear of their new surroundings. Persephone's heart was pounding at the sight. There was no life anywhere outside. The silence was eerie, with no birds chirping, no leaves rustling, and no water burbling over rocks.

She splashed the reflection, tossing water everywhere in her panic. Dressing with a wave of her hand over her body into her gown, she left to find Hades. He had to listen to reason and take her back.If she could get to Olympus, she knew Zeus would listen to her and help her find Demeter. She would convince her mom that Hades was not the monster they all made him out to be and stop this madness.

Her mom would surely be upset. For how long, Persephone couldn't imagine. When one is immortal, it could be ages before Demeter would accept their love. Damn it! Why do I have to choose?

The feelings she had always felt for him welled in her chest. The pain of loneliness was too much to bear. Was this what it felt like for him?

Persephone would bring back the light and life to the surface. She knew it because she'd already done so. Combining her powers with Demeter's was the key to beginning the new cycle. It had to work. The freezing ice and storms would remain forever, and no world would be left if Persephone didn't try.

The hairs on the back of her neck rose, sensing someone was in her room behind her. The exact dark figure she'd seen lurking in her dream appeared from the shadows. She pulled her sickle to face the lean man with dark eyes drifting with sand. His light olive skin showed his bare chest under a dark coat, almost touching the floor as he walked closer with boots that made no sound. Medium curls of black dusted his collar, and glowing gold eyes thickly lined in kohl stared down at her, giving her a sense of unease.

"Who are you?" She asked, narrowing her eyes.

"I would ask you the same question," he replied with a smooth as honey tone in a high baritone, tilting his head and looking her up and down with little to no change in his stoic demeanor.

Persephone reached a hand to her back to hold the hilt of

her blade. "I asked you first."

"Fair enough," he said with a shrug. "My name is Morpheus, and I am the god who molds and shapes your dreams." He took a deep bow before her. "At your service, my queen, Persephone."

"So you do know who I am," she said, still suspicious of the god.

"I know of you and have often woven your dreams, but no." He shook his head. "We have never met."

"What do you want?" She asked, uncomfortable being alone in Hades' room with him. "Why have you come here?"

He stepped forward. "Because the dreams you and Hades possess are becoming more disturbing."

Persephone backed away. "You can see them?"

"Yes." Morpheus looked down at her with a sly smile. "It's been interesting shaping your most recent dreams. But the prophecies are still unclear to me."

Her embarrassment flamed in her cheeks.

"How much have you seen?"

"Enough," Morpheus smiled and walked around her in a slow circle.

"What do you mean?"

"Aren't you and the Dark Lord the cause of this?" He asked, tilting his head. "The end of the world."

"I was going to say my mother," she said with a shrug.

"If no mortals and immortals are alive, there are no more dreams." Morpheus stopped circling. "Meaning I would cease to exist. If I return you to Demeter, she may relent... Or I could kill you, and the issue would solve itself."

"There is another way," she replied, pulling her blade. "I've seen it."

He shook his head. "I can't risk it."

Morpheus took his hand from his pocket and pulled a poppy plant from his coat. The dewy red flower, with a small drop of water, dripped onto her forehead before she could react.

A soothing feeling overwhelmed her body as the sedative took control of her. Before she hit the ground, Persephone was asleep.

Persephone opened her eyes to a nightmarish place of darkness and emptiness. She cried out for anyone to hear her, but no one responded. Running back and forth, she tried to find a way out. Nothing could prepare her for the intense loneliness and helplessness she felt. Her tears soon wet her cheeks as she called for Hades or anyone who could hear her pleas. No one answered.

Despair began to creep up on her spine. Was this what Hades felt inside the belly of Cronos? To have no light, no love, only loneliness. It was an unbearable feeling. Her heart began to break thinking of how he must have suffered. He must have felt the fear and horror she felt now. All the original gods had experienced nothingness, apart from Zeus.

Persephone continued to search and fight off her emotions. There had to be a way out. She wouldn't give up. *Morpheus would pay for this*, she thought as her anger began to take over her fear. Searching deep into her gut, she called for her powers, but they didn't come. Damn it! She couldn't feel them. Which meant she wasn't in her world. Persephone remembered the dark figure before she arrived and discerned that she was asleep, trapped in this nightmare. How could she escape?

The wind drew her attention from her thoughts. Inside her head, Gaia's voice reminded her she could choose them both. Six months, six seeds. Yes. That was it. She remembered her mission when she'd awoken earlier. She would consume six seeds and spend half a year with her mother and the other half with Hades. How else could the world find warmth again if she was gone? The mortals and immortals needed her above as much as she needed him in their home below.

Each time she went with Hades, she would have to leave him. But it would only be for a short time. They would all have to deal with the separation to keep the world alive and have what little happiness Persephone could find that her mother was unable to. Persephone knew she would find Demeter and make her mother understand no matter the consequences. As for Hades... Where was he? How would he know what had happened to her if she couldn't leave? She cried out with everything she had, fighting against the nightmare.

"Persephoneee...," the familiar voice said behind her.

She turned to see her other self, standing in the dark in the same gown Persephone had worn at the party.

"What are you doing here?" Persephone asked, secretly relieved to see her.

"I thought you'd be glad to see me," she replied with a smile. "But if you want me to leave, I can."

Turning away, Persephone reached out and grabbed her other self's arm.

"No, wait." Persephone sighed. "I need you to help me get out of here."

The other's smile widened. "It's refreshing to hear you say so."

"Where are we?"

"We're under attack by an epioles," the other replied, looking around. "The God of Dreams took the vision of before we met Gaia and is using it to immobilize our body as the monster feeds."

"Do you know how to get us out of here?" She asked the other.

"There is only one way," the other said, tilting her head.

"What?" Persephone tucked her hair back out of her face. "What is it?"

"We must become one," said the other, holding out her hand. "Only then will we be strong enough to fight back."

"What will happen if we do?" Persephone felt uneasy. "Will you take over me, or will I remain dominant?"

The other smiled wide. "I don't know."

Persephone thought about the offer. *If she took over, would I even exist?* She wondered.

"There's only one way to find out," the other replied, hearing her thoughts. "Don't forget. I am you."

Persephone narrowed her eyes. "If I do this, will you let me lead?"

The other nodded. "If that is what you wish."

"How can I trust you?"

"The better question is," the other tilted her head. "Can you trust yourself?"

She looked around, hating the darkness. "What choice do I have?"

"There's always a choice," the other countered.

Persephone flexed her hand, wanting to trust she could control the other. She hated taking a back seat to her own body.

"If you don't like sitting back," said the other. "Then the only option is to join me and become one."

"What will I become?" Persephone asked, glancing at the offered hand of the other.

"Who we are meant to be."

Reaching out, Persephone chose trust over fear and gripped the other's hand. Both their heads shot back as the power coursed through her body like a bolt of lightning striking a powerful blow.

Suddenly, she was awake with her hand around the throat of the monster sitting upon her. The power coursed through her as before, though she was in control this time. Her anger boiled from the violation, feeling its tongue retract from her throat. Her grip crushed its larynx as it thrashed until its life drained from its body, turning it into dust, taking every drop of its life force into herself.

Rubbing her eyes clear of the fog, Persephone rolled over to her hands and knees, coughing when she saw a beast of a male holding Morpheus by the throat against the wall, cracking the surface with his helpless body flailing. His feet dangled as Morpheus struggled against the clawed hand of Hades that held him in place as though the dream god weighed nothing at all.

"Hades?" She uttered, weak, sitting up with the room spinning until the creature's energy gave her complete clarity.

Hades turned his head to her. His eyes burned completely black, with his blue flame exploding from both eyes. He turned back, his body engulfed in the blue fire mixing with the darkness that usually surrounded him, crushing Morpheus in his grip.

"Hades, No..," Persephone stood and crossed the distance between them, stopping just shy of coming into contact with a flame that radiated a powerful aura of heat. "Let him go."

"I came looking for you and found you in the Epioles' grasp," Hades growled, bringing Morpheus close to his elongated fangs. "You dare try to harm my wife?"

"I'm sorry, Lord of Darkness," Morpheus replied, choking. "I was trying to save us all."

"Hades, please," she pleaded. "He doesn't matter right now."

Slowly, Hades set the struggling immortal down, growling in his face again, then forced the miserable being to his knees.

"Tell me, God of Dreams, how should I punish you?" Hades' tone was so menacing it chilled Persephone to her bones and thrilled her at the same time.

"There are other, more important issues than this." Persephone walked over and placed a patient hand on Hades' arm, attempting to calm him. "Let him go, and I will explain everything."

Reluctantly, Hades shoved the god into a heap at his feet.

Hades cocked one brow. "Those that harm you must always receive punishment. This time, my love, I will have justice."

"Agreed," she said, touching his cheek and pulling his gaze to hers. "First, we have more important things to discuss, and no more time is left."

Hades calmed, and the room grew dark, leaving them as shadows with light in the distance illuminating Hades enough to see he'd returned his control.

"Get out," he growled to the cowering god who crawled and stumbled away from Hades.

Morpheus fought to run and eventually found his footing enough to escape. His form disappeared in a blue cloud that swirled over him.

Hades clenched his hands, fighting for control with his eyes closed. When he looked back at her, his eyes were soft and loving. Pulling her forcefully against him, Hades gently touched her cheek.

"No one is more precious to me," he said through strained breaths.

She smiled up at him, feeling her heart melt at his touch.

A cough sounded behind them. Thanatos stood, keeping his eyes averted.

"Speak!" Hades barked.

Thanatos bowed. "My Lord, Hermes has arrived... With reinforcements."

"He dares?" Hades began when Persephone touched his chest.

"What does he want, Thanatos?" She asked with more patience.

"Zeus is not pleased with your refusal." Thanatos sighed, placing his hands on his hips. "I'm afraid he insists you return to Olympus with Persephone. Now."

"Or what?" Hades growled.

Thanatos cleared his throat at Hades' intimidating tone. "I'm told you will be imprisoned for any refusal, no matter how polite."

Hades touched his head to hers, breathed deep, then released her.

"Prepare my chariot," Hades said, walking past them both.

"Should I prepare the queen's things?" Thanatos asked with a hard swallow.

Hades turned on his general and glared. "She's staying

here."

"What?" Persephone couldn't believe what she was hearing. "Hades, see reason. Zeus will punish you if you don't bring me."

Hades turned to her and brushed a gentle hand down her cheek with sadness in his eyes.

"I know," he whispered. "I don't want to lose you, so I have to go."

"Wait," she protested. "If you hear me out, I know what to do."

"My Lord." Thanatos following Hades. "You can't do this. You'll be humiliated in front of the entire court of Olympus if you don't send her back. My lord, please! Is this all really worth it?"

Hades stopped and turned his head with the most violent glare she'd ever witnessed.

Grabbing the God of Death by the throat, Hades roared. "Thanatos, if you tell me to send her back again, I will have your head. I said. Ready. My. Chariot."

Thanatos shook in his grasp. Once released, the god disappeared to obey his orders.

"Don't go," Persephone ran up and wrapped her arms around Hades from behind.

Hades turned and gently wrapped his arms around Persephone, bringing her tighter into his arms.

"He will kill you if you don't take me back." Persephone felt tears form in her eyes, thinking of how terrible Zeus could be.

Hades smiled, softening his eyes. "He needs me too much to kill me. I'll be fine."

He held her back by her arms and stepped away from her.

"Why won't you give in?" A single tear fell down her cheek. "I'm not worth all of this."

"You're worth everything to me." Hades brushed her hair back behind her ear and cupped her face. "The difference between Zeus and I is that he would sacrifice anyone, including Hera, for the world, but I would sacrifice this entire world for you."

"I can't let you do that," she gasped, shaking her head.

Hades smiled. "I wasn't asking permission."

Persephone's hand burned with need the moment it separated from his. She stared off at him and watched him leave. A horrible feeling welled in her gut. She knew that Zeus was only benevolent if you were of use to his grand schemes. But if anyone disobeyed, may Gaia help them. They would beg for a death that would never come.

Without thinking, she rushed to Hades, wrapping her arms around him, refusing to let go.

"If we are to be together," she said, choking back her tears. "We must face everything together. Including my father."

"Persephone..." He swallowed hard. "I can't let you go."

"You won't have to," Persephone said through her tears. "At least not for long. Besides, I have a plan. If you trust me, I will make this work. But you have to take me with you."

Hades let out a sigh. "What's your plan?"

"I will tell you," she said, letting him go as he turned to face her. "Once I have the proper pieces in place, I will succeed. I need a little more time before I can tell you all the details. Just know that, no matter what, I will return with you."

"How?" He growled under his breath. "Zeus will take you from me at his first opportunity."

"I know," Persephone said with a wicked grin to one side. "I'm counting on it. I need everyone to think I'm in one place while I gather the distraction I'll need for the final plan."

"A distraction?" Hades raised one brow. "How are you planning to distract Olympus from what's to come?"

"That's the point, Hades," she said with guilt, making her stomach sick. "I won't have to. You will."

"I don't want you there without backup," he argued, growing more incensed.

"I will gather a team to ensure I return." Persephone smiled and clapped her hands together. "And I know just who to choose."

"I have doubts," Hades said, pulling her close.

"Just trust me," she said, placing a gentle hand on his cheek. "I don't. Not in us. But I will need you to hold on for as long as you can so that I can make this right."

CHAPTER 18
PUNISHMENT

Hades drove his chariot, snapping the reins hard with her in his arms, cradled close to him. The mountains were a blur as they rushed through the valley where giants had cut paths long ago. Routes that were now empty of life while the winds blew so fierce it was challenging to stay on the chariot. Four black horses galloped in unison through the thick fog until they met the mountain's base. Shooting vertically up the slopes, driving them to the top of the mountain, they leveled out, landing hard on the uneven grass, stuttering to a halt.

A shiver ran over his body, and he stepped off the carriage to the ground that crunched beneath his feet. The dead grass was strange to see on an always-perfect landscape. It was freezing up here. So much colder than it had ever felt before.

He noticed no creatures prancing around, no garlands of decorations, no laughter. As comfortable as that was to him, he knew it was far worse than he could have imagined. Reaching out his hand, Persephone took it, stepped down from the chariot, and nestled into his arms. Nyctimus and the rest of Persephone's team would be close behind, waiting in the shadows for their command. At least they weren't defenseless.

Guards with a centaur leader approached with hooves that clicked aggressively toward Hades with each step. His horses neighed aggressively at the armored threat. The centaur was at least four feet taller than Hades, forcing him to look up at the broad-chested half-male-half horse. His blue eyes were shrouded in long waves of dark hair pulled back behind his strong jawline.

"Hades, God of the Underworld," he said formally with a bow, bending one front leg. "We are to escort you to Zeus himself."

"Don't bother," Hades said, tilting his head while glaring. "I'll find him myself."

One came close to touching his arm when Hades lit his eyes with his blue flame, making the uneasy guard reconsider and back away. Without another word, Hades walked between them with Persephone under his cloak as the guards followed behind.

The leaves on the ground lay covered in frost, leaving the trees and bushes bare, craning against the strong winds that howled. The once lush green landscape was brown and barren, covered in decaying foliage. Flowers and garlands that had adorned the palace were all gone, leaving the building to appear almost naked, were it not for the statues and colorful archways. The light in the sky had changed from a bright blue to an amber hue, and an eerie mist drifted by. Were it not for the chill in the air and the sight of their breaths, Hades had found it quite beautiful.

The colors reminded him of Persephone's changing appearance, which now seemed more permanent with her darkening hair and reddening lips. Her skin was still her usual olive hue, and her curls remained. But her walk was more confident and sensual than before. Something had changed in her after the epioles, but he wasn't sure what had happened. To see her blended as though both forms were one left him wondering. Perhaps she would tell him what had changed when this was all over.

He kept her covered from the cold and held her tight as they made their way through the courtyard, where their statues stood covered in dark vines and dead leaves. He paused at Demeter's statue with her arms in the air, wondering where she was in all this chaos. Persephone peaked her head out and stared at her mother's form with a sigh. She turned her head to meet his eyes and touched his cheek with a smile.

The centaur behind them coughed into his hand, signaling they should continue. Hades narrowed his eyes at the intrusion but decided to go into the main entrance without argument.

Eventually, they stood at the door where Hades had escorted Persephone inside. Thinking back on that moment, he remembered feeling so angry about the prophecy and having to do the ceremony again. Yet her beauty and kind eyes had enchanted him in the garden where they'd met before, and secretly, he was glad he would be her guardian so he could spend more time with her. Now, Hades was grateful for the warning of what was to come.

He kicked the door open and walked through, arms draped in his cloak to be warm. Even in the throne room, it was uncomfortably cold. Zeus raised his head to glare at Hades, watching with a clenched jaw. Persephone remained hidden in Hades' cloak, shielded from the cold.

Zeus stood and lit his eyes with lightning. "I told you to bring her."

"Yes." Hades said in a dead tone. "You did."

He opened his cloak to reveal Persephone to the crowd that gasped at her appearance. No longer the floral maiden, she stood draped in black lace over tyrian fabric with jewels and armor adorning her gown that dragged on the floor. Her crown was small but pointed as his, and she had her dark kohl eyes narrowed on her father.

"What have you done to her?" Zeus demanded, eyes wide

in horror.

"Only what she desired," Hades said through a glare.

"Damn it, Hades!" Zeus's voice boomed in the hall. "I gave you an order! You were to bring her back as she was or suffer the consequences."

"I already told you." Hades tilted his head up at Zeus with narrowed eyes and a growl. "She's mine."

Zeus gestured to the outside. "Do you see what's going on out here?"

Hades raised a brow. "I would have to be blind not to."

"Don't be coy with me, Hades." Zeus stepped forward. "Demeter is wracked with grief. If I had known this would have become such a problem, I would have never agreed."

"Yet, you did agree." Hades' eyes narrowed even further. "If I'm not mistaken, you and Poseidon had quite a few nefarious ideas on the subject. You also said you would handle Demeter." Hades looked to the ground and then up to Zeus, head cocked to the side. "If you can't control Demeter, what makes you think you have the strength to control me?"

"Hades, you go too far," Zeus' eyes flashed. "I would be careful. Your next words may be the last I allow you to utter. I am your king, and you will obey my orders."

"King," Hades scoffed and gave a short smile to one side. "Your realm is in tatters, your females can't stop fighting, and you have an endless supply of offspring. Who, I might add, do nothing but cause problems for all of us. To say nothing of your queen, who, unless you've forgotten, is still locked up in my dungeons. Forgive me, but you haven't been able to control anything for a long time in your realm. You make a mockery of the very idea of a king and ruler. You're so selfish you couldn't possibly understand the love that I feel for Persephone."

The crowd gasped at his rebuke and confession. It was the first time he'd declared his love for her publicly. The way his heart pounded at the thought of her in his arms so close to being ripped from him made his blood boil. She deserved better than to be torn between the two realms.

Zeus fumed, baring his teeth. "You will bend to me, Hades."

"Or what?" Taking a deep breath, Hades prepared himself. "I am neither your servant nor required to bend. I am the King of the Dead and an entire realm of the deathless. My army far outweighs yours. You forget I'm the one with the Titans. I will not bow to the whims of an adultering, childish, so-called ruler who can't even manage to control his lovers or his kingdom."

"If it's control you wish," Zeus said through clenched teeth. "I think I'll start with you."

"Do what you will," Hades said, not moving. He clenched his fists by his sides, closed his eyes, and bowed his head. "I know fighting you would rip our realms apart. And you can't kill me, or there will be no one to control the Underworld since none of you have enough power to contain the Titans without me. While I have no choice but to submit to your punishment, I will not bend to your demands. Persephone is mine, and I will not give her up."

"Hades," Persephone whispered with tears shimmering in her eyes, pleading for him to be careful.

"It's alright, my love," he said, bending to gently kiss her lips, causing everyone to murmur with shock and criticism. "I trust you to find a way out of this, but you'll have to trust me to endure this first."

"Why are you doing this?" Zeus asked, exasperated, his reluctance clear on his face. "You love her enough to force me to humiliate you in front of these lesser beings and let the world perish?"

"I would let a thousand worlds die to keep her," Hades said, gazing lovingly into her eyes and touching her cheek before turning back to glare at Zeus. "Do what you will to me. I don't care. But I will have my wife regardless of whatever punishment you devise."

"Very well, Hades." Zeus squared his shoulders and raised one arm to the sky. "I have decided you will take

lightning to your body for your blatant disobedience. You will suffer an agony of which you've never felt. Your blood will boil. Your flesh will rip and repair over and over. The electricity will wreak havoc on your entire body in blinding agony. You may never recover."

Persephone gasped and covered her mouth, looking at Hades with tears welling in her eyes. He shook his head at her to say nothing. Slowly, he let her go and stepped forward with his chin raised.

"Persephone is mine," Hades said, eyes narrowed at Zeus. "Do what you will. I won't stop you. But I won't give her back to you or anyone else, no matter what you say or threaten to do to me."

He could see the court was both impressed and filled with fear for his resilience. No one dared go up against Zeus, and his refusal was changing their attitudes toward him the more he stood his ground. From their sneers and mockery now changed to murmurs of appreciation and sighs of endearing love, Zeus was losing his own court.

"I think I'll start with taking my daughter back," the God of Lightning said with a glare.

Nodding toward his guards, they grabbed Persephone and pulled her away from Hades. His response was immediate as he punched the one closest, sending the centaur flying back. The other blocked her with his body and pulled a sword. More galloped into the room surrounding her.

"Hades, don't!" She cried out to him, shaking her head, their eyes meeting, reminding him she had a plan.

Zeus reached out, and chains appeared around Hades' throat, choking him. Two more appeared, grabbing his wrists and holding his arms wide. Hades glared at the ground, filling with rage while holding it inside. His instinct was to fight, be free, and tear apart this place. This was the only way to make them see he wouldn't give in. Hades knew that he could be permanently damaged but would endure it anyway. The agony of losing Persephone and being unable to touch or even love her was far worse than any physical pain Zeus could muster.

Zeus called to the sky with a hand raised. The nimbus clouds rolled in, swirling above them in a dark storm. Hades stood illuminated from below where the once moving floor ceased churning, stopping with the central circle around him. His breaths came faster as he prepared for the pain he would face. Eyes drifting to the sky, Hades watched as the power of Zeus' lightning built.

Suddenly, it hit. His skull felt like it was splitting apart. The shock of energy drove downward from the crown of his head, radiating through his body, was almost paralyzing. Hades planted his feet firmly, refusing to show any weakness, and stood when he desperately wanted to fall to the ground. Again and again, he took each lightning bolt, struggling to stay upright. His eyes lit with his powers, making Zeus step back a moment.

Closing his eyes, Hades fought to control the power, trying to save him. He pushed it down deep inside, locking it away. It fought against him, trying to claw its way up and out of him to fight off the lightning. Hades refused to let it, instead feeling its rage battle against him as the lightning continued to strike. His jaw clenched so hard he prayed he didn't break his teeth.

Each of his breaths was on fire. The force of energy driven through Hades lit up his veins. His claws dug deep into his clenched hands that pulled against the chains to hold on as the blood pooled at his feet. Another strike made Hades struggle, fighting his instincts more than the lightning.

He knew Zeus would expect him to submit. But Hades was just as mighty, and if this were the worst of what he had to endure, he would take these strikes over and over for thousands of years. Arcs of electricity erupted from his mouth when he let out a roar that only strengthened his resolve as he stared down Zeus with hatred.

Hours had passed with no rest to the strikes that gave Hades only a few seconds to recover before the next. He could faintly hear Zeus demand that he give in, but Hades refused to speak. As God of the Underworld, he would never give in. Zeus knew it. One of them would have to break before the other.

The only thing Zeus loved more than justice was his reputation. Zeus would appear weak if he let Hades go. So, this would continue for as long as it took to force Hades to submit. Hades resigned himself to an eternity of this if it meant he would win.

His survival forced his mind to begin to disassociate. The thought of her smile gave him the strength to keep going. Each time he wavered, he thought of her eyes, how they gazed into his with so many emotions. When his eyes closed, he went to a locked away place in his mind. A place where they could be happy with one another. Where all of this was just a dream, and they could be together.

He walked with her through the Elysian Feilds to a place where he'd built a cabin for the two of them. They sat enjoying wine and laughing as Persephone told him stories of her adventures above. The food on the table lay prepared for them to indulge when they wished. Persephone prepared platters to enjoy while they sat on the shared cushion by the fire. No one bothered them in this special place. It was quiet and peaceful.

The warmth of the sun he'd created shone on her pale face, illuminating her radiant smile. They walked the hillside, observing the beings that arrived, greeting one another with warm hugs and smiles as they were reunited. None of them noticed any others aside from their personal loved ones. They faded into the distance as they walked hand in hand to their resting place. As the evening approached, Hades would walk with Persephone to their special place to stay.

Holding her in his arms, Hades kissed his beloved and made love to her each night they spent together in the simple bed that remained a mess. At dusk, they would watch the sunset over the horizon filled with children and happy families settling down for the night. And each dawn, he would wake with her in his arms.

His mind replayed this fantasy as he waited, hoping Persephone would find a way soon to free him. And so here, in this place, he would wait for her. A space between the pain he felt and his mind where he would escape, trusting that she would return.

***

Persephone paced back and forth, wringing her hands. She had to get out of this room. Once the punishment commenced, Persephone was taken and locked in her old chambers. Hades almost turned when they grabbed her arm. He would have destroyed everyone in the room if she hadn't stopped him. She couldn't see what happened after he was chained but heard the first few blasts. Still able to listen to the thunder, her room shook each time the lightning struck. Persephone would not rest until Hades was free. Refusing to waste any time, she called on Thanatos to meet her.

"Thanatos, how is he?" Persephone asked, unable to stand still. "I know you don't report to me, but I need to know."

"I am loyal to no none other than Hades." Thanatos bowed his head. "In his absence, he has commanded that you are his proxy. Once you consummate your union, you will also take my place and fully command his army."

Persephone's eyes widened. "Consummate?"

Thanatos coughed into his hand. "Intercourse to finish the marital requirements."

Persephone felt the blood rush to her face. Thanatos recognized her blush immediately. He dropped to one knee and crossed his arm in a fist over his heart.

"Queen Persephone," Thanatos said, never making eye contact. "I am your servant. Your will is his. What can I do for you? Whatever it is, I will sacrifice to see it done."

She sighed. "Your loyalty is appreciated, especially in a treacherous place like Olympus."

Persephone bent over in pain, placing a hand over her

heart, feeling it ache.

She turned to where the light was illuminating the clouded sky. "Can anyone even withstand that kind of torture?"

"I know my Lord is strong, but..." Thanatos looked up when another bolt shook the palace. "I don't know of any who weren't permanently injured or worse from Zeus' means of punishment."

Persephone knew she had to do something. Zeus wouldn't listen to her. She knew that now. Her original plan to reason with her father ended the moment he saw her changed. Pacing again, she scratched her chin, trying to think of a way to free Hades. There was no time to negotiate with anyone while he suffered. If they wouldn't listen to her, then only one option remained.

"Wait! I've got an idea." She smiled to herself. "Find Nyctimus and the others and have them meet me here."

"What are you planning?" Thanatos put his hands on his hips, looking down at her. "Zeus will not release Hades unless you sacrifice yourself to Olympus."

"The sacrificing ends tonight," she said, assured of what she needed to do. "He could die."

Thanatos closed his eyes as the thunder echoed. "Hades would gladly die for you."

Persephone straightened her shoulders. "I'm not going to let him."

"What are you going to do?" He asked, turning to her.

"Bring Hermes to me," Persephone nodded to reassure herself. "I need to speak to him privately. And Thanatos. Be sure to clear a path for our return. I need the door open when we get there."

Bowing, Thanatos disappeared. She took a deep breath and tried to remain calm with her frustrations mounting. Several minutes passed when she heard a rustling of the curtains on her balcony door.

"Hey, Persephone," Hermes said with a wry smile,

hovering at her balcony. "Look, I just want to say I'm sorry. I had no idea Zeus would react this way."

"Tell me," Persephone said, leaning both hands against the table. "Is he still alive?"

Hermes scoffed. "Yes, but I can't imagine he would want to be."

"Hermes," Persephone said, clearing her throat for his attention, her ire clear in her tone. "How bad is it?"

"I've never seen anything like it," Hermes said, shaking his head. "To take one lightning bolt from Zeus is terrifying enough, but constant and in front of the whole court, in the middle of the throne room, no less."

Persephone clenched her jaw and looked away. She felt sick to her stomach.

Hermes sighed. "No one has ever dared to insult the king in any matter... Well, maybe Demeter. But it's brutal. Zeus is not handling it well, either. He says Hades will suffer without rest until he submits and agrees to leave you here."

Persephone stood back and crossed her arms. "How strong are your wings?"

Hermes scrunched up his face as though insulted. "I can carry anything so long as I have a hold of it. I'm way stronger than I look, you know."

Persephone pursed her lips. "Then I'm going to need a favor from you."

"A favor requires a favor in return," he said with a smirk.

"What's that?"

Hermes wrang his hands. "Could you put in a good word for me to the nymph, Daeira?"

"You're thinking about romancing a nymph at a time like this?" She asked, narrowing her eyes.

"Well," he said shyly. "Seeing Hades confess his love for you did something to me. I don't want to wait until my moment is gone, and you're so good with nymphs."

"Not all nymphs." Persephone sighed, pinching her nose. "Who is she?"

"She has the most radiant smile when dancing in the well of Kallikhoros," Hermes said with a wistful grin. "She is one of the many daughters of Oceanus. Do you think she would ever look at me?"

"A simple nymph and Zeus' messenger?" Persephone shrugged. "I guess there are worse matches. However, I have to be honest. I don't think it will work."

"I know." he frowned, looking down. "But no one thinks you and Hades will work either. I just want a chance. Maybe after you free Hades, you could travel to Eleusis. Say something in my favor? I just need a minute to talk to her."

"Are you sure this is the favor you wish to owe?" Persephone asked, feeling sorry for the heart-sick god. "No money or jewels?"

"I just want to talk to her," he said, drawing his eyes from the ground. "Even if she hates me, I want to know if she'll give me a chance."

Persephone thought for a moment. "I'll tell you what," Persephone smiled and patted his shoulder. "I will go to her after we get Hades back to the Underworld. I have a plan to return if you trust me. Will that be enough?"

Hermes smiled wide like a youth who'd found sweets. "Thank you so much. You won't regret this." Hermes stood tall, smiling from ear to ear. "Now, what was that favor you wanted?"

Persephone landed in Artemis' room, carried by Hermes, and found her sleeping. Startled awake, Artemis lept into Persephone's arms.

"Are you crazy!?" Artemis shouted. "What are you doing here? I thought you were in the Underworld."

"Shhh!!" Persephone grabbed her arms. "Listen, I have to rescue Hades, and I need your help."

Turning to the balcony, Persephone signaled to her group to come up. One by one, they gathered with Nyctimus to stand in the shadows, keeping watch.

"What are they doing here?" Artemis put both hands on

her hips. "And how do you propose we get him out from under the lightning without taking damage?"

"They're here for me. Artemis, meet my crew from the pits," Persephone said, gesturing for them to come forward. "Of course, you know Nyctimus."

"It's an honor to see you again, moon goddess," he said with a sly smile.

Artemis blushed and waved.

Persephone pointed to each one. "Next, we have Castor, her brother Pollux, Phoenix, and Wadjet."

"It's good to meet you," Artemis said with raised brows. "Never thought I'd get to meet beings from the Underworld. Especially ones so good looking."

"Artemis, focus," Persephone scolded. "Tell me more about what's going on with Hades."

Artemis nodded. "Honestly, it's unbelievable he's lasted this long. I've never even heard of anyone taking multiple strikes from Zeus. One or two is usually enough to make the strongest give in. How he has lasted so long is starting to make the court talk."

"What are they saying?" Persephone asked, leaning close.

"They think Zeus is making mistakes in handling this situation," Artemis said, shaking her head. "It doesn't make any sense. Why doesn't he just make Demeter submit? She's the one causing all of this."

"Because he loves her." Persephone looked into the moon's light. "He would never hurt her. No matter what she did. Even if she destroyed the world." A smile crept over her face when she turned back to the others. "What would any of us do for love?"

Artemis sighed and leaned against the column. "What wouldn't I do?"

She looked over to see Nyctimus staring at her. Their eyes locked on one another for a moment.

Coming out of her dreamy daze, Artemis cleared her

throat. "Okay, what should we do first?"

"We have to get rid of the guards," Persephone said with her hand on her chin.

"I can ask Ares, Eris, and Enyo to do that." Hermes replied with a smile. "I'm sure they've been itching for some mischief lately."

"Nyctimus," Persephone said, looking to the group. "You and the others will have to create a distraction of a magnitude that would warrant a hunt. I want chaos."

His large, perfectly white grin locked back with Artemis. "I think we can manage that."

Persephone nodded, then turned to her best friend. "Artemis. We need a way to unlock the shackles."

"He's locked up with Hepheastus' trap on the floor. Without him, I'm afraid we won't be able to get Hades out."

Persephone closed her eyes, clenching her fist. "Then I need you to find Aphrodite and convince her to convince him to release Hades. Hephaestus would never listen to either of us."

"Do you really think he will risk his life for Hades?" Artemis asked, shaking her head.

"No, of course not." Persephone squared her shoulders. "He'll risk his life for Aphrodite. Who better to know what love means than her? Tell her that I love him and I'm taking him home."

"You love him? After all that he's done? Even after everything that is happening around us?" Artemis placed a kind hand on her arm. "Persephone. He's not the good guy here. He's the villain."

"Perhaps," Persephone said with a sad smile. "If he is a villain, as you say, he's my villain, and I want him back."

Somehow, Aphrodite convinced Hephaestus to release Hades, as Persephone had asked. Her story had moved them both enough to risk the wrath of Zeus.

"Ah! I am such a sucker for a good love story," Aphrodite said, looking off into the distance with sparkling eyes. "Graces.

You three stand guard while Hephestus and I enter the room to release Hades. Distract anyone who comes along with whatever you've got."

The three females nodded and ran off to help as instructed. Persephone remembered the first time she had met them all. A shame she wasn't here for a social call, or it would have been nice to catch up.

"Now, Phaes..." Aphrodite's buttery tone seemed to cast a spell on Hephaestus. "Be a good god and follow me closely."

He nodded with his cheeks burning. "We have to unlock the chains with three different keys."

"Well, did you bring them?" Aphrodite asked, nuzzling up to him.

Hephaestus coughed into his hand and nodded. "I made them the other day when Zeus had planned this."

"Zeus was going to punish Hades regardless if I showed up, wasn't he?" Persephone asked, choking down her anger.

"Yes," replied Hephaestus. "Zeus has been unbearable since Demeter started messing with the weather. He's been furious and taking it out on anyone who comes in close contact with him. He recently raped a few mortals and a goose while he searched for you to appease Demeter."

"Are you serious? I mean, really? That's disgusting." Aphrodite scrunched her nose and gagged. "That poor goose."

"And the mortals," added Artemis, narrowing her eyes.

"Yes, of course... those poor mortals." Aphrodite waved a dismissive hand. "Can we get back to the issue at hand?"

"Right, we must stay concealed," Hephaestus signaled them to follow him.

They led her to the throne room, hiding in the shadows. The doors she'd first entered when she arrived, what felt like centuries ago, seemed smaller somehow.

An explosion rang out. The distraction of her old team had worked well, and when she opened the doors, the guards had just left to find what chaos had occurred outside. What she saw in the next moment ripped her heart open, and she fell to her knees, staring through tears at the one she loved in the most horrific pain she'd ever witnessed. Her breath left her body. She tried to say his name, but nothing came out.

His eyes had gone completely black. His claws dug into his hands as a lightning bolt struck. She felt her soul cry out as he took the hit, momentarily closing his eyes. His skin ripped apart in eclectic patterns as it trailed through his body, leaving a glow in its wake. She could see the blood under his skin, boiling. He stood with only his jaw clenching to show he was even conscious. How he could still stand was beyond her comprehension. Unable to stop herself, instinct overtook her when she saw another bolt coming, and Persephone ran to him.

Persephone wrapped her arms around his neck and kissed him. When their lips connected, her powers erupted, creating a shield of darkness and vines that took the hit. The smell of burning and the intense pressure of the pounding blast almost knocked her back, but she held him tight, amazed he could have withstood this. Her vines grew for the first time since coming to the surface. Once she heard the clicks from Hephaestus' keys, her vines ripped them apart, releasing him. Hades slumped forward, leaning heavily in her arms. Hephestus grabbed Hades' arm and put it over his shoulder, helping Persephone to carry him away before the next lightning bolt struck.

"Hades, wake up!" she yelled, trying to lift his head to look at her.

He seemed lost and unable to comprehend what was happening. As if he'd retracted into his mind to deal with the damage done to his body. They moved him as he walked with staggered steps away from the circle. He stood hunched over, breathing hard with his teeth still clenched. Another strike came, but they were all out of the way this time. Persephone cupped his face, calling to him. His black eyes slowly returned to green, gazing at her with such tenderness. He reached up a hand and touched her cheek, then pulled her into a deep kiss.

"I knew you'd return to me," he said in a husky whisper.

Artemis came running into the room. "We've got company. Come on, let's get him out of here. Both goddesses took his arms and wrapped them over their shoulders. Struggling with his slow steps, they found a hiding place on the balcony when the guards returned and managed to lug his heavy frame behind the curtain. He slumped against the wall while Persephone looked to see the centaurs searching for their missing prisoner. Upon finding him gone, they sounded the alarm.

"Good luck getting out of here now," Artemis said, struggling with his size.

"We have to try," Persephone said, adjusting his weight higher on her shoulder. "We have to make it to the stables to Aethone. Even if all we can take is her, she'll get him back safe."

"What if you get captured? They'll never let you see him again."

"It doesn't matter. As long as he's safe, I won't complain."

"Can we talk about that later? This god is the density of a dying star!"

Persephone stopped and narrowed her eyes at Artemis.

Artemis scrunched her face. "Sorry, not dying. Very much alive."

Persephone started walking again without another word.

"Persephone," He whispered through a scratchy throat.

"Shh. I'm getting you out of here."

"I can hear them getting closer," Hades rasped. "You should run."

"Don't talk right now. We have to hide." Persephone hefted his weight on her shoulder and walked faster.

"Could you all be quiet?" Aphrodite said, glaring back at them as she crouched and kept watch. "It's almost as if you've already forgotten your training."

His head wobbled as he tried to look at her, but he was too far gone. Hephaestus came over and helped the two goddesses lift him, and they dragged his limp form through the shadows, avoiding any of the guards. Showing them a secret way out, Hephaestus opened a wall behind a tapestry, and they hurried to the stables.

The beast's hooves kicked the stalls, trying to get out as they sensed Hades and Persephone approaching. Artemis ran over and opened the pens to let out the stallions and Aethone. With her hands up, she guided them to connect to the chariot. Hades found the strength to pull himself into the chariot, then slumped to sit at Persephone's feet.

Artemis came over to the side of the carriage. "You'd better go. Everyone is on high alert now."

"Apologies for having to meet again this way. It's not what I wanted."

"We can talk anytime." Artemis grabbed Perseophone's neck and touched foreheads to say goodbye for now. "Now go. Get out of here. Save your beloved."

Persephone was about to say something when the doors slammed open, and centaurs burst through along with Hestia.

"Persephone!" Hestia pulled her blazing sword. "Your mother's been missing you."

"Go!" Artemis yelled, pulling her bow and notching an arrow. "I'll give you a head start."

Hephaestus pulled his hammer and joined Artemis to take on the guards next to Aphrodite. Ares, Enyo, and Eris blasted them from behind and ran into the stables to stand beside Artemis.

"Never thought I'd see the day we'd be protecting Hades," Ares said with a smirk. "Guess he's going to owe us."

"Shut up, Ares." Enyo rolled her eyes. "Your quips aren't even funny."

Eris lit her eyes with a dark purple and tilted her head. "I'm just glad we get to cause a little mayhem. It's been boring without you, Persephone."

"We'll meet again soon. I promise." Persephone said, nodding to her old group, emotions welling up that they came to help.

"I'll bring the beer and cannambrosia!" Leaping into the air, Artemis began to hail arrows at the guards who took cover.

Hephaestus brought his hammer down, breaking the ground open and throwing the two centaurs galloping toward them back, destroying the side of the stable.

Aphrodite flew into the air, flipping with poised grace with her sword, and slashed one of the guards down his chest, goring him open.

Exiting the stables, Persephone was about to snap the reins when Hestia appeared before them, sword blazing with flames, lighting up her face filled with anger.

"Get out of the chariot, Persephone," Hestia said, eyes lit with a red flame Persephone had never seen.

She swallowed the lump in her throat. Closing her eyes, Persephone found her courage.

"No."

"You dare defy your mother and Zeus like this?" Hestia's confusion marred her beautiful face, then turned to rage. "Demeter is destroying the All Mother because of Hades' treachery."

"That's not what's happening," she said, gripping the reins tighter. "I mean, yes. Hades did abduct me and take me to the Underworld... and yes, I'm sure Mom has been sick to death from worry over my disappearance, But that was before... and you know, Hera... oh, never mind."

Persephone stopped her stumbling of words and squared her shoulders.

"I will find a way to make all of this right," Persephone said, heart pounding in her chest, knowing she was no match for the goddess of the hearth. "If you let me go, I will find her and end all this suffering."

Hestia swung her sword in a circle, ready to fight. "I can't let you do that."

"I wasn't asking," said Persephone, narrowing her gaze on her generally sweet aunt.

Persephone sighed and closed her eyes. When she opened them, they lit up with her tyrian flames, and the darkness poured from her eyes as she allowed the remaining powers of the Underworld to well up inside her. The other part of herself she kept hidden from everyone came forward, causing Hestia to hesitate and lower her sword in shock.

Persephone could feel her other dark self's presence in sync as their objective was the same. Without a battle, her two consciousnesses balanced and coexisted. The other growled, ready to murder anyone who came near Hades.

"So he has claimed you." It wasn't a question from Hestia, she knew.

"In truth, " Persephone said, pausing to look down at her hand, emanating a dark energy that tipped with the color of her eyes. "I think I've claimed him. So I'm taking him home, and you will let me." Persephone turned her gaze to Hestia, tilting her head to the side and raising a confident brow. "In case I wasn't clear, dear auntie, that wasn't a request.

"Persephone, I...," Hestia stepped forward but stopped.

Persephone pulled her weapon, spinning it to open the scythe that blazed with her powers, slamming its weight to the ground with a crack of the soil with a clear threat.

Hestia stepped back, eyes wide. "Where did you get that?"

"Mom gave it to me," Persephone said with a shrug. "Hestia, I have always had a deep respect for you. I ask that you respect my wishes and let me handle Demeter and the one I love."

The sounds of battle raged behind them. Persephone could hear the team she once fought alongside, audibly enjoying themselves as laughter and familiar banter rang out among them. They wrecked the entire area, fighting off guards. She was running out of time and needed to go. If she had to fight Hestia, she would. But she prayed it wouldn't come to that.

"You? You love him?" Hestia asked, eyes wide. "Is it true

that the dark one has found love?"

"Please, Hestia." Persephone held the reins hard, feeling the horses trying to move. "Let me take my husband home, and I will find my mom and fix this."

Hestia stood, eyes darting back and forth in thought, weighing her decision. Finally, she nodded, and the flames in her sword left her a dark shadow in the night.

"Go." Hestia stepped aside and kept her gaze on the ground. "I didn't see anything."

Persephone relaxed her powers and nodded, brows drawn at the mercy Hestia offered. She snapped the reins, causing the horses to lurch forward. Standing firm, Persephone braced herself for the powerful force of their flight. She turned back one last time to see fires erupting across Olympus as her team fought for her. The light in Hestia's eyes showed a sweet smile, and he gave an approving nod before the light extinguished. She didn't know why Hestia's approval felt like a win, but the eldest goddess was almost like a mother to her. She would find a way to stop Demeter once she rescued Hades. They could negotiate if she could get to the Underworld before being caught. If not, this would all be in vain.

CHAPTER 19 SEEDS

They rode hard, blazing through the woods to get to the Underworld's entrance. Olympus behind them exploded with chaos and fires erupting. The distractions were working. No one pursued them. She thought they had a clear path to the gates, but Persephone's worst nightmare came true just before they reached Thanatos.

Demeter appeared standing next to Hecate, who held a torch to illuminate them under a waning full moon. Persephone halted the horses as her hands shook, holding the reins. Steeling her resolve, she exited the chariot, keeping her shortened weapon in her hand.

Demeter was haggard in appearance. Her usual beauty was rough, with wild hair and a tortured look in her eyes. Her usually green robes were now red and orange with gold lining. Persephone felt the fear well up inside her as her dark powers emerged to reinforce her magic.

"Kore," Demeter said with relief, opening her arms. "I knew I would find you. At last, you can return home with me."

Persephone swallowed the lump in her throat and squared her shoulders.

"I can't do that, Mom," she said, brows drawn as she turned to Hades. "I have to help him."

"Look at you." Demeter tilted her head, observing Persephone's changes. "He's possessed you. Hades deserves Zeus' punishment."

"No one deserves that," Persephone replied, astounded that her mother would be so cruel.

Demeter gestured for Persephone to join her. "I know you might hate me right now, but I'm doing this for your good. Come over here and return home with me at once."

Persephone shook her head. "I know why you are doing this, but I can't let you."

"Step aside, Kore." Demeter's eyes blazed with gold fire. "You don't know the forces you are messing with in this conflict."

Demeter reached out her hand and formed a golden fireball, hovering over her palm. Persephone knew if she let her, Demeter would take this opportunity to kill Hades. She couldn't let that happen.

Persephone stepped between her mother and Hades. "I won't do that."

"He stole you away from me!" Demeter seethed with rage.

For the first time, Persephone saw what others had. Though always loving and kind to her, her mother was capable of vicious violence and cruelty.

"I..." Persephone stopped when Hades walked past her to step between her and Demeter.

"She's mine," Hades said, shuffling on unsteady legs to put himself between the two goddesses. "Zeus agreed to our union when we met. There's nothing you can do here, Demeter."

The murderous growl from Demeter chilled Persephone to her core. Hades held firm. Even with the scars of the lightning still glowing and coursing over his body, he tried to protect her. Only the black cloak hid the majority of the damage done to him.

"You monster," Demeter seethed.

"That's rich coming from you." His voice scratched, no longer smooth and deep. "This is your handiwork,' he said, opening his arms to reveal the extent of the damage he sustained.

Demeter glared with a snarl. "How dare you blame me for your treachery. You brought this on yourself."

"Look around you, Demeter." Hades tilted his head and narrowed his black gaze. "The world is dying because of you."

"How can I grow and harvest life when you've stolen my heart?" Demeter stood in her billowing robes, shaking in anger, pointing an accusing finger at him.

"So now you wish to steal mine? I would rather die than let you!" Hades roared back, his fangs and claws flashing out with his rage. "You kept her from me. I didn't know if she was alive after what Hera did to her. Do you know what that did to me?"

"You don't deserve to know anything." Demeter's hair blew wildly around her. "She is mine to protect, not yours."

Hades' gaze stayed on the ground as he fought for control.

"My wife belongs to me." Hades began to walk forward with such menace that Demeter's eyes wavered. "Her body is mine. Her blood is mine. Every strand of hair on her head is mine. The air she breathes is mine. Her soul, which you were so careless with, belongs to me. No matter what you say, Demeter, she is mine, and I will kill you if you try to stop me. Then, when your soul returns to the source, all of this will end."

"She will never be yours, you monster," Demeter snarled, extending her staff.

Persephone loved how possessive he was at this moment. Wishing she didn't feel so aroused by his aggression, Persephone knew she would have to fight her mother if this continued, or Hades would lose. Worse, yet, he could die. This time, she wasn't giving in. She would make them both realize she would go where she wanted from now on, and neither one would control her anymore. Even though she loved them both, it was time to decide her fate. She took a step forward and stood by his side.

"I'm taking him home," Persephone said with her flame lighting up her eyes. "Afterward, I will find you, and we will discuss what future I have decided upon. Until then, Mom, please. Let us go."

"What have you done to my daughter? What have you done to your eyes, Kore?" Demeter stepped close to them and glared at Hades with pure contempt. "You better not have stolen her virtue, or so help me. I will kill you."

"I haven't done anything to her that she didn't beg me to do," he said with a tilt of his head and a sly smile.

"Hades!" Persephone glared at him. "You're not helping."

***

He wasn't concerned for himself, but he knew it would break Persephone's heart if her mother were hurt, so he resigned himself to being the diplomat. He stood before her, ready to fight anyway. His body was in so much pain he could barely stand, but he would fight until his death to stop Demeter.

"Persephone, what's wrong?'Demeter asked with fear in her tone. "Has he touched you?"

Persephone stuttered. "Well, I... He... that is, we...."

Demeter could see the truth written all over Persephone's blushing face. Gold eyes lit with the glow of rage as Demeter roared like a lioness.

Hades stepped toward Persephone but stopped as he felt a burning in his chest. Demeter struck him with a fireball. Hades launched across the open dirt grounds, slamming into the base of a large tree, and landed on one knee with his claws buried into the soil. His hands shook. The damage from Zeus' lightning drained his abilities to the point where he could barely stand.

"Hades!" Persephone ran over to him, cradling his face to

look into her eyes.

"I'm okay." Gently touching her chin, he brought her lips to touch his.

Once Demeter saw this, she screamed a warrior battle cry filled with pain and hatred, lunging at Hades with her staff striking downward.

Persephone, by instinct, held up her hand and put up a shield in time to block Demeter and used her vines to snare her mother, wrenching her backward.

"Mom, no!" Persephone moved to block Demeter's attack but was pushed out of the way so fast she hardly saw Demeter's swing.

"Get back!" Demeter cried out, shoving Persephone several feet away. "I will kill you, Hades, for defiling my daughter!!"

Moving swiftly with her staff, she landed several hits to his face using her speed and agility. Hades jumped back, dodging her last strike, and appeared behind Demeter, staggering. He was too weak to use his powers, so all he could do was call his bident and block at the last moment before Demeter cleaved in his head. She was screaming like a crazed beast. With a twist of her staff, the grain pieces shot from the tip with a simple flick of her wrist.

Hades knew he had to avoid those barbs, or he would lose function in his limbs from the poison. Moving like the skilled ancient warriors that they were, they fought with a similar harmony as he'd fought with Zeus. Every thrust she made, he parried. If he thrust, she whirled her spear to deflect and flip out of the way. Her dress's fabric seemed to float eerily around her, and she used it to try to tie up his bident. Even with his injuries, Hades moved too quickly for her to catch him.

"Why are you holding back, lord of the dead? I thought you were better than this?" She spat with hatred.

Another stab of her spear went straight to his head, but he craned his neck to the side and spun out of the way.

"I don't want to hurt you, damn it!" He blocked her

thrusts and moved to the shadow to get behind her.

She knew his tricks, anticipated his shadow move, and stopped him as he emerged.

"Well, that's too bad because I will hurt you!" She brought the butt of her staff upward and hit him in the chin, throwing him backward into a large rock and smashing it to pieces.

Demeter leaped into the air and descended upon him to fling her barbed grain. Moving just in time, Hades twisted to the side, avoiding the grain as it embedded into the stone. He got back up with his sword ready.

"ENOUGH!!" They both stopped at her voice.

Turning to see Persephone in tears, they both relaxed for the moment.

"Both of you stop. Just STOP!!!" She screamed with tears in her eyes.

He felt horrible to do this in front of Persephone, but he didn't know how else they could have avoided this outcome. He stepped back, feeling ashamed to have upset her.

Demeter lowered her spear and moved to go to her daughter, but Persephone held up her hand to stop her.

"I'm so tired of people fighting over me and trying to determine what my fate will be," Persephone said with tears spilling down her cheeks.

Demeter positioned herself between Hades and Persephone, rendering a growl from Hades.

"I suppose you thought you could steal her away from me? That you could manipulate her to your side?" Demeter turned her hateful gaze on Hades.

"Demeter, we don't have to fight like this," he said, feeling his head spin.

Persephone's mother pointed her finger, shaking. "You, Hades, are no better than Zeus, Poseidon, or any of the other gods that take from us goddesses and expect us just to accept it with a smile and act as though you haven't betrayed me time and time again."

"That was never my intention," Hades replied, vision beginning to blur.

"While you and Hera schemed to betray me and my love for Zeus, I became pregnant with Persephone," Demeter countered. "You made him choose Hera as his wife. You knew we had a love affair, but you insisted on Hera. The choice has made him a serial adulterer. He may not have turned out that way had he chosen me."

Hades hated having to relive this mistake of his past. She would never move past this. He now understood why. Demeter was so upset that she took her daughter and hid her away safe until she was mature, unmolested by the turmoil and schemes of Olympus, ensuring that the influence of Zeus's corruption did not raise Persephone. Because of her hatred for him, Hades knew Demeter would never accept him as her daughter's husband.

Hades stepped forward, showing no one he was on the brink of collapse.

"Demeter, I wish we could end this rivalry between us." He let out a heavy breath. "I had no idea of the unfortunate events that would play out between you and Zeus. I wish I could go back and make a different choice. You know I would. But It's over now. You need to move on."

Her look of shocked indignation said he had screwed up with her yet again. There was no winning this battle.

"Move on?" she asked in a choked whisper before she narrowed her lit eyes. "You try moving on when someone you love chooses another."

Hades shook his head to clear it. "Demeter, I am sorry for the role I played. If I could go back and change things, I would. Zeus has been terrible to Hera. I know now that my actions ruined your life and the lives of many others with Hera's jealousy. But don't let your jealousy ruin what Persephone and I have."

Demeter scoffed. "I should have known you were up to something on coronation day. You were acting strange around

Persephone. When you touched her, and she passed out, I should have gone with my better judgment and taken her home straight away."

Hades glanced at Persephone. "Yes, you should have."

"But I didn't. I let you all convince me that having her be around her fellow gods was a good idea. That she could train as a warrior, and nothing would happen." She stepped closer. "You lied to me. You all did. I should have known not to trust any of you, especially Zeus. I promise you I will never make that mistake again."

"Mom!" Persephone yelled, distracting Demeter. "I know this will be hard for you to understand, but Hades didn't force me to save him. Remember that I was already on my way here when the incident happened. I wanted to see his world and experience all I could even before he took me from the Meadow."

"Why, in the name of Gaia, would you want to do that?" Demeter asked, shaking her head in disbelief. "What reason could you possibly have to see his dismal world?"

"Because it was his." Persephone stepped between her mother and Hades. "I didn't mean for our love to blossom, but it did. Despite what you and everyone else think of him."

"Blossoming love?" Demeter narrowed her eyes at Persephone and then glared up at Hades. "You call abducting my daughter to this gloomy, desolate place an act of love? Have you all lost your fucking minds? Does consent mean nothing to any of you?"

"Mom, I'm in love with Hades and wish to stay with him. I need you to understand," she said in almost a whisper, but his heart soared at her words.

He was stunned that she would say that openly.

Demeter groaned with a heavy sigh. "I know you think you love him, but it's all an illusion. Sooner or later, he will break your heart."

Persephone looked uncomfortable and folded her arms around her waist.

"I'm not a maiden anymore," Persephone said with cheeks burning. "We are husband and wife, and you will eventually accept my decision."

Fuck. He knew this wasn't going to end well.

"What did you just say? You can't be serious," Demeter said, eyes wide, staring at both of them. "He steals you from me, from our home, our world! And you would stand there and defend him? No. I will not have this. Your bewitching of my daughter is over, Hades." Demeter moved to her daughter, grabbing her by the arm forcefully. "We are leaving. Now."

"I won't be going with you," said Persephone, wrenching her arm away.

Demeter stopped and looked at her daughter with disbelief.

"What did you just say?" Demeter said with a warning tone.

Persephone held out her hand to show them the pomegranate seeds hidden in her pocket.

"Where did you get those?" Demeter demanded.

"I'm sorry," Persephone whispered as she went to Hades' side. "But I've decided."

Hades turned to see the deep red seeds that looked like rubies ready to burst. He couldn't believe what was happening. They looked so delicate in her hand as she shifted them around.

Hades had seen this stubborn side of Persephone too many times to count. Demeter, however, had never seen this side of her daughter before, judging by the constant look of shock, confusion, and disgust on her face.

Those looks on Demeter's face were painful to him, knowing his desires had caused this. Hades understood that he wouldn't be able to make things right. Perhaps Persephone could. His fears of her not returning were only partly quelled.

"Kore," Demeter said in a warning tone. "If you eat those, you will be trapped down there forever."

"Six seeds for six months each." Persephone gazed into

his eyes for understanding. "I will accept my role as Queen of the Underworld and Hades' wife. And I will fulfill my role above with you for the next six months."

"Six months?" Hades growled with his eyes narrowing. "I won't agree to that."

"Neither of you will be making this choice." Persephone looked up into his eyes, pleading. "I need you to agree to my terms, or both of you get nothing. Six months. It's the only way, my love."

Hades' jaw flexed. "Fine, agreed."

The seeds would draw her back, but her terms of six months with him and six months with her mother was not what he'd envisioned. And now Zeus couldn't force him to give her up no matter what punishment he chose. Hades had won, so why did it feel so hollow?

Looking into her mother's eyes, she surrendered the seeds into her mouth. Her eyes rolled back into her head as a dark cloud surrounded her.

"Kore! Stop!" Demeter screamed, leaping toward her daughter to try to catch her before she ate them.

But it was too late. The energy surrounding Persephone pushed Demeter back, and the darkness wrapped around her.

The ground beneath them began to shake, and a phantom wind emerged, surrounding Persephone. The tempest grew, making her gown creep with dead tree branches. Her crown grew larger, igniting with her flames, revealing the side of her she kept tightly contained.

Persephone's eyes glowed and lit with the same dark energy surrounding her. She looked down at her gown. At last, she appeared whole. Both worlds combined must have made her a terrifying sight to behold to her mother, who stood in shock and horror at what was happening to her only daughter.

"What have you done!?" Demeter exploded with fury and fire. "Now, you can never leave the Underworld!" Demeter turned her hateful gaze at Hades. "You did this. You turned her against me! You fucking coward!!"

She hurled a fireball at Hades, hitting him square in the chest, sending him hurling back, slamming into the rock.

Hades held himself up with one hand as pain wracked his chest. He coughed up blood. Seeing it for the first time since the Titanomachy, Hades felt fear that if Demeter did try to take Persephone, he might not be able to stop her. His body was on fire. It felt like his blood was still boiling from the lightning. As his joints ached, his skin felt like a million needles were stabbing all over. The last hit from Demeter hurt him more than he realized at the time. Taking on Demeter after Zeus' punishment was stupid, but what could he do? He would instead take a thousand strikes from all of the gods if it meant Persephone was safe.

"Demeter." He said with a laugh, dusting off his pants as he stood. "Is that any way to behave with your new son-in-law?"

Hades wrapped an arm around Persephone and pulled her chin up to face him, kissing her with all the passion he could muster.

He didn't know how much longer he could remain upright. Hades' vision began to fade. He blinked to clear them, feeling his head swim and his stomach churn as the world spun around him. He couldn't show weakness. Not now. Not when he was so close to his goal.

If he was being honest with himself, the truth was he needed Persephone. He couldn't live without her. Not anymore. He'd rather die than lose her again. If Demeter finished him, Hades knew he would die, knowing that only one of the best of the gods defeated him. It was a small comfort.

He pressed his forehead to Persephone's "Let's go home."

"Hades, I need a moment with my Mom," she said, kissing him once more. "Will you wait for me while I speak to her alone?"

"I don't have much time," Hades whispered in her ear.

Persephone nodded and turned to face her mother as he backed away.

"It's too late," Persephone said with confidence. "I've made my decision, and it can't be undone."

"The Underworld is not your home, Kore." Demeter's eyes flashed with emotion as tears filled them. "I am your home. The meadow is your home. I would even allow Olympus to be your home with your father. But the Underworld will never be your home while I still have breath in me."

"I will see you again, but for now, I need to take him home," Persephone said, squaring her shoulders.

"I will not allow it," Demeter snarled.

"Allow?" Persephone clenched her teeth. "You don't have a say in this any longer. How many more must suffer with what you allow? Haven't we all suffered enough from your demands? Hades took the punishment of Zeus' lightning because of your temper. And now you seek to control and isolate me. And for what?"

"I was trying to get you back."

Persephone clenched her fists. "Killing everyone unless you get me back is wrong! I am not worth killing all of Gaia."

Demeter placed her hand on her chest. "I would do anything to keep you safe."

"Now you know how Hades feels," Persephone said, angrily pointing to his slumped form. "You didn't tell him I survived even though he had a right to know as my guardian."

"He has no rights!" Demeter raged.

Hades decided to give Persephone another minute, then he would have no choice but to force them down to the Underworld. He was losing strength, fast. He needed to get to his throne, or else he'd fall into a coma, completely drained of his powers. Unconscious, Hades had no access to the energies he needed to revive. Only a god equal to his power could wake him. He surmised the only one willing to was still arguing with her mother.

Demeter pointed an accusing finger. "He stole you from me!"

"I would have gone even if he hadn't," Persephone said,

narrowing her eyes at her mother. "I was already on my way to him when Hera stopped me."

Demeter shook her head in disbelief. "I never could have imagined my only daughter betraying me for a monster."

"If he's a monster, then so am I."

Persephone's eyes began to glow, lit with her flame as she stepped in front of Hades in defense.

Her dark powers drifted around her. The phantom wind whipped around Persephone as her fire erupted around her body. Demeter stood wide-eyed, clutching her chest in horror at her daughter's appearance.

Pulling her crescent blade, Persephone clicked the handle, and it opened. Extending her scythe, she slammed the sharp edge to the ground in a loud crack.

"Kore, you know you can't defeat me." Demeter glared at Persephone for the first time with a single tear falling. "Don't make me do this. You might as well give in so we can go home and forget this ever happened."

"I will not," Persephone said through gritted teeth.

"You're starting to piss me off, little one," Demeter said, flaring her nostrils.

"The feeling is mutual," Persephone replied, bending her knees with one foot back. "Words won't make you listen. Perhaps action will."

Persephone lunged forward, striking a hard blow.

Demeter stepped to the side and deflected the scythe with her staff.

"You dare strike at me?" Her mother demanded, eyes wide.

Focus, Hades, he commanded his failing powers. He inhaled deep into his lungs for strength, and as he looked up, to his surprise, Demeter cracked Persephone right in the chest with her leg, sending Persephone flying backward.

Reacting on instinct, Hades used his remaining strength to get to her. Catching her in his arms, he knelt, holding her, staring into her eyes for longer than he meant to. His chest welled with emotion. She chose him. Completely and forever, she'd chosen him. He smiled at her, holding her to his chest.

"Persephone," Hades whispered, touching his forehead to hers.

Wrapping her arms around his neck, passionately kissing as though their lives depended on it, Persephone soon let him go and stood, grabbing her weapon.

Demeter snarled at the show of affection. "I will end you, Hades. You've taken the only thing I hold precious in this world."

"Let me show you what I've learned without you," Persephone said in her dark side's voice.

Hades couldn't hold her back. Persephone lept into the air, bringing her scythe down hard, forcing Demeter back as she blocked. Demeter gracefully slid backward from the force and readied her staff as she stopped. The ground shook with each blow as the two goddesses fought, each one able to counter the other. The billowing fabric of their gowns floated around them with each twist and flip in the air.

He watched, unable to stop them, feeling his energy ebb the longer it took them to work out their anger. Pride and fear welled in his chest as he witnessed Persephone's power defend them against Demeter. He hated that he could do nothing but watch. He couldn't even stand anymore.

Demeter blocked another attack but failed to stop Persephone's punch to her chest, sending her flying into the rock face. Falling to one knee, Demeter held her chest and glared, eyes erupting with golden flame. Fury marred her face as she stood and spun her staff, sending barbs at Hades.

Hades raised his arm to block, but Persephone moved in front of him, twisting her blade, deflecting each one. Moving too fast to see, Persephone rushed her mother, kicking her in her gut into the air, then flipped in a spiral and kicked again, slamming Demeter into the ground. Coming down with the scythe, Persephone barely missed as her mother rolled out of the way. She swung at her daughter, missing each hit as

Persephone stepped from one side to the next, then flipped backward at the final thrust. Raising her blade, she blocked her mother's staff as they locked together.

Usually, Demeter would have ended the fight in minutes, but Hades knew how much power Persephone now possessed.

Their feet danced in kicks and blocks until Persephone forced them apart in a split kick that struck Demeter in the chin. The blood spurted from her mouth as she hurled backward, landing hard. Demeter wiped the blood from her mouth with an appreciative smile.

"You have learned a few new tricks," she said, standing. "But I haven't finished teaching you a lesson for your wretched disobedience."

"You don't want to do this, Mom," Persephone warned.

"It's clear you need a good spanking, Kore." Demeter spun her staff and readied to fight again.

The dread of Demeter's words hung heavy in the air. Hades needed to warn Persephone of what her mother was about to do. He knew her fireballs were her next move.

"Persephone!" He called out to her.

She turned to Hades, eyes widening at his condition. When she turned back, Demeter smiled with a wicked grin as her hand lit with fire.

Without hesitation, Persephone flipped forward, dodging the first fireball. Twisting into a backward spiral, she avoided the next two. Her face turned to rage when Demeter's eyes met Hades, and she turned to aim one at him. Closing the distance in less than a second, Persephone grabbed her mother by the throat and raised her above her head, eyes blazing with rage.

Demeter grabbed Persephone's arm, trying to release her grip when her eyes bulged with genuine fear. Hades sucked in a breath as Persephone began to siphon the life force from her own mother. Fearing she'd lost control, he struggled to get up. His weak limbs barely held him as he stood to stop her.

"Persephone!" He yelled. "Stop!"

Persephone turned to him and smiled. It was different than before. This time, he could see she was in control. Tilting her head toward her mother, she narrowed her eyes.

"I tried to warn you, Demeter," she said in that haunting voice. "You should have listened."

Demeter gasped for air, unable to move as her body aged.

Persephone brought her down to her knees. "This is the last time you will seek to control me."

Letting Demeter go, the goddess collapsed to the ground. She looked at her hands, which showed signs of aging. Tears filled her eyes as Demeter looked up at Persephone.

"What have you become?" She asked with horror and tears in her eyes.

Persephone straightened her shoulders. "Who I was always meant to be."

CHAPTER 20
MOTHER

The exhilarating feeling of being charged without the internal struggle was everything she had hoped it would be—both energies of a singular mind with one purpose.

Protect him.

Her mother crawled forward with a hand out to touch Persephone's face when a gentle hand gripped Demeter's arm. It was Hecate who met her gaze with sadness and remorse.

"Demeter." Hecate pled with her eyes to stop. "Persephone has chosen. There is nothing you can do any longer. It's time to go."

The goddess looked back and saw Persephone standing beside Hades, holding him up. Tears in her eyes, Demeter sobbed.

"Come." Hecate wrapped her other arm around Demeter, lifting her to her feet. "It's over."

"Goodby, Kore," Demeter said through tears that stained her aging face. "May I never see your wretched face again."

Refusing to look back, Demeter faded into the distance until she was gone. Her tear-stained face was the last thing

Persephone saw before her heart broke at the pain in her mother's voice.

Hades dropped to his knee, spitting more blood on the ground. Persephone caught Hades in her arms. Seeing the blood spurt from his mouth, she panicked.

"Hades!" Persephone tried to pull him up to stand. "Are you alright?"

"Get me to my throne," he said, coughing up more blood through ragged breaths.

She gasped, covering her mouth. A chill went up her spine. All thoughts left her but to get him home. Persephone rushed him to the chariot, her lungs heaving from exertion with sweat beading down her brow, barely able to walk with his weight.

Persephone covered him with his cloak and grabbed the reins. She napped them hard. The agitated team sprung into action, galloping toward the Underworld's entrance. Thanatos met them at the gates. As she had asked of him previously, he held the door open using his powers until they were safe. They descended into the darkness, where she could feel the warmth of home once again.

Past the river Styx, through the darkened caverns of myst, beyond the entrance where Cerberus barked in concern for its master. Finally, they arrived at the stables. She could feel the fear emanating from the four ebony horses who tore away from their restraints, knocking over the stable helpers to be near Hades. Aethone was the most concerned, shoving the stallions aside, whinnying at Persephone with a plea in her red eyes to help him.

Persephone and Thanatos lifted Hades out of the chariot, barely able to hold up his hulking frame. They rushed him to his throne, his feet shuffling to keep up with them. Persephone ignored the gasps of the court when everyone saw him. Knowing Hades hated to appear weak, Persephone needed to get them out immediately.

"Get out! All of you." Her voice boomed in that haunting

voice she was becoming familiar with using. "Now!"

The crowd hurried out of the throne room until it was empty.

"Hades will need to recover for several days," said Thanatos, who continued administering aid. "He can't leave his throne while he regains his powers and heals."

"Find Hecate and bring her here to help him," she said, rising from one knee. "There's no time to waste. I must find Demeter and restore Gaia."

"Yes, my queen," Thanatos said with a deep bow.

"I don't want you to leave," Hades whispered, grabbing her arm to stop her. "Let me heal so I can keep you safe. I just need time."

"There is no more time, my love." She gently took his face and kissed his lips. "I will always return to you."

He cupped her neck to bring her closer to deepen their kiss.

"I have loved you since the moment I first saw you." He kissed her again. This time with more urgency. "And now I can call you mine for eternity."

"Focus on healing yourself," Persephone said with her brows drawn. "I need to use Hecate's scrying mirror to find Demeter. I promise I won't be gone long."

Hades nodded. Sitting upright on his throne, Persephone watched as his eyes turned black. Teeth growing into fangs, he clenched his jaw, gripping the arm of his throne with claws digging into the stone. Blue fire exploded around his body. The strain showed on his creased brow as he focused his energy on drawing from the Underworld.

His powers surrounded him as the blue light flickered with the dark cloud that engulfed him inside. She could feel the power emanating from him, but it would take time before Hades healed. It was strange to see him so vulnerable. Zeus' powers must have been excruciating to experience. Persephone knew that Zeus would have to make an example of his refusing the God of Olympus' order. But did it have to be this cruel and damaging?

She wanted revenge for what they did. Forgiveness was beyond her. All this destruction and fighting over her? Were they all mad? She could never have imagined that things would turn out so awful when the first vision arrived. The devastating look in her mother's eyes broke her heart. Still, Persephone was grown and able to make decisions on her own. She was queen. It was time she started acting like it.

Persephone waved a hand over the scrying pool. The ripples soon cleared to reveal the outside world was changing again. The colors were fading, and the trees and plants had all grown barren. The wind whipped the last leaves from their branches. Animals scurried to find shelter. Many lay dying from the cold. It would have been shocking if she hadn't already seen these images. Her mother was making it worse, and if things continued to progress, Persephone knew the ice would come soon and cover everything.

"Damn it, Mom," Persephone grumbled as she searched. "Where are you?"

She slapped the water in frustration, then began to pace back and forth, crossing her arms. Reaching her peak of anger over her failure, she realized she needed more help.

"Hecate!" Persephone yelled into the pool.

"My Gods, you don't have to yell so loud," Hecate said, appearing sitting on the side of the large pool. "It seems all the attention I get lately is always so aggressive and negative. I really need to clear these bad vibes surrounding me."

"Where did you take my mother?" Persephone asked, walking up to the Titaness.

"Take her? I merely escorted her away from the situation you caused," Hecate said with a shrug.

"You and I both know this was inevitable," said Persephone, narrowing her eyes at Hecate, who appeared with a thick strip of white at her temple against her raven hair.

"The chaos you're able to cause is truly inspiring my darkling," Hecate said with a sly smile.

Persephone pinched the bridge of her nose for patience. "I need to find her and speak to her. Alone."

"Why can't you find her in the reflections?"

"I don't know." Persephone turned away, placing her hands on her hips as she paced.

"That's strange." Hecate tapped her chin. "She could easily hide from many of us, but not you."

"I've looked everywhere." Persephone clenched her fists to avoid striking anything. "The surface is getting worse, and I need your help to devise a plan to stop her."

"You've already made your decision, my dear," Hecate said, leaning back. "I'm afraid you'll have to lie in this naughty bed you've made."

"I ate six seeds," Persephone said, facing Hecate. "Dividing the year into six months means half of it I will be with Hades, and the other half I can return to the surface and work with Demeter to wake the world from the frost. Gaia told me I had a choice, so I've made mine. There's no changing it now."

"Your mother won't accept this," Hecate said, shaking her head. "She wants you home permanently."

Persephone folded her arms. "Demeter said she wanted me home and Hades punished by Zeus, and she got what she asked for. She never specified how long I had to return to Olympus."

"Oh, you clever goddess." Hecate said, clapping her hands. "Seems you're beginning to get the hang of the politics of this world after all."

"Hades is just as unhappy about it as she is," Persephone said, resuming her pacing. "Now, neither can do anything about it."

"Yes, the bargain has been struck." Hecate walked over to the carafe of wine sitting on the table by the fire. "The good news is, you don't have to keep starving yourself."

Hecate handed Persephone the wine in the chalice that remained empty since she had arrived. Taking the glass, she sipped the flavors of pomegranate and chocolate, sighing at the warmth that filled her belly. It was exquisite. Not too sweet, but enough to satisfy her aching stomach. She tilted her head back, enjoying the heady feeling that warmed her all through her core.

"Thank you." Persephone continued to drink the remaining wine until it was gone.

Licking her lips, she sat, wondering where her mother would have disappeared.

"When did you last see her?" Persephone asked, holding her glass out for a refill, which Hecate smiled and obliged.

"The last place I saw her was near Athena's city."

"You mean Poseidon's city?"

"Ah, yes." Hecate gave a sly smile. "They're still working that out."

Persephone waved a hand dismissively. "It doesn't matter what it's called. What happened after you took her to this city?"

Hecate frowned and looked down at the floor. "Demeter crumbled to the ground and wailed for several minutes. Then she just stopped. It was eerie, to be honest. Then she got up and removed her robes. Naked, she walked west toward a town called Eleusis."

Persephone took another sip. "Did you try to stop her?"

"What a stupid question," Hecate clicked her tongue. "Of course I did, but she hit me with a powerful force that knocked me back several feet. Her power surprised even me. Then the snow came and covered her tracks behind her."

"Snow?" Persephone asked, raising a brow.

Hecate nodded. "Yes. That's what it's called."

"And you didn't see where she went?" Persephone groaned. "I thought you could see everything?"

"I can see nothing past indecision," Hecate filled her glass and drank it. "Besides, she whipped up one monster of a storm that chilled even me to my bones. I watched her naked form go pale as ice, and her hair turned stark white. Once she was gone from view, I sought shelter in the nearest cave. Until you called, I was stunned to see what she could do. She'd manifested a new form. Once the Goddess of Grain, she is now the Winter Goddess. I've never seen anything like it in all my years."

"No wonder I couldn't find her," Persephone said, finishing her glass and setting it on the table. "She's no longer connected with me."

"What madness," Hecate grumbled. "How could she do that?"

"You must have missed the betrayal in her eyes when I chose to take Hades home," Persephone replied with a side-eye.

One brow raised as Hecate nodded. "That's true. Demeter is one to hold a grudge. But we both know how much she loves you."

"And I love her." Persephone looked at her hands that fought against her mother. "In that moment before she left, the pain I saw broke my heart. I can't allow her to destroy our world because of me. She can't control me anymore. No one can. Not even my husband."

"You've grown so much since you arrived on Olympus." Hecate sighed. "It was inevitable that you would change. It's hard for a mother to accept when it's time to let go."

"Will you help me find her with your abilities combined with mine?" she asked the Titaness.

Hecate popped over to sit in the oversized chair, crossing her legs. "It's in all of our best interests to find her as quickly as possible. The outside damage affects all realms, and we must get you to the surface to rebuild."

The Titaness filled her glass with the other full carafe.

"Hades won't like that I have to leave," Persephone said, sitting forward and offering her glass to be filled.

Hecate topped off Persephone's glass and leaned back in her chair. "What choice do you have now, my darkling?"

Persephone sighed, resigning herself to the next six months without his touch. It would be torture for her as much as he. She knew she had a duty to both worlds.

How she was to manage was beyond her imagination. All she knew was that without Demeter, Persephone couldn't fix the damage to the surface.

***

Hades felt the magnitude of energy the Underworld produced from Tartarus to the upper levels. Pain ripped through his body. The damage he'd sustained was draining his life force. He needed power from his entire realm to heal. Hades rolled his eyes back, digging deep, drawing from every space.

The violent force of his entire realm slammed into him.

The surge was like riding Aethone at top speed while spiraling through the air. It was everything he could do to hang on. Healing was going to take a while. More importantly, he had to take only enough to recover but not break anything in his realm. Vaguely aware of his surroundings, Hades focused on every problem he could find in his body, starting with his failing organs. So many areas had been damaged nearly to ruin. Though he was immortal and would heal, his throne would speed up the process exponentially. Regretting how terrible the unfolded events had gone, his only comfort was that Persephone had made it home with him.

Wanting to be with her and help her find Demeter, Hades felt helpless, unable to be of use without his powers. All he could do until he recovered was disassociate and hold on to his throne to escape the searing pain. His mind began to go to the place he knew would be a relief from his reality. The only place he could speak to her...

Surrounded by mist, Hades sat alone in his mindscape on a small deserted island surrounded by black waters and mist that was calm and quiet. The pain was a distant feeling he could recognize but no longer feel. Only the draw of power from his realm could reach him here.

Here, he only needed to think about her when a light shone brightly before him as a female figure walked toward him. Her presence cut through the fog, illuminating the island he sat upon alone.

"Rhea?" Hades asked the figure, squinting and reaching up to shield his eyes.

"Hello, my beautiful little one," she said with a gentle smile, towering over him as large as his father. "Are you fighting with your siblings again?"

Her light dimmed enough to no longer blind him as she walked on the dark waters onto the shore in her bare feet. Her sparkling white robes dragged behind her but never showed signs of being wet. Her thick, dark brows surrounded her golden eyes, which complimented her golden beige skin.

"No more than usual," he said with a slight chuckle, feeling comfort at the sight of his mother.

Her bright, white hair glowed around her disapproving face. "You laugh, my son, but the situation has appeared to get out of hand."

Hades cleared his throat, looking to the ground in shame. "I tried to prevent this."

"Did you?" She asked with a raised brow.

Hades growled, turning away from her. "You always take their side."

"I'm not taking anyone's side," she said, bending down to sit. "I simply wish to know your heart."

Hades scoffed. "My heart is what got us into this mess."

"Your heart is the most gentle of all," Rhea said, leaning on one arm. "You didn't want any of this pain or deserve it."

Hades turned away from her again, feeling shame and remorse for Persephone. If he hadn't taken her, none of this would be happening.

"This is all my fault," he said, head bowed.

"Prophecy is never kind," said Rhea with a heavy sigh. "But the events that continue to unfold could not be prevented. I wish it were easy, but love never is."

Hades sighed, pulling his knees to his chest. "Demeter is furious and heartbroken. Zeus is on a rampage to punish those disobeying him. Persephone can only be with me for half a year. I will have to draw enough power to heal, which may have dire consequences for the magic that holds the seals in place over the Titans. Ultimately, I'm helpless to watch these events unfold and witness the damage left in the wake of my decisions. I can't stop the storms from coming. Nothing has gone right for me."

Rhea nodded. "I felt the same helpless feeling when I watched my babies one by one be consumed by your father. My heart still breaks that I wasn't strong enough to protect you."

"How could you have stopped him?" Hades looked up into her radiant face. "Cronos was too powerful."

"After Hestia disappeared," Rhea began, keeping her eyes to the ground. "I suspected it was your father, but I had no proof. I couldn't see what he was doing. I should have run away with you then. I should have saved you, but I couldn't leave without help. We had fought together against Ouranos, our father, as you did with yours, and won. Then Cronos and I fell in love for a long time. To be betrayed by him by hiding the prophecy that destroyed our family and taking away my children, I will never forgive him. To say nothing of what he made me do as an accomplice."

Her murderous look of rage was even more frightening when her eyes turned white, and she bared her teeth. Taking a deep breath, she closed her eyes and regained her calm.

"If I hadn't taken Persephone from Demeter..." Hades shook his head. "Maybe I should have waited. You probably felt the same way she did. That's why you left with Zeus and why she left with Persephone. And I had a role to play in her fear for Persephone's safety. Our world is unkind. Perhaps I am the monster Demeter calls me."

Rhea touched his hand, but he felt nothing. "Trust Persephone. Trust that she loves you and will always return."

"If I hadn't been so impatient..." Hades wrapped his arms

around his knees.

Rhea looked at her hand's transparency and placed it in her lap. "Demeter would never have agreed. She's too stubborn, like her father."

"Persephone inherited the same trait," he replied with a slight smile.

He liked how headstrong she could be. How much passion she held for the world was intoxicating. And the rarest of all was how she could see through to the inner being to know if it was friend or foe. She was fearless.

"Hades, you deserve love," Rhea said, drawing up her brows. "Nothing in this world would make me happier than to see you at peace."

Hades swallowed hard. "How can I be at peace without her?"

"You will endure, my son," Rhea said, straightening her shoulders and clasping her hands together.

"How?"

"You are the strongest and most vulnerable of my children. As we all do in these immortal vessels, we must use that strength when things do not go our way. We do what we must and persevere, no matter the obstacle. She must love you very much to choose to stay in the Underworld. Take heart in knowing you can be with her, even a little," Rhea said with sadness shadowed in her eyes. "Many of us are not so lucky to have such a connection with another."

"Maybe you're right," he said with a sigh. "I'm lucky to have her at all. But for how long? And what should I do about Zeus and the others?"

"Zeus will calm eventually, and Demeter, though stubborn, loves Persephone." Rhea smiled. "She will come around to your union. Her pride is hurt, and her temper hasn't run its course. She will need time, but she will relent."

"And Persephone?" Hades asked, extending a leg out and leaning on one arm. "How am I going to live without her for so long? I want her to stay with me."

"Let Persephone go to Demeter first," Rhea said after some thought. "Have faith, my little one, that all will be well."

He shook his head. "I don't want her to leave. Not yet. I need more time with her."

"Hades, you are a god. You have all of eternity with her," she replied with a caring smile that always made him feel better.

"You're right," he said, swallowing hard. "I can't keep clutching her so tight to me anymore."

Rhea nodded. "Persephone will return every half year. You get to have your queen and save the world if you just let go and trust she will return."

"Trust." He swallowed his feelings. "I'm afraid to trust."

"Have courage as Persephone does when facing hardship." Rhea tilted her head to meet his eyes. "She trusted you, so now you must do the same."

"Though I had doubts, she did save me from Olympus." Hades smiled to himself. "She nearly burned the place to the ground."

"She did, didn't she?" Rhea chuckled, covering her lips. "She deserves an elevated position of the gods for succeeding."

"Persephone is already my queen, elevated by my status," he said, feeling pride that she was so brave.

"True," Rhea agreed. "However, in this instance, she earned her place. Not through might or brute strength, and certainly not on her own. But by using her intelligence, her friendships, and by listening to her heart."

"She knew once Olympus was on fire, it would signal Demeter."

"Persephone took the risk of captivity to save you," Rheia said, holding her head high. "For that, I will be eternally grateful to her."

"When she asked me to trust that she had a plan, it never occurred to me she would destroy all of Olympus to bring me home," he said, feeling his emotions well inside of him. "I didn't know she loved me enough to do such a thing."

"Even the blind could see how much she loves you," Rhea said, tilting her head. "Her only struggle was Demeter accepting it."

Hades bowed his head. "Their connection is fractured because of me."

"Fractured but not broken." Rhea countered. "Persephone will use that connection to find Demeter and repair it. You'll see."

"She'll be gone before I wake up." Hades sighed. "If she hasn't left already."

"Yes." Rhea nodded. "Until you wake, I will stay with you so you're not alone in the dark. I know how much you hate being alone."

A single tear fell down his cheek as he wrapped his arms around his bent knees.

"I wish you were really here," he whispered.

"I am always with you, my little one. Even when the light shines the least."

CHAPTER 21
RETURN

Persephone left the room after days of searching. How many? She didn't know anymore. She'd stopped counting after nine to focus on finding Demeter. The last stage of the vision had finally arrived. The storms had frozen everything. The harvests were gone, and a drought fell upon the world. Hades was still recovering, and she was beginning to worry that it was taking so long.

Sitting gnashing his teeth, still surrounded by the flaming glow of his powers pulsing around him, he'd not moved this entire time. Her desire for Hades was burning as hot as the blue flame surrounding him. She needed him now more than ever, but his recovery was more important than her desires. Hades would have to stay there for as long as it took to heal, possibly several more days, perhaps weeks, to regenerate his powers. She knew that now was the only chance to leave and find Demeter.

There was no other choice. As much as she hated her decision, Persephone knew it was the only way to have them both and save everyone. Without Hades, she had to find another way out. There was only one creature that would dare take her.

Persephone paced and watched the events above in the reflection. Waving her hand over it, she scanned for her mother, finding nothing. The rage boiled inside her when something caught her eye, and she froze. Persephone saw an elderly mortal hobbling near a newly built temple with a statue that was an uncanny resemblance to the Goddess of Grain. She repeatedly saw this aged yet still beautiful human woman and couldn't understand why until it dawned on her. The human female may have hunched shoulders with white hair, but Persephone knew it was Demeter.

"There you are," Persephone said to herself as she ran out the door to the stables.

"Saddle Aethone," Persephone demanded to the stable worker.

"My queen, the mare is only allowed to be ridden by my Lord, Hades," the short male with horns said, shaking and bowing at his waist. "I could not do so against his will."

"Get out of my way," she said, pushing past him. "I'll do it myself."

"My Lady! She's too dangerous." He reached out a hand and stopped before he touched her.

Persephone's eyes lit with her fury. "So am I."

Opening Aethone's door, Persephone went in and greeted the horse.

"I need your help, old friend."

Aethone sniffed around Persephone, then whinnied in a tone of disappointment.

"Apologies," she said, petting the mare's nose. "I didn't bring you anything. There wasn't time. I promise to remedy this when we return."

Aethone tilted her head and then nodded. Grabbing the saddle, Persephone prepared Aethone.

"My queen, wait." Thanatos appeared and stood in her way of the stable door. "You can't leave. He would kill me if I let you."

"There's no time to argue about this," Persephone said, getting onto Aethone's back.

"He needs you here," he replied, grabbing her reins.

"I will return," she said, touching his hand and gently removing it. "I promise."

"But..."

"Thanatos, I need you to trust me and care for him while I'm away." She pulled the reins to turn the mare toward the door. "Tell him I found her and will make this right."

Leading her out of the stables, she whispered into Aethone's ear where to go, and the horse took off galloping into the air.

The snow drifted, covering the battlefield. Blood soaking the mounds of bodies was a stark contrast to the white blanket that showed Aethone's footprints. To her relief, the smell of death reeked less than it would typically due to the cold.

She scanned the area and the skies to see the gods invisible to mortal eyes. Winds howled over the snow drifts, and hovering above the battlefield, facing off, were Athena and Poseidon. They pointed to their armies, shouting commands forward. Persephone watched as the humans fought with great skill and bravery for the city by the sea. She wished she could stay long enough to greet her old friends Ares, Enyo, and Eris, who were somewhere on the field relishing in the fight. She missed their adventures, she thought, resigning herself to her goal. Persephone turned Aethone to ride west toward the last direction Hecate had seen the Winter Goddess. The village of Eleusis.

Demeter's godly essence ceased to be trackable about halfway there, so Persephone dismounted and continued on foot. Her promise she'd made to Hermes had fortuitous timing. How convenient she would find her mother in the same place as his lover. Two birds with one stone sounded like an ideal situation.

First, she would discover Demeter's location. After

making peace, Persephone would need to find Daeira, the nymph of the well of Kallikhoros, and set a time and place to meet with Hermes. With a wish of good luck and a pat on the back, it was up to him to make it work.

Persephone walked for miles holding Aethone by the reins, looking for clues that Demeter had been there. After a few confused looks from passersby, it became apparent Persephone appeared underdressed for the bitter cold. Though Persephone knew the cold only as an inconvenience, to others, it was deadly.

Not wanting to stand out, she waved a hand over her appearance, summoning plain brown leather with warm fur lining that formed over her body, covering her fully. Her bright red hair was like a beacon in the snow, so Persephone figured a covering over her head would make her blend in with the humans. Persephone found a light tan himation hanging on a clothesline, forgotten, so she took it down.

The cloth was solid and immovable. She warmed the stiff fabric with her flame until the fibers softened enough to wrap over her shoulders and cover her head. Over by another cottage was an abandoned horse head cover decorated with red beads and wool meant to drape over the horse's eyes. The blanket beside it covered in snow was a dark brown. Persephone took them both and covered Aethone's wings and eyes so the humans wouldn't be frightened of the mare.

"That's better," Persephone said to Aethone. "Are you comfortable?"

Aethone nodded and nudged Persephone's arm.

"I know," she said, petting the mare. "I'm worried about him too. It's just a little bit further. Once we get to the village, I promise we can rest. I'll see if I can find any fruit there for you. Although, judging by the looks of things, that may not be possible."

In time, Persephone came to a small village that was still developing. There was a palace and a market that was lively and loud. But the most popular place appeared to be the temple, filled with crowds of humans as it received the final touches of construction.

Folks of all ages and creeds gathered together, seemingly starved to skeletons, as they prayed for the harvest to return. She followed them up the path where her mother's visage appeared, walking with symbols of the harvest carved surrounding her. The relief on the wall was vibrant, resembling the youth and beauty of her mother. Demeter's figure appeared similar to her statue on Olympus, where Persephone once stood beneath, feeling insignificant. Now, she only felt worried, not knowing if her mother could recover. The mortals painted the goddess's long hair gold with green and gold robes holding a sheath of grain. Simple columns held up an enormous roof over a building that, upon entering, revealed a room the size of a small arena.

Entering the temple with the crowd, walking past the praying emaciated humans, what she saw at the altar was beyond comprehension. A man wearing a crown stood beside her mother, offering a goblet filled with perhaps wine. She didn't know. But the effects of the wine seemed to send the humans into a trance-like state with their hands out as though seeing visions.

Demeter, once the most powerful Goddess of Grain, was now living as a human. Though she showed signs of age, she was still beautiful. Hecate had been right. Her hair was as silver and white as the snow that fell outside the temple. Her robes were white with a laurel of ice crystals on her head, and her skin was pale like the mortals, with no goddess light shining beneath it. Though unrecognizable to others, the sorrow in the older woman's eyes was unmistakable. This was her mother.

The king raised his goblet. "Once our beloved Doso, now our venerable Goddess Demeter, we honor this temple with this wine and remaining food from the harvest for all of you."

"Thank you, King Celeus," Demeter said, handing him herbs to add to the wine. "Your generosity pleases me and will bring much-needed sustenance to the people."

"We are blessed to have a harvest at all, thanks to you." he bowed and drank the wine. "If only we knew how to bring the plants and trees back to life...."

Her smile faded. "Only my daughter's return will herald the warmth of spring. Then you will sow seeds into the soil as I teach you the ways of agriculture. Until then, there will be no harvest, no bounty, and no more beasts to sustain life on Gaia."

"Isn't there anything we could sacrifice to appease her enough to return?" King Celeus asked with his brows drawn.

Demeter shook her head. "Survive as long as you can, and pray my daughter returns before the end."

Persephone was shocked to find her mother revealed to mortals and led them in the worship of her. What in Gaia's name happened during the time Demeter was here? She couldn't let her mother see her yet. Persephone ducked out of the crowd and searched for where Demeter's chambers would be.

It didn't take long for Persephone to find a door with symbols of grain and harvest painted on it. Stepping inside, she closed the door and looked at the barren room. The walls, bedding, and even the furniture were snow white. Shards of ice on the lighting and curtains made a tinkling sound as the cold breeze blew through the room. Instead of torches with flame, the light was more like dancing blue sparkles swirling in a spiral.

The door opened behind Persephone. She turned and stood still as Demeter entered. The woman in white froze in place with only her hands shaking.

"Mom?" Persephone hoped the older woman would remember her. "It's me, Persephone... I mean Kore."

The wind whipped Demeter's white hair from her face as she stared at her daughter for what felt like an eternity.

"Mom, it's me, Kore." Persephone held out her hand and placed it on Demeter's arm.

"Kore?" she asked, seeming to barely have a voice when she spoke, shaking her head as though not believing this was real. "No, not Kore... Persephone." Demeter hissed with hatred in her eyes, wrenching her arm away from Persephone's grasp. "My daughter died the day you were born."

"You must trust me." Persephone stepped closer as Demeter backed away.

"No. No matter what trick this is, I will not submit to the gods. I have no daughter!" Demeter rushed to the window and shouted to the sky. "You hear me, Zeus? I will not fall for your tricks! Curse you for what you've done!"

Lightning struck in response to the hail storm the winter goddess rained down upon the village she pretended to help only minutes ago. Screaming into the storm, the goddess raged until she had exhausted herself. Coughing and looking like she would faint, Persephone rushed to her side and helped her mom sit by the empty fire.

"I don't regret loving Hades." Persephone knelt in front of Demeter. "Just because I love him doesn't mean I love you any less. You can't ask me to choose you over him."

Her pale, wrinkled hand reached out to touch Persephone's cheek. "You've changed so much. I can't bear to see what he's done to you."

"Hades didn't do this to me," Persephone leaned against her mother's hand. "There have always been two sides of me. I made the choice to make us a singular being. To stop fighting the darkness that has always been inside of me. You must have known she was there, or you wouldn't have taken me away."

"That's not why I took you away," Demeter said, shaking her head. "But once, when you were very small, you touched a flower that withered in your hand. I was so upset. I scolded you mercilessly until you cried. You never did it again, so I thought nothing of it afterward."

"You knew I could do this?" Persephone asked, wishing she could remember.

"I thought it was a mistake." Demeter sat back in her chair. "To see you now and to have felt this ability of yours, it was heartbreaking. I blame myself for this. Had I not returned you to Olympus, we would have lived in peace."

"We can still live in peace," Persephone said with a heavy sigh. "But we can't go back to how things used to be. We have to find a way forward."

"You shouldn't see me like this," Demeter said softly through her tears.

"We've both changed." She reached out a hand to her mother. "I still want you in my life. Will you come home with me?"

Hand shaking, Demeter timidly reached out and touched her daughter's hand, slowly grasping it with tears filling her eyes.

"Home," Demeter said through tears. "Whose home? His or mine?"

"Ours," said Persephone, taking her mother's other hand. "I promise I will always come back to our home."

Demeter brought Persephone close, embracing her as only a mother could. They wept together. Tears of regret, pain, and loneliness fell from their eyes as they held one another.

"I missed you so much," wept Demeter, gripping her daughter tight. "Please forgive me."

"Shh. I'm here, and that is all that matters."

Demeter held her for a long time before releasing her. "How is this possible? Hade has bound you to the Underworld.".

"Yes, that's true. I will always return to him," said Persephone, wiping her mother's tears. "Right now, I need you to return with me."

"After all that I've done," Demeter said, looking down at her swing hands. "I can't go back."

"Yes you can," Persephone said, wiping her face. "Help me to thaw our world."

"How?"

"I had a dream," Persephone said, waving a hand over the mirror, showing Demeter her vision. "It revealed to me that if I eat six seeds, I can spend six months in the Underworld and six months with you on the surface. I told Hades this when you caught us at the gates, and he agreed to share my time with you.

"He did?" Demeter looked touched by the gesture. "But... I thought the rule was forever."

"The duration is," Persephone nodded. "However, it's up to Hades to set the rules for this binding law and can allot the time as he desires. I realized through what I'd experienced from dreams and prophecy that the rule is I must return if I eat from his realm, but he can decide for how long. Thus, he gave up six months of the year so I could be with you."

"He did that for us?" Demeter stood and held Persephone's hands facing one another. "You really do love him, don't you?"

"I do," Persephone replied. "And I know he loves me."

"But what if..." Demeter said, trailing off.

"Hades is not Zeus," Persephone said. "I've learned that over time. I think, eventually, you two will grow to be allies. If only to be mine."

"You want us both in your lives?" asked Demeter.

"Yes. I do," Persephone said reassuringly. "Please come with me, and let me show you how."

Demeter shook her head. "I don't know how to forgive Hades."

"Maybe start by making peace and working from there." Persephone smiled. "You don't have to like him. I just need you to support me."

Demeter thought about this for a while. She turned, took a deep breath, and nodded to Persephone.

"Okay," Demeter said, swallowing hard. "I will support you and be there for you. Your happiness is all that matters to me. Perhaps for your sake, I may be able to forgive him, but only a little. That doesn't mean we're going to become friends."

"That's fair," Persephone said, chuckling. "Will you come with me then to make our world bloom again?"

"I will," Demeter said, nodding. "But only while you are

with me. When you go to Hades, the world will wither and sleep until you return. When the first blade of grass grows, and the birds begin to sing, the world will know that my Persephone has returned to me. Until then, I shall appear as I am and live in my Temple, where you can always find me waiting for you."

Persephone smiled and embraced her mother, trying to hold back tears but failing. Their connection returned when her lips touched the older woman's cheek, and the goddess's light burst to life, burning bright under her once pallid skin. Demeter's old exterior faded away. The magic that turned her mortal fell all around her, dissipating into the ground.

The Goddess of Grain was renewed and stood tall, transformed into her green robes, holding her long staff as her white strands changed to golden curls. Her visage was older than before, but only slightly. Now, with a forty-year-old mortal's appearance and a few strands of white, Demeter turned and smiled at Persephone. The same smile the young goddess had known all her life. To see it again after everything that had happened had brought Persephone the joy and peace she'd craved for so long.

"First, we have to make a blade of grass," said Persephone with a nod.

Demeter transported them outside to a field where a grove of trees surrounded them, completely void of life.

Removing her boot and placing her foot into the snow, Persephone reached out to the core of Gaia, and the snow melted and cleared away. Grass with tiny flowers bloomed under her foot and spread when she placed her other foot, now bare, to the ground.

Demeter gasped with wide eyes. "It worked!"

Persephone held her mother's hands, creating a wide circle with their arms.

"Now, we must bring everything back before we can join the others," she said, smiling at her mother.

They channeled their energy by facing one another.

Soon, the light from the circle that appeared around them rose and coated them in its radiant glow. The rays beamed upward into the sky, creating a dome of golden light. The storms cleared. Everything on the horizon and beyond glittered with sparkling dust that rained from above. The life-giving energy moved outward on the breeze to wake the world. Trees yawned and shook off their branches as the dryads emerged from their hibernation. The green leaves and flowers broke through the icy surface and blossomed across the land, filling their world with color.

Watching the cold and snow recede, they could see the crops growing. The shimmering dust fell delicately all over Olympus, causing bursts of growth that sprung to life. It made Persephone smile to be close to her mother as they worked together to bring everything back. When the last blossom opened, the birds came out of hiding, signaling to the world that it was time to wake up. Helios cracked his whip, driving his chariot across the sky, waving down at them with an approving nod.

"Come on, Mom, let's go home," Persephone said, then stopped momentarily.

Remembering her promise to Hermes, she turned to Demeter.

"One last thing before we go, have you heard of a nymph named Daeira?" Persephone asked.

Demeter rubbed her chin and thought for a moment. "I do know her. She is near a fountain spring, not too far from here. If we walk, we can get there in a short time."

"I have one more promise to keep," Persephone said, holding her mother's hand. "Then we must go to Olympus."

Demeter nodded and held Perspehone in her arms as they walked with joyful smiles toward Eleusis.

***

Hades had been informed by Thanatos where

Persephone was. He tried to relax, knowing her mission and that she would return to him soon. She couldn't refuse if she tried now that she would be forever bound to him. Besides, she had Aethone with her, so he knew she would be protected.

"Where are Poseidon and Hestia?" He asked Thanatos.

"Poseidon is licking his wounds from the loss of the city of Athens on the shoreline." Thanatos closed his eyes as though receiving a message, then opened them. "Hestia is on Olympus trying to calm Zeus, who has spent the past few hours raging with lightning storms over a town called Eleusis."

Hades nodded. "Send a request to Hestia to meet me where Poseidon is."

"Yes, my Lord," Thanatos said, bowing deep. "It's good to have you back."

He stood, fully recovered, on the sandy shore. As he descended his chariot, his stallions stomped, agitated by the whipping winds. Hestia and Poseidon were already there, arguing. Their agitation over the storms was apparent as they both paced back and forth, leaving footprints in the sand, washed away by the snow drifts. Once they noticed Hades, they approached, and all clasped forearms in greeting.

"That bitch stole my city from me," Poseidon raged, shaking his fist at the new temple on the top of the acropolis now named Athens. "I'll get it back, mark my words."

"There's no time to worry about a damned city of mortals," Hades said, giving a side eye at Poseidon.

"Is this why you brought me here?" Hestia asked, folding her arms. "To argue about whose city it is when we have far more pressing issues? Such as the location of Demeter? Zeus is raging up there, and he refuses to cease his storms as he yells into the aether."

"I came to tell you that Persephone has found her and is working to bring back the flora as we speak," Hades said to assuage their fears.

"You honestly think Persephone can get Demeter to stop

this?" Hestia asked.

Hades nodded. "I trust her completely."

"Forgive me if I don't share the same sentiments," Poseidon said, rolling his eyes. My ocean is beginning to freeze, which is how I lost to that cunt on the hillside."

Hestia scoffed. "Athena's skills of war even exceed mine. I doubt you had any chance in the first place against her."

Poseidon's hand went to his chest as though wounded. "Hesti, how could you? You dare suggest any of these new brats could compare to our might?"

"You should have seen Persephone battle Demeter," Hades said with a sly smile. "This next generation of gods have many new talents we would be wise to heed before assuming we'd win on seniority alone."

"Agreed." Hestia nodded. "If we're not careful, it'll be us in Tartarus while they run the show."

"Speaking of the show," Poseidon huffed. "What is Demeter trying to prove with all this chaos? If you ask me, no female is worth this much trouble."

Hades narrowed his eyes. "It was worth it to me."

"Do tell Hades." Hestia pointed to the sky. "How was all this worth it?"

"Persephone had eaten the fruit of my realm," he said with a small smile, looking down. "She will always return to me."

They both gasped with wide eyes.

"Hades," Hestia said with her hand over her mouth. "How could you force her to do such a thing?"

Poseidon nodded. "For once, I agree with Hestia. Though I must admit it, I didn't think you had it in you to be so duplicitous. Especially after you told Zeus and me that you wouldn't entrap the goddess."

"I didn't..." Hades said, then paused, looking up into the sky.

Suddenly, the storm ceased. The gods turned to see a bright beam of light igniting the clouds.

"Persephone," Hades whispered, shielding his eyes from the light. "She found Demeter."

"Thank Gaia, " Hestia said, standing beside him, pointing. "Look at the shore."

Green grass and flowers bloomed over the roving hillside as the ice and snow receded.

"Good," Poseidon added. "Half of my ocean has ice bleeding from the shorelines. It's going to take ages to melt."

Hestia sighed. "It's a shame there won't be so many by the hearth, but it's to see the grass return."

"So this leaves the issue with. Uh. What did Hecate call it?" Poseidon asked.

"Seasons," Hestia replied with a groan. "Zeus and Tethis had three new goddesses born recently."

"And another twelve called the Horai, or hours of the day," Poseidon said, rolling his eyes. "We best not tell Hera."

"I wouldn't dream of it," Hades said, crossing his arms. "Besides, Hera won't be able to be imprisoned for much longer."

Three gods came riding over to them from the melting battlefield and smiled with a wave. Ares, Eris, and Enyo landed from their flying mounts and approached Hades.

"Well, if it isn't our old boss," Ares said, extending an open hand.

Hades greeted each one, clasping arms.

"We just received word from Hermes that Demeter has been found and arrived on Olympus with Persephone," Enyo said with a smile.

"Such a shame," Eris frowned. "I was beginning to enjoy the abundant misery."

His old team was excited to see him, making him smile at their filial attitudes. Eris would serve his needs the most moving forward. The other two would as well, though less so. He would forever feel indebted to them for helping him escape with Persephone.

What surprised him the most was the participation of Artemis and Aphrodite. Hephaestus would do anything for

Aphrodite, but the rest risked the wrath of Zeus for him. Hades would never forget Hestia looking the other way in the most important moment of their escape. His filial kinship towards her was even stronger than before. It was the friendships that Persephone had cultivated that inspired him. She was a light in his constant darkness. Persephone was far more clever than he'd ever imagined. It was the sexiest thing about her. He would have to take responsibility for their actions, ensuring they didn't receive punishment from Zeus as he had.

"How did you do it?" Ares asked Hades. "What made Demeter give in?"

"Persephone ate six pomegranate seeds and will to return to the surface to keep the earth from being in a drought for too long," Hades replied, crossing his arms. "Every six months, she will return. It appears she convinced Demeter to accept the terms."

"So you decided the six seeds she ate will correlate with six months?" Hestia asked, wide-eyed. "And this repeats every annual cycle? Hades, you must be insane to agree to that."

Hades shook his head, "No, She decided on her own. I agreed to her terms. Besides, when she's with Demeter, the surface will flourish. This solution should please everyone enough."

"Everyone but you," Hestia argued.

"And for the other six months?" asked Poseidon. "What are we to do then?"

"Persephone has a plan," Hades said with a slight smile at her cleverness. "She will convince Demeter to put the world to sleep to reawaken upon her return."

"I have to deal with six months of this shit!?" Poseidon yelled, throwing his hands in the air. "How could you do this to me?"

Hestia clicked her tongue. "Hades. I appreciate that you found a solution of sorts. But how will you manage that much time away from her? It's quite the sacrifice, and after how Demeter has treated you all these years? I don't even think I'm that benevolent."

"For the time that she will be ruling with me, she will be my queen and wife in all ways," Hades said, letting his arms rest at his sides. "She will be powerful and invaluable to my realm."

"I'm sure she'll have plenty of work on her hands," Poseidon teased. "But since Zeus will need her warrior skills occasionally, maybe you two will have more opportunities in other instances." Poseidon smiled and winked at Hades.

Hades nodded in agreement. "You're right. It's just that it's hard to imagine her far away in a place I can't be."

"Maybe you can have conjugal visits or something," said Hestia with a shrug. "Demeter isn't always there, and there are plenty of opportunities to see Persephone."

"I think it's time we see just how ready Persephone is to be queen," said Poseidon. "Are you ready to be with her forever?"

"Yes," Hades replied without hesitation.

A smile broadened across Poseidon's face at Hades' answer. "Then tonight, let us consider you two to be official. There's just one last thing."

"Nonsense, Poseidon," Hestia said, narrowing her eyes. "Persephone is perfect for Hades. A better match I have yet to see. She's proven herself enough."

"She still has to prove herself worthy of Hades," Poseidon said, looking to all the gods. "Maybe the Underworld accepts her, but can anyone argue that Hera will be furious when she's out? Your queen will need assurances of her position."

"Poseidon has a point," Ares said, facing Hades.

"What exactly are we talking about?" Enyo asked, raising a brow.

"The gauntlet," Eris said, rolling her eyes. "Don't you know the top gods have to fight in each realm to become undisputed leaders?"

"Can we run it?" Ares asked, excited.

"You'd die in the first trial," Eris replied in a dead tone.

"Persephone could barely challenge the three of us," Enyo argued. "What makes anyone think she'd have a chance in the gauntlet?"

"Persephone is more than capable of killing a god," Hades said when they all stared at him in disbelief.

"But can she kill a Titan?" Asked Poseidon with a raised brow.

Hades glared. "Do we want to risk Gaia's wrath to find out?"

Poseidon groaned. "I'm still reeling from Zeus' wrath on you. To say nothing of what he plans to do to your accomplices."

Hestia smiled. "Well, one thing is for sure. We should all return to Olympus and sort this out between you and Zeus."

"I don't think he wants me there," Hades replied.

"Nonsense," Hestia said with a shake of her head. "Zeus only did what he had to when you challenged him. You would do the same in your realm."

"No. I wouldn't." Hades narrowed his eyes at Hestia.

"We all know why you did what you did," Hestia gently touched his arm. "Persephone appears to have made peace with Demeter, so now we must make amends with Zeus. I really don't want to see what Zeus would do to those who helped you escape."

The three younger gods looked at one another, swallowing hard nervously.

Poseidon nodded. "She's right. We all need to go back to make peace so we can focus on our work instead of creating another war of the gods."

Hades nodded. "I will speak to Zeus on their behalf."

"Thanks, boss," Ares said with a nervous laugh. "I wouldn't want to sit under his lightning for one moment, let alone how long you did."

"Again, you'd be dead with the first strike," Eris replied in her dead tone.

"Will you stop!" Ares yelled, glaring at the dark goddess.

Enyo clapped a hand on Ares' shoulder. "She's right. Maybe we can get out of this relatively unscathed with Hades putting in a good word for us."

"Come," Hestia said to the gods with a smile. "We better catch Zeus in a good mood while there's still time. I bet he's more than relieved to see Demeter again."

They returned to Olympus, finding the palace covered in blooms. The yard was bustling with merriment and smiling beings running around to redecorate. There were still small piles of snow on the ground, but for the most part, the flora had returned.

They left their mounts in the stables and began to leave when Hestia stopped and noticed Hades wasn't with them.

"Are you coming?" She asked over her shoulder.

"Soon," Hades replied. "There's someone I need to speak with first."

Hestia nodded and left with the others as Hades walked away from the group and went to a familiar stable door. He found his mare giving the stable satyrs a difficult time, knocking over their food buckets.

"Aethone!" He yelled, making everyone freeze. "What have I told you about behaving?"

Not to. Aethone chuckled, speaking into his mind.

The Satyrs hurried away, leaving them alone except for Broutzos, who waved a hoof at Aethone, making lewd suggestive noises. The mare rolled her eyes and kicked a bucket of manure that slopped onto the surprised Hypocampus' face. Hurt in the stallion's eyes, he slinked into the water and disappeared under the surface.

His anger was only for show. Petting her mane, Hades let out a heavy breath.

"Thank you for keeping her safe," he said, rubbing her nose.

You're not mad? She asked, hanging her head.

"I should be mad," he said, narrowing his eyes. "Furious

even. But you did what I couldn't. You brought her to her mother safely. So I'm grateful."

She is a clever goddess with a strong heart, Aethone said, holding her head high with a smile. *Do we get to keep her?*

Hades chuckled. "Yes, my red-eyed beast. We get to keep her."

Mulling over his thoughts, Hades left Aethone with her stall repaired and new hay for her to rest. Feeling satisfied with her care, he went to find Persephone.

As Hades entered the main hall, he stopped, surprised to see Demeter who approached him.

Her appearance stunned him. With strips of white within her golden hair, Demeter had grown older than she'd ever been. He had no idea what she'd been through, but it must have been difficult for such a change in her to occur.

"Hades, can we talk?" Demeter asked calmly rather than in her usual stinging tone.

Hades nodded. "Of course."

Demeter cleared her throat and looked up at him without malice for the first time since they were young.

"For the sake of Persephone, I feel that you and I should come to some sort of truce," she said, seeming almost to vomit the words but composed herself enough to continue. "When I first realized you were to be her protector while she was here, I was angry it was you but secretly relieved." Seeing his surprise, Demeter continued, "I knew you would keep her safe no matter what. Even if it was just your duty."

"I will always protect her," he said, his gaze moving to the ground. "Just as you have all her life."

She gestured for him to walk with her toward the garden. "When did you realize that she was to be your queen?"

He cleared his throat nervously but decided that honesty would be best with her.

"We shared a vision during the coronation that revealed all this to us," Hades said, walking beside Demeter. "Including what you would do to the world. Albeit, we couldn't see any details in how it would all come about."

"You saw what I would do?" She asked quizzically. "My rage was foretold?"

"Yes." Hades nodded. "At first, I resisted. I knew there would be no easy solution for it to work. But over time, being around her, I found myself enchanted and couldn't help how I felt. I didn't intend any of this to happen, Demeter."

Demeter stopped her stroll to look into his eyes.

"No, I don't suppose you did," she said with a sigh, then continued to walk. "I will agree to a cease-fire with you for my daughter's sake. But on one condition."

"What are your conditions?" He asked, dreading what she would say.

Demeter paused. "When Persephone is on the surface with me, I want you to remain away from my home. I may have to share her with you, but regarding our work, I don't want your presence there."

He thought about what she was saying. He knew she wanted time with Persephone, but she didn't know about the key he now possessed.

"While I may accept my daughter's choice in you, that doesn't mean that I have to welcome you into every private place I have," she said, walking again beside him. "My home is one of those places. It's my one sanctuary, and I want it to stay that way."

"So I can see her during any other time, just not in your home?" He asked, understanding why she would want privacy as he would.

"Yes," said Demeter. "If she is at a ceremony for Zeus during her time with me, by all means, spend what time with her you need. I want you to stay out of my land, my home, and my way. Do this, and I will cease my constant challenges of you in public, and you will leave my daughter to me when it is our time together."

If it would make Persephone happy, he felt he had no choice but to accept the offer. For now.

"I agree to your terms," Hades said finally. "You will not see me when her time is with you."

"Thank you," said Demeter, nodding. "Since I imagine there is nothing else to discuss..."

"I would like to ask one thing," he said, cutting her off.

"And what is that?"

"I wish to be formally married tonight," Hades said, folding his arms. "I don't want any more challenges to our union from here on."

Demeter stiffened but remained calm. "Okay. I will speak to Zeus and prepare her for the challenge... I mean ceremony."

"She's going to need a dress," Hades replied. "One that will blend both our realms."

"You leave that to me," Demeter answered. "I suggest you prepare yourself as well. It's not going to be easy convincing Zeus to officiate after what I've heard occured."

"I will," he said, trying to hide his concern. "He will see reason when we speak."

"For both of our sakes," Demeter said with raised brows. "You'd better be right."

She turned and left him. Never in his wildest imaginations had he imagined a truce with Demeter, especially not after what happened. But things were beginning to work out despite the obstacles.

An uneasy feeling washed over him like a shadow. Hades looked around for the source but found nothing. Something was off, but he couldn't quite place it.

EPILOGUE

The ceremony was brief, but the flowers and decorations were beautiful and a delight to see after such terrible events. Adorned in their dark colors, Hades and Persephone looked ever the Underworld rulers that they were. Even their guests wore black and tyrian colors to show their support. Her sleek gown formed her body while a belt held her wide-hipped train layered in dark tyrian petals drifting with magic that sparkled in cascading light. The top pointed upward in bare branches with a sheer bodice with dark lace to cover her breasts. As always, Hades was in black leather with his robe draped over one shoulder, clasped with his silver sigil, and a hand held out to hold hers as they stood together in front of guests from the three realms.

Zeus had come around and officiated the wedding with a smile and offerings of gifts and well wishes to the new King and Queen of the Underworld. He even pardoned those who assisted in Hades' escape. Begrudgingly, Zeus acknowledged the teamwork it took to do so and admitted how proud he was they could pull off such a task.

They left the feast early to their new chambers with a door carved with a flower surrounded by flames, framed by two pomegranate trees. The fire shone bright and lit the room when they entered, and a trail of white petals from the narcissus flower led to their bed.

Persephone grabbed him by the nape of his neck and pulled him close to give him a long, slow, passionate kiss. Their hands moved over one another, removing pieces of clothing as they sought to be free of their heavy garments. All that was left was his pants and her simple dress as the rest lay in a pile at their feet.

"Hades. Take me to our bed," she moaned into his mouth.

He pulled her dress open, lifting her while cupping her ass with one hand, bringing her thighs around his hips, and did as she asked. With her hand pressed to his chest, she could feel his heart pounding for her. Reaching up, she cupped his face, bringing him back into a kiss that made her head spin with desire as he sat down on the bed.

His kisses were aggressive, opening her mouth, licking her tongue, and nipping her bottom lip. He raised one hand to cup her head, bringing her in closer. Persephone sat straddling his erection that threatened to rip from his pants. His other hand gripped her hips under her dress, rocking her back and forth against his restrained shaft, making her legs shake with tension. The anticipation of what Hades would do next with her in his arms filled her with excitement.

He kissed her neck behind her ear, sending shock waves down her body to her toes. She moaned even louder, grinding slowly, feeling the pressure intensify. She moved her hips in slow circles, eliciting his moans that sent electricity down her spine. The way he smelled aroused her. His dark sandalwood and fire scent drove her wild. *He smells so fucking good*, she thought as she drank in his essence.

Tonight, she wanted to take her time without interruptions. Persephone leaned down, kissing his neck, feeling his moan vibrate in his throat with each wicked stroke of her tongue. He pulled back for a moment, holding her face with one hand that she kissed tenderly. Hades met her gaze and then drew his eyes to her lips as he devoured them again.

"Are you sure you want to do this here?" He asked, voice rough with desire.

"Yes," Persephone moaned breathlessly.

Hades smiled that wicked grin she loved. "We're not alone. Someone could hear us."

"Let them," she purred, nuzzling and kissing down his cheek to his neck and ear, eliciting a sexy moan. "I don't give a damn who hears."

She sucked on his lobe, then left it wet, gently blowing on it, feeling his body shake with chills. His salty skin tasted delicious. She couldn't get enough of his responsive moans that only added to her excitement. He sat her upright, pulling her gown off her shoulders to reveal her taut nipples. Hades slowly kissed them individually. The wet heat he left with his tongue, followed by the cool breeze as he blew on them, made her body tingle. He reached up to cup her right breast and brought it into his eager mouth, holding her close. Her moans turned to a cry for more as he sucked her nipples, tugging and teasing, stroking her with his thumb between licks. Moving back up her neck, they kissed, filled with all their pent-up frustration, desperate for release.

"Say it," he said, growling low in his chest. "I need to hear you say it."

"I love you," she whispered, reaching down his chest to his swollen shaft. Rubbing it, she felt it flex in response to her hand. Sliding her dress down over her hips, Hades lifted her and let it drop to the floor. Gently setting her down to lay back, he stood and removed his pants, then nestled his body between her legs.

He caressed her naked pussy, then grabbed his cock, gliding it back and forth. His cock stopped right at her entrance and slid in just barely before pulling back and sliding against her once more.

"Don't tease me, Hades."

He chuckled low in his throat. "I wouldn't dream of it."

They moved together, slowly exploring each other's bodies and desires. Each time, he penetrated her just a little more. She liked how he kept her wondering if he would go all the way in. But he didn't. Persephone tried to slide down his shaft, but he held her in place, allowing her excitement to build with each stroke. As he pinched her nipples, watching her reaction, her body began to pour down his cock.

His weight felt glorious on top of her. Persephone surrendered and opened her legs wider. She didn't know what to do next but didn't care, choosing to let him lead.

Bracing himself up, he reached down, touching her bud. The blinding pleasure forced her head back as her back bowed forcefully, rendering a moan from inside of her. She almost didn't recognize her own voice. Persephone pulled him back to kiss her whimpering mouth as her body vibrated with need.

"Hades," she whimpered. "Please."

"You want me inside you?" he asked, teasing her with his tongue.

"Yes," she said in a husky whisper.

Holding his cock, he fed it into her slowly. He kissed her neck to distract her, allowing her time to get used to his size.

"Relax a little more, and I'll go deeper," he whispered in her ear while he kissed her.

He brought her mouth to his and started to massage her clit. It was still so sensitive his touch was almost too intense at first. The more his fingers moved in a circle over her bud, the more her body responded as her orgasm began to build again.

"You're mine, Persephone," he breathed in her ear, rubbing her mound in slow circles until her hips matched his strokes.

Lifting her leg over his hip, he finally slid his cock deeper as far as he could. With each thrust, his muscles strained, trying to control his movement. Opening her legs wider, she moved her hips to meet his. She felt her body warm at her core. With each thrust, they soon found a rhythm. Slow at first. They touched and explored one another's bodies, kissing and moving as one. The deeper he entered her, the more she loved how good and full she felt.

Persephone could feel her orgasm building. Hades' pace quickened as he thrust a little harder each time, making her drunk with pleasure. She could feel his hands everywhere, caressing her, pinching her nipples. His mouth left her panting and gasping for more. She needed him closer if such a thing were even possible. Driving himself into her more aggressively, which she found surprisingly delicious, Hades grew more demanding.

Neither one of them cared about anything else.

Persephone moaned and clawed into his back every time he hit her in the spot at her core, making her shake uncontrollably. She met him with her hips with everything she had. Hades was driving both of them to the edge. She gripped his neck and shoulders while staring into his eyes, pulling her legs higher as he went deeper into her core.

"Ah! Don't stop!" Persephone screamed as their bodies slammed together.

Holding on to him, she felt herself falling over the edge. She tensed, and her eyes rolled back as she came hard, calling out his name. Her body jerked with spasms, and she could feel his body flexing and straining to release. Tucking his head between her shoulder and neck, he thrust harder and faster, building the intensity and making her cum in rapid succession over and over.

"Ah! I'm cuming..." She screamed.

"You want me to cum for you?" He asked, thrusting even harder.

"Gods, yes!" She cried out. "Ah! Please cum for me. I want you to fill me."

"Mmm. That's my good flower." Hades growled with a light chuckle. "I like it when you beg me."

"Hades, please," she panted. "I'm going to cum again... Please fill my pussy."

"Yes, cum on my cock," he moaned in her ear. "Fuck you

feel so good."

Her stomach fluttered at his words. They turned her on so much she started cumming again.

"I'm gonna cum, Persephone," Hades groaned deep in his chest. "Fuck, I'm cumming... Ah!"

She held on tight as his growls turned to a roar that shook the walls. He held onto the headboard to pull himself deeper inside as he came, filling her womb. Throwing his head back, Hades moaned, sweat building on his brow as his cock flexed with each spurt. Careful not to crush her, he leaned on his forearms, trying to recover his breath.

They stayed there for several minutes, moving slowly. Eventually, he pulled out of her, leaving a sense of emptiness without him.

Pulling the blankets over her, he tucked her into his arms and settled behind her. She felt like she was high. Her head swam with every nerve dancing with pulsing energy. She couldn't help but brush her hands over her breasts and luxuriate in their sensitivity.

They lay together for a while, staring at the fire. She felt calm, soothed. Finally, she felt peace.

"Did you enjoy that, my love?" he asked, stroking her hair back out of her face so he could look at her.

"Mmm... Deliciously so." Turning to face him, she smiled. "I need to clean up. Let's go play in the pools for a bit."

Hades kissed her lips. "Of course. Whatever my wife desires."

His cock lay against her straightened leg, miraculously growing again. She reached down and stroked him with tender fingers, making him moan again. Her stomach danced at how sexy and erotic he sounded when she touched him.

He laughed under his breath. "You keep doing that, and we'll have to start this all over again."

"Promise?" she asked, pulling his lips to hers.

***

Hades carried Persephone to the pool to ease their sore bodies. He could feel his heart pounding as he lazily kissed her neck and breasts above the water line. Straddled over him, he slid into her tight pussy, making her moan against him. He loved the feel of her running her fingers through his hair as he touched and caressed her. Hades never wanted to leave this moment. Feeling his cock inside of her and her worshiping kisses made him realize what he had been missing out on all of his life.

Love.

"Let's stay like this forever," Persephone said between kisses.

"You may want to revise your plans for future happiness," said Hecate, popping into the room.

Appearing just above them, Hecate lounged on the smooth stones.

Groaning in frustration, they both sat up, rolling their eyes. Hades got up and walked into the pool deeper to throw water over his face and hair before getting out and drying off. He waved a hand over his body, dressed in his leather pants with a leather vest. His boots and weapons finished his look as he leaned over the table, grabbing the carafe.

"Hecate, we really need to work on your timing," Hades grumbled, grabbing three glasses and pouring them each some wine.

Hecate looked at them innocently, taking her sip.

"What? At least I waited until you were both done. What a show for you two. Phew!" She said, fanning her face with her hand.

Persephone drank from the goblet Hades offered her while she sat in the water. Sitting up, she brushed out her hair with her fingers.

"We can discuss new boundaries about my quarters

later, but for now, tell us what happened," Hades replied, drinking his wine.

"Oh, you'll find out soon enough. I simply wanted to warn you to get dressed and meet me outside on the main balcony in five minutes."

This wasn't good. With a wave of her hand, stepping out of the pool, Persephone dried herself and changed into her fighting gear rather than her dress. She wore her usual dark tyrian leather with her weapons appearing along with her wedged boots.

A knock at the door drew their attention when Thanatos appeared inside the room without an invitation.

"Thanatos?" Persephone said with her eyes wide.

"My queen," Thanatos answered with a bow. "My lord," said Thanatos, bowing as Hades came up behind her. "I'm glad I found you. We have a situation."

Hades looked down at Persephone and then at Thanatos.

"What is it?" Hades growled.

"I have bad news," replied Thanatos. "Hera's escaped, and she's freed the Titans."

"How is that possible?" Hades asked, feeling a sinking feeling in his stomach.

"The only way it would be possible is if you drained too much energy from the Underworld in your recovery, my Lord," Thanatos replied, looking down.

"Someone would still have had to get into the depths of Tartarus and release her," Hades countered with a glare.

"Few could ever make it that far without harm," Thanatos replied with a hand to his chin. "I will send my daemons to find out who."

"Go," Hades commanded. "Find out who let her out and prepare the Underworld for battle. I'm going to need an army to capture the Titans. Find out who got past the Hekatonkheires and prepare all three. We're going to need them."

"Right away, my Lord." Thanatos bowed, then

disappeared.

Persephone stood next to Hades, looking up at him with her brows furrowed.

"What is he talking about, Hades?" She asked with worry in her tone.

Hades cursed under his breath. "When I was healing, I must have broken the seal that holds the Titans in their prison. Hera would have sensed this and must have found a way out. It takes tremendous power to keep the seal active, which means this is my fault."

"It can't be your fault," Persephone argued. "If anything, this is all my fault. I was the cause for all of this."

"It's not your fault, Persephone," Hades said, knowing this had all occurred because of his choices. "I won't let you think that."

Persephone frowned. "If I had gone back, Zeus wouldn't have punished you, and you wouldn't have had to use the Underworld's power."

Hades took both of her hands in his. "My love, from the moment I first touched your hand and gazed into your eyes, I was willing to sacrifice anything, including my life, for you. I would do it again, even now."

She smiled up at him with pink rosebud lips. Brushing back her hair from her cheek, Hades leaned down and gently kissed her.

"We need to find Zeus," Hades said, brushing water from her cheek. "I have to tell him his wife is on her way home and to prepare for war."

"I don't imagine he's going to be too happy," said Persephone sarcastically.

Hades chuckled. "No, I don't imagine he will be."

"Hades?" Persephone asked, beginning to shake. "Now that Hera is free, what should I..."

"Don't worry," he said, interrupting her. "I won't let anything happen to you. Besides, After what I've seen, I think you can handle your own against her now."

"Something she said to me when I paid a visit isn't sitting well," she said, shaking her head. "Hera told me she plans to take Zeus' throne."

"Oh?" Hades raised a brow. "I'd love to see her try."

"We warn Zeus." Persephone's worried face concerned him. "If she succeeds, we're all in danger."

Hade nodded. "Then we shouldn't waste any time."

He led her out of their chambers and into the hall where beings of all kinds were running in fear. *This isn't good*, Hades thought to himself.

"Come." Hades grabbed Persephone's hand. "We have to get to the throne room, fast."

Disappearing with her, they reappeared near the balcony and saw everyone had gathered on it, staring off into the distance.

The wind kicked up as the sky turned red. The air became moist and overheated. Sounds of thunder and a great roar echoed in the distance. The mountain shook beneath them, causing them to reach out to hold on to each other for stability. In the distance, she saw something birthed from the ground that took a monstrous form. Rock and lava poured from its mouth as it began its trek toward Olympus. More Titans emerged from the rift behind it, clawing their way out.

Dred crept up his spine as he realized the danger before them. He swallowed hard and saw the terrified look on everyone's faces, including Persephone's.

Hades pulled her to his chest and placed a loving hand on her cheek.

"Persephone, listen to me," he said, feeling her shake in his arms. "Stay with me. No matter what happens, I will protect you."

"No." Persephone shook her head. "This time, we'll protect each other."

Hades touched his forehead to Persephone's. "May we meet again, in this life or the next, if things go wrong."

"No matter what happens,' Persephone said, taking his

hands in hers. "We'll face it together from now on."

They stood hand in hand, looking back at the beings ripping apart their world. More giant beings of varying elements emerged as if being birthed from the core of Tartarus. Hades could sense their fear in the air as they murmured amongst themselves. Zeus pulled his lightning bolt with one hand and rallied them together.

"Gods!" Zeus looked at each one as he spoke. "You've been preparing for this for some time now. Remember. Give no mercy. For none will be offered in return."

"Zeus." Poseidon grabbed his arm. "We can't let them go out and fight this. We need help." he turned to Hades. "We need the Hekatonkheires."

"With you both by my side. We can win anything." Zeus clasped arms with Poseidon and then Hades. "And you, Demeter. Will you fight alongside me?"

Demeter stuttered. "Zeus... I."

Pulled into Zeus' arms, his lips met Demeter's in an aggressive smoldering kiss.

She resisted at first, pushing against his chest with her fists. Soon, her hands opened, and she reached up to the nape of his neck and pulled him closer.

Everyone in the group turned away in awkward silence as the two embraced for a few stolen moments. Persephone's eyes were wide in shock.

Suddenly, Zeus pulled back and cried out in pain, holding his head. As though some phantom force overtook him, Zeus dropped to his knees. His bolt fell, crashing to the base of Olympus, shaking the mountain with a powerful explosion.

"Zeus!" Demeter called out as Zeus collapsed into her arms, unconscious.

"What's happening?" Poseidon asked in a panic.

"We can't stop them without Zeus," Demeter said, shaking the unconscious god, unable to revive him.

Demeter looked to Hades with genuine fear. "What are

we going to do?"

"Call Hecate. Figure out how to wake him up," Hades replied, knowing the Titaness could help. "We'll buy you time to revive him."

Demeter held Zeus close to her chest, brushing back a strand of hair behind his ear. She looked up to Hades and then to Persephone. He instinctively placed an arm around his wife. Demeter nodded, then brought her cloak over Zeus and disappeared with him.

"How could she have possibly gotten out?" Persephone asked.

"Who? Poseidon demanded.

"Yes," Hestia said, appearing on the balcony in flames. "I'd like to know who let out the Titans."

"I must have drawn too much power when I healed," Hades replied, feeling guilt well up within him.

Persephone shook her head. "Even if you had, someone had to open the gates. This has been Hera's plan all along."

"Hera?" Hestia asked, turning to Persephone. "Explain."

"Hera told me that if she were to escape," she said, wringing her hands. "Her first plan was to take Zeus' throne."

Hestia's eyes darted to the tumultuous sky, then back to Persephone. "Then what?"

"She didn't say," Persephone said, wrapping her arms around her waist.

"Then who is responsible for incapacitating Zeus?" Poseidon asked, pointing to where Demeter and Zeus had disappeared.

Hades glared over the horizon. "I'm not sure, but whoever it is will regret it when Zeus wakes."

Persephone closed the distance between them and entwined their fingers. "What sort of being is powerful enough to put Zeus to sleep?"

He wondered the same thing. Only a few beings were capable of such things, and they undoubtedly came from his realm.

"We can't focus on that right now," Hades said, taking a deep breath, resigning himself to what lay ahead. "First, we must find a way to revive him, capture the Titans, then Hera. After that, we can decipher who would dare attack Zeus and their motives."

They all stood lined up on the balcony, watching the horde of Titans approaching them in a nightmare made reality. Her grip was tight, and he could feel her fear growing along with his own. If he didn't find a way to fix this, they would all die, and there was no way to tell how any of them would be reborn or if any of them would be necessary enough to be granted another life.

Ares came over to Hades and cleared his throat. "So what's the plan, boss? What are the rules of engagement for something like this?"

"There is only one rule... Never fucking lose," Persephone said with a sly grin up at Hades, quoting the same line he'd told her when she fought in the arena.

Eris and Enyo, always the shadow of Ares, were followed by Artemis, who'd only just arrived with her bow in hand.

"Looks like it's time to put our mischief to good use," Artemis said with a wink at Persephone.

"Just like old times," Enyo said with a nod.

"Yes," quipped Eris, smiling as she gained energy with everyone's apprehension. "It has been a while since we've been allowed any fun."

Nyctimus lept over the balcony, landing with his group close behind. His eyes glanced at Artemis and then to Hades when he bowed. "My team is yours to command, Lord Hades."

"Agreed. My team will follow your lead, brother," said Poseidon, who had genuine fear in his eyes at what he witnessed in the distance.

"And mine," Athena said, stepping forward with Zeus' group.

With these teams surrounding him, Hades knew he had a fighting chance. But it wasn't a good one without Zeus and

Demeter.

More Titans emerged with deafening roars, making their feet unsteady. Many held back tears. Others' eyes glinted excited at the prospect of a battle they'd only read about in legends. *Fools. They'll be the first to die*, he thought to himself.

"We're going to need some help," Hades said, addressing his team. "Thanatos will command my army and bring the Hekatonkheires. Until then, no matter what, don't hold back. I expect all of you to use every one of your powers to the fullest. We are no longer playing war games."

The severity of Hades' tone visibly sent chills down their spines as he observed them all, considering their immortality. Their nods told him everything. They would fight to the death, and while the other teams may not enjoy it, he knew his team would.

Hades smiled his wicked grin at the group, met with glints of mischief and joy in their eyes as they smiled back, nodding toward each other.

Hades pulled his bident and extended it to its full height. Persephone did the same with her scythe. Instinctively, the rest of his team followed his lead and pulled their weapons, Artemis notching an arrow at the end.

Hades' eyes drifted to Persephone's. "Unleash everything you've got. No gods are dying today. Do I make myself clear?"

"Even in the afterlife, I will follow you," Persephone said with such tenderness he almost lost his resolve to let her fight.

In the end, he knew what no one else did. She was the most deadly warrior to enter this battlefield, and he loved her with all his heart, soul, and being.

Persephone smiled. "You ready?"

He grinned and kissed her again.

"Alright, Gods!" Hades roared, eyes turning black, teeth extending, staring down at the monstrous beings emerging before them. "Let's hunt."

THE END...

To be continued in Book 3...

BOOKS IN THIS SERIES

Persephone & Hades is an epic Greek Mythology Adult Romance with themes of love, family, and the seasons. Set in ancient times, these two gods must find a way through adversity in order to forge the love they are destined to share.

Persephone & Hades

Remember Persephone... The Gods are not your friends.

Summoned to Olympus, Hades arrived in time to meet the one who'd plagued his dreams. Used to being alone, he dared not hope that she would want him in return. But the more time he spent with her, the more he began to desire her not only for her beauty or for her skills in battle, but her ability to surprise him. He wanted her, but there was no way that her mother, Demeter, Goddess of the Harvest, would ever allow them to be together.

Persephone was drawn to the Lord of the Underworld from the moment they'd met in the garden on Olympus. Frustrated and confused about her fate, Persephone fought the seductive lure of the darkness growing within her. Provided she survived the Olympic trials, and the manipulations of Hera, Persephone must find her own place in the Pantheon regardless of her feelings for Hades.

Their destinies now intertwined, Persephone has a choice to

make. Either choose to give in to her desires for the Dark God whose touch she craves, heralding the end of the world as they knew it, or resist and instead return with her mother to the meadow for eternity, denying the darkness that calls to her.

Persephone & Hades 2

From now on, you're mine, and I will always protect you...

The moment he'd sensed Persephone's energy in the world again, Hades froze in place, his rage dissipating as he stared up at the sky he couldn't see. Hope. The seed, now bloomed, was sending a signal, causing his whole body to pulse with power. Hades dropped his accusing hand, pointed at the daemons before him, and stood from his throne when he felt her. Go to her, his body screamed, knowing there would be little time to succeed in his plan.

Persephone could see no sky or sun, nor feel the cool breeze on her cheeks. Like a gentle beckoning, she felt a whisper welcome her as it echoed in the distance, barely audible, but there in her mind. It was unmistakable. She was no longer home. The power surrounding her was warm, an energy that wrapped around her body as a mother would to a child. She shook her head to clear it. Feeling the powerful male behind her, she turned to face him.

"Hades? What have you done?"

The events of the battle with Hera were devastating. Lives were changed, and the innocence Persephone once held was shattered. Hades would never forgive himself for failing to protect the one he loved. Vowing it would never happen again, he made a decision that would change the world forever and change the love that he had developed with Persephone. There was still one last obstacle to be with her... Demeter.

Persephone & Hades 3

Persephone & Hades III will be the epic conclusion to the battle of the Gods against the Titans. Publication TBA

ABOUT THE AUTHOR

Tabatha Grove

Tabatha Grove has studied Greek Mythology most of her life and enjoys writing stories about the gods that resonate with humanity. Her love for research and history led her to obtain degrees that would help her pursue her true passion of becoming an author.  Persephone & Hades II is the second book in her trilogy about Greek Mythology Gods.

Tabatha has a Bachelor of Science (B.S.) in History, an Associate of Applied Science (AAS) in Visual Communication with Advanced Graphic Design, and certification in Digital Imaging and Prepress Technology. Her love of art, history, literature, and her autistic son drive her passion and enrich her life. Her hope is to enrich others with her stories and offer a new perspective on this classic romance tale that has brought so much joy to so many around the world.

AFTERWORD

Thank you to everyone who has supported me and my work. For more news and updates on my next book or ways you can donate, visit

www.tabathagrove.com

Made in the USA
Middletown, DE
30 September 2023

39493921R00225